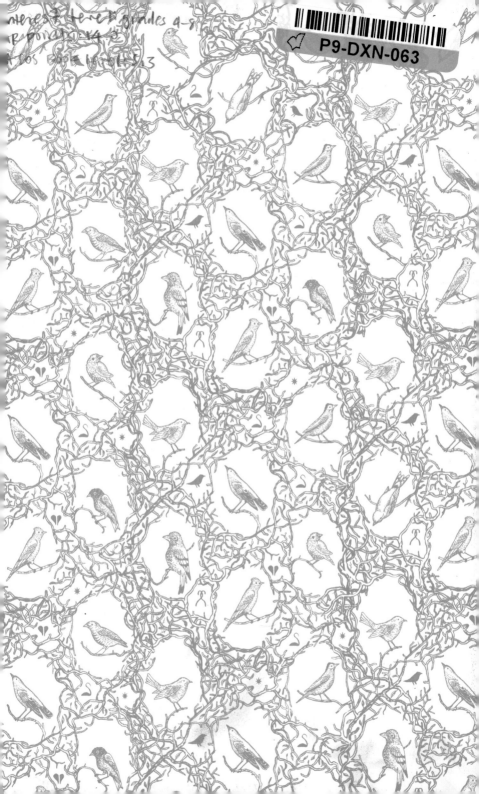

SUMMER and BIRD

by
KATHERINE
CATMULL

DUTTON CHILDREN'S BOOKS
An imprint of Penguin Group (USA) Inc.

DUTTON CHILDREN'S BOOKS
A division of Penguin Young Readers Group

Published by the Penguin Group
Penguin Group (USA) Inc., 375 Hudson Street, New York, New York 10014, U.S.A.
Penguin Group (Canada), 90 Eglinton Avenue East, Suite 700, Toronto, Ontario, Canada M4P 2Y3
(a division of Pearson Penguin Canada Inc.)
Penguin Books Ltd, 80 Strand, London WC2R 0RL, England
Penguin Ireland, 25 St Stephen's Green, Dublin 2, Ireland (a division of Penguin Books Ltd)
Penguin Group (Australia), 250 Camberwell Road, Camberwell, Victoria 3124, Australia
(a division of Pearson Australia Group Pty Ltd)
Penguin Books India Pvt Ltd, 11 Community Centre, Panchsheel Park, New Delhi—110 017, India
Penguin Group (NZ), 67 Apollo Drive, Rosedale, Auckland 0632, New Zealand
(a division of Pearson New Zealand Ltd.)
Penguin Books (South Africa) (Pty) Ltd, 24 Sturdee Avenue, Rosebank, Johannesburg 2196, South Africa
Penguin Books Ltd, Registered Offices: 80 Strand, London WC2R 0RL, England

LIBRARY OF CONGRESS CATALOGING-IN-PUBLICATION DATA
Catmull, Katherine.
Summer and Bird / Katherine Catmull.—1st ed.
p. cm.
Summary: In the world of Down, young sisters Summer and Bird are separated and go in very
different directions as they seek their missing parents, try to vanquish the evil Puppeteer, lead
the talking birds back to their Green Home, and discover the identity of the true bird queen.
ISBN 978-0-525-95346-3 (hardback)
[1. Fantasy. 2. Adventure and adventurers—Fiction. 3. Sisters—Fiction.
4. Birds—Fiction. 5. Puppeteers—Fiction.]
I. Title.

PZ7.C2697Sum 2012
[Fic]—dc23
2012015587

Published in the United States by Dutton Children's Books,
a division of Penguin Young Readers Group
345 Hudson Street, New York, New York 10014
www.penguin.com/youngreaders

Creative Direction by Deborah Kaplan
Designed by Lori Thorn
Set in Minion Pro

Printed in USA First Edition

1 3 5 7 9 10 8 6 4 2

*For my beautiful mother
and my beautiful, inscrutable sisters*

(and for Ari & Kait, who gave me the idea)

CHAPTER ONE

THE INSIDE CLOSET

The evening before that terrible morning, Summer and Bird were at the edge of the forest. As the light left, they were half together and half apart. Summer was sketching the barks of trees. Bird was lying on the grass with her wooden recorder, playing several two- or three-note song fragments over and over. "You sound like a treeful of birds," said Summer. Bird said nothing. "Annoying birds," Summer added, still sketching.

Whether by accident or not, the sisters looked like their names: Summer was twelve, with sandy hair and sky-colored eyes; Bird was nine, sparrow-brown all over, with gray eyes that changed from light to dark and back again, like storm clouds.

The light was almost gone. An owl hooted, a long *woooo-oof, woooooo-oof,* with a rise at the end like a question or warning. "Something smells like apple pie," said Bird, turning toward a small stone house a few dozen yards away. After a pause, she said, "I think that *is* apple pie."

"Oh, I love apple pie," said Summer. The girls gathered notebooks, pencils, recorder, and ran home.

If Summer and Bird had stayed, they might have seen the Great Gray Owl up on a high limb of a white oak, tiny yellow eyes in their great circling cases staring at the house. The house sat all alone in a long green field, within sight of the river, at the edge of the forest. It was a long bike ride to the school bus stop and the nearest neighbors, but Summer and Bird had always lived in the long green field, and liked it.

Yellow owl-eyes watched the house for long minutes, until a window facing the forest flew open: *chunk*. But no light came on; the room behind the window stayed dark. From the white oak, the rising *wooooof* came again.

Silence.

Then the owl fell like a stone, wings arched above his back, and disappeared inside the open window. If Summer and Bird had stayed, they might have noticed something bright and hard dangling from the owl's left talon, something that glinted in the last light, something like a small brass key.

The wind rustled the trees. Farther inside the house, someone was telling a long story about a substitute teacher.

The owl reappeared on the windowsill. He paused, lifted his wings, and drove through the air back toward the forest. His talons were empty now.

Inside, Summer was annoyed to find there was no apple pie for dessert after all.

Later on, when the girls were in bed, the night was no darker than usual. But for a long time, Bird lay awake, afraid to dream.

The next morning, their parents were gone.

Summer woke up first, as usual. She had dreamed that she was flying, but a painful half-flight, where she struggled to stay a foot or two off the ground. Her arms and back still ached with the effort, and her chest felt as though something had been torn away.

Just a dream, and she almost always dreamed. But as she slipped into her freezing clothes, whispering "Oh, cold" so as not to wake Bird, something did feel wrong in the house. She couldn't see why yet, but the house felt different.

The house felt quiet.

Summer walked down the silent hall and pushed open the door to her parents' room as softly as she could. The bed was empty. Her father's cell phone sat charging on the dresser. The low, square bed was a mess of tangled sheets and blankets, pale gray and green like the walls of the room. The bedroom closet yawned open on a tangle of clothes and shoes inside—and on something else, something odd, something that almost caught her attention. But that almost-thought was blown away by the freezing wind gusting through the open window.

Why in the world was that window open?

Summer closed the window. The silence in the house felt like the ice on the sill. From room to freezing room (Why was the heat not on?), on bare feet, she looked for her mother, her father, her small black-and-white cat; but there was nothing alive, only furniture and silence.

Still barefoot, Summer ran out to the front yard. Their old green car was still in the driveway. The bicycles were all in their rack. "Sarah!" Summer called, looking along the ground and under hedges for a slinking or sleeping cat. Nothing moved but a few last dead leaves skittering across the ground. It was so cold for almost-spring.

"Mom?" she called, in a smaller voice. "Dad?"

Winter never altogether vanishes, even in the warmest summer. You can always find it lingering, if you look.

At a noise from the house, Summer ran back in. But it was only Bird, finally struggling out of bed. Pulling on socks and boots, Summer told Bird what had happened, carefully, trying not to scare her. But Bird's face took on a strange expression, and she sank inside herself.

Practical Summer went into the kitchen to start a fire in the ancient black iron stove. The stove had come with the house; it was ridiculous to use it, their father always said, instead of a normal gas or electric one. But their mother loved it. She said food cooked best over burning wood, that the ghost of the wood made the food more nourishing. Their mother had long, unruly black hair, with long white streaks, like chalk on blacktop, and that was the kind of thing she said. Summer loved her, but did not believe that wood or food—or houses, for that matter—held ghosts. Bird said Summer was being stupid, that their mother obviously talked in poems, and poems were always true. Many things were obvious, to Bird and to their mother, that were not obvious to Summer or her father at all.

Lighting the fire was much harder to do alone than when she helped her mother, and the paper burned too quickly, and the stupid logs wouldn't catch, and a sliver of wood jammed into her finger, and Summer wanted to cry.

But she didn't. And soon a flame jumped up, and the room grew warmer. Summer pulled out a heavy pot and boiled water for oatmeal. Bird came in, still barefoot. Bird, like their mother, almost never got cold, even on the coldest mornings.

But even when the table was set and the milk and salt and sugar put out, and the oatmeal steamed before them, neither Summer nor Bird ate much at all.

Bird looked through the kitchen window at the bent black fingers of a cherry tree. "Leaves should have started by now," she said. "I wonder why there's still no leaves."

"What?" said Summer.

Bird didn't answer. Her eyes were dark. With her foot, Summer gently touched Bird's leg under the table, and when Bird looked up at her, she smiled. Of course that made Bird want to cry. But she did not cry; she took her hot, swelling private grief and held it tight in her heart until it was small and cold. Her eyes were like a cloudy sky that won't storm and won't clear. After a while, Summer said, "So. We have to tell someone."

"No," said Bird. "It will get them in trouble."

"They might already be in trouble. Something terrible might have happened." A kidnapping, Summer thought. Or they'd fallen to the bottom of a well somewhere, legs broken. She thought of people saying: If only the older girl had called someone in time, it all might have been so different. She felt panic rise up, but she hid it, so Bird wouldn't see.

"We could call Mr. and Mrs. Matocha," Summer began. These were their nearest neighbors, a couple of miles away.

5

"No," said Bird, tearing her toast into pieces. "They will call the police. The police will take us away from each other, and take us away from Mom and Dad."

"They won't!"

"They will. They'll have to. "

"But Mom and Dad will be back soon," said Summer. "They'll be back in an hour, probably! You're being stupid!"

Bird's eyes were set in dark circles. She said, "If they'll be back in an hour, then we don't have to tell anyone. We can just wait." She stood up. "While we wait, we could look for clues."

"One hour—" Summer began. But Bird was already running down the hall, straight for their parents' bedroom. Before Summer had even reached the end of the hall, Bird saw what Summer had only almost-seen.

"The inside closet is open," she called.

"The inside closet" was what Summer and Bird called the half-size door in the back of their parents' closet. It was locked, and it had always been locked, since before they moved in, since before the girls were born. They had never had the key. Their father and mother had tried to pick the lock or pry the door many times, but it wouldn't be picked or pried.

"Let's just enjoy the mystery then," their mother had finally said. And so the Inside Closet game began, a good one for slow days. Might be a box of treasure in the inside closet, Summer would say. Might be bones and hair, Bird would reply; might be rats or bees. Might be another universe, Summer would say. Might be a ball of fire, Bird would say. And so on.

But now the clothes on her father's side of the closet were roughly pushed back, and Summer could see the inside closet door swung wide. A small brass key lay on the floor in front of the closet.

They moved closer; they knelt down; they bent their heads into the dark hole.

Treasure or bones?

A smell. A green, living smell: spring wind over a river. "It smells like the river," said Summer.

Bird said, "It smells like Mom." Her eyes adjusted to the dark before Summer's, and she reached inside. They both sat back.

In one hand, Bird held a long gray-and-brown feather with white spots; in the other, a folded piece of paper.

Summer ignored the feather, grabbed the paper out of Bird's hand. "It might explain," she said, flattening the paper out and sitting back on the stone floor. "Yes, look, it's a picture letter from Mom." Bird's eyes clouded over with little-sister darkness, but she slipped the feather, an owl feather, into her pocket, and sat back to watch Summer.

She knew it was an owl feather, because her pocket already held the burnt fragments of another owl feather, which matched this one almost exactly.

Bird was a girl with secrets.

~

Twenty minutes later, Summer still sat on the floor, studying the picture letter. Bird was curled up in the inside closet, a tight ball. Her eyes were closed and pressed against her knees. "Mom, Mom, Mom," she said into her knees, so Summer couldn't hear.

The old digital clock on their father's dresser flipped, flipped, flipped.

Since they were small, their mother had left them notes on special occasions, like birthdays, or after big fights or soccer goals. They were written in pictures instead of words, at first because they hadn't yet learned to read, and later because the girls loved the game of decoding the pictures. Especially Summer loved that game. An eye, a sun, a fish, a smile: I saw Summer swim, it made me happy. Sun always meant Summer. A bird always meant Bird. It was a special mother-game; their father never could get the picture letters right.

Summer sat back against the wall to think. "Let me see," said Bird, uncurling from the closet. Summer didn't respond. "Let me SEE," said Bird. She took the edge of the thick paper between two fingers and pulled. The paper tensed for a moment. Summer let go.

Their mother drew her notes with black ink and a calligraphic pen. The thick black strokes made a knot in Bird's stomach.

The first picture was something she hadn't seen before: a heart, in two pieces.

Then a sun. That was Summer.

Then a small, funny bird. That was herself.

Then—a hook of some sort—or a snake, coming out of a—out of a flower, or a boat, or something. "Summer, what—"

"It's a swan," said Summer, still looking at the ceiling. Bird saw it now: of course it was a swan. They had never had a swan before.

The last image also made her pause. It was almost like two swan necks, twining near the top. But then she saw: "Our gate!" she said out loud, with pleasure. "Mom's gate."

It was more of an archway than a gate, really, and it looked almost like the woods it led into, until you got close. The gate stood over the beginning of a sort of natural path into the forest. ("Animals come and go on that path, and have for many years," their father, who was an ornithologist, had once said. "Five years?" Summer had asked, when she was less than five years herself. "Ten thousand years," he said. "Or more." *Ornithologist* meant studying birds, but it meant knowing about trees and water and other animals as well.)

At the edge of this old path, when she was first married, their mother had planted two willow saplings about five feet apart. Over the years, as the trees grew taller, she wove their tops together so that they grew together, and then grew down, twisting around each other, to make a living arch. When Summer and Bird asked why she had made it, their mother only laughed and said, "Don't you like it?" When they said yes, she said, "Good enough reason."

But Summer liked to find reasons that were better than good enough. "Maybe it's so the animals know the way out," she decided, once.

"Maybe it's so someone else knows the way in," Bird had replied.

In the picture letter, the drawing even showed just the beginning of sprigs around the sides of the gate, just as it was now, at the beginning of spring.

Two-pieces heart. Summer. Bird. Swan. Gate.

Bird turned to Summer, who was faster at puzzles. "What does it mean?"

No hesitation. "The first part means she loves us the same amount each. One heart in two pieces, one each for Summer and Bird."

That made sense, Bird thought. Anyway, maybe it did.

"Then the swan means—I'm not sure. I think—the swan is swimming, or like gliding, so I think it might mean 'move,' or 'go.' Yes," she said, sounding more confident as she spoke, "it means, I think it means 'move fast,' or 'go along quickly,' something like that."

"So, and the gate?" Bird asked.

"I guess," said Summer, more slowly, "I guess it just means 'the gate'?" That didn't sound right. It wasn't how the picture letters usually worked. But what else could it mean?

There was a pause. Bird said, "So it means, so the whole thing means…'I love you both the same. Move fast, move fast…'"

Summer looked at her. "Through the gate. That's what it means. 'I love you both. Move fast through the gate.' Bird!" Summer was excited now. "The whole thing is just a game. It's nothing bad. Mom's hiding in the forest, she always goes into the forest, she *loves* it in there—"

"Yeah, she goes in a lot," Bird said slowly, "but it makes her so sad and strange afterwards, I don't know if she exactly loves it in there—"

"Whatever, okay, but the point is she goes in there all the time! And now maybe she's going to show us *why* she goes in there, she's going to show us, I bet! That's what the note means: she wants us to come find her!"

(That's what Summer thought the note meant. And Summer was smart, but not always as smart as she thought she was.)

They ran out of the bedroom to pack for a hike. In the hallway, Summer slipped on the rug by the back door, caught herself, and ran on. Someone was always slipping on that rug. In fact, if Summer and Bird had been awake the night before, they would have seen their father slip in the same way, on that same rug, as he ran after their mother, who was already outside and half running, half limping through the grass.

They would have heard nothing, because both their parents were urgently silent. They would have seen that their mother was wearing no clothes at all, but was struggling to slip on what seemed to be a feathery white robe. They would have seen their father run after her as she disappeared into the dark, one arm in the robe, then another.

They might not have noticed, as their father did not, the small black-and-white cat, light and silent, running just behind her.

Maybe in the dark it would have been hard for these unsleeping girls to see the slow transformation of their now limping, now running, now flying mother as she headed toward the river. But they would have heard, as their father did, the sighing of air as what he was now chasing—no longer a woman, but an enormous white bird, like a great white sheet in the wind—lifted above the bank, above the water, and flew with strong wing beats down the length of the river.

And they could never have run fast enough to see their father jump into the canoe he kept on the river, his hands shaking as he spun the padlock. Nor would they notice, as he did not notice, the cat curled in the stern, green eyes on the swan now flying down the river in the direction of the low, full moon.

The huge swan beat the air with all the strength in her wings; their father beat the water with all the strength of his arms on the oars. Was he thinking about leaving two small daughters alone in the dark house, sleeping? He forgot to think of them at all, only of what he loved and was losing.

Was she thinking of two small daughters?

11

Yes: the daughters filled her heart so full that love and grief spilled over, and her heart, even her alien swan heart, wept inside her.

But when you find your soul, you have to go. When you find your true shape, when the wind lifts you up, when you remember who you are, you have to go.

CHAPTER TWO

NO BREADCRUMBS

It took longer than they expected to get started. Their father had taught them that on a long hike, you always brought enough food to be gone overnight, and an extra set of warm clothes—to be safe, in case you got lost. Summer made a list, but Bird kept thinking of more to bring—it was fun now, it was a game. And then the packs would be too heavy to carry, so they'd have to unpack some and think it through again. When Summer packed a notebook for observations, Bird wanted her notebook and pencil, too.

"For writing down observations?" asked Summer.

"Yes, and stories," said Bird.

"We don't need stories," said Summer.

Yes we do, Bird thought stubbornly, stuffing her notebook, with its cover of pink-and-purple birds studded with plastic jewels, into her pack. She watched Summer, wondering why she was still here when all the others were gone.

Summer kept notebooks filled with observations and sketches she had made of the plants and creatures who lived in the field and at the edges of the forest. They had separate sections for plants, animals, insects, and stars.

Bird did not observe scientifically, but she knew things, especially about birds. Summer would read the almanac, consult her father, and go to the river every day for weeks, waiting for the migrating flocks to pass over. One day Bird would join her, and that was always the day the birds appeared.

"How did you know?" Summer would demand, and then decide: "It's probably a coincidence."

"It's not coincidence," Bird would say. "It's just obvious. Your body just knows."

"But *how* do you know?"

"How do you know if a story is a good story or not?" asked Bird. "Like that. You know like that."

Bird liked stories, and she remembered all the songs she'd ever heard. Sometimes she would sit playing her recorder at the edge of the woods, to charm the animals. They never came, but sometimes she could feel them at the shadowy edges where the meadow and dark trees met. And even if animals didn't come, birds often did, lighting on branches to watch her and listen.

For food they packed dried apples, nuts, raisins, chocolate, cheese; some buns and crackers. A big aluminum water bottle each. At the last minute, Summer grabbed a box of matches from the shelf by the stove, just in case, and Bird said, "I'll get my flute to bring, too."

"It's a recorder, not a flute," Summer called after her.

"A recorder is a *kind* of flute, and flute is a better word," said stubborn Bird, returning with recorder in hand.

They stood in the kitchen, jackets on, packs on their backs. Seeing Bird's pink backpack with the cartoon mermaid, Summer's heart sank. Bird was so little, and it might be a long hike, hours long. Was this really what the picture letter said to do? But to her heart, a note sending them on a hike made more sense than their parents disappearing without a word. "You could stay," she said to Bird. "You could stay with the Matochas, and I could go in alone."

Bird looked surprised, then dark. "It said a sun and a bird. It didn't say just a sun."

"Never mind," said Summer, before a fight began. "We won't be gone long. It'll be fun. We'll find Mom, and maybe Dad is with her. And if we don't—we will, but if we don't find her and it's getting dark, we'll come home, and call the police, or someone. Okay? Let's go." They locked the house and headed for the gate.

When the sun shone on the valley where they lived, it was bright and clear; and when the clouds came in, it was gloomy-dark. But some days, like this day, the small thick clouds flew across the sun, so that the whole valley was bright and dark, bright and dark, and that was the light the girls liked best.

At the edge of the forest, at their mother's gate, Bird began to sing. "Two little cygnets," she sang, "starting on their way." It was from an endless nursery-rhyme song their mother used to sing when they were small. "The path was dark,/And they went astray."

"We won't go astray," said Summer. Bird didn't answer, but with a twist of the pink backpack, she stepped ahead of Summer, and entered the forest first.

The song was right about the path, at least, because it was darker immediately, though the early-afternoon light was still alive around them, moving among branches and leaves. The air grew colder, more clinging, with different, worrying smells. It smelled like things dying and other things growing out of the dead.

(Which is what life always smells like. But our senses are sharper when we're afraid.)

They guessed that they were supposed to follow the ancient animal trail, and at first it wasn't hard, since they had followed it many times— though never out of calling distance of home; that was a strict rule. The rule had been broken only once, by Bird, when she was very small. "The air showed me to go there," she said tearfully when she was finally found. "The air bent that way, you could feel it, the bending made me go."

"She is tired and frightened," their mother had said, and gathered her up to bed without scolding her at all. After that, she and Bird often went for walks together. Summer sometimes watched from a window as her mother's head bent low to speak in Bird's ear.

She never took that kind of walk with Summer.

At first, the trail ran straight as skis. Summer practiced tracking, in case she could see signs of her mother. Bird stopped, seemingly at random, to examine a half-hidden red flower, a chalky stone, tiny green-gray leaves in a circular pile.

"What are you looking for?" Summer asked.

"I will know when I see," said Bird. "It will tell me."

Summer could think of nothing to say to this stupid remark, but it made her feel alone. So they walked together, alone.

As they walked farther and farther from calling distance, they became more accustomed to the forest, or perhaps it became more accustomed to them. Birds sang and called around them, an enormous conversation.

"All these birds—I hope Mom is nearby," Bird murmured. Their mother spent hours watching birds, though more often from a window than among them. In any case, despite the birds, there was still no sign of their mother at all.

They walked a long time, many hours, more silently the longer they walked. Finally the path became almost surely…not there anymore. Two small voices:

"No, wait, I see it there. Is it?"

"Yes, I think so…wait, no."

Summer wished—she wished like anything, she wished too late—that she had remembered to blaze their path as they followed it. Snap twigs, tie rags, cut bark: she knew how to do this. But in the excitement, she had forgotten. She had been dumber than Hansel and Gretel, hadn't even left an edible trail back. They were much deeper into the woods than they had ever been. Following this path backward toward home would soon be impossible, might already be, unless they turned back very soon.

"We have to turn around now," said Summer, stopping. "We ought to be there by now. She ought be here by now, if the note…if I read it right. We've walked too long. We need to head back. We need to go—" Her voice stopped.

"We need to go where?" whispered Bird in the almost-dark.

But Summer had lost the path.

It was quiet for a long time. As the light dimmed, the birds grew louder. Bird looked up through the darkening trees. "I think it's too late to go back, anyway."

Summer felt sick. She saw that Bird was right: they had walked so long that it was too late to start back, even if they knew the way, which they didn't. And even if they did, the dark would catch them long before they got home. This had been a stupid, stupid idea, and she would be in terrible trouble when any adult found out about it. Imagine explaining to neighbors, teachers, police: my mother drew some pictures, and I thought they said I should take my little sister deep into the woods. What had she been *thinking*?

But the other thought—the thought that they had no idea where their parents were, and no one had left them a note, and they were all alone—had been too terrible. Even this stupid, stupid idea had seemed good compared to that.

"Yeah, it's getting pretty late, I guess," she said, with false calm. "Might as well set up camp for tonight." Bird's face was blank, which meant she was upset.

"Then tomorrow we can figure out what to do," Summer continued. "It will all make sense in the morning."

That last part was just what their father would have said, which made Bird want to cry, and made her hate Summer a little, for her strange, fake voice. For pretending to be their father. She knew it was too late to go back; she already knew that, she had already said it herself. Everything was wrong.

~

In this strange almost-spring, winter returned after dark, especially in the forest.

"We need a fire," said Bird. "It's getting cold. Even I'm kinda cold." Bird, who could run coatless through the snow.

A campfire was dangerous, and Summer had never made one without help. But it was cold. "Just a short one," she said. "We won't leave it burning all night." She arranged a circle of rocks to keep the fire confined and tame.

Bird was singing a soft, made-up song while she hunted for sticks. "Cheese toast and chocolate," she sang.

"Stop singing," Summer snapped. "And we can't use up all our food tonight."

"We're going home in the morning," said Bird. "And we need to warm up." Then she sang, in a warbling, babified voice, "Where the story begins,/A thousand birds of a feather/Call to the cygnets/'Let's sing together!'"

Summer laughed in spite of herself. "It's 'journey begins,' though, not 'story begins,' I think," she said.

"Are you sure—is it?" said Bird.

They each tried to remember their mother's voice, singing that song to them. They stopped laughing.

When the dry wood was gathered and circled with rocks, Summer opened the box of matches. She knew how dangerous it was to light an unprotected fire in a forest, and her mind ran with visions of how badly wrong this could go, what fire could do to trees, to animals, to girls. Her hands shook as she leaned toward the little pyramid of kindling and struck at the box.

Nothing. She struck again. "Why isn't it working?" said Bird in a high, complaining voice. Summer slashed at the box a third time, as hard as she could.

The match caught—but the box flew out of her shaking hands and into the kindling, and in one second it blazed up huge, a tall center flame with a smaller flame on each side.

Bird said dreamily, "It looks like a red bird."

Summer was able to rescue three matches and a few pieces of the dark strip from the box for striking, all of which she carefully stored in a small plastic bag. But as they ate melted cheese on warm buns, her terrible mistake clung to her heart, and she did not enjoy their dinner the way Bird did.

Lit a fire. Lost all but three of our matches, she wrote in her journal. *Ate a bun and cheese and half a chocolate.*

Then:

We shouldn't have come.

For a while the moon was full and bright above, but then even the moon abandoned them. Bird sat across the fire from Summer, tangled dark hair spilling over her knees, writing in her notebook.

"We should sleep together to share warmth," Summer said.

"Okay," said Bird, still writing, not moving. She was writing a story of birds flying home across an ocean. They were almost home. After a while, she said into the dark, "Mom must have meant us to end up here, I guess. We just don't know why."

Lying on her back, eyes open, Summer said nothing. She watched the dark shapes in the dark sky. When she finally fell asleep, she slipped in and out of anxious dreams of a forest in flames, birds screaming. Above the flames stood a tall, gray figure, thin as an iron spike, a human figure but with a long, narrow beak. The beaked thing watched the screaming, burning birds without expression.

Later, in another dream or half-dream, Summer thought she saw Bird awake by the fire's embers. The dream or half-dream Bird threw a long gray-and-brown feather onto the coals, and they blazed up wildly. Two tiny yellow eyes appeared in the blackness.

CHAPTER THREE

THE
PATCHWORK
BIRD

n the morning, in the sunlight, sleepy Summer said, "I dreamed you put a feather in the fire."

"Strange dream," said wide-awake Bird. "Look up."

On a low, bent branch just above the girls was a small bird—so small that even after Bird told her to look, Summer almost missed it. She had never seen, in life or in books, any bird that looked like this. It was covered in tiny, precise squares of color: a dusty blue square, a rusty orange square, a grass-green square, a rain-cloud square, a raspberry square—dozens of tiny squares on this tiny bird. A deep indigo-black square folded across its little throat, and its beak was a sharp bit of sky.

At first it was still as a toy. But then it turned its beak away from them, to turn its eye toward them: head turned away so eye could see, the bird way.

Kuuuuh, kuhhhh, said the bird—a raspy sound, not like a bird at all. Like static; like a snake on dry leaves. Like a human cough or whisper.

"*Kuuuuh, kuhhhh,*" Bird repeated, standing up. Her face was tense and alive.

Haaaaaa, said the bird.

"*Haaaaaa,*" Bird repeated.

"Shut up," said Summer, struggling to sit up. "I can't hear when you do that," she added, which wasn't true.

Maaaaa, said the bird. *Maaaaa. Muuhhhh.*

"It doesn't know what it's saying," said Summer.

"You shut up," said Bird.

Mother, said the bird, *your mother needs you.*

Summer screamed. The bird startled up, and Bird moaned, "No." But then it settled back down to the branch. The whole world fell silent around them, a waiting silence.

Song, song, the bird rasped. Bird's face was bright as a moon. *The song is the path,* the bird said. *The path is down.*

And then the bird began to sing: a lovely, liquid song, a bird's song. After a few seconds, it stopped. It cocked its head toward Summer, who looked at the ground, angry and lost, out of her summery element.

The bird sang the same notes again.

And then, and then: Bird understood, and she sang the song back.

The bird turned away from Summer and gave its full small voice to Bird, singing that same short phrase again. Bird began to sing it back, but stopped in frustration. "My voice won't go right," she said. "It's too hard."

"Use your recorder," said Summer, still looking at the ground.

She felt mean. She had screamed, and Bird hadn't. She had burnt the matches. She had missed what the stupid bird was asking her to do.

Bird pulled the small recorder from her pocket and tried the phrase that way. She played it again, then once more to be sure. The bird sang a new phrase, and Bird tried to play that back as well.

This went on for a long time, the bird singing a short passage, Bird playing it on her recorder. Summer sat on the ground after a while, her head still down. The bird seemed tired, and its songs grew softer, but when Bird put her arms down to rest, or catch her breath, the bird fluttered its wings anxiously.

"I think she came a long way," said Bird, when the patchwork bird had paused for a minute, its head bent, its body trembling with small breaths. "I think she's tired."

Summer said nothing. The bird lifted its head, and sang again.

Finally, Bird stopped, put the flute down, stretched her neck. "I have it now," she said. She looked at the bird for confirmation.

The bird was gone. "She flew away!" cried Bird, searching the trees. But it was unhappy Summer, still staring at the ground, who saw the bird first, where it lay on the ground, sky and grass and raspberry limp across a dead leaf. Its side rose and fell, stopped. Rose and fell, stopped.

"She is dying," said Bird. She reached down.

"Don't TOUCH it," Summer shouted, too late.

Bird held the tiny patchwork thing in both hands. It was made of silk and air and bones; it weighed nothing. She held the bird to her chest, so it could feel her heart beating and remember how to do it.

The bird's body pulsed against Bird's hands.

On the ground, Summer hid her head in her arms. Poor Summer, poor heavy head.

The bird's body pulsed more slowly. A small wind came up, blew through Bird's fingers, ruffled the many-colored feathers.

The pulsing slowed and slowed against Bird's chest. After a while, it stopped. The patchwork bird was dead.

But Bird's heart pounded on.

They buried her beneath the bent black tree. Bird cried snottily the whole time. "She died to do that," Bird sobbed. "She died because it was so hard to come here, and to tell us her song."

Summer's two pink lips made one flat line.

"Now what?" said flat-mouthed Summer when they had finished. "Are we supposed to follow the advice of a talking *bird*? If it wasn't just our imagination, making bird sounds into *words*. I have never seen a bird like that!"

Accusingly: as if this were the bird's fault.

"I have never seen a bird like that," she continued. "Never, and I don't believe—" She stopped. (Don't believe what, Summer? Your eyes? Your ears? Your fingers still gritty with the dirt you dug to bury a bird made of raincloud and rose?)

Bird leaned her head against a tree. Her recorder was zipped into her jacket pocket; its strong wood held the bird's song now, as did her own fragile bones. Her mouth drew down hard, but she didn't cry. After a while, she turned to look at Summer. "I learned the song," she said.

"So what," said Summer in a hard, flat voice. "We're still lost."

Bird said, "She said Mom needs us. Mom *needs* us. I will find the way. The song is the path. I know it is."

An ugly laugh from Summer. The ugliness was shame: shame she had lost the path, put her sister in danger, failed the bird, failed their mother.

"You don't know the way," said Summer in the same ugly voice. "We're lost." And she sat on the ground.

But Bird knew the song. And though she did not understand it yet, she had sung it over and over and into her bones. Bird's bones often knew what she did not, and when your bones know, they move you in the right direction, if you let them. Her mother had taught Bird that, but she had never taught Summer.

"If this were a story," Bird said. "If this were a story—"

"That's so, so stupid. It's not a story."

"The bird trusted me! Mom needs us! I am trying! I think it's right."

Summer closed her mouth and watched.

Bird stood quiet, tried to make her mind easy. As if she were telling a story, she tried to feel it through. She felt the flute in her left hand, pulled it quietly up to her mouth, and began to play the bird's song, all the while thinking: *If this were a story—and not a stupid, baby story, an excellent one—what would be the right way to go?* She walked a few yards back the way they had come, then stood in a clearing: first in its light center, then moving to the dark edges. She closed her eyes, took the flute from her mouth, and dragged her hand along the trees, idly, as she moved around the edge of the clearing. Her hand ran across the rough bark, feeling for crevices, stopping her mind.

Then: a clear, calm "Oh," and she disappeared.

Summer had followed just in time to see Bird, and then the space where Bird had been, and wasn't anymore. She felt a stab of shock and fear; and then, overwhelming the fear, a stab of terrible loneliness. Everything she had been holding back since yesterday morning was alive in her at once. She had lost everyone now; now there was no one at all.

Summer ran to the spot where Bird had been. Nothing. She called out in a voice so loud it hurt her throat: "Bird! Bird!" But nothing answered, not even the normal forest sounds, shocked to silence by her screams.

Summer sat down on the cold ground, trying not to cry, trying to think.

Then she heard a soft, distant sound. "I'm here," said the distant sound in what was almost Bird's voice.

"Where, where?" Summer shouted.

"I'm here," said Bird's voice, tiny but strong. "I found the path. The new path is down, Summer. We're going down."

From a maple branch far above the two girls, the owl who had accompanied them all this way, just out of sight, lifted himself into the air. Leaving the girls, he flew for hours, through ways in the air that only birds know, until he found another high perch, this time along a stone balustrade in the eye of an enormous stone swan. Standing against the railing was a tall, thin figure in a straight gray dress, like a stone column, like an iron spike. On her head was a large mask, long-beaked, small-eyed, with a slash of white on each side. In her right hand she held a small, terrified brown bird.

When she saw the owl, the masked figure lifted the trembling bird to her face and held it there for a moment. Then she opened her mouth, thrust the living bird inside, and swallowed it whole.

She turned to the owl. "Now tell me your news," she said.

The owl leaned forward and spoke in her ear for a long time.

It was snowing down there.

Summer had made her way down with difficulty. As Bird's thin, distant voice instructed her, she trailed her hand along the trees, but it took some time. "Don't GO somewhere, you are always going in your head," said the voice. "Just feel with your hand, let your hand look." And there was a sudden space—more than a space, almost a vacuum, as if the emptiness seized her hand and tugged. The space seemed hardly big enough for her arm, let alone her whole body. But as she let herself be pulled farther in, the empty space shaped itself around her. And suddenly the ground beneath her feet pulled away, as if it were alive.

Bird should have been hurt in this fall, Summer thought, as she slipped and slid down the undulating black ground. But in fact she was not exactly falling. The Summer-shape of the emptiness held her tight, almost too tight—she felt choked. She felt as if the air had turned into a snake, and swallowed her. She felt afraid.

Then the Summer-shaped hole in the air gave a sort of cough, and spit her on the ground.

"Did that hurt? The leaves caught me," said calm Bird when Summer finally joined her. It had hurt a little, in fact. And it was far, far colder here below. In fact, it was snowing, in slow, thick flakes. How could snow be falling here, but not above? She turned to look at the hill she had just slipped down, to find a path back up the hill and out of this place.

But there was no hill, only thick trees on flat ground. Behind her was not where she had come from.

Bird stood a little ways away, behind a snow-veil, still.

"Where—what do you think this is?" asked Summer.

"This is our right path," said Bird, still calm and sure as a queen. She turned and began to walk.

"To find Mom, to help her?" Summer asked.

Now Bird hesitated. "Well, it must be," she said finally. "Yes. I know it's the right path, I know that. So it must be the path to help Mom."

"But how do you know it's right?" said Summer.

"From the song," said Bird. She started walking. "And I know because it's just—obvious."

"Wait, wait," said Summer, scrambling behind her. "I'll lose you, I can't see you, I'll lose you. We need to stick together."

Bird stopped. "Then come," she said. "Because it's time to walk. If we're on the right *path*," she added, with some of Bird's old petulance, "then it's time to *walk*, right?"

"Yes," said Summer, not quite sure how to take this sudden reversal in roles—why was the little sister suddenly in charge? "Besides, I'm cold, and walking will warm me up."

"I'm not cold," said Bird. They walked.

Snow hung between the sisters, and a snow-curtain obscured the dark, bare trees. Where were the leaves that had been so many shades of early green above? What had happened to the new springtime, how had it turned back into winter? However hard she thought about latitudes and altitudes and freak weather conditions, none of the answers Summer came up with made sense.

"Why are we going this way?" Summer asked, in an attempt to re-establish her authority and the correct order of things.

"Because it's the right way," said Bird, still walking. "Also, we're walking in the direction that would take us home, if we were still up there in—if we were still Up," she concluded. "So don't worry."

They continued on.

On the inside, Bird was less calm. She was full of a frightening new energy. Her bones felt charged with electricity, and the energy moved outward from her bones and through her skin to charge the air around her. She felt great joy and great fear. It made it hard to talk. The electricity in her body knew where to go.

Time passed and passed again, and they continued to walk. Summer's mind kept saying, "Time to stop," but Bird was not stopping. "Rest," said Summer out loud, surprising herself. Bird stopped and turned to her. Then she sat down.

The falling snow seemed to hang still in the air, so that the world trembled toward them through static or shattered crystal. Summer watched as Bird, a small shape dissolving in snow, rose to her feet and pulled out her recorder. Then Bird played: but not a tune. It was the song she had learned from the bird, short bursts of little notes, some rising up round and sweet as a peony, some snapping like a handful of twigs. The sound-bursts came fast. Summer didn't know Bird could play so fast.

"What are you doing?" asked Summer, in a disintegrating voice that seemed to come from the tops of the trees.

"Calling my path," said Bird though haze and distance.

"Calling our path?" repeated Summer, not sure she had heard.

The snow-shattered Bird did not reply. She lifted the recorder above her head and threw it, like a spear, between the two trunks of a forked tree, and into the depths of the wood. The flute didn't arc—it flew straight as a hawk. It looked as if it would never fall. It looked as if it would fly through the snow-shattered trees forever.

And then, abruptly, the air cleared. The snow stopped.

"Come on," said Bird in her flat, normal voice. "Let's keep going. It's getting dark."

An hour later or more, as the dark grew close, the air around them changed, felt lighter, breezier. The trees grew fewer and farther apart.

"We are coming out of the long woods," said Bird softly.

"It's dark," said Summer. "We need to stop."

"We will soon," said Bird. "Just a little farther, that's all. I think that's right. I think we'll find Mom, maybe, and be able help her. That might be right."

She did think it might be right. But she wasn't sure.

CHAPTER FOUR

THE FIRE PLACE

The sky had cleared, but the air had grown colder. They had walked out onto a wide plain, blank with snow. "This is where our house would be, if we were Up," said Bird. But there was no house—no house, no mother, no father. Only the skeletons of a few low trees stood between them and the icy wind.

Above them hung an overturned bowlful of stars, a billion stars, lighting the plain in spiky, shivering light. Summer sat down, and Bird walked out into the silent, starlit plain. On the cold ground, Summer thought: *The stars like us.* Then she scoffed at the thought. The stars didn't care, she knew. "The stars don't care one way or another," she said aloud.

"The stars care," called Bird, just the outline of a small girl in a large empty space. "The stars love us. The stars care." The electricity in her blood still sang. She was only half Bird now, and the other half song. She liked it that way.

She stopped by a low, bare tree that leaned crookedly toward the ground, a skeleton of white-gray wood only a few feet taller than she was. Its limbs splayed up at odd angles, like bent arms and legs. "Come here!" she called to Summer. Then: "No, wait!" And she ran back, arriving breathless. "Bring our stuff," ordered Bird. "Bring it all. Bring the matches especially."

Summer said, "Bird, I thought of these shrubs, but there's not enough. We'd waste a match and it would only burn for a few minutes. We should get some wood from the forest." She looked over her shoulder; the forest looked far away.

"Come on," said Bird intently, and Summer stood up. Her legs were so stiff and painful she almost cried. It seemed impossible to think of walking but she began, one foot in front of the other, loping behind Bird, hot tears turning to tiny diamonds in the icy wind.

"Your face is all jewels, Summer," said Bird when at last they stopped. "It's shining with stars like the sky. Summer, your face is like the sky." Summer barely heard. She sat by the crooked little tree, then lay down. Sleep opened its dark mouth and swallowed her.

Bird was shaking her. "No," she said clearly. "I need you to help. And you can't sleep so close to this. You can't, Summer. Summer, I'm not big enough to do matches, I don't know how. You have to do it. Summer, wake up and do the match."

And feeling as if it were all a dream, the glittering icy sky against her glittering icy face, Summer opened the plastic bag with red frozen fingers, clumsily trying to choose one of the three remaining matches, to push the magic bit away from her across one of the dark strips, just as she had learned at her mother's stove. Nothing; and nothing again; and for the first moment since they had come to Down, Bird looked uncertain and scared.

And for some reason, seeing Bird afraid gave Summer strength. She focused her mind on the match. She held it more firmly. She dragged it more bravely and briskly along the dark strip. And it caught.

"You did it!" said Bird. "You lit the match—oh, Summer—now throw it on the tree. Throw it, hurry Summer, before it goes out!"

Summer hesitated. It went against everything she had been taught—against her every instinct, to throw a burning match into the world, onto a living tree. And there was nothing here to burn, it was silly: this tree or bush would burn in the snow for a few minutes and then be gone.

Gone, like almost everything alive that she loved.

Then Summer felt angry. And in her anger, she threw the burning match.

Nothing happened for a dreadful moment. Then a crackle; then a flash of sparks, like hot bright crumbs shaken from a cloth.

The little tree was all fire.

"I knew you would know how to do it," said Bird.

"It won't last," said Summer.

"It will last long enough," said Bird.

And it did last, much longer than made any sense at all. They lay together on the bare ground by the bright, undying little tree. The smoke-scent was spicy and sweet, like incense or perfume. Bird curled up against Summer and fell asleep. Summer felt the warmth of Bird and the sweet-scented fire at her front, and the icy blackness at her back.

She could feel the bones in her own shoulders, and they felt small. *Don't let the fire go out,* she thought. And then she thought, *I have to ask Bird why she threw away her recorder—did she do that? Or did I dream it? No, she did it, I think she did.* As she fell asleep, she thought she heard, very faint and far away, a bird's song—the patchwork bird's song. And she felt she knew that it was a heartbreaking song, the saddest song in the world, and somehow profoundly comforting as she fell asleep.

That night, Summer woke once, or seemed to wake. The fire had gone out, but she still felt warm. Where the fire had been stood an enormous red bird, a bird larger than a man, with two long blue feathers spilling from its head. Beneath each eye was a half-circle of green jewels. The great bird lifted one wing, and a rush of warm air surrounded Summer. She thought of one Christmas night when her family had walked a freezing mile to a friend's house. They rang the bell, stamping and laughing and wiping cold noses, and then the door opened, and light and warmth and music rushed out. This bird was like that opening door.

I thought it was the fire, she thought. *But it was this bird. The warmth was always coming from this bird.*

Summer stood up in the icy air and moved toward the bird, drawn by the heat and the slow pulse in its long throat. *Not heat that burns,* she thought, *but heat that comforts.* Red feathers ruffled in the wind. When she was close, the bird lifted its great wing, and Summer flinched for a moment—but then the blood-colored feathers were over her, pulling her close, warm as a morning quilt. Hidden safe against the bird,

Summer looked out through a red silk curtain into the night. She felt her muscles soften and her eyes sting. She began to cry. The pain she had carried in her stomach since that terrible morning, only yesterday morning, when everyone but Bird was gone, began to fade. Instead of a whole universe of pain, she felt only an ache.

Summer did not know how long the bird held her, because she fell asleep inside the red silk room, the pulse of the bird's blood against her face.

CHAPTER FIVE

A GREAT BIRD AND NO BIRD

A great bird and no bird. That sentence echoed in Summer's head as she hovered between sleep and waking. *A great bird and no bird.* She wrapped her arms around her cold self. *A great bird*—it was like a riddle. And for a moment, her eyes still closed, she thought: *Wait,* was *there something about a great bird? A great red bird?* But as her eyes opened, what she saw made the thought disappear. She closed her eyes quickly, then opened one just enough to see.

The burning tree was gone. In its place, standing in a small pile of ashes, was an old man. He looked like he might have been standing there a long time, and could go on standing longer. He looked as if he were about to laugh (for as long as Summer knew him, he would always look like that). He stood lightly, tall, with thick, disheveled gray-and-black hair. His skin was lined, but warm and clear, as fresh as a child's, caramel-colored but with an ashy, silver cast. He wore a long, ash-gray coat and a long gray scarf, and from what Summer could see through her barely open eye, the clothes beneath the coat were gray as well. A gray cloth bag sat beside him. He scanned the plain. He looked happy and listening.

Summer, secret, watched him from behind her lashes. When a birdcall trailed across the silence, he smiled again. Something about him made Summer feel relaxed for the first time in a long time.

Then the old man looked straight into her barely open eye. "You found the tree," he said. His voice was rough, as if it had been a long time since he had used it.

"Bird did," said Summer, feeling foolish. She sat up.

"What bird?" asked the man.

"Bird, my sister, Bird, is—" Summer looked over her shoulder, then all the way around, then around the man. It was past dawn, and she could see the plain, when last night she could see only stars. Scattered patches of snow were melting on the whitish-gray clay. On her left, she could see the edge of the forest she and Bird had walked through. Ahead was a shining slice of distant water. To her right was a soft row of mountains, white at the top, then green and brown patched with white. Behind her, a long, narrow dirt road stretched down the empty plain to the horizon.

And on all four sides, no Bird. Bird was nowhere at all.

"My sister's gone," said Summer. Her voice sounded shocked and strange in her ears. "Where is she? Do you know?" She thought, but did not say, *Did you take her? Who are you?* With Bird missing, the old man seemed less comforting.

"I do not have the pleasure of knowing your sister," said the man. "How did you find this tree?"

"Bird found it," Summer repeated automatically. Her mind was racing—if this man had taken Bird, then why would he be here, asking about her? Or was he here to capture her as well? But the man did not seem especially interested in either of them. And Summer saw that Bird's pink backpack was gone; her water bottle was gone; and the bag of food had been pulled out of Summer's own pack and left half empty on the ground. The plastic bag that had held the two remaining matches now held only one.

A square of notebook paper was half tucked under Summer's pack. *THE LAST PART OF THE SONG WAS JUST FOR ME,* it read in Bird's scratchy, familiar printing. *DON'T GET MAD ABOUT IT. I MIGHT BE GONE A LONG TIME.* Then a little picture of a bird, like in their mother's picture letter.

The ground looked far away. The paper in her hand looked small. A long time? Meaning an hour? Meaning a day? Meaning a month or a year? She turned around, looking for tracks, but the snow was melting and the ground was hard. "She's gone," Summer said out loud.

"Did Bird set the tree on fire?" the man asked, interrupting her thoughts.

The question was abrupt. Was she in trouble? "It was Bird's idea," was on her lips to say, and she felt immediate shame, even though she hadn't said it aloud, and even though it was true. "I did," she said instead, which after all was also true. "I lit the match. We were really cold. I'm sorry if we shouldn't have, or if that was your tree." She turned and looked over the ground, crossing back and forth, looking for what— tracks? Would Bird leave tracks?

"Bird found it, and you lit it," said the old man. He still seemed about to laugh. "I would like to meet Bird as well."

"Well, she's not here," said Summer. She stopped moving, stopped looking for invisible tracks. "She left." Her lip trembled, and she felt furious with herself. Carefully: "Will you help me find her?"

The old man's smile became a degree more kind. "If she ought to be found, then I will try," he said. "Let's sit down and make a world."

"What do you mean, 'make a world'?"

"That's what my people say to mean 'Let's talk,'" said the old man. "What's your name?

"Summer."

"Summer and Bird," said the man. "Well, that's right. Birds are happiest in summer. And summers should have many birds." He smiled as if he had made a joke.

"I only want my Bird," said Summer. "Did you see her go?"

"I did not," said the old man in the gray coat.

"What's your name? Please," said Summer, remembering "please" at the last minute. "And where did you come from?" She was suddenly at the edge of tears again. He should be helping her.

"Oh, my name," said the old man, as if that were a long story he did not have time for. "You can call me Ben. And I came from where the fire was, of course. Why don't you tell me something about how you came here?" he said. "Perhaps I can help."

Although his explanation made little sense, a knot or two loosened in Summer's heart. "We came—well, we began when—we're looking for our mother and father. And cat, I guess," Summer began. And she told him the story, beginning with the terrible morning, and the empty closet, and the picture letter. The picture letter seemed to interest him particularly, but he let her finish, and when she got to the patchwork bird his smile did not leave, but changed, with layers of sadness and thoughtfulness. "That is remarkable, that is—And your sister has learned her song? That is remarkable. That is outstanding." He was quiet for a while. "You were good to bury that bird," he said. "That was right to do. Thank you for that."

Then he said, "May I see your mother's picture letter?"

Summer felt unexpected gratitude. The puzzle of the picture letter had felt heavy in her pocket all this time. She opened it for him.

"Oh," he said softly. "Well, look at this. Look at this." He nodded his head, and whistled a low whistle. After a time he looked up and said, "What did you choose this letter to mean?"

That was a strange way to put it. "We thought...well, I thought it meant—" Summer began, and then stopped. She tried again. "I thought the first part, a heart in two pieces, that it meant 'I love you both equally.'"

"Ah," said Ben. "I had not thought of that. I like that. Now, I thought it meant 'a heart that is broken.' Or perhaps, instead—or also—'a heart that is torn in half.'"

Summer reddened. "I didn't think of that. I guess it could be that, instead."

"Or that, *also*," said Ben. "And the sun and the bird, is that you and your sister?"

"Yes." (Defensively.) "Or I think so. It always means that."

"It might mean that and other things as well," said Ben, scratching his nose with a long bent finger. "*You* might mean that, and other things as well." He turned his smile toward her. "But yes, I think so, too: Summer and Bird. And then what did you think of this next one?"

"It's a swan," said Summer. "And so I thought—well, we never had a swan before, but I thought"—this was the hardest part, the part she had felt least sure of—"it probably meant like gliding, or moving fast. You know, like a swan," she added, feeling how wrong it sounded.

"And what did Bird think?"

"I didn't ask her," said darkening Summer. "Anyway. I thought it meant we should move fast."

"Because you wanted to move fast," said Ben. "I don't say you're wrong—this letter was sent to you. But it is easy to get it wrong, when you care a great deal about the answer. Let's start more simply. Why can't a swan just mean itself? It might mean 'I am a swan,' you know. Or it might mean 'You are a swan.' Or one of you is."

"That doesn't make sense," said Summer. "My mother is obviously not a swan."

His head cocked, Ben looked at her through one eye. "All right," he said agreeably. "You might also look at the context, and try to guess the syntax. Do you know what syntax means?"

"No."

"It means what things mean when they sit next to each other. Like: a fox chasing a chicken is one thing. A chicken chasing a fox is another. This swan in this place could mean 'My heart is torn between my girls and a swan.'"

"Except none of that makes sense," said Summer, stubborn. "She wouldn't leave us for a swan."

"What is this last picture?" Ben asked. "It looks like two swans, or perhaps a gate."

"It is a gate," said Summer, and explained how their mother had made it. "I did start simpler with that one," she added. "I thought it just meant that gate, and that she had gone through it, and so we should go through it."

"It might mean just exactly that," said Ben. "But it might also mean more than that." He was infuriating. "It might also mean, for example, you and your sister, who are also two trees your mother planted—that between the two of you, the two of you working together, you might create a way forward. Or, listen, Summer—turn around and look at me—or a way back. Gates work both ways, you know. Maybe you and Bird are the gate."

"What gate? And how am I supposed to know which of all those things it means?"

"Maybe it means them all. Nothing important means only one thing." He ran his hands through his hair so that it stood up awkwardly around his head, then got to his feet. He seemed to have finished this conversation. He arched his long-boned arms out wide and behind him, long fingers spread, and looked up. For a moment, Summer felt he might actually launch into flight.

"You said you would help me find Bird," she said. The old man looked down and smiled, and Summer felt that he was smiling down at her from a great height. Then he laughed and dropped his arms.

"It can wait," he said to himself. Then: "I'll tell you what. Let me draw my own picture letter, and see what I can see." He looked around the campsite, picking up and dropping various small stones and sticks, as if looking for one that suited his purpose. He seemed to be enjoying himself. Then he sat down on a large flat rock and began to draw in the dirt.

Summer sat down, too, because she couldn't think of what else to do. The hem of the old man's gray coat fluttered in the small, cold wind. His brown skin was ashy, as if he had slept where the bush had been. He was sketching and erasing on the ground, and humming to himself.

The great bowl above the plain was silvery gray now, and the plain was white and cold, and Bird was nowhere.

"We need to hurry," said Summer. It was rude to speak to adults that way. But she felt rude, and also scared.

"We are hurrying," Ben said, his voice as friendly as ever. "This is hurrying. Oh, this is interesting." And he drew and wrote and erased. Summer moved toward him to look. At that moment he was drawing what seemed to be a frog. Then he drew an odd tree next to the frog, if it was a tree—a tree with a top like a mushroom. Then he erased the frog and the mushroom tree, thought for a while, and wrote: *broken bridge.* Then he erased that, and drew more figures: stars and birds and a staircase and a gate.

"Those are pictures like the ones my mother used to draw."

The old man looked up, and turned his gray head to the side to look at her out of one eye. "I know they are," he said. "I know she did. You are such a surprising person," he added. "And that makes me happy."

He continued to draw. With every drawing and every erasure, Summer knew, Bird was moving farther away. "Please, why are you— what are you doing?" said Summer, trying not to sound upset but knowing she sounded that way anyway.

"I draw on the ground to see what I am drawing, and that helps me know what to do," said the man.

"That is the stupidest thing I ever heard of," said Summer, as rudely as possible. With no warning, her heart was hot thunder. This was like Bird in the forest, looking for stupid signs everywhere, reading meaning in birdcalls and broken bark. ("You read meaning in broken trees, when you're being a tracker," Bird would say. "I read FACTS in broken trees," Summer would reply.)

But it was like what she had done, too, reading meaning into their mother's stupid, childish pictures. It had led them here. It was horrible and useless and wrong.

"You should try it sometime," Ben continued, unaffected. "It isn't the drawing part that's hard. It's understanding what the drawing means afterward." His voice was calm as seawater at the edge of the sand, in and out. "It's very easy to get it wrong, especially if you care about the answer. It's easy to confuse what you want it to say with what it actually says. But it's useful, and of course also very interesting." He straightened up. His hair, which never seemed to stay in one place for long, fell in his eyes. His smiled deepened, and the wrinkles around his dark eyes deepened with it. "So here's what I see," he said.

"I see that your sister will need your help, but she doesn't need help today. I see that you will find her, but not today, or tomorrow, or the next day.

"I see that she is hungry, but not for food. And I see that she is with her family—"

"My family!"

"—but not with your parents."

This was a fairy-tale jumble. This didn't help at all. "But which way did she go then? Where is she?"

"That I don't know."

"Then where are my parents?"

Ben stood up. "That's not a good question right now," he said, as if that were an answer. "And I have something important to do."

"Then I'll find Bird on my own!" said Summer defiantly. But there was nothing to defy; Ben did not seem to hear. He was gazing around the plain with its few, bare bushes. "I am not spoiled for choice," he said with relish. Then his gaze stopped on a low tree, forty or fifty yards away, very much like the little tree Summer and Bird had burnt. "There you are," he said, and moved toward the tree in swift silence, like a hunter.

Like the tree is going anywhere, thought Summer, trailing behind—shy because she had not been invited, curious because she was Summer. Against the white horizon, Summer could see every line of the low-spread tree, every twist of the smallest branches. A few dark green leaves still clung to a branch here and there. She had to go find stupid runaway Bird, but she had to see what Ben was doing first. She could not tell whether he knew she was there or not. He focused on the tree like a cat on a bird; but as if the cat loved the bird (and was somehow, always, about to laugh).

Summer pulled her jacket closer, against the cold and the pointlessness, as Ben reached the tree. He took a branch in one gentle hand and began to murmur something, almost like a chant. Summer leaned forward.

It wasn't a chant. It was a nursery rhyme, a ridiculous, baby nursery rhyme.

One two three, Summer heard Ben say. His hand moved among the tree's many branches, the way a mother strokes a baby's face.

Four and five
I caught a fish alive
Six seven eight

Nine and ten
I let him go again.
Why did you let it go?
Because it bit my finger so.
Which finger did it bite?
The little finger on the right.

With this last word, *right,* Ben's hand stopped.

"Thank you," he said softly to the tree. "We both thank you." (Summer thought: *So he does know I am here.*) She saw a flash; saw a knife in Ben's hand; saw him slice off a chunk of wood as wide as her own palm, but much thicker. A sweet smell—the incense smell of the burning tree, Summer realized—filled the air. A few drops trickled from the cut tree down to the frosty ground.

"It's bleeding," said Summer, stupidly aloud. "The tree is bleeding."

"Or crying," Ben said. "It might be crying a little." He turned to her with his more complicated smile. "You should thank the tree, too, Summer," he said.

"Thank you," said Summer, before she could think. "I'm sorry." Hearing herself, she felt ridiculous. She said, "That smell. We smelled it when our tree burned, too. What is it?"

"It's a myrrh tree," said Ben, tucking the knife and the piece of wood somewhere in his gray folds. He gave the tree a last stroke with his hand.

"Gold, frankincense, and myrrh? Like that?" said Summer. "Like We Three Kings?"

"Yes, like that," said Ben. His long legs took him swiftly toward the camp, and Summer could not keep up.

Months later, in a lonely and terrible place, Bird would hear a story about Ben, although she didn't know it was Ben at the time. She would hear the story from an old, mad bird. It was a story about how, years before, a woman the birds called the Mask, but whom Bird called the Puppeteer, had sent her puppet birds to trap an old man in a tree, "in an eggwood tree, upside down," the old bird said. "She magic-close the tree, and there he stay. There he stay, long legs bent in long bent branches. Long arms twisted in twisted branches. Old head pressing hard gray wood. There he stay."

"For how long?" Bird asked.

"Thirteen years," said the mad old bird. "If he still in there."

But he wasn't.

CHAPTER SIX

THE BIRD QUEEN

The Puppeteer was full of dead birds.

We call her the Puppeteer, but birds call her the Bird Eater, or the Mask. They fear her. She was a dancer and a puppeteer—not in Down, in Up, in the real world, as you might think of it. She made bird puppets to use in her dances, tiny, delicate things in brilliant colors. Your eye made a trail behind them, a smear of ruby or cerulean in the air like a long tail, because you couldn't bear to let the lovely color go. All her tissue birds were like hummingbirds, were lighter than air, were glints of bright color all around her.

The Puppeteer wanted to be a bird. She wanted to fly, but she didn't know how to begin. Instead, she learned bird dances. She traveled the world to study wild cranes and their dances. She took pictures and videos and studied them, practicing for hours.

She ate as little as she could, to make herself light and flyable. She didn't even eat when she was hungry. She thought this would make her more like a bird, but it wasn't much like real birds—real birds eat all they can. They walk around with their mouths wide open sometimes, they're so greedy to find food. A bird is happy to get fat. But the Puppeteer hated her human flesh, so she starved herself, and her bones grew brittle and thin.

In her dance, she controlled the bright paper birds with invisible wires and threads. She played the human: heavy, tied to earth. Her dances weren't pretty or delightful, but they were magical, and even though she only put up one or two handwritten signs in whatever town she performed, people crowded to see them. Word would spread, and a hundred people or two hundred people would gather in whatever field or meadow she had made her stage. They called her a dancer and a puppeteer and an artist. They might have called her a witch, and not the good kind, either.

One early golden evening, a year before Summer was born, the Puppeteer performed her dance in a long green field beside an old, abandoned stone cottage—the cottage that would one day become Summer and Bird's home. She had also performed in this meadow the night before, which was unusual—she did not normally like to perform twice in one location.

But this time, she had a special reason for revisiting this spot. After the performance, the Puppeteer believed, she would have what she craved most in the world. She would become not just a bird, but the queen of the birds.

It was late summer, nearing fall, and the weather was cool, and the wildflowers were dead. Scores of cars parked on the grass, and a hundred or so adults and children stood waiting. Some put money in a battered bucket marked FOR THE DANCE.

As it grew closer to twilight, the Puppeteer's soaring, delicate birds appeared, like magic, out of the trees. She walked out behind them. She was dancing "human"; she was awkward and heavy. She sagged. She waddled, clumsy and stiff, beneath the soaring, delicate birds. The birds darted and dipped in the air above her. The human longed toward them. She grew angry. She clawed with her hands at the streaks of cherry and tangerine sailing above her.

Then, among the paper birds, a real bird appeared. This was part of the dance—the Puppeteer counted on a real bird coming, and one always did, sometimes more than one. Her puppet birds drew them in. This bird was not much bigger than the tissue birds, but it was not as pretty or colorful, and not as delicate. It was coarse and imperfect compared to the tissue birds, and for that reason it put the puppet birds to shame. The audience could not take their eyes off it. That always happened, too.

In the dance, the awkward human flailed at the birds, clutching, hungering, pathetic. Then her hand froze in mid-claw: Caught one. The tissue-paper birds trembled above her, hovering, waiting. Her hand rose up to her surprised, stupid human face. She peered inside her fist. Then, quick, she slammed the fist against her open mouth, and swallowed it.

Some of the audience gasped, because she seemed to have swallowed the living bird. But their friends whispered, "No, no—that was just a trick, if you were watching closely, you could see, it was all sleight-of-hand." That's what some people said. But others, for the rest of the dance, would swear they could hear the wings of that bird beating inside her, terrified, like a wild heart.

Those others were right. She *had* swallowed the living bird. She swallowed one in every performance. Here's why: for the few hours that that terrified, fluttering bird remained alive inside her, she could understand the bird language. After performances, she would wander in the woods, listening to the Great Conversation. Sometimes she tried to join in herself. But the only bird who would speak with her was the owl. She said to the owl one time: "You and I have this in common—we both eat birds." The owl said nothing. It was true and not true.

Here are some of the things the Puppeteer had learned from listening to the Great Conversation. She learned that the birds had a queen, called the swan queen, who had disappeared. She learned about a place called the Green Home, now lost, which was a thorn of grief and beauty inside every bird. Most interesting of all, she learned about the swan queen's robe, which let her choose to be either a swan or a woman, depending on whether she wore the robe or not.

The more the Puppeteer learned, the more she wanted to be the bird queen; and above all, above everything, the more she wanted that swan robe, to be the beating heart inside it—the way a living bird was sometimes the beating heart inside her own chest.

Bird-eating was one kind of magic, a secret kind. The other kind, a theater magic, was what happened to her dance after she ate the bird. With a bird-heart, her dance lightened. Now she was only half heavy human; she was also half radiant bird. She danced like a crane, her head thrown back, her long throat stretching up. (Some in the audience could still hear, could almost see, wings beating in anguish inside her chest, and felt uneasy.)

Then the dance became more violent; dangerous. The human was hungry again, and danced a hunger dance. One by one, she swallowed (seemed to swallow) all the tissue-paper birds. The audience were quiet as cats.

Now the dancer dropped to her knees. Something painful was happening inside her. She twisted and rocked on her knees, rising high, dropping low, rising high again, as if she were the puppet now, jerked and heaved on the sky's string. Jerked high, one last time, almost to the tips of her toes, she opened her mouth wide and gave a long, wailing cry.

It was the first sound of the whole performance. The audience drew back.

At the tail of the long cry, a single tissue-paper bird seemed to fly out of the dancer's mouth. It was all the colors of all the other paper birds, twisted together. The audience applauded. The rainbow bird swooped above her, alone, then lit on her shoulder, by her ear. The dancer stood still as ice, listening.

Then the bird flew off a yard or two toward the river, and hovered in the air. It flew back to her, and darted away again. Everyone in the audience could see what that meant: Come. The dancer came. Darting and retreating, the tissue bird led her toward a particular spot on the riverbank.

Here's why.

The night before, after her performance, the Puppeteer had wandered through the woods eavesdropping on the birds, as usual. Alerted by their excited chatter, she had discovered what might be— what surely *must* be—the object she most desired: a silky robe of swan feathers, hidden in a hollow tree. But as she clutched the robe, sensing its power, the sky was beginning to gray toward morning, and the bird inside her was already dying. It was too late to learn how to put it on, how to use it to become a swan, to become a queen. And without that knowledge, the robe was useless to her.

Then, as she stood in the almost-dawn, half wrapped in the robe, she had heard voices, a man and a woman; had seen a flashlight moving through the trees. Quick and soft, she had gathered up the robe and run through the woods to the empty stone cottage nearby. There she found an inner closet—you might call it an inside closet—with a small brass key in its lock. She stuffed the robe inside, turned the key, and whispered certain words that made the door and the lock unbreakable for as long as she kept the key.

All that had happened the night before. Tonight, she had returned with a plan: she would swallow another bird, disappear into the forest as usual, and while tonight's bird lived within her, eavesdrop on the bird conversation until she understood how to use the robe. Then it would be hers forever.

But the Puppeteer was vain. And in her vanity, she had added one extra piece of trickery, one final bit of astonishment, to her performance that night. Earlier in the day, she had discovered a place where she could cross the river on a series of rocks, just below the surface. If she finished her performance at just that spot, and crossed the river there into the forest, it would look as if she were walking on water. The audience would be astounded. Their mouths would hang open.

And that, the Puppeteer could not resist.

But though she did not know it (except the part of her that chose this field, this river, this place to cross), that little stone path in the river led straight to a Puppeteer-shaped doorway to Down.

So as the Puppeteer put one foot on the bank on the far side of the river, the doorway caught her, just as Summer and Bird's doorway had caught them, and she slid through to Down. The robe lay locked in a closet in that empty stone cottage, out of her reach. And that was that.

To the audience, it looked as if the dancer walked across the river, on the water, and then disappeared. It was thrilling. They applauded the theater magic, waiting for her to return. But she didn't return, and the applause trailed off. After a while, they left.

Night fell on the FOR THE DANCE bucket, sitting on the grass alone.

CHAPTER SEVEN

RAVEN AT THE CROSSROADS

After cutting the piece of myrrh wood, Ben returned to his rock and began to work the wood with his long knife. Summer couldn't tell what he was making, and she was shy to ask.

"That sounded like a nursery rhyme you said back there," she said instead. "That 'One two three four and five, I caught a fish alive.'"

"So it is," said Ben, carving.

"But you're old," said Summer. "Why would you say a nursery rhyme?"

Ben looked up. "What do you think a nursery rhyme is?" he asked.

Summer's tongue struggled with what should have been an easy answer. A nursery rhyme was just—everyone knew what they were. "It's just—it's like, a poem, for babies and little kids."

"It is that," said Ben. "But it is also more than that. It is made of rhymes and rhythm that sink deep into a small child's bones. A nursery rhyme shapes your bones and nerves, and it shapes your mind. They are powerful, nursery rhymes, and immensely old, and not toys, even though they are for children."

"But they make no sense!" Summer protested.

"Ah, well," said Ben. "Sometimes sense hides behind walls. You must find a window and stick your head right in before you can see it."

After that, he was no more help at all. Summer knew that if she was going to find Bird that day, she was on her own.

∽

She had four directions to choose from, and she chose the road, because she wanted to move. She wished she had her bicycle and could ride across this cold flat plain with hair and jacket flying behind her, heart and feet pumping. She wished she could howl like dogs and birds. Do birds howl? Was Bird howling?

The long dirt path seemed to begin, or perhaps end, at their camp in the center of the plain, for no good reason Summer could see; and it ended, or began, somewhere past the horizon. "You will find her, but not today or tomorrow" rang in her mind, but she set her boots on the path anyway. After she had walked for a minute or two, she began to run. Over pounding feet she thought: *Stupid Bird, stupid* baby, *to run away and do this to me. I don't care what happens to you, Bird, I just want to be done with watching you, tending you. I only want to watch myself.*

(Then: *Maybe I am already done watching her,* Summer thought. And she quickly thought about something else.)

After a while, running, walking, running again, she could no longer see Ben or the camp behind her. But the horizon looked just as far away as when she started. She could see, though, that in the distance, another path crossed her own, and in that crossroads, a tiny black figure stood. As she walked closer, she saw it was a raven, with smooth feathers as black as a puddle of tar on a road. One of its eyes was black, and the other was blue. It did not move.

Summer stopped a few feet away. More to herself than to the bird, she said softly, "Hello, raven."

The raven opened its beak and, just as softly, exhaled a small sigh. Warm air clouded around the sigh. Summer lowered herself to the ground until she sat cross-legged, facing the bird.

The raven cocked its head, so that its black eye gleamed at her. She felt her own blue eyes gleaming back. The air between them began to swim and shimmer. ("Left my eyes open too long, probably," she explained to Ben later. "Or some pollen.")

Then the world leaped into focus. Though she had not turned her head, she found she was looking at the forest to her right. She saw each leaf, and the lines and veins of each leaf, and the wind brushing the feathers of the birds half hidden behind those leaves. The forest was made of new colors, thousands of them, for which Summer had no names.

But the world was also flat, somehow—like a photograph of a world, but a photograph that showed the grain of every pebble, the waving antennae of a family of ants on the ground near her feet.

(Were they feet, still? Her toes felt long and thin and crooked now, and strong.)

Sounds were sharp and separate—a bird toe shifting on gravel. A sigh. A birdcall hundreds of yards away.

And then she smelled the world. The delight of it almost rocked her backward. The patches of new snow smelled of minerals, a diamond smell. A strong smell of urine from near the forest—but not a bad urine smell, a friendly one. A dark spicy-sweet smell of nuts from a young beech tree a little farther in. It was as if she'd taken off a blindfold and could finally see.

Alive to every sight and sound and smell, Summer felt a joyful wariness. Confident as a tightrope walker—*I might die, yes. But I won't. Unless I do.*

She tilted her head to the right and saw the flat picture of a yellow-haired girl, face and hands streaked with dirt, wisps of grass and dead leaves caught in her hair. The girl looked shocked; looked lost within herself.

Summer laughed out loud at the yellow-haired girl; it came out dry and harsh. She felt the opposite of lost inside—she had never felt so alive in the world. Her back and arms, which were no longer arms, were bursting with dangerous power.

It might have lasted ten minutes, or two hours, the time was that rich and full.

And then the dirt-smeared girl across from her blinked. The air swam, and then was air again. A door shut against the new name-less colors, against what sight and sound and scent could be. Summer was herself again, blind and deaf and uncertain, looking at a raven on the road.

The raven watched her for a moment. Then it flapped its wings and flew away.

Hours later, Summer gave up on the road that never got any closer to the white horizon. *It could get dark while I am still out here,* she thought, and turned back, even as she turned thinking angrily, *Everything I do is because I'm afraid. I wish I were more like Bird.* And thinking of lost Bird, she cried a little. She cried and walked and cried until she was back at the camp.

Ben was still carving. The sky was indeed growing darker, and night was coming. A whole day gone, and Bird not found, and night coming on. As the sun slipped down the sky, it paused for a moment behind Ben's head, bent over his work. From where Summer stood, it was as if a golden disc shone behind his head for a few moments, then dropped away.

Stupid. It was just the sun.

For a long time, Ben did not speak, only worked his knife over and over the bit of wood, making it smooth. Summer sat down, miserable, on the chilly ground. She opened her journal, but did not know how to begin to describe what had happened in the last two days. Instead she wrote: *Bird left last night. Looked for her down the road. Will look again tomorrow,* then snapped the journal shut. Summer was beginning to shiver as the sunlight faded. Even the ashes from last night's fire were gone.

"It's cold," she said finally. "And I only have one match left. I can't use it just for you and me, and not for Bird." The burden of her misery spoken out loud, she began to cry again. In the dim light her tears disappeared as soon as they dropped from her cold cheeks. It seemed like all she'd done down here was cry. Bird hadn't cried.

Ben looked up, surprised. Then he gave his almost-laughing smile. "We won't freeze," he said. "I am not so new on this earth as it may seem," he added in his voice that said "joke," though Summer did not see what was funny.

"Why don't you make a fire?" said Summer, adding, unkindly, "Don't you know how?"

Ben cocked his head again to look at her with one eye. "I do know how," he said. "I know a lot about fire. But I don't want to burn any more of these trees only to keep us warm one night. What a terrible waste that would be."

He fished inside the gray cloth bag that seemed to be his only possession. "In any case, there are other solutions. Or there should be…this may…no, more light than heat, and that won't do, what we want…ah!" he said happily, pulling out an iron pot that seemed too large to have fit in a bag no bigger than Bird. The pot was rusty under one lip.

"There's nothing to cook in it," said Summer, anger hiding inside her voice. "And there's no *fire* to cook with."

"I didn't really fetch it for cooking," said Ben, "not this time. But it has kept the heat of many years of cooking, so it's quite warming…aha!" he announced, tugging at something inside the bag. "I knew it was here." He held up what looked like some old red knitting. "This will keep you warm," he said, balling it up and tossing it to her.

Summer darkly doubted it, but she unfolded the knitting, with reluctance, as it did not seem very clean. It was a sweater, the color of a dusty tomato, full of holes, and far too big for her. It looked as though it might smell bad. She put it on anyway, and found it smelled sweet, as if it had caught some of the scented smoke from the burning myrrh tree. It was much warmer than she had imagined, and comforting, too.

"Good," said Ben, though she had not said a word. "Come sit closer to the pot."

She did, and felt warm air—not the billowing heat of a fire, but a peaceful radiance, coming from the pot. She put her hand out to touch it, then pulled away. It was hot. Ben was right: it would be good to sleep near tonight.

Thinking of sleeping out again reminded Summer that she had not yet said aloud the worst part of her burden. "Ben," she said softly, so softly that he looked up from his carving.

"Yes?" he said, softly too.

"Bird is out there in the cold. Bird hasn't got any sweater or pot or friend. I didn't find her," Summer said, and she began to cry again. She thought of her mother and father, vanished, and how (she thought) they would hate her, if she let something happen to Bird. The pain in her chest swelled huge and hard.

Ben said, "I know she is out there alone. I am sorry for that. I think she might be being…watched over. But that doesn't mean it isn't hard and dangerous." He put down the wood and the knife. "Listen, Summer-shower. When you and Bird set fire to the bush, it changed some things. And it helped me, a great deal. I have to go soon. But I want to repay you somehow, you and your Bird. And also, I need to ask you for just a little bit more help. What do you think?"

Summer looked up at him. "You're going?"

"Not tonight," said Ben. "I haven't finished what I'm making." He paused, then said, "Why don't you tell me about your walk today."

So Summer told him about the walk, and about not finding Bird, and about the raven.

"That was an animal teacher," said Ben, "or, you might say, an animal friend, who came to remind you of your animal soul."

"My animal soul," said Summer. "I don't know what that means."

"You have a soul, of course," Ben said. "And of course also you have an animal soul. Did you think you didn't have an animal soul? Now that would be sad." Saying "sad," he laughed. "How could you not, Summer-rain? Where else could your animal self live, but in your animal soul?"

"I don't have an animal self," said Summer, stiff from being laughed at. "I'm not an animal."

Ben looked at her quite seriously. He felt her arm, down to the wrist. He looked a long while into her eyes. Then he laughed again, dropped her arm. "Well, you scared me for a minute," he said. "But you are definitely an animal."

"Are you an animal, too?" Summer asked.

"Oh, me especially," said gray-and-dark Ben, returning to his carving. "We all have an animal teacher or friend to teach us about our animal souls."

"Is it always a bird?"

"No, no. A bird, often. But other times a dog, perhaps, or a horse. It can be anything. What you need, is what comes. A bird to call you, a horse to bear you, a dog to guide you. What you need is what comes. And it comes to everyone at some point, all over the world, not just this world, but your world as well."

"Then how come I've never heard of anyone"—she wasn't sure how to say it—"meeting an animal the way I did? I've *never* heard of that."

"Ah, well. When a person's animal teacher comes, will they be paying attention enough to see it? That's another question. You have to be awake. You have to be paying attention. And you have to have enough sense to understand the bird. You have to have enough trust to follow the dog. Enough courage to mount the horse. See, that's the trick of it."

Summer felt calmer from the sweet-scented warmth of the

sweater. She began to feel sleepy. Ben said, "Are you warm enough?"

"Yes," she said.

"I'm glad," he said. "That sweater is your first gift."

"My first!" she said, almost laughing. "How many gifts are there?" But Ben didn't laugh. "There are three," he replied. "Two are from me." And then: "While you're falling asleep, I would like to tell you a story."

"Is it a true story?" asked Summer.

"Yes. It is true right through," said Ben. And he began the tale.

"Haven't you wondered why there are so many birds still here in the winter? Some birds always stay—cardinals, that's right, and lots of robins and wrens stay, too, even in the snow—but not so many birds as are here now. It's very bad for them, and hard for them, those birds who usually cross the border at this time, to have to stay."

"What border?"

"The attainable border of the birds. You don't know it? Well. When the cold comes and deepens, and the frosty nights are longer than the warm days, the birds begin to leave. That's how it's always been. They gather at a particular lake, almost all the birds do. Where you're from, when you see birds leaving in the fall, that's where they're going, to that lake. When they have all arrived, the queen of the birds leads them to the Green Home. The queen is like an arrow in the sky, pointing the others on.

"The birds fly a long time, many days and weeks. The journey makes them thin and strong, or it kills them. They fly over a sea so blue it is almost black, and the rising water-winds hold the birds up like a hand, and the sun sparks off the water and hurts their eyes."

"I know this story," Summer interrupted. She was half asleep but half remembering something as well. "It's from that song, that 'Two Little Cygnets' song."

Ben gave her his cocked-head, one-eye look. "I don't know that song."

"Everyone knows that song," said Summer. It's like 'Rain rain, go away,' like that. Like a nursery rhyme. Anyway, I thought everyone knew it. My mother sang it to us all the time when we were little. 'Two little cygnets/Flying to the queen,/To her stone-white castle/Near a'—something -een. 'Near a mountain green,' maybe. And then the queen, like, leads them on this trip, and later on it says something like, 'The sea blue as nighttime,/The wind like a hand,/Two little cygnets/Looking for land.' See, like you said, like a hand. Anyway, it's just a baby song. It has about a million verses. I don't even remember most of them."

"Hmm," said Ben. "That is very interesting. It might be a children's song, but perhaps it is also—"

"Oh, ALSO. Everything is ALSO," Summer said.

Ben smiled. "Also a great deal more than that, I was going to say, quite right. But let me finish my story." And he continued. "The birds fly over a thousand miles of lumpy green, like heads of broccoli.

"They fly over a thousand miles of yellow sand and rock.

"They fly over a sea so green it is almost blue.

"They fly through terrible storms. In a storm, they wait in one of those broccoli trees if they can, if they're over land. It does not storm over the yellow rocks and sand often, but when it does, the storms are terrible, and the birds hide in rock crannies."

"What if a storm comes when they're at sea?"

"They make a tighter band, and ride it out as well as they can. Some are blown far from their families, and land alone on ships or islands. And some of them die.

"The very last thing they fly over before they reach the attainable border is a low mountain, which is covered in soft grass at the bottom, dark trees in the middle, and snow at the very top. Two paths lead up the mountain, and at the very top, they cross. Where the two roads cross is a small house made of stone, with one chimney that smokes all day and night."

"I know that part!" said Summer. "On a mountain crossroads/The little house stood./ Two little cygnets say/'Something smells good.'"

"Aha," said Ben. "Well, every year, when the birds fly over, the woman who lives in the house, who is very old, sees them through her window. She always comes out, and puts her hand up to shield her eyes from the sun, and watches the birds pass."

"And the old woman watches/On the mountain alone," Summer sang, "While the birds fly past/To the Green Green Home, the Green Green Home, the Green Green Home." She sat up on one arm. "That's the last line. So what happens next?"

Ben paused. "Well. After that, the birds reach the attainable border. The border is where earth and sky meet. You can see it from here. You can see it from everywhere. Even now, with the moon just past full and all these stars—do you see it? The place where earth and sky meet, where the stars stop? It's the farthest thing you can see. That's the attainable border. The queen leads the birds over the border, to the Green Home."

"But how can they go beyond? If that's where earth and sky supposedly meet, how could they get through?"

"Because at one special time of year, which is the time the birds fly there, the border opens. Earth and sky open their mouth, and the queen can lead the birds through. Or that is what used to happen. Thirteen years ago, the birds gathered at the lake, but their queen never came. They waited for days and then weeks, but she never came. That had never happened before. Every queen teaches the next queen the way before she dies. But this queen had not died, at least as far as the birds knew. She had simply disappeared. She never came to the lake that year, or any year since, though many birds still gather there. She has abandoned them."

That seemed to be the end of the story. Lying on her side, looking at the horizon, Summer imagined the birds, thousands of them, floating silent on a lake, as the day waned and the dark came. Bobbing in the dark, ten thousand birds, waiting. Her mother's song ran through her head, and the memory of her mother's voice made her sad. The plain's silence deepened. She was glad she was not alone. "Why couldn't they just go to the Green Home without the queen?" she asked.

"They didn't know the way," said Ben. "Only the queen did. Well—only the queen, and one other, but he hadn't yet heard of the trouble, and once he did, he was"—Ben hesitated—"he couldn't come. But some brave birds, or desperate birds, have tried, because they miss the Green Home so much. But they have all died trying."

"Why do they keep trying, then?"

"Finding your real home, imagine what that must be like. Imagine how you would feel."

Summer was quiet. "Then why did they ever leave the Green Home in the first place?"

"Why don't you leave your Christmas tree up all year?"

"Because it isn't Christmas all year."

"Well, the Green Home is a seasonal home only. It is only there in the right season."

"Then why did some birds not go even in the season? Why do some stay here?"

"The birds who stay—they stay to care for one another, and for the land, and for you, and people like you."

"Which is the better choice? Which one is right?"

"Every bird has to decide that alone in her own heart."

It was silent for a while. Wind traveled hard above them, but the air was still below.

"What is it like, on the other side of the border, in the birds' real home, the Green Home?" asked Summer, sleepily.

Ben was silent a long while. Summer thought he had not heard her, or had chosen not to answer. Finally, he said softly, "I can't really say. I forget, when I am not a bird."

But Summer was already asleep.

That night Summer dreamed that she was looking for her cat in the woods. It had run outside: a house cat shouldn't do that, a house cat should stay in the house. And her mother won't like it that she's gone in the woods to look. Dreaming Summer walks and walks along the path, but woods have so many moving shadows, how do you find a small black-and-white cat among them, especially if she does not want to be found?

The woods are quiet. She is afraid to call the cat's name out loud.

Then, from a low thicket, the cat's green eyes glitter as they always do. Summer reaches under carefully, but something terrible must have happened—the cat must have lost all her hair somehow, she must have been sick, or in a fight. Summer's hands are wrapped around bare, raw flesh. Her stomach turns. But she pulls. She pulls, and pulls again—and the cat keeps coming. The naked, hairless cat is much too long. Something is wrong.

She is holding a snake, a snake as thick as a cat, a snake with green glittering eyes, and a half-circle of tiny green jewels under each eye. She and the snake stare at each other. Then, slowly, the snake begins to weave against her arm, rough bare skin sliding against hers. She can't move, watching the snake's green eyes, as deep as cave pools.

Then the patchwork bird is speaking in her ear. But it doesn't sound raspy and foreign, it sounds like someone she knows, but she can't remember who.

The voice says: "Snakes are old birds."

The snake's snout is very near her face now. She knows that it will eat her.

And then she wakes up.

CHAPTER EIGHT

WHERE IT BEGAN

In their first night in Down, in the snowy woods, her blood electrified by the song of the patchwork bird, Bird had thrown her recorder into the woods. With it she sent a wish: choose where I should go. All that night, as they walked, as they set camp, as they lit the fire, she longed to find the place her instrument had chosen.

So later that first night, when the fire was burning strong, and Summer's arm around her had grown heavy and soft, Bird pulled herself away. She walked through the blackness, blinder and blinder the farther she got from the flames. With her pack, with her water and some of the food, and with one single match, Bird walked into the dark. Her boots crunched on the light snow. Cold air slipped under her jacket hood like a mother's hand. Her breath was smoke. The moon had sunk away, and the night was almost perfectly black, except for the tiny circle of yellow light behind her and the million glittering stars far above.

Once she stepped into the woods again, the stars were no help. But blackness does not matter so much when your bones know the way. The patchwork bird's song sang furiously inside her, pushing her on. Her bones heard the song and led blind Bird to the twin trees, helped her between them, slipped her through thick brush and beneath bent trees, even in the blackness.

Little yellow eyes in round gray cases watched from above.

Maybe she had walked three hours, maybe more. An electric song drove her small body. Finally, her legs buckled; she could go no farther.

As she dropped to her knees, her limp hand fell on smooth wood: her recorder. The song had led her truly, just as it promised. She took the cold wood in her hand, lay down, and fell asleep.

She dreamed of growing wings.

She dreamed of a feathered crown.

When she woke, it was past dawn. Light glowed between the branches here and there, complicating the dim. All around her was the call of birds.

Silence. Birdcall, silence. Birdcall. Silence. Birdcall, and an answer, another answer. Silence. A song.

Bird sat up and listened. Her eyes closed. The bird music sank into her, like a song you used to know but forgot long ago. You hear a piano play it some day, and for a minute you feel a happy pain, but you don't know why. Bird felt like that.

Bird sat in the cold and listened for a whole day. She ate two pieces of dried apple and drank some of her water. She copied Summer's little pile of kindling from the first night, copied the way she struck her match, and made a small fire. Soon after dark, when the birds went to sleep, Bird slept, too, pushed up against a tree, the hot fire warming her face, coat pulled tight around her. She woke up twice in the night to feed the fire.

The next morning she tossed a few twigs to keep the embers alive, but she did not get up. When the air moved from black no-light to gray half-light, she stayed where she was, lying on her back, and watched. At first she could only see the confusion of leaves and branches and light and shadow above her, songs emerging, but no birds. Once in a while a branch would tremble, as if some tiny creature had leaped away. But she couldn't see what leaped.

Bird stayed still and watched, with her ears now as well as her eyes. Everything faded but the sounds—a trill, an unsteady chirp, a frustrated scream. One bird's uncertain call: *Chirp. Chirp…chirp. Ch-chirp.*

The stiller she lay in the chill air, the calmer she became, and the more her eyes and ears opened. At first her mind raced with wanting, wanting to hear and see and learn. But after a time, her mind was as still as her body.

And once her mind was still, she began to see. Just a little at first— a flash of wing as it passed through a patch of light. A twig that trembled not from the wind.

Once she saw a whole bird, hiding among patches of light and dark. It had rough brown wings and a soft gray face and breast—no special bird, but Bird saw it. She saw it open its mouth and call.

The bird seemed to sit so Bird could see her, and Bird felt gratitude. The bird was short and fat and moved in quick, efficient bursts. *Birds are efficient: like Summer,* thought Bird.

The bird paused. She moved. She called, and Bird saw her beak open, her head lift, and heard the tiny burst of sound.

The bird called; and another bird came. Together they flew off.

Something like "Come," Bird thought. And she sang the notes in her head, softly. Something like "Come."

She ate the rest of her dried apple slices and a few nuts. She drank half the water she had left, although she wanted more. And when the birds went quiet in the cold dark forest, she stoked her small fire, and slept.

So Bird slept in the forest with the birds that night, only a weak, flickering fire between her and the black cold. Summer slept under the stars, wrapped in Ben's red sweater. But each of them fell asleep turning over the same questions in her heart: Where is my mother? Where is my father? Where are they, where are they, where are they.

The answer was that they, too, were in Down, but far apart, and far away.

Their father sat in a boat that sat on dry land.

Their mother lay deep in the ground, but alive.

And their father's heart and their mother's heart each longed for their girls, just as the girls longed for them. A full house of longing hearts, though a house split open and scattered, far from where it began. But even scattered as they were, the strands of longing from those four hearts met in the sky and twined in harmony, making one sad, silent song.

But another heart, a discordant heart, had thrust among them. This heart had spoiled the family's music for many years, though they did not know it. And this heart's ravenous longing sounded not like any music, but like the scream of a cat, or a hawk when it kills. This was the Puppeteer's heart, and the Puppeteer's long claw was coming very near one small, cold, sleeping girl.

Soon, Summer and Bird will each hear the story of how their lives began: how their parents met and came to be together. Summer will hear something like the true story, and Bird will hear it mutilated, deformed.

It took Bird a long time to get over the way she heard the story first. But Summer told her the true version, much later—the very beginning of the story, before the Puppeteer made it all go so sad and wrong.

Here's what Summer said:

"When our father was in college he took a class in Nature Something, something about ecology, or birds, or something. They did field research on a river where migrating swans would visit once a year. But the swans were late that year. The students took shifts with binoculars and notebooks and tape recorders, waiting for the swans.

"It was his second shift, his second turn. And it was late in the day; the twilight was coming in. He sat in the woods just off the bank, hidden, so as not to scare the swans, who weren't coming, who weren't ever coming, he thought. His hands felt gritty. He was bored. He held the tape recorder by its wrist cord and let it twirl, back and forth. He drew pictures in his notebook of trees and Chinese mountains and a woman's face.

"Then he saw it. Not a flock of swans, like he'd been waiting for, but just one swan. She must have sailed over the woods across the river, he thought later; but to him it looked like she had come burning through the clouds aimed straight for him. She had a fat gourd of a body, he said, wings like an angry angel, and an impossibly long neck. The proportions were all wrong—they could not make a beautiful creature. But her beauty broke his heart, he said, and (he said; he told me this) his heart has never healed again.

"As she drew near the water, the swan arched her wings, lifted her long throat, and, at the last moment, dropped huge, hilarious black feet flat onto the water. Dad said his first sight of those huge feet made him so happy, he had to cover his mouth so that he wouldn't laugh out loud. Her celestial beauty, he said, and her huge, hideous feet. She skimmed across the water on those flippers, arching her wings higher, lifting her face, until her feet sank—like a water-skier when the boat slows down, he said—and the swan settled on the surface of the river, making its wings into a new shape, close against her body. Like an origami of wings. She sailed like a floating chariot.

"So it was almost dusk, right when things look wet and strange, and the swan's feathers glowed. The wind ruffled and played with her feathers. Dad wanted to ruffle and play with them, too. The swan turned and glided toward the shore near his hiding spot. He pulled back a little, so as not to scare her, so as to be secret.

"He was supposed to be taking notes and estimating her size—she was almost as tall as he was—"

"She was, I know," said Bird.

"—and her wings spread wide were longer than that," Summer continued.

"But he wasn't taking notes, like he was supposed to; he was just watching. She was supposed to be with a whole flock of swans, or at least her family. But she was alone, she was all by herself.

f them was doing what they were supposed to do.

reached the riverbank and climbed up a little ways on flat ugly feet. Dad covered his mouth again. Those feet always made him laugh, he said; his whole life, after that, those feet never stopped making him happy.

"It was quiet, except for the sound of the river, a rushing sound underneath the quiet. The swan paused on the bank as if she were listening, and for a minute he thought she heard him breathing, because her head ducked toward his hiding place, just for a minute. But then she settled down on the bank.

"And that is when something amazing happened, even more amazing than a swan sailing out of the clouds straight at him. Dad stopped talking for a minute when he came to this part. He looked at something on the ground. While he was quiet, I waited in the picture he made in my mind. The river runs on, *rushhhhhhhhh*. The light is darker at the edges of things. His notebook lies on the ground, open to a drawing of a mountain in fog.

"Then he said this: he said the swan began to move inside her skin. Inside her skin, he said. The feathers began to slip and slide in a wrong way, as if the skin beneath them was no longer attached to the body. As if they were not feathers and skin, but a heavy robe she shrugged and wriggled off. The feathers shook. The swan's shape swelled and shrank and twisted.

"And then the robe of feathers did slip off. And a woman stood there, a thick white pile of feathers at her feet. A strange-looking woman in the strange light, but beautiful to our father. Her hair was black with white streaks, like chalk on blacktop."

"I know," said Bird.

"She was very pale," Summer went on. "She wasn't wearing any clothes; the feathers in a pool at her feet, those were her clothes. The moon was rising. She stretched her throat to the moon and yawned, a big, noisy yawn. And then she stepped to the edge of the bank and dove into the water.

"As her legs disappeared under the glitters of moon, our father saw that the woman had one human foot and one big, black swan flipper. He laughed out loud."

CHAPTER NINE

CRANES OVER
THE RIVER

The next morning, haunted by her snaky dream, Summer woke up with a tight, angry heart. But then Summer never woke up easy and slow, only fast and anxious and ready to move.

Ben was asleep, sprawled at an awkward, hieroglyphic angle, cradling something between his body and the ground. Summer said out loud what she had only felt the day before. "Stupid girl, stupid BABY."

Ben's eyes opened. "You or your sister?" he asked, as if he had not been asleep at all.

"My sister, obviously," said angry Summer. "Stupid baby to run away like this. I bet she didn't mean to be gone so long, but she's lost now. I bet she is."

"Where do you bet she went?" said Ben, still angled on the ground.

"I don't know, how would I know?" said Summer, quick and furious. But then she thought: *Where* would *Bird go, if not up the road?* This time she would think it through.

So as Ben straightened his gray layers, then sat down to his knife work—it was his carving that he had cradled so tenderly in sleep—Summer looked around. Woods: we came from there. Road: tried that. Mountains: yes, maybe. Water...oh: *water.*

Bird loved water. After summer breakfasts, she would race straight to the river, plastic goggles dangling from one finger. "You go, too," their mother would tell Summer. "Bird's too young to swim in the river alone."

"But she's a great swimmer, she's better than me!" Who ever plans to spend a ripe summer morning babysitting?

"It doesn't matter. She's too young to make good decisions. Go."

In this cold, though, surely Bird would never have tried to swim? But too late: now that Summer had had that terrible thought—little brown Bird, too young to make good decisions, putting a careful foot in freezing, unmerciful water—she must go.

"I have to go to the water," she said to Ben, slipping the red sweater off and folding it into her backpack.

This time Summer did not run, but walked across the white clay plain, at first in wide zigzags, looking for small footprints. But hard clay keeps its secrets, so she gave up and aimed straight for the water.

No track. No wind. Ground so bare that when she stopped to rest there was nowhere to sit, so she squatted to sip the warm sweet tea Ben had scooped from his iron pot into her aluminum bottle. Tea seemed to be all he ever ate. With the tea, she had one chocolate and two crackers, which wasn't enough.

After another hour, the river grew from a sliver to a ribbon, with the distant-traffic sound of rushing water. Her heart rose as she imagined Bird, hungry and cold, but fine, sorry she'd been so foolish, grateful to be saved.

And then a broad river, its near bank low and lapped by shallow waters, the far bank indistinct, snowy ground with scrub, then a line of trees.

Water-sound rushed along the quiet plain.

And no sign of Bird—none of her now, and none that said she'd been here. Summer walked up and down the bank. Nothing. As far as Summer could tell, she was the first person ever to reach this white-and-gray piece of river-sky-ground. No Bird. Only disappointment, aching legs, and the death of her stupid hopes. She sat on a rock. A white-gray mist rose out of the water, obscured the riverbank for a while, then melted into the white-gray sky.

White on silver on gray on white, thought Summer: it was like being in someone else's old black-and-white photograph. She untucked her own hands for reassurance: red-chapped, blue at the nails. *I am not a photograph.*

Why had she come? Why had she been so stupidly sure? And where—she felt a sword of anger in her chest—where were her parents? *They* should be looking for Bird, not her. "Mom!" Summer shouted furiously, for no reason but to hurt something, if only the air. "Dad!"

As if in answer, a call came in the air—a high, soft, guttural cry, and then another. *A bird?* Summer thought. *A bird* purring? She looked up, shielding her eyes from the white sky: a goose?

But the bird beating a wide circle above the wide water was much too big to be a goose. It looked as tall as she was, with outstretched neck, long thin legs trailing the air behind it, and enormous wings. It was whiter than the white clay, except for a sunset-red strip down its head, and black-tipped primary feathers along the edge of its wings.

A crane: it was some kind of crane. Automatically, her father's daughter, Summer tried to figure out what kind of crane it was. But identification begins with habitat and time of year, and she had no idea where she was, or whether it was supposed to be winter or spring.

The wheeling crane turned, began to fall through the air directly toward her. Summer jumped up and stumbled away, her heart jumping up and stumbling, too. But girl-eyes misjudge what bird-bones know. The crane pulled up in the river shallows where the ground was flat, ran a few steps, its wings lifted high, then slowed and settled and stood, silent, ten or twenty yards from Summer, silhouetted against the silver-gray water and sky.

Now the cold air was still again. No wind, no snow, no Bird: only another bird, however extraordinary. Summer turned to leave. But hearing another faint call, she glanced back. Her crane stood calm and alert as a reed. But above the crane…

A snowstorm? A sky filled with fluttering, glancing white, moving with the wind. But it wasn't snow. It was cranes, more cranes, an enormous flock of them. And now they began to sing out. Dozens, scores— a hundred?—flapping, guttural, bird-purring cranes. The flock dove and wove and swirled, and the air was thick with them, whiteness fluttering among red-streaked white, each white wing edged with rippling sable.

Summer's face was lifted up; her pack hung from her hand. The storm of cranes had calmed the storm in her heart. She watched the croaking, purring whirl over the river settle into a flock of long-legged, long-necked, long-beaked white birds who stood quietly in the shallows. One lifted a foot and put it down again. There was a long pause.

Then two of the cranes separated from the others, walking in slow high-steps. Wings back, their two necks long, breast to breast, they danced and leaped. Then they strutted one behind the other, in perfect unison, their beaks thrust upward and open to the clouds as if to drink the faint color from the sky.

Summer knew a lot of things, but she had never known that birds danced.

The two dancing cranes ran together, side by side, splashing water against their feathers, and lifted into flight. Necks thrust forward, they made a new dance against the sky. They wove, met, crossed. One flew almost straight up; the other flew straight-as-an-arrow across. They curved and met again, then swooped apart.

And then Summer dropped her pack and said, "Oh." The birds were not dancing, she saw. They were painting. As they flew, their wings left dark marks against the white sky. The graceful black lines swooped and curved, shot straight, crossed, thrust upward, following the track of the flying cranes. The black lines hung against the sky, as if the birds' black-tipped wings were dipped in ink, and the white sky was a piece of paper.

The cranes who filled the river's edge stood silent, necks at full length, watching, the water lapping over their feet. Summer, too, felt her whole self alive, full of witness.

And then her father's scientific training snapped in. A camera! *Oh, too* bad *I don't have mine,* Summer thought, and even as she thought it she grabbed up her pack, pulled out her notebook and pencil, sat on the cold rock, and began to draw. Glancing up, she drew even faster, because now she saw that the first lines were beginning to dissolve, crumble into soot or ash in the air, fall to the river below. Had she missed any? She sketched as fast as her hand could move, glancing up and down to get it right.

As she sketched, she guessed. At first she thought it was some sort of hieroglyphic language she did not understand. But gradually, as she traced the angles and lines and curves, her hand told her heart what it must be.

"It's a map," said Summer out loud, to no one.

By now the two painter cranes had landed among the others. As they settled on the water, the high echoing clattering cries began again. Already half of the map had dissolved. Summer bent to work harder. She finished just as the last black curve dissolved and dropped into the water.

Summer looked at what she had. The map was made of thick lines, often more curving than straight, some perpendicular, some parallel, many crossing. At one nexus, many of the lines crossed at the same point. One long, horizontal line crossed the whole map.

What would cranes map? Their own migration? The way they had come so far; or the way they had to go?

Maybe it was a drawing of the winds.

Maybe it was for her.

Much later, after a long, cold walk made shorter by the crowd of questions in her mind, Summer showed the map to Ben and told her story. "How could they do that?" she finished. "And what is it?"

Ben looked away and made a face as if he were trying not to smile.

He said to the air, "The map is your second gift. It is a precious gift, and I am very, very pleased."

"I knew it was a map! Can you help me read it?" she asked. And without waiting for an answer: "Where does it lead? What is it a map of?"

Ben paused. "For the cranes, it might map one thing. But you caught it—like catching a fish in a fairy tale, do you understand? So for you it would map something else. It will have its own path, for you. You just need to find out what that is. To use it, you must know two things: where you are, and where you're going. You must also decide how to hold the map—that is, you must also choose your north." He added, "A map is a song. It's different when different people sing it. Think of it like that. You will make this your own song, sing it your own way. I hope you will. It will only work for you once, Summer. So choose carefully."

Summer was so tired that it all almost made sense, almost seemed reasonable. But not quite. She looked in her journal at the drawing she had made of the sky and wrote on the page beside it, *The Crane Map*. And then: *Where you are, and where you're going.* And: *Remember to choose your north.* Finally: *A map is a song.*

Then, just in case, she carefully tore the map from her notebook and put it in her jacket pocket.

It was quiet for a little while. Ben said: "The cranes are the oldest of all. Older than me, and I am very old, even older than I look. No one knows all that they know. No one knows everything about them. They know the oldest things."

Summer wrapped up in the red sweater, lay down near the iron pot, and tried to set her questions aside so she could sleep. From where she lay, she could see how carefully Ben was carving, with how much attention and love.

"Listen, Summer," he said, his knife moving along the wood like a seeing hand. "Remember this: when you find the place where you should be, it doesn't matter if the door is locked. You are the key."

Half asleep: "How will I know when it's time to use the map?"

"You will be lost, of course. Hush, I need to work."

Summer put her hand over the crane map inside her jacket pocket. *I am lost* now, she thought. *But when it's time, when I find Bird, when I find my parents, I have the map, and we can all go home.* Then she fell asleep, her first peaceful sleep in this place.

Much later that night, Summer woke up. Ben was sitting in the dark, carving.

"You'll cut yourself carving in the dark," said Summer, soft.

"I can see by the stars," said unstartled, almost-laughing Ben.

They were quiet for a while. Then they spoke at the same time:

"I didn't get a story tonight."

"I think you should have a story now." And he told one.

"This story is about a chickadee," Ben began. "You know what a chickadee is, don't you? The fat little black-and-cream-and-gray bird."

"I *know.*"

"This one flew higher than a chickadee is meant to; she did it because of something she dreamed. She lived in that tree right there, at the threshold of the plain and the forest, a tree that is hung with berries in winter. So a good tree, for a chickadee.

"But this chickadee kept dreaming the same dream, in her night perch. She dreamed of a sun that was half risen or half set, she couldn't tell which.

"In the dream, half the sun was hidden under the horizon. The half she could see threw its colors against this white plain, this one we're on. It threw every color—and not pale rainbow colors either, but deep jewel and fire colors, reds and purples and an emerald green that darkened at its last edge into indigo. The rays of color shone all around the half-sun and shone also across the plain, as if the sun were looking into a mirror.

"The chickadee had watched the sun go down every night of her life, but even from the highest tree, she had never seen the sun do that. It only became smaller and colder and disappeared, sometimes with a little color in the sky, sometimes not. So now the chickadee also woke in the dark every morning to watch the sun rise. But no matter how tall the tree or how pretty the sunrise, it was not what she had seen in her dream.

"So one day the chickadee left this place to find a tree tall enough so that she could see the rising or setting sun of her dream. She flew away one midnight, without a word to any bird, because she didn't want any fuss or dissuasion. 'Dissuasion' means—"

"Talking her *out* of it, I know," said Summer.

"What she did not know is that one bird saw her leave, with his large night-seeing eyes. And after a minute or two, this bird flapped quietly after her.

"The chickadee flew for a long time. Maybe many years—I don't know."

"Redwoods," said Summer.

"What?"

"She should have flown to California, to the redwoods," Summer said. "The sequoias, they're tallest."

"Ha," said Ben. "You are quite right. Except that birds know some trees that you do not. She flew north, where the trees reach up to the wind. She found remarkably tall trees, and met strange birds whose calls were hard to understand. Once she stopped by a big lake, and from the tallest tree at the water's edge saw an amazing sunrise, color after color climbing the sky in clouds, and reflected in the lake like a mirror. This sunrise was so extraordinary that the lake itself has never forgotten it. Once it was cool and gray, but now it is warm and many-colored. The imprint of that sunrise remains. I could show you that lake, I've seen it.

"But for all its beauty, the sunrise at the lake was not the vision of her dream. Still, it strengthened the chickadee's heart and seemed to point her on. So from that night on, she flew straight toward the place where she first saw the sun each morning—she flew east.

"She had many more adventures, some terrible, some rich and strange, and met many strange birds. Sometimes the birds she met turned from her in fear and flew away. Those birds had seen her dark companion, a few trees behind.

"But the little chickadee never saw the one who followed her.

"At any rate, after long weeks, the chickadee found the World Tree."

"What is that?" asked Summer.

"The World Tree?" said Ben. "Oh, it's—too many things to tell tonight. But for the purposes of this story, you should know that it is very tall. Taller than any tree you've ever seen. Much taller than any tree the chickadee had seen, and she had seen many. She flew to the top, where the air was thin. That's not as easy as it sounds. It was a job of many weeks, many cold nights resting on branches higher and higher up, living on fewer and fewer berries and the dew that clung to leaves. But one day, she arrived at the very top of the tree, exhausted, hungry, and proud.

"The chickadee looked around in the cold wind with finding eyes.

Her little feet clung like iron to the topmost branch of the World Tree.

"And sunset came. And it was an extraordinary sunset—ravishing, heartbreaking. But it was not the little chickadee's sunset, not the sunset of her dream. All the long night she stayed awake, exhausted as she was, her eyes dry in the cold wind, waiting for the sunrise, her last chance. She waited without hope or fear or anxiety, or any of that. She was past all that. She just waited.

"And finally, the sunrise came. And it was the half-sun vision of her dream, exactly that, or even more. And the bird's heart filled up with joy, such powerful joy that her heart dissolved, right into her throat, and emerged from her throat as a song. Her liquid heart became the most beautiful song the world had ever heard—we sing it still, we still sing that song—a song that met the sunrise and joined with it, two pieces of beauty dissolving into one joy, one song.

"And then the chickadee could think of nothing more perfect to do than fly straight into that sun. But she was too tired, and the wind was too strong. Though she beat her wings, she was caught in the cold and battering winds around the tree, and they tossed and pushed and smashed her down to the ground.

"And the owl carried her body back. And because of the owl, we know the story, and the song."

After a long, drowsy silence, Summer said, "Do you remember how you said that a map is a song?"

"I do," said Ben.

"I still don't understand that," Summer said.

Ben paused. "Another way to look at it," he said, "is that a song is a map."

Summer thought about this. "Like how birds sing their territories?"

"Yes, like that."

Then after a pause, sleepily: "A map is a song, a song is a map. Everything keeps turning into something else."

"That's right," Ben said. "That's important. Chick a dee dee dee, Summer-rain. Good night."

A few hours later, and not so far away, as the third morning hinted at the edges of the sky and the calls began again, Bird had a strange feeling. Although she was still lying on the soft forest floor, cushioned with dead leaves and damp, freezing black dirt, she felt that she wasn't lying there at all. She felt that she was floating in the air, halfway between the forest floor and the branches of the birds. This was odd; but it made the birds much easier to see. Also, there were many more birds than she had realized. They sat in branches and called to one another. They chased and tumbled each other. They flitted past sharply, then dove toward a seed or a berry, or a loose twig or feather for a nest. Bird, floating, if she were really floating, watched them all with her still, gray eyes. And the calls grew in meaning in her mind. *I found food. Do not touch me. Please play. Who will make a home with me? Danger!*

A shadow flew across a patch of light. A big bird, far bigger than the others, though not as big as Bird. *Why is it flying in the day?* thought Bird, and then wondered why she thought that.

Then the owl disappeared.

CHAPTER TEN

THE THIRD GIFT

Summer had slowed to a walk hours before.

"So it's the mountains," she had explained to Ben that morning. "She wasn't on the road or at the river. We've been through the forest already. It must be the mountains. I know this time."

Ben had said only, "I will be here." And Summer had run.

But now she was walking. She had run and walked so far that the ground was no longer white clay, but black dirt with sprouting green. Real trees had sprung up, not little scrub trees but the winter skeletons of oaks, and tall fir trees that made a rushing river sound in the sky. The mountain foothills rose up ahead, lower slopes patched with snow.

But Summer wasn't seeing or hearing any of this. She was caught inside her mind, lost inside two stories playing over and over: the morning her parents were gone; and the morning of no Bird. She pushed and dug at the pain in those stories over and over, the way you dig at a loose tooth, tasting the blood.

Caught in these stories, Summer didn't see the firs or the foothills. And she never saw the fog come in, until, startled by a too-close bird-call, she looked up and saw: nothing.

A cloud of nothing had eaten the world. Fog. Only a single tree a few feet away stood black and vivid against the mist. The mist moved, and then there was no tree; then there was part of a bush, bearing part of a bird. The fog sucked up sound, shook Summer from herself. She walked gingerly in the silence, not knowing what might be beside her or ahead.

(We never really know what might be beside us or ahead, but most days we walk as if we do.)

For more than an hour, Summer walked in the silence of only-this, each object appearing like a single picture framed against a wide, blank wall, then disappearing again. The cool wet nothing clung to her. Once she saw a black bird skimming and sliding in the fog, silent and frictionless.

The fog calmed her. It was a world of nouns, except for that single bird, that flying verb, that might have been a crow, or a raven. Her raven, the blue-eyed, black-eyed bird? But the thought dissolved with the fog. She saw that she herself was a solitary thing among solitary things, and she walked on, eyes open, alone and present and ignorant in the world.

✺

Very near to Summer, too near, but out of hearing and out of the fog, a dozen birds stood in a ring. In the center was an old, ragged, half-bald crow, whose wing hung at a wrong angle, as if it was broken. The old crow's beak was bound tight with iron wire.

A tall, masked figure, thin and gray as that wire, paced around the circle, speaking. "Betrayer" was one of the words she used. "Traitor" was another. "Most of you are too young to remember," she said, "but thirteen years ago this soldier dishonored his queen"—the birds looked up in surprise—"dishonored her, by dishonoring me, who rules in her stead as we wait for her return." The masked figure continued smoothly, "When we faced a terrible enemy, he turned like a coward and fought against his own brothers. For thirteen years he has eluded us, but now he stands before you. Bird court, I ask you for the harshest sentence: death."

The birds were silent. Impatient, the masked figure asked, "Well? What's supposed to happen next? It's your court."

Small claws shifted on the ground, and then a jay spoke, in English, in a voice harsh and high, but uncertain. "Customarily, the accused speaks a few—" he began, but stopped when the Puppeteer turned her cold, blank face on him.

"You wish to hear the words of a traitor? Why is that? Why does that interest you?" She looked around the ring. "Does anyone else long to hear the lies of a traitor?" The jay shifted from foot to foot, eyes on the ground, and shook his head.

"Then do it!" cried the Puppeteer. "Do it now! Kill him, in the ancient bird way! Kill him, as all traitors deserve!"

A large, iridescent black grackle broke from the ring and waddled up to the crow. He struck at the old bird's back with his beak, hard. Blood dripped from the ragged black feathers.

"What's wrong with the rest of you?" the Puppeteer demanded. "Show you are loyal to your queen! Do it!"

The other birds—some reluctantly, some with an ugly strut—

moved toward the crow, who stood steady, looking above and past the birds, his broken wing grazing the cold ground. He took another blow to his back, and one near his eye, and staggered briefly. The big grackle raised his beak to strike again.

Then, from above them, came the long, wailing alarm call of the Great Gray Owl. Instinctively, all the other birds froze. It repeated twice, then three times.

The Puppeteer gave short, high scream of fury. She seized the bloody crow in her long fingers. "You were too slow," she said to the bird court. "Now I must go. I'll deal with this crow myself. I have a place to keep creatures like him until his death can be useful to me."

The ring of birds were left staring at one another and at the ground.

Not far from the ring of birds, but alone in the fog, Summer heard rustling grass behind her. She snapped her head around. For a moment, nothing moved. Then a small creature dissolved out of the misty light.

It was a bird, but not a flying bird. It was a fat starling, sleek, iridescent, freckled all over in tiny streaks of white, and it strutted along the ground. The starling stopped at her feet and gave her a hard look through a little black eye. Summer almost laughed. "Hello there, bird," she said softly, remembering her raven, not wanting to scare it off.

"Hello," replied the starling. Summer's breath caught. She had heard of starlings who had learned to speak, like parrots. But this starling spoke easily, horribly easily, in a human voice that was kind and warm. Horribly kind and warm, coming from a starling. Worse, it was a voice she almost recognized.

"Who are you?" said the starling, still kind, still warm.

"I'm Summer," said Summer, then, pressing her fingernails into her palm so as not to shake, she asked, "Who are you?"

"I am the watch," said the starling. "I am the guard."

Summer realized why the voice was familiar. It was her mother's voice. She felt as if she might be sick.

The starling-mother's voice grew icier. "If you are Summer," she said, "then where is Bird?"

"I don't know," said Summer.

"You don't *know*?" asked the starling, raising her little head sharply, her body a gesture of alarm.

"I lost her," said Summer, finding hardly enough air inside her to get the words out. "I—she ran away."

The starling-mother took one bird-step toward her. "But how could you?" she asked. Her feathers trembled. "What was more important? How could you be so inattentive, care so little, to let your sister run away?"

"I was asleep," Summer cried. "It was night!"

I am arguing with a bird, she thought. *It is not my mother.* But when the bird spoke again, Summer's heart was wrenched open.

"I don't want to hear excuses from you," said the starling-mother in a cold, even, no longer kind tone. "Your excuses don't interest me. The responsibility for this terrible thing is only yours. She is too young to make good decisions. She could be dead. Her death will be your fault."

Summer did not cry or protest. She was struck dead inside. Part of her said: *But I was asleep. How could I?* But that part was weak and faint, and she despised it. A tall, glowing part of her agreed: *My fault. My fault, forever.*

But there was a third part of her as well, a new, farther-seeing part of her, and that part said: *Run, Summer. Run away from the voice that says all that. Even if it is the voice of your mother. Especially if it is. Run.*

Summer ran, she ran hard and fast in the other direction, shreds of mist clinging to her hair, the cold of the fog inside her. *That was poison,* she thought, she and the new voice inside her thought together, in chorus for once. *That was poison. I would have died if I'd stayed and listened to that bird. I would have died, not Bird, not stupid Bird.*

It is not my fault she is gone, said Summer's pounding feet. It is not my fault. It is not my fault. But I will find her. If she wants to be found.

High above the swan's stone walls, in the swan's eye, the tall masked figure in the long gray dress stood like a stone pillar. On the railing of the balustrade, she set down a small puppet: a tissue-paper starling. She watched Summer as she ran away.

Stupid child. Run away now. My fog will never clear for you. My doors will never open to you. I want the other girl, the brown girl, the gray-eyed girl, the one who talks to birds. I want my Bird, bring me my Birdling, to my dark nest. When she opens her mouth to cry I'll feed her what's inside me, until she grows to become me, a me that speaks with the birds. I want to sing, too, I want my song to be part of that Great Conversation.

("It doesn't work like that," Bird would later miserably say to the Puppeteer. But that was much later.)

As Summer ran from one bird, Bird lay deep in the forest with many. She had no more water or food, so she sucked a piece of bark and listened. The birdsongs and calls began to twine together and become one sound, a sound that was small and bird and large and sky at the same time. The sound of birds was the same as the sound of sky.

Bird and sky are the same, thought Bird.

The single birdsong grew and shifted. It sounded almost like a song Bird knew, or almost knew but could not quite remember. She listened hard. She tried the trick of relaxing her memory so the song would come out of hiding and show itself. *I know you, song. I know you.*

It was an ice-cream-truck song. Or it was a song her mother used to sing to make her laugh. One of those. Or a song she and Summer invented one half-warm spring day under a cherry tree shedding white petals around them. But no, because also it was something to do with crying, if crying were a song. Listening to the great twined birdsong around her and the soft, barely heard song inside her, Bird felt afraid. There was something afraid in the song, too. A child crying in grief. A fight in another room.

Cherry blossoms. Muffled anger in the next room. *It is too big a song for me,* thought Bird. *This song is too big for me, I am only one small Bird.*

And the song said: We are all birds together. It is not just your song. What a ridiculous idea, as if you could sing this song alone! Much too big! You never could! It's the song of all the birds together. Sing with us.

It was hard to find the right thread. Bird found it. Bird sang.

〜

It was close to evening now. Summer had somehow, after many wrong turns and sickeningly unfamiliar paths, made it back to camp. She had wept out most of the story to Ben, although she said only that the starling had said "horrible things," not what it had said, nor that it had her mother's voice. Ben had listened with careful attention and let her cry into his knee, resting one of his old hands on her shoulder until she felt herself again.

She sat up, wiped her nose on her shirt, and went to her pack to dig out crackers and a piece of chocolate. "I'm sorry I stopped your carving," she said.

"I am sorry I cannot help you in this trouble," said Ben, "because it is serious and real. You will soon see why I cannot." She had never seen him look so serious. "Summer, you have not stopped my carving," he said. "I am finished." She saw that he held something closed inside his right hand.

"I am giving this to you, Summer," he said. "It is your third gift, but it is also—yes, 'also'—a favor that I must ask." Instead of handing her the object, he dropped it to the ground. It bobbled and rocked across the hard pale ground to Summer's feet.

She picked it up. It felt smooth and warm in her hand. "It's an egg," she said. A pale wooden egg, so pale it looked like a real egg. It fit beautifully in her hand, comforting to hold.

"Thank you," she added, remembering politeness, but also feeling grateful.

Ben looked almost sad—or if not sad, something Summer could not identify. "Please don't lose it," he said. He gave her his side-cocked head, but his one open eye looked to the side, not at her. "You need it. But also, it needs you."

"What do I need it for?" Summer asked.

"You will find out when you need it," said Ben. He paused. "Why don't you ask me why it needs you?"

Summer flushed. "Okay: Why?" she said in a sarcastic, false voice that made her feel worse.

Ben's face was almost truly sad. "It needs you in order to become itself. It's so important, Summer-y. I trust this egg to you. Okay?"

Summer could not help feeling bitterly that too much had been trusted to her in the past, and that she wished with all her heart nothing would ever be trusted to her again. But she wanted this egg.

"All right," she said, sullen. "I will take care of it."

She slipped the egg, warm as a cat, into her pocket. They spent the rest of their evening in silence. Summer felt that they were far apart, and it made her lonely.

Late that night, with Summer curled up by the warm pot, Ben said, "That story I told you last night—do you remember?"

"Yes, of course. The chickadee and the sun and the World Tree."

"Good. But that story is told another way as well. In this other version of the story, the owl does not bring the chickadee home, because the chickadee does not die in her fall from the tree.

"Instead, the snake that lives at the bottom of the World Tree swallows her.

"That seemed terrible to the bird at the time, as you can imagine. But what the chickadee did not know was that being swallowed by the snake saved her from the owl, who had followed her all this way to kill her.

"At least, that's one way the story goes. No one actually knows why the owl followed the chickadee. Owls are a mystery.

"At any rate, the chickadee traveled all through the bowels of the snake. And the bowels of the snake traveled through the bowels of the earth, where the furnaces of magma would kill a bird that was not inside the World Snake. But still, not knowing what would happen, not knowing she was protected from the earth's fire, not knowing her escape from the fatal (perhaps) owl—well, you can imagine the chickadee's grief and fear, what a terrible dark time she had, being squeezed through the endless, dark, wet muscle of the World Snake.

"Often she thought she could not live, and often she longed to die."

Summer turned and pulled the sweater around more closely. She was listening.

"But one day—*pop*—out came the chickadee, in a whole new land: the land on the other side of the horizon. And she knew that it was her true home, and she felt great peace. And perhaps she ought to have stayed—most people would have stayed, wouldn't you? Only the chickadee whose heart had turned into a song didn't want to keep this joy and peace all to herself. She wanted to share this true home with the other birds.

"So she began her long journey back, looking for a path from her true home in the land on the other side of the horizon, back to her first home, where we are right now. She looked for a route that would not involve going through the snake, because that was so unpleasant and would take so long, even if the snake were willing to eat all the birds of the earth, one at a time. Probably it would not be willing; the World Snake does not do favors.

"And she had many adventures, both wonderful and terrible ones, and eventually discovered the attainable border of the birds, which was a way, although it was not by any means an easy way. The birds might have been better off inside the snake. And she made a map to this marvelous place, which she called the Green Home, a special kind of map, and gave it to the queen of the birds."

Summer turned on her back and looked up at the stars. "Is it the same Green Home that is in that nursery rhyme song, and across the attainable border of the birds?" she asked.

"Yes."

The night was silent for a little while.

"Ben?"

"Yes?"

"Which of the endings of the chickadee story is right?"

"Maybe they are both right."

"No, don't say both this time. How can they both be right?"

"It's easier than you think," said Ben. "Go to sleep."

And Summer did go to sleep, her hand in her pocket, around the warm egg.

CHAPTER ELEVEN

EVERYTHING BURNS

A few hours past midnight, Bird swam out of sleep, trailing fragments of the night's bird-conversation like seaweed in her hair. The bird-world slept; only Bird was awake. So she picked up her recorder and played the low, electric patchwork song, both to have the bird-company of it, and to prepare, now, for the last part of her journey. The song was not quite finished with her, or she with it. It had one last place to send her. And although she could not quite understand what that place was, she had felt some pieces of it: something about birds; something about castle; something about queen.

These were only pieces, half understood, but Bird wanted them to be the whole, finished puzzle. She had always known she was *not the same*. Now she knew why (or wanted to believe she knew why).

She was meant for a bird queen's castle.

Meant for a crown?

Light dawned in a corner of the sky. A few small songs and calls brightened the air, as the song of the patchwork bird brightened Bird's blood. A raven landed on a stump a few feet away from Bird and watched her through one blue eye.

Bird thought of her mother, the queen of her heart, and hardened against her. *Mom wouldn't let me,* she thought. *She would say I wasn't old enough. She'd say "not yet, not yet," like she always says, like she always says every time. She said "not yet" to all my questions, and then she left me alone with Summer.*

"Well, I don't care," said Bird out loud, said Bird, who cared so much that she couldn't bear to touch the hurt. "I don't care. I ran away from Summer, and I will make my own castle. I will be my own queen."

And then they'll see they were wrong, she thought.

The fire was guttering out; it needed feeding.

Birds don't tend fires, she thought.

(But birds have hollow bones, are feathered dinosaurs wrapped in down, beat their wings for warmth—Bird, you are no bird, at least not yet.)

Neither do queens tend fires, she thought. *And this is not my world any longer.*

She stood up unsteadily. She lifted her pink-and-purple notebook with its plastic-jeweled birds. She held it for a long moment.

Then she threw it into the fire. She threw the pencil after it.

She opened her pack, pulled out all her extra clothes—jacket, pants, shirt—and threw them in the fire as well. She threw in the bags that had held her food.

Then she threw the pink mermaid backpack itself into the fire.

The fire swelled up.

"HUNGRY fire," said Bird. "Hungry fire." She had the clothes she wore and the recorder in her pocket. Everything else was burning, just like her anger was burning, and swallowing up everything in its hungry mouth.

For a moment, she felt tall and free. A bird. A queen.

And then, just as quickly, she felt despair. Because of course: Summer would find her. How had she forgotten that? Summer knew tracking—she'd read a whole book about it. She knew the right things to look for, the stupid broken twigs and torn grasses that were somehow different from all the other stupid torn twigs and grasses. Summer was tracking her right now, probably; she could be here any minute.

(Or so Bird thought—but she was thinking with her little-sister mind, which saw her big sister as much bigger than she really was. Little sister, she is only your size, inside. Summer is as lost as you.)

And a much worse thought crowded in: Summer would never give up, would track her all the way to the bird queen's castle. And when she did, she would take it over. She would be in charge of it. She would keep it all for herself.

Not fair. The end of this journey, the queen's castle, was for her, not for Summer, Bird was furiously certain of that. Desperation made her small, fat heart beat like a bird in a house, banging and fighting against the walls. She had to do more than get to the castle; she had to stop Summer from following her there to steal it all.

And then she thought: a map.

Summer loved maps. Summer believed in maps. They had once argued about this: It isn't real, a map, Bird had said. She had no interest in the lines and squares and colors and how they might be laid upon the world. Boring. The world was the world, it showed you where to go. The lines and squares were nothing.

But Summer loved maps. Summer would follow a map even when it was wrong. Once they had fought their way through a hot half-hour of bush before Summer would admit that the path on their father's old map was wrong, or that she had read it wrong.

Bird thought: *I will make a map, and leave it for Summer.* "Here I am—here's where I've gone—come find me," the map would lie. Summer would follow, and end up nowhere at all.

(But all maps take you somewhere, Bird. You can't make a map that goes nowhere. You will map your own—something. Your own heart? Longing? Guilt?)

Bird looked at the black- and-blue-eyed raven, who may or may not have been looking at her—it's hard to tell with birds and their sidelong eyes. Then she grabbed a long stick and pulled her half-burnt notebook to the edge of the fire. Its pink-and-purple birds were charred over, the little plastic jewels melted black. But the pages were still mostly whole. She flipped it open with the stick to a blank page, and with a bit of warm charred wood, began to draw. *Where will I send her?* she wondered.

And answered: *The opposite of where I'm going, of course. So I will send Summer—home.*

At the center of the white space she drew an X with an O around it. A kiss inside a hug. How their father signed his notes to them.

Around the kiss, she drew a path. It wandered and crossed itself, it moved south and west and northwest as it liked (as the anger buried in Bird's mind liked). A tangle of lines. It would be quite hard to follow. *It shouldn't be easy,* thought Bird.

But maps, even false ones, are true to something. Bird, drawing away, doesn't know that. Doesn't know she is mapping her own crisscrossing, backtracking heart. Doesn't know how much her crisscrossing, backtracking heart longs for home. For kiss; for hug.

And at the end of the ashy black maze, what did Bird draw? What would be right?

A bird, to represent herself, and a sun, to represent Summer. At the start of the road to the kiss, the hug. A bird and a sun going home. Summer would understand, would think she had found their parents. Summer would follow the map, thinking she was joining Bird on the road back to mother, back to father; back to kiss, back to hug. "When she hears the song/That a true map sings," Bird sang absently to herself, "That's when a cygnet/Finds her wings."

A few yards from the fire, apart from the other trees, stood a lightning-struck oak. On a spiky twig of that oak, Bird impaled the false map. Then she stood in the empty, smoking camp, the heart of her small apocalypse, without food, without pack, without warmth: burdenless.

Then she turned and ran off into the woods.

Is it really so easy for Bird? Can she walk away from her family with only a little sadness?

Perhaps she is walking away from something else as well. Perhaps she is walking away from something she did—something that she doesn't want to think about.

Perhaps she feels a little guilty. Or more than a little.

The evening before that terrible morning, someone opened the window to their parents' room so that the owl could come in. And the owl unlocked the inside closet. And that's how this story began.

Who invited the owl into that home?

She only wanted to learn the birds' speech. She didn't mean for everything else to happen.

But it did. It did happen, Bird, running Bird, who wants not to be Bird any longer, but only a bird.

The blue-eyed, black-eyed raven did not follow. She watched Bird go. She waited a while, unmoving, except for feathers that ruffled in the light, cold morning wind. Then the raven hopped and flapped up to a broken branch near the false map. She looked long and carefully at that scrap of paper. Then she took the paper in her beak and flapped off in the opposite direction of Bird.

Now the blasted tree stood bare again in the cold wind. Smoke from the dying fire slipped into the ragged bark, in and around the tiny cracks, making a home.

"And now," said Ben, "I have to go."

Summer's heart fell to the ground. It was the morning after he gave her the egg, and they had only just finished breakfast. "Where are you going?" she asked, her voice too high.

"Somewhere you can't come."

"What about Bird?"

"You will find her and lose her and find her again."

"Will I see you again?"

"Not in the way you mean."

"What other way is there?"

"Summer. Let me have the egg for a minute." Pulling it from her pocket, she walked toward him. He looked older—he had looked older every day, she realized, his hair a little grayer, his eyes more tired. Now his hair was all gray, and his eyes were gray as clouds, and they mostly looked at the horizon, not at her, and his about-to-laugh smile had become thin and stretched, though it was still there, she could see. He took the egg and held it to his stomach, then held it to his heart, then held it to his mouth, and whispered something Summer could not hear. Then he handed it back to her, warmer from his hand.

"The egg is so important to me," he said. "And it may be important to you. I think it will be."

"I *said* I would take care of it," she said, sounding angry, feeling heartbroken.

"Then I trust you," said Ben.

"Have I heard all the stories I need to hear?" she asked, stupidly. But he answered as if it were a good question.

"No, you haven't. But you don't have time to hear any more from me. So listen for stories wherever you go. It won't always be someone telling them; sometimes they come in other ways. And Summer, when you tell yourself stories, make them true. And make them surprising. That's how you will know they might be true."

He paused. And then he continued, "You have an interesting story of your own to follow now, Summer. Someday someone like me will tell your story over a warm blanket at bedtime. Or your sister's story. Or both—it might be only one story. But it's hard to say before it's finished—otherwise it wouldn't be surprising, and it wouldn't be a very good story."

He stood up and shouldered his bag. "So. You have three gifts—gifts or burdens—to take with you on your journey. You have the sweater. You have the egg to protect and to be protected by. And you have a gift that is not from me: you have the crane map to use when you are the most lost. Maybe it will take you home."

"Maybe, or for sure?"

Ben shrugged. "Everything is maybe. Nothing is for sure." This did not seem funny, but he laughed, fully laughed, for the first time. It was a laugh like warm honey on morning toast, like warm honey on her heart. Summer thought: *His laugh makes his face young.*

"There's not much left of me to go," he said, with joy. "But the part that is left is going now."

A wind was coming up. Summer could hear it in the trees off to her left, could hear it rising across the plain. Then it caught her from behind, blowing her hair into her face and eyes. But it wasn't a cold wind—it was a warm one, as if someone had opened a huge, hot oven and let the air roar out. She felt warm for the first time in days. "Please take care of the egg," Ben said into the wind. His voice was blown back and away from her, almost before she could catch it. He smiled, a wide, lighthearted smile. "But don't worry too much," he added. "You worry too much, Summer. Don't worry."

He squinted in the wind. Above him, the clouds cleared around the sun, and in the sudden wash of light, Summer realized she had never seen this place in full sun before.

Ben lifted his face to that sun. The wind beat his hair back, now gray and white, not gray and black. He kept his eyes fully open. He was still smiling his wide-open smile. The wind grew harder and louder, and Summer felt afraid, as the old red sweater whipped around her and her hair whipped her face. You go blind when you look into the sun with open eyes.

"Ben," she called out, to warn him; and the wind carried her voice straight to him, but he didn't seem to hear.

His face to the sun, his open eyes, his smile. Even looking into the sun, his eyes were dry.

Then Summer saw that his eyes were no longer eyes. They had become two white flames.

The tips of his ashy hair had begun to smoke.

His face turned up to the sun: Ben was burning. He was burning, but the flame was coming from the inside. It happened quickly. He grew drier, hollower. He seemed to weigh less and less. His skin looked dry and thin as paper, wavering around the flame within.

"Ben!" she screamed.

Hollow, paper-thin, flame-eyed Ben opened his mouth, and a song emerged. But it wasn't only Ben singing. It was Ben singing, and the fire singing with him. A dry, bright, dancing song. A song made of incandescent blue and yellow and red, peace and fury and pain and love. A map of a life. It consumed him from within.

When the flame broke through, Ben was all flame. At that last moment, as he hovered in the air, the ghost of the old coat blowing about him, his old face broke into one last huge smile, like a child's. His face dissolved into the smile. Through the singing, flickering heat she could see his outline, face still raised to the sun. Then only his outline remained, a rough gray pencil sketch of her only friend.

And then—as if what was left of him was light as ashes, as if he were *made* of ash—the wind picked him up and swirled him away. The sketch dissolved in the wind. And there was nothing.

Summer stood still for a long time, as the warm wind died and the cold air congealed around her. Ben was dead. Ben was gone. And one more time, Summer was left behind, alone.

The sun was hidden again. In the gray morning light, the plain looked huge and empty.

CHAPTER TWELVE

LOST

In the silence, Summer stood alone for a long while. He was gone. Like her parents, like her mother, Ben was gone.

She walked to Ben's gray rock, the rock where he carved, and told stories, and drew his picture letter to see what he could see. She sat down. She didn't cry. She felt as if her heart had dried up with Ben's ashes.

She faced the fourth direction: the forest, the way they had come, the only way she had not yet looked for Bird.

But the forest was big, and Bird was small.

I'm sitting on his rock, Summer thought to herself, *so I'll try it.* It made no sense, but it was the only thing she could think of to do.

She would draw a picture letter, and see what she could see. And while she drew, she would think about Bird.

Bird. Summer tried to let the idea of Bird, the feeling of her, sink inside her. What could she think of that felt like Bird? Summer took her pencil and journal from her pocket and began to draw. She didn't look at what she was drawing. She looked up, and remembered Bird.

She thought of Bird's writing. She was always writing something, about green evening light, or the smell of onions frying in butter, or the uneven *plop* of the faucet they always left dripping for Sarah the cat. The dripping faucet was against the rules, but they all did it anyway, even her father, who had made the rule, because sitting by the sink, staring at the dry faucet, Sarah looked so trusting and sure.

Remembering the trusting cat, Bird's scribbled pages, and her father's rules he couldn't keep, Summer's dry heart filled up unexpectedly. Then it brimmed over, and she began to cry. Her picture letter was finished.

Through wavering tears, she looked down, and found that she had drawn three things.

A heart, large and full.

A recorder, like Bird's. But *flute is a better word,* Bird had said: so call it a flute.

A claw, like the claw of a bird.

Summer wiped her tears. Okay. She had done the drawings, as Ben had, as her mother had. But what did they mean?

A few days ago, Summer would have scoffed at that question. But now she would try, try to learn to read this kind of picture.

A heart. Maybe Bird's big heart, stuffed with feeling. Or some other, bigger heart?

(*Or some other, bigger stupidness?* asked the old Summer, bitter-voiced, her face turned away inside this new Summer).

Summer pushed on. A flute is music, or song? Bird said once, "A flute tells a story." Is it a story?

The claw, the claw of a bird. A predator? Was her Bird danger-ous? Or was she in danger? Summer thought of that dream (if it was a dream) of Bird and the tiny yellow eyes across the fire.

She paused.

Now what? She had tried. She had had one or two ideas. Nothing happened. A new idea elbowed in: this was pointless. Mother and father were gone. Bird was gone. Ben was gone. And this was stupid, stupid, stupid and pointless.

Summer grabbed her pack and started walking toward the trees. Soon she wasn't walking but running.

A heart, a flute, a claw. It pounded in Summer's head as her feet pounded the ground. A heart, a flute, a claw. The three images began to weave fleeting stories in her mind.

A heart plays a flute.

Or: A claw catches a heart.

Or: The flute beats away the claw that tries to snatch up the heart!

Close to the forest, Summer slowed to a walk. At the edge of the trees, she stopped. And without looking for a good place or a safe place or any place at all, Summer lay down where she was and, with no warn-ing at all, fell asleep. It was not yet noon.

As she slipped into sleep, the heart, the flute, and the claw slipped from her mind. But in her heart and her bones, the three pounded on.

∽

An hour later, Summer woke up, still lying in the sun, one eye hidden in her arm, one open on the forest. *Flute,* she thought. Oh, *flute,* of course, because Bird had thrown her flute into the forest. She'd have gone back for that. Of course, of course, of course.

Summer got to her feet, slipped on her pack, moved. *And the claw is birds,* she said to herself as her feet moved fast into the forest. She would use the flute to talk to birds; so listen, then, listen for the sound of birds.

And the heart—*well, I don't know about the heart,* thought Summer (her own heart pounding away unheard), *but maybe I will find out.*

Soon she was well into the forest. Darker. Dark. But she had found the path, the path she and Bird had half made and half followed through the veiling snow that first day.

She had forgotten how much colder it was in the forest. All the more important to find Bird, then. Where was it they had stopped that first strange night? Summer recalled the curtain of snow, the ache in her legs, looking through static. She stopped walking and closed her eyes, trying to remember, like remembering a dream.

The feeling of floating. Bird throwing her flute. Its long flat arc through the forked tree.

Her eyes opened. That tree. She would recognize that forked tree, as long she stayed on the path.

Summer walked on, faster now, for an hour, then for two. The woods were quieter than she had ever known woods to be; they were barren of birds. She heard not a single call or song.

The air grew even colder, and she stopped to untie her jacket from around her waist. Reaching for the sleeve, she turned just slightly. And turning, she saw it, on her right, unmistakable: two thick black trunks rising from the same set of roots. The forked tree, through which Bird's flute had flown. The flute of Summer's picture-map.

She moved closer to the double tree. Beyond it, she heard a rushing sound, like a waterfall or an ocean. The sound was hissing, crashing, burble and clatter, rising and falling.

The sound was almost familiar.

And then she realized that it wasn't water. It was birds. It was as if the whole missing forest of birds had flown to one spot, just through those twin trees. A rising, roaring chitter of birds, all different songs and calls, a whole chorus.

So that was two pictures from the map, wasn't it? Claw, flute?

Heart?

She thought: *That flute flew straight as a spear. If I keep that twin-tree straight behind me, and walk straight as the flute flew, then I will find Bird, and I will find my way back.*

She held her egg close to her heart and pushed forward as best she could, through vines and brush, through the rising birdsong, straight as a thrown ball.

As she reached the chattering, bird-loud clearing, the one where Bird had lain for so long, a branch whipped Summer's face. Because of that, as she broke through the trees into the burnt and ruined camp, she closed her eyes.

But even once she opened them again, Summer's mind could not grasp what she was seeing.

Her body saw, though, or thought it saw. Her body gave a long, high wail before she knew the sound was hers; her hands flew to her face as if to block her eyes from seeing. The birds around her went silent.

But her hands were too late—she had seen, she had seen. She had seen the charred remains of the fire, and in those charred remains, the edge of a sleeve, blue-and-black plaid fleece. Just the edge, thrusting out of the blackened wood where the fire had been. Summer was shopping for school clothes with their mother when she bought that jacket for Bird.

Someone must have tied rocks to Summer's heart and threw it in an icy river, because it sank hard and cold and forever.

When you see something as terrible as what Summer thought she saw—her sister, dead, and her fault, her fault, forever—time slows down as it does in an earthquake or nightmare. Like an earthquake, without warning, the ground under your feet goes away, and you are falling, in a falling world, a much worse world: the world where that terrible, unimaginable thing has happened.

Now this will always have happened, for the rest of your life: you took your little sister into the forest because of a stupid, childish idea, and because of your childishness, she is dead. Bird is dead. Bird is dead. Bird is dead.

Summer's hand reached automatically for the only comfort she had left in the world, Ben's warm wooden egg in her pocket.

But the egg was gone.

And when she realized that, a strange thing happened. Summer's human mind was now collapsed in grief, shattered by this one last loss. But in its place, her animal soul, her raven mind, came alive inside her.

This was the gift of the raven with one blue eye.

Summer-raven stood still at the edge of the clearing, her eyes closed. Summer-raven felt no grief. She was present here, and only here, no other thoughts.

The chilly early-evening wind ruffled at Summer-raven's face, carrying scents to her in waves.

She smelled the warm, breathing smell of snow-damped earth.

She smelled her own dirty clothes, and the remains of the cheese in her bag.

She smelled something dark and musty—maybe animal droppings? Mushrooms?

She took another breath, slower now. She heard a bird in the distance, lonely.

She smelled pine.

She smelled the remains of the fire, smoky and just a little sweet, like incense in a church.

Her mind stopped for a moment on that smell. Sweet, like incense. And then, before her thinking-self could choose, her feet turned and walked directly to the fire. There it was, her egg—it must have flown out when her hands flew up in front of her face. She leaned forward to take it, focused on the egg, now burnt on one side. She kept her eyes from the terrible other thing in that fire.

(If only she had looked at what she thought was so terrible, if she had looked just a *little,* how much sorrow she could have saved herself.)

But then Summer did see something, just next to the egg, and like the egg, half burnt, half whole.

Bird's notebook.

At the sight of the small pink-and-purple journal, the grip of Summer's animal mind broke, and the ocean storm of her grief roared back. She thrust the egg in her pocket, grabbed the notebook, and ran.

She stumbled, choking through the brush, tormented by the words of the fake mother-bird at the swan castle: "She could be dead. Her death will be your fault."

How can the squirrels still chatter? she thought as she ran, not looking where she ran, not noticing what branches slapped her face. *How can that bird still call? This happened.*

Still safe in her jacket pocket was the map, the now half-useless map, the crane map that she had meant to use to take them both home. Now it could only take one girl home.

∽

Summer ran a long time. She ran out of breath and blood and light and time. In her mistaken shame, she could not bear for the sky to see her, so she ran deep into the woods, as a small wounded creature looks for a place to hide. She ran until she walked, for hours.

And though she paid no attention to where she was going, in those hours her feet found a new path.

(Our feet find paths, if we are not paying attention. They find a way. Sometimes we're lucky with the way they find. Sometimes not.)

The path, once she saw it, seemed to start from her feet, in the middle of thick woods, in the middle of nowhere. It was narrow and studded with the backs of half-buried rocks. But it was clearly a path. *Keep walking,* she said to her feet. She had no intention of stopping for the night, or ever; she had no intention of sleeping or eating again.

But our bodies betray us, and Summer's body insisted: I am thirsty. I need water.

Maybe she would come to water soon. Paths lead to water.

Maybe on the other side of this hill.

At the top of that tree-thick hill, Summer stopped. The path forked here: one track went down the hill to the left, and one down the hill to the right. She put a hand around the charred egg in her pocket and listened. It did seem like she might hear rushing water coming from below, to her right—unless that was the wind in the trees. She walked a few steps in that direction. The rushing sound was louder.

But then, from the left, she smelled smoke. It smelled like—it must be—something cooking, something savory and delicious. Her stomach awoke and cried with pleasure and longing. Even the egg in her pocket seemed warmer at the scent. Her legs shaking, she abandoned the rushing water sound and ran in the other direction, toward the wonderful smell her faithless, betraying body longed for. Skidding and stumbling, she slid down the rocky hill. If there was cooking, there would be water, too. She could eat and drink, both.

∽

It wasn't water that Summer had heard to her right, just wind rushing through the trees. But in the low dell from which Summer was now running, even though there was no water, there sat a little boat. Its oars were crossed across the bow, and the man inside was lying on his back, resting, watching the birds in the trees above him. He watched the birds not in an idle way, but with an intensity that suggested he expected to learn something important any minute. On his chest was a map or maze scrawled on notebook paper in thick black charcoal. *Kiss, hug,* said one end of the maze. *Summer, Bird,* said the other. The man had been studying the map intently since dawn, when a raven had dropped it in his boat and flown away.

The man propped himself on his arms. For a second, he was sure he heard a sound, an un-animal-like stumbling through the bush, almost like a person, maybe a child. He sat very still for a moment, listening.

But the sounds got softer, not louder, and then disappeared entirely. It was nothing after all, Summer's father decided. And he lay back again to watch the birds, and think about the map.

CHAPTER THIRTEEN

AND NO
BIRDS SING

As Bird followed her sure, song-brightened bones to the bird queen's castle, birds followed. In fact, as the day went on, she collected a whole flock of small birds, who fluttered and darted around her. Remember Cinderella and the helpful songbirds who fluttered around her in the movie? It was exactly not like that at all. These were real birds, unsmiling, unreadable, alien, dashing toward her and away, chittering in their many-one language. Not always your idea of clean, birds. One clawed at Bird's hair again and again. Another sat on her shoulder, not prettily, but digging its claws into her shirt and skin to withstand Bird's bumpy stride.

The one on her shoulder sang a piercing phrase, over and over in her ear: *Go back, go back, go back.*

That's what all the birds were saying. The birds opposed her path. They crowded the air and branches around her, they sang and called, they tugged and dug. They watched her with their beady alien eyes. They said: *Go back.*

But Bird was not only following the patchwork song, which she believed was meant for her; she was not only running from Summer; she was also running from her own guilty, hurting heart. So there was nowhere to go back to. Nowhere to go, nowhere to return.

Reaching the castle took more than a day of walking for short-legged Bird. Her bird companions saw a gray-faced, blue-lipped, brown-haired girl who was beginning to look very ill. Still, she walked grimly on, in a cloud of agitated gray and brown wings, among birds whose anxious calls and chatter echoed the worried clamor of her own heart, if she knew it. But Bird did not want to hear her heart's bad news, when the song was sending her, *must* be sending her, to her destiny. So she walked in a fog, not hearing her heart, not listening to her birds.

Summer had walked in a fog once, and toward that same castle, though she never found it. Now Bird walked in a fog, too, only Bird's fog was on the inside. But inside or out, all fogs lead to the Puppeteer. The Puppeteer works through fog.

Bird was starving and ill and walking in the wrong direction, all because she would not listen to the birds who fluttered above and around her. After all those years listening to real and recorded birdcalls, longing to know the real language; after what she had done to come to this place; after those three long nights in the forest alone, when she sometimes thought she was going crazy and sometimes thought she was dying—after doing all that to learn their language, now she refused to listen to them. She thought the birds were on Summer's side, that they wanted to send her back to the little-sister place. But really they only wanted to keep her from the misery she was walking so stubbornly toward.

Late in the day, the bird chatter grew quieter around her. One by one, birds were dropping away from her fluttering brown parade. Because it took all her concentration to keep her feet moving, Bird didn't notice. The birds were leaving. By the time she saw a clearing in the trees ahead, only two wrens were left, darting near her head and crying their bubbling cry.

But when she stepped out of the forest and into a strange, silent garden, she was alone.

Or so she thought. One bird still accompanied her, but he sat far above where she could not see, watching with his keen owl eyes.

⌒⌒

It wasn't a bright garden, but a dark one. The grass was dried and blackened and patched with snow. Dark flowers grew in neat beds—blood-red flowers, and indigo blues, and dark purples, all reaching toward the no-color of black.

A night garden. A winter garden. But the strangest thing about the garden was not the dark flowers but the bird feeders. Dozens, maybe more than a hundred bird feeders and birdbaths crammed the grounds. One birdbath was a tall fountain bubbling against a bright red mosaic bird with jeweled crests; another was a modest brass bowl propped on a tree stump; another was a stone goblet almost as tall as she was, carved with feathers and beaks and claws. One large copper bath hung from chains from a tree branch, creaking back and forth in the empty wind.

Bird moved slowly among the feeders: iron cages with blocks of seed, long tubes of nyjer, hummingbird nectars in shiny glass, or little brass and wooden shacks with tiny rails and platforms for bird feet.

The feeders were clean and cornucopian, bursting with seeds, sticky with suet.

But there were no birds anywhere, only an eerie silence, a wrong silence, in the trees.

"And no birds sing," whispered Bird to herself, remembering a poem her mother had read her. She was half delirious from sleeplessness and cold, from hunger, from walking so long. She felt as if she were floating.

And so it was floating and hazy that Bird came through a thick grove of trees and saw the enormous swan. She blinked. She thought she was dreaming. It was impossibly large, its lovely head reaching past the tallest oak trees, well up among the firs. Whitish-gray and cool as stone, the swan stood still against a dark hill. Bird stood still as stone herself, hardly breathing, watching the great bird. The swan never moved; not even a feather ruffled in the light wind.

And within a few breaths, even Bird, dizzy and starving as she was, saw why: the swan was not just still as stone: it *was* stone, pale gray stone, every feather carved and unmoving. It was a swan statue. Or no—she revised the thought—not a statue, either. It was a swan *castle*, a castle with huge, fluted wing-walls and a tower as narrow and curving as a swan's throat. What she had taken for the swan's deep black eye was not an eye, but the castle's entrance, the only entrance Bird could see, more than a hundred feet in the air.

A castle is for a queen. But a castle with a door in the air—that's a castle for a bird queen. It had to be.

But how do you knock on a door that's a hundred feet in the air?

Bird followed the swan's stone gaze to a lake, a big one, still as a silver plate, and so big that she could only just see it melting into green-black forest at its far edge. The stillness of that silver lake gave her a sharp, surprising twist of homesickness—why? Silver and green are Christmas colors, she thought. Maybe that's why that lake makes me feel so happy and so terrible.

Just then a voice, a thrilling voice above her, said, "They're waiting for you, Bird." She turned her head so fast it made her stumble—the voice was that familiar, and somehow cut Bird's heart with joy, somehow answered her homesickness. Although she couldn't think why… she almost could, but then she couldn't.

A small, spotted bird leaped down to a closer branch. "They're waiting for you," said the bird again, in the wonderful voice.

Perhaps because she was so exhausted and ill, or perhaps because the voice cut so near her heart, Bird asked the question that had plagued her deepest heart all this time. "Really for me?" she asked. "Are they really waiting for me, and not for Summer?"

The starling cocked its head in an affectionate way. "Oh, Bird," she said. "This place wasn't meant for Summer. It was meant for a queen. It was meant for you. Go in."

"By myself?" asked Bird. Despite the music of the starling's loving voice, she was beginning to feel a profound loneliness. *And no birds sing.* Only this starling, who sounded nothing like a bird.

"Go on," said the starling, with more firmness now. "I must stay here and guard the grounds." Then, kindly: "You'll see. The castle wants you to come."

But whose castle is this? wondered Bird. She had heard everything she ever wanted to hear—meant for a queen, meant for you—and she suddenly felt unsure. *Are the people in this castle good people? If they are, where are the birds?*

The starling watched Bird with cool, bright eyes. "There are birds inside," she said simply. "They are waiting for you."

And so Bird understood, or thought she did. That's why this place was birdless, of course, she thought—for some reason, they were all *inside*, in the castle. With the queen. Or waiting for a queen. "Thank you," she said to the starling with joy. "You're welcome, alouette," replied the starling. *That's my mother's name for me,* thought Bird. And—*Oh! That's my mother's voice!* She spun around.

But the starling was gone. The copper birdbath creaked in the wind.

Bird turned back to the swan, and a small sound like a laugh came out of her. While she'd been talking with the starling, the castle had utterly transformed. Before it was cool, unreachable—now it was warm and welcoming and hung with lights, rippling ribbons and garlands of brightness spilling from the swan's head and down its sides. The gray stone was draped in long festive sweeps of red and saffron cloth. And in the swan's side—how could Bird not have seen them before?—were huge wooden double doors, and they were flung open. Inside were warmth and light; were delicious smells that made Bird feel faint from hunger. The light and the warmth and the smells called her on.

Birds in there, there must be, in that warm and glowing castle, and she needed birds. And maybe they needed her.

She walked through the wide, welcoming doors.

∞

Inside, Bird found a room that was made for birds, and was full and noisy with them. It was bare of any furniture, and dark, curving wooden beams lay like rib bones against the swan-colored walls. The walls rose curving upward until they narrowed at the swan's long throat. *It's beautiful,* Bird thought. But the graceful lines of the castle's throat were spoiled by a gleaming golden stairway, elegant but cold, metallic, out of place, spiraling up from the dirt floor into the high, dim recesses of the swan's head. *That will choke the swan,* Bird thought. Then she shook it off as a foolish idea.

The hall was saturated with cozy, even light, though Bird couldn't see its source. A warm draft poured from a huge fireplace at the far end of the hall.

It's beautiful, Bird thought again. And the room was full of birds, many of them bright tropical birds with fat, curving beaks, colored like children's drawings, red and green and yellow and blue. Others were pitch-black with beaks like fire, yellow tipped with red. Bird saw magpies, too, black with white patches, and a few more white-freckled starlings like the one outside.

But bird-loving Bird was distressed and disoriented, in fact almost stumbled back out of the castle. First, because the birds—all the birds, scores of them—were scattered across the black earth floor, standing or strutting or puffing along the floor. The walls were hung with perches, and the beams half concealed the crumbling remains of nests; but not a single bird flitted up to watch her from above. Not a single bird sailed the warm smoky draft up the swan castle's throat.

Worse, all the birds were speaking human languages. It took Bird a minute to understand that, tuning in through the echoing chatter. Most were speaking English, but she did catch some Spanish as well, and perhaps other languages—all in human-like voices. Bird felt a little sick.

A parrot strutted up to her. He had a pale green eye with a black dot at the center, and the eye jerked back and forth as he spoke.

"Welcome, welcome," he said, in the voice of a tiny old man. "She's waiting for you upstairs."

"Who?" said Bird, upset by this creature, but also full of sadness for him, and also almost ready to laugh. "Who is waiting?"

"She is," said the parrot.

"She is, she is," echoed the other birds in their doll-voices, crowding around her, shuffling back and forth on the dirt floor. Yellow and black, blue and red and white-spotted, the birds stared up at her, unblinking.

Bird felt her face and neck get hot. Did they mean the queen? She had thought that she might be the queen. Was there another? She put the heat into her voice, to get it out of her. "Why aren't you speaking your *own* language?" she asked. "You sound *stupid* speaking mine."

A shocked silence. The fireplace crackled and spit. One bird laughed, a high, hideous cackle, then stopped. The parrot drew himself up. "We don't speak *forest language* here," he said in his tinny voice. "This is her castle. That would be an insult to her."

"Why do all these birds live inside?" Bird persisted. "Why do they live inside on the floor of a *house* when they could live in trees with the sun and stars?"

"They like it here," said the parrot, not looking at her, not looking away.

"We like it here, we like it here," chanted the birds around her in their broken-human voices.

Bird opened her mouth to ask again, but the parrot waddled past her toward the spiraling staircase. "Follow me," he said. "She is waiting."

The other birds stood still, watching, as Bird walked slowly to the staircase and, following the little green-and-yellow bird, began to climb. She did not like staircases in general, and this one had no railing, and empty space between the shiny metal stairs. She made her hands into fists and pushed on, one foot on a step, then the other. The stair uncurled like a golden ribbon on a birthday present. It wound upward through the warm air the way a bird would, if a bird were flying up the castle's throat.

Bird had not eaten in so long, and she had walked so far. Her legs were very tired.

The parrot plodded just in front of her, fluttering slightly from step to step, then walking, then flutter-hopping again. Bird suddenly laughed, then gasped, as the force of the laugh made her waver on the step. She was very high up now, and could barely see the crowd of birds watching from the floor below. There was no rail to catch her. She felt a poisonous flood of terror, and could not move her leg another step.

"Why have you stopped?" asked the tiny-old-man parrot, his head cocked. His head was blue-green on top, with a black-and-yellow throat. His face was zebra-striped. Bird leaned forward and held on to a step above her. She felt the room turning around her; she felt sick. Her legs trembled, and her blood trembled inside. She laughed again, her eyes shut tight. "Why don't you *fly*?" she asked in a choking voice. "Why are you *walking* up these stairs, you're a *bird*."

Bird did not see, but the parrot sagged a little. He didn't answer, instead asking, "Have you rested? She is waiting."

Bird pressed her face against the cold step. The old children's song, their mother's song, popped into her head: "Two little cygnets,/Climbing through the air/One flies to the top/And one takes the stairs." She almost laughed; it sounded more like crying. Groping with damp hands at the steps above, her eyes half shut so as not to see below, she half crawled, half climbed, half pulled herself up the cold, curving stairway behind the parrot.

Fear of heights—that's funny, for a girl who wants more than anything to be a bird.

$$\sim$$

It felt like an hour, getting to the top. When she arrived, her fingers were too weak to grip, but she pushed her hands down and pulled herself across the floor, belly down. She kept pulling, to get as far from the edge as she could. She lay on the cool wood floor, shaking.

"Bird," said a warm, golden voice above her. The voice was like the sound of wine pouring into a glass. "Hello, Bird. Welcome. Now you are where you belong."

The warm voice ran over Bird like a hand. Her breathing calmed. She opened her eyes, and then sucked in her breath. Just a few feet away was a small heap of filthy cloth, from which two dark, animal eyes were peering at her.

And then the figure shifted in her mind, and she realized she was looking at herself. She blinked. The room was lined with mirrors. A soft light came through a high window that ran the length of the longest wall, just below the ceiling. It was hardly a window, more of a crack, only a few inches high. But a slant of light came through.

Bird turned on her back, confused by the multiple images of a thin, ragged girl. She propped herself on her elbows. Then she saw, at the other end of the room, a tall woman, erect in a gray dress, a slender gray column. A woman—Bird thought she was a woman—who wore a large bird mask. The mask had a long beak, red then black, not thin, that looked sharp as two knives locked together. On either side of the beak, the mask was black; above that were two strokes of white, wide as a paintbrush, on either side of the small round eyes. The top of the mask, which folded over the top of the woman's head, was the color of half-dried blood.

"You are a wild Bird," said the masked woman. "Do you see yourself?"

"Yes," said Bird.

"Watch me closely," said the figure behind the mask. "And when you are ready, join in. Dancing is the bird's other language."

She gave a long, high-pitched cry: *aaaaAH, AH-ah, AH-ah, AH-ah.* She lifted her chin high, pointing up. One knee lifted, a sharp square angle to the floor, while her arm lifted, too—back behind her, and up. Bird thought: *I've seen her, in the Egyptian hall, at the museum.* Her movements were sharp, violent and sharp, shoulders square and tight, pressed back as her elbows lifted above and behind.

The bird-mask lady held an angled pose; then came the high, strange cry again.

Bird thought: *I know that cry. It's like a bird cry, although it is not one. She is supposed to be a bird. What bird is she supposed to be?*

The masked figure screamed or cried again. She turned slowly in the mirror, cocked her head at Bird. Bird looked at her own reflection in the mirror; saw the mouth of her mirror-self open, felt an answering scream. The two figures in the mirror cried out together, and mirror-Bird's cry lay under the bird mask's cry, with enough difference and enough sameness to create an answer and a harmony.

"I will teach you the dance language," said the masked figure. "You need to learn it, for when you are the queen."

Was Bird wishing she had never come? Was she longing to be outside, knocking the guard starling to the ground, legging it back to the forest and Summer—Summer, whom she had misled and abandoned? Was Bird feeling the terrible thing she had done now?

No. As exhausted as she was, as hungry as she was, Bird was flooded with happiness, or something like happiness. She had heard the words "When you are the queen." She knew, she believed she knew, that this was where she belonged.

Bird looked in the mirror, at herself, and the bird mask poised above her. She cried her own name. A little bright explosion of a name.

An egg of a name.

Well: to the Puppeteer, the woman behind the mask, it was an egg. The one she had been hoping for; the one she meant to nurture.

CHAPTER FOURTEEN

RED HOUSE, BLACK DOOR

The path to the savory smoke led Summer through the thickest part of the forest, a tangle of black branches and vines that grew denser as the smells became more delicious. The path was now so narrow that at some points it was only a few inches wide, providing no buffer against the forest. Summer didn't care. The slashing branches and tearing sticker vines hurt, and she was glad they hurt. The hurt almost made her forget for part of a second what she had done (what she thought she had done). She pushed a little harder than she had to, to make it hurt a little more.

And then the path broke through the trees, and it was there in front of her: a little red house, no bigger than one biggish room. It had a black pointed roof and a thick black door, with one thin, twisting tendril of smoke rising from a square black chimney. The clearing around the house looked like neither the white-gray winter of Down nor the early spring she'd left behind at home. It looked like deep autumn, a carpet of red leaves beneath a gray sky. The whole thing looked a bit decayed, a bit collapsing—except that the dark red paint was still shiny, almost wet.

The black door, on the other hand, was old, scarred and beaten and sludged over with the dirt of many years' winds and mucky sleet. But the strangest thing about it was that it had no knob. It had a lock and a keyhole; but no knob, no lever, and no way that Summer could see to open it.

Why does it need a lock if there's no way to open it anyway? Summer thought. She moved closer, picking her way through the rattling dead leaves, and underneath those leaves, the rotted black muck of the leaves that had come before them.

No one has cleaned this door in a long time. Summer moved nearer the door. She felt distant and detached, as if she were in a dream. *This door is filthy.* She didn't want to touch the filthy door. The iron of the lock and hinges was rusted over, probably frozen stiff.

"Probably frozen stiff with rust," said Summer out loud into the quiet. Her voice sounded hoarse, not like her own.

The keyhole was large, and Summer could see something inside. A bit of muddy color, and a dim light. And was that movement? She knelt in front of the door, the dampness of the earth sinking through her pants and into her knees.

Kneeling, she was at just the right height. Holding herself carefully so as not to touch the filthy thing, she put her eye close to the keyhole. She thought she saw what might be the edge of a table, and the glint of some shiny dish, and perhaps, oh please, was that the edge of some food? Was it meat? Was there fresh bread? If she could only—

And forgetful of the filth, Summer pressed her eye against the keyhole.

As her face touched the door, something happened. It was as if a strong hand pushed her tight against the lock, pressed her eye into the hole. No—the force didn't come from behind. It was as if a vacuum from *inside* the house sucked her toward the keyhole, sucked her eye against the opening. Summer struggled and fought, her hands pushing and scraping at the filthy door she had meant not to touch.

But it didn't matter how she fought. She felt the skin of her face pulling through the keyhole. She felt her right cheekbone pushed against the hole, too, and then, impossibly, somehow *bending and twisting* through the hole. Now one whole side of her face slid into the hole, and her hair was catching at the edges of the lock. Now the rest of her head squeezed like dough through the keyhole. Summer had the dreadful sensation that she was being swallowed by a snake, as the keyhole closed around her somehow rubbery shoulders. And then, with a struggle and push, her shoulders were through, followed almost at once by the rest of her: *pop.*

The house sat silent in the forest again, a few dead leaves gusting up beside it and dropping away. It looked just as it had when Summer arrived—unless you happened to see the few blonde hairs caught on the edge of the keyhole, tossing in the cold wind.

∽

Scraped and shocked and sick, Summer lay tumbled against the other side of the black door. She found her breath, righted herself, and sat against the door, which did not seem much cleaner inside. She felt for the egg: safe, and ever warmer, warm as a cup of tea. Then she felt around her face and shoulders for broken bones or torn skin. Traveling through the keyhole had not hurt, but the sensation of her bones twisting and softening as she was sucked through the hole made her feel sick to her stomach. She wouldn't think about it again.

But everything seemed to be in place, her bones as hard and real as ever. She stood, brushing the last leaves and dirt from her pants and jacket. She turned to look back at the dreadful door.

No knob on this side, either. And now the keyhole was gone, too.

If she had found this house (or: if it had found her) just a few hours earlier, she would have felt excitement and fear: How will I get out? Is anyone here? Are my parents here? But now the idea of seeing her parents made her stomach turn. She couldn't ever face them again, after what she had let happen to Bird. Just as well to be trapped in a cabin forever.

The floor was rough, dusty wooden planks, bare except for one rag rug, made of bits of old cloth that might have once been brightly colored but were now gray. (Something about that gray cloth reminded her of Ben; but the thought went away.) The walls had once been painted a deep sky-blue, but now the paint was peeling, and white cracks ran through it like shooting stars. Taking up most of one wall was a stone fireplace, a low fire fluttering and snapping inside it, with a large center stone in the shape of a bird's head—a bird Summer did not know, except that she did almost remember it from a dream of a great red bird, those two mosaic plumes, sapphire blue, rising from the stone head.

A window (a way out?), narrow and filthy, was set high, near the high ceiling, lined in peeling white paint. No wonder the light was so dim and dirty.

All this she saw in a second or two. Then her attention was riveted by a small wooden table, perhaps once painted red, on which sat a loaf of warm bread, steam still rising, and a big jug. A black iron pot hung over the fire, something wonderful-smelling bubbling inside. That was the smell that had brought her here.

(Something familiar about the pot, too—those starry nights sleeping in the open air, curled next to a warm pot. She felt she almost ought to know whose house this was, and the egg, warmer still in her pocket, almost hot, seemed to be trying to tell her. But Summer was too hungry to follow that thread.)

Stew cooking, bread just made: the owner of the house must be somewhere near. "Is anyone here?" Summer said aloud into the dusty silence. The dust absorbed her voice and made it sound thick and small, the cry of a fat mouse. She was near tears from hunger, and even her knowledge that this food belonged to someone else could not keep her from it.

I won't eat all of it, she said to herself, and half stumbled toward the shelf where she had spotted an iron mug, a clay bowl, and a wooden spoon. She scooped spicy-savory scented stew into the bowl, tore off a hunk of bread, and began to eat.

Summer was ravenous, and the stew was delicious—beans and vegetables simmered in a sauce spiced with cinnamon, she thought, and pepper, and some other spice she couldn't name. And maybe mint? She poured what she had thought was water from the jug, but it was pale gold, and tasted spicy as well, like flat ginger ale. The bread was delicious. It was all delicious. Burying her grief and guilt, she ate and ate and drank until she was too full to have another bite. In fact, she broke her promise to herself and ate and drank every bit.

She sat back. She did not feel sated or sleepy—on the contrary, she felt bright and alert, perhaps more alert and alive than she'd ever felt. Her senses were sharp as a raven's. The crumbs and smears of sauce in the bowl smelled complicated, savory; the last of the embers in the dying fire added a smoky tang. Now she could see the rich red the table used to be. When she looked up, the flowers and vines painted around the shelves seemed to dance and crawl along the walls. Bright-eyed, she followed them as they circled lower on the wall and then looped around toward—what? She could not quite see. She stood, her feet as light as her head, and moved (or glided, as it felt) toward the wall.

It was a small latch, almost the same color as the wall. In fact, she realized as she reached out to touch the latch: This was not a wall. This was a door. This was the way out.

Summer pulled on the latch. It stuck. She pulled again; stuck. Heat rose in her face. The stupid thing ought to open. Why wouldn't it? It seemed so much on the verge of opening, so close. She pulled again. Not quite, still stuck, but it felt as if just one more pull, one really hard pull, one yank—

A cloud of dust rose soundlessly in the doorway. Summer had stumbled backward; she sat on the floor, surprised. The dust motes patterned and unpatterned in the dirty light.

As the dust settled, Summer could see more clearly. Where she had expected to see the forest outside, she saw a hallway—a long, long hallway, stretching off past what she could see in the dim light.

Summer felt disoriented. This was such a small house; this was such a long hall. It didn't seem possible. And yet the hall stretched before her, lit as if by faint sunlight, but with no windows or skylight she could see.

Dust rose in the pale light.

Summer hesitated, then stepped inside. She made her way down the dusty hallway, moving farther and farther from the small, high window's dirty light. She left her pack behind; she left her red sweater behind. She left her whole life behind.

A summer-haired, sea-eyed girl is walking down a dusty wooden hallway. She once had a name, but she has forgotten it. Along the hall are three doors: one on the left; one on the right; and the last at the far end of the hall.

The left-hand door is cracked open. The summer-haired girl slips in.

A room made of six blank pages: white floor, white walls, white ceiling. In the center of the floor, a white box, tied with red ribbon, the ribbon ends teased up like the crest of feathers on a bird's head.

A present.

The girl opens the box. It is full of colored chalk, thick pieces, like colored birds' eggs tumbled together in a nest.

The girl who cannot recall her name chooses a piece of chalk and begins to draw.

She fills one wall with a sun, amber and saffron, throwing off threads of corn-colored light. She gives the sun a burning tangerine heart.

On the opposite wall, she draws a bird, electric blue and iris, ash and steel, every sky color in the white box. But the girl draws the bird on the ground, not flying, and draws with extra care the bird's rusty, curling feet.

On the third wall, between the sun and the bird, she draws a swan, as white as the wall, so white it seems like part of the wall. The lifted throat, the curving wing, the blossom of tail feathers: she outlines these in lilac and black, longing colors.

Across from the swan, also between the sun and the bird, she draws a leafy gate made of spring and clover, forest and moss, every green twining together, each side leaning and bending toward the other in a high arch. But the girl draws the arch too high, and although she stands on tiptoe, though she stretches her arm, she cannot reach to make the arch ends meet.

The summer-haired girl turns to look at her work. Then she kneels on the white floor. She draws a heart as large as a tree, a heart in two pieces, in the colors of lava and fire engines, of roses and rubies, of blood.

Now her box is empty. She has used all the chalk. She looks at the sun, the swan, the bird, the gate that doesn't meet, the torn and bloody heart. She can't remember her name. She doesn't know why she drew these things. But grief blooms in her throat, and she begins to cry.

As she cries, it seems to her the walls and floor cry with her. The white swan on the white wall trembles and vanishes, reappears, vanishes. The sky-bird with its crooked brown feet shivers and twists as if it stands in a flame. The heart split at her feet streams in rivulets across the white floor, like rays of sunrise across a white plain.

This is the gift of the first room: to see with clear eyes your own bleak and luminous pain.

Still clinging to an empty box, the girl runs from the melting, burning colors and her own hot tears. She runs across the hall to the next room and slams the door shut.

Another blank, white room; but this one is calm and cold. Her ragged breath makes puffs of fog and begins to slow. Her pounding blood slows. Her tears come slower and slower until they move sluggishly, choked with ice.

Her heart slows. Her tears stop.

She stops.

Now the girl's hair is snow, not summer. Now her swimming eyes are frozen seas. Now her lips are dusted white and still.

She stands, cold and white, in the cold, white room. Her heart sits protected in a nest of ice, almost not beating at all.

She stands that way for a long, long time.

And then, in her chest, a single point of hot pain burrows through.

It hurts, thinks the girl with milky, frozen eyes. (What hurts? She can't remember.) *It isn't fair,* thinks the frost-girl. (What is unfair? She doesn't know.)

The pinpoint flame of anger and grief becomes a hot needle, then a hot knife.

It melts the ice-nest around her heart, making space for it to beat again.

It melts the frost that binds her lips.

It melts the sea in her eyes.

This time, the summer girl doesn't run. Carefully, she slips a hand inside her chest. Carefully, she takes the hot orange pain in her hand like a pulsing bird, slips it into the empty white box, and ties the red ribbon again. Then she folds the box up very small and tucks it back inside her heart.

"You'll be safe there," she says.

This is the gift of the second room: to protect you from the worst of your pain, but to keep the pain safe, so that you never lose its colors or its lesson.

Then she walks out of the room and down the hall. She stands before the last door. She closes her eyes, opens the door, and steps through.

Air rushes around the girl, a waterfall falling up. No: she is falling.

The summer girl opens her eyes to blue. She is falling through an immense sky, a huge and cloudless empty blue. Her ears are full of rushing silence. She feels tinier than a flea, falling toward nothing, because there is no ground, not below or beside her. There is only sky, in all directions.

This is the gift of the third room: falling.

A sleek black bird flies past the falling bit of summer. As it flies, it turns to show her one blue eye. And as she watches the black bird beat past, her stomach jerks; she is not falling anymore, she is yanked up. Leathery talons grasp her upper arms, drag her like a puppy through the blue. She hears wings crashing above her, like wave after wave in a storm. She is afraid to look up to see the size of a bird that can carry her so lightly in its claws.

Claws, thinks the summery girl in the blue sky: *heart, flute, claw.* Not knowing what she means, but wanting to say it, she says it aloud: "Heart, flute, claw."

One enormous black feather falls gently past her. This bird could fill a cathedral. Her legs drag through the thick, rushing air.

Together she and the great black bird pursue the small black bird—a raven, its black tail fanned out. The raven is fast as a fat black arrow; the raven is getting away. The summer girl is not sure whether she is sorry or glad, or even whether they are pursuing the bird or going somewhere together. *One black raven/Flying through the blue,* she remembers, but can't remember why.

The deafening wing beats of the enormous bird begin to slow. Looking below, hanging by her sore arms, for the first time the summer-haired girl sees something besides blue. She sees a patch of green, far, far below her, a small, dark green swatch swimming out of gray mists. The beating stops as the great wings straighten. Bird and girl plunge downward, and the patch of green grows larger and larger.

The patch is the top of a tree, the girl realizes. The rushing air pulls her face tight and her hair back. It must be the tallest tree in the world, she thinks: taller than mountains, taller than mists. All alone, this single tree raises its green head among the clouds.

The tree grows larger and closer.

A roar of air. They are going to hit the tree! And yes, rough twining leaves and branches tangle all around as the talons release her and are gone. The summer-girl slips and scrambles and clings, no time to even lift her head to see the bird who saved and abandoned her. She's clinging to the top of a huge, swaying tree, too far above the ground to see anything but swirling mists below.

Terrified, she wraps her hands tight around the slim branch. She tries to wrap her legs as well. But in the fierce, high wind, the swaying branches twist out of the girl's hands, swing away from her scrambling legs. The girl fights, kicks her legs wildly, tries as hard as she can. But her hands are not strong enough. She slips; she falls through the cold misty air…

…and finds herself thumped to the bottom of a huge, rough basket, sheltered from the wind it sways in. She is rocked in a cradle of woven branches.

A nest. The giant bird had left her in a nest.

Quiet at last, safe for a moment when she thought safety was gone forever, she knew herself again: Summer. *I am Summer,* she thought. *My name is Summer.* Shocked, she sat up straight. *I have parents, gone; and a sister, dead. I am in a swaying tree far above the earth, in the nest of a giant bird.*

She started to cry, stopped herself, then wondered: *Why? Why stop? Why not cry? I am at the top of the world, all alone, no one can hear me, and my sister is dead because of me, and I will probably die here.*

So Summer cried as hard as she could. The crying shook her whole body, like being sick. She made ugly wailing sounds. Her tears ran fast down her face and slipped down her neck, making the cold air colder. Summer wiped at her face, then plunged her cold wet hands into her pockets to warm them. Hands in pockets, body curled tight as a comma, Summer wept into the rough grass and twigs of her rocking sky-nest, among the wisps of cloud.

In her right pocket, Summer's hand knotted into a fist as she wept. But in her left pocket, her damp hand caught tight around the wooden egg. It fit her hand, and comforted her.

Many thousands of feet above the earth, hung in a basket in a great, gray-green tree whose roots ran down to the center of the earth, Summer sobbed until her sobs finally ran out. She lay curled in the basket, swinging in the wind as it sang through branches, holding the warm rough egg. Remembering its sweet smell, and Ben's distant, kind eyes, she pulled the egg out of her pocket and held it to her face. Its fragrance was deep and sweet—not sugary-sweet, but warm and spicy, like the scent from their fire the first night. It smelled so much like the fire, and the fire bird, that Summer began to feel warmer, and calmer. She felt how her body ached, and she wanted to cry again, but then all she wanted was sleep. So she slept.

∽

In her dream, the egg fell from her hand as she slept and rolled across the floor of the nest. In her dream, as she slept, unknowing, something long and sleek poked its head through a tiny gap in the weavings of branches and vines that made the nest. Wriggling a bit, in Summer's dream, the long, dark, shimmering thing slithered toward the egg.

In her sleep, Summer stirred unhappily.

In her dream the serpent rose up a bit as it reached the egg, as if to breathe its scent. Like a cat, the snake rubbed its mouth across the burnt, black side of the egg, once, twice. Then slowly, with great care, it began to wrap its long, long, dark-glinting body around the egg. As it wrapped itself, it drew the egg upward, until it stood on its thicker end. The snake coiled around the egg in neat, regular spirals. Finally, the serpent's tail rested on the floor of the nest, its body wrapped about the egg, its head swaying above, as the nest was swaying. As the serpent's head rocked, the egg rocked gently, too; and the serpent-entwined egg rocked gently, back and forth, back and forth, on the floor of Summer's rocking nest.

Summer's eyes flew open. She felt sick and terrified and lost.

The egg had fallen from her hand. But it was still there, tumbled on its side on the rough brown floor of the nest. And she saw no snake, no snake anywhere.

But still the lump of revulsion in her throat took a long time to go away.

CHAPTER FIFTEEN

IN THE
WORLD TREE

It was afternoon when Summer woke up. She felt rested for the first time in a long time. She felt rested, and she felt empty. As she turned on her back, the crane map in her jacket pocket made a papery sound, and she thought: *I'd like to see that supposedly magic crane map get me home from here.*

The edge of the nest was far above her head, as high as the roof of a house, she thought, or higher. Even stretching out her arms, Summer could nowhere near touch the other side. The nest must be at least twice as long as she was.

Above her was a gray, misty sky—no blue, no clouds. Or perhaps she and the nest were inside a cloud. She must be very near the top of the tree, because there were only a few bare branches above the nest. Nothing but gray, and a few bare branches, as far as she could see.

She stood, bracing her feet against the swaying, feeling small. The enormous nest was empty, except for herself and her egg. She was a little hungry (how long ago was that meal? a few hours? a frozen life-time?) and terribly thirsty. Although she knew it wasn't wise, she fin-ished off the last of the canteen water and ate the last six raisins. She thought, without feeling: *I will die in here if I don't find food and water soon.*

Remembering the birds' nests that she had climbed trees to see at the edge of the forest near her home, she thought: *These walls must be made of vines and branches, woven together. I'll find a handhold or a foothold and climb up to look over.*

But first, she pulled the egg from her pants pocket, brushing ashes from the side that had fallen in the fire. The burn was almost even, so that the egg was now exactly half black and half its own warm near-white. But it still held the shape Ben had given it—only on the black side, the wood was rough and charred now, instead of smooth.

"I'm sorry," said Summer aloud to the egg, and held it close. Then she tucked it into a hollow on the nest floor, charred side down. No matter what happened to her in this climb, the egg would be safe.

Now she returned to the wall and pressed against it, looking for a handhold—until she felt something square and hard in her jacket pressing back. An acrid smell of smoke came with it as she pulled it out, and her stomach turned: Bird's old journal, greasy with soot, lumpy with melted plastic. Summer walked to the other side of the nest, set it down without looking, and walked back. She might open it. But not yet, not yet.

Now the egg was safe, and what was left of Bird was safe. Again, Summer slid her hand across the nest wall, until she found a largish crack at hip height. Her right boot fit into it. She found fingerholds above, and pushed up. Starfished, she felt for another foothold on the

left, found a narrow edge, more fingerholds, pushed again. Clinging like a lizard, she felt with her right foot—but something snapped
under her left foot, and her fingers tore away, too weak to hold her
whole weight.

For a while she lay on the floor of the nest, nursing a ragged, bleeding fingernail. Then she stood up to try again. This time she chose her
holds more carefully, and while the swaying made it harder, after long
minutes, she was up, her head and shoulders well above the edge of the
nest. Resting her forearms on the knobby edge, she looked down.

The tree swayed, sharp and sudden. Summer felt sick, her stomach
lurching sideways. She clutched hard at the edge of the nest. The swaying softened, a rocking in the wind. Clinging to the edge of the nest,
eyes closed, Summer took three deep, shaky breaths. "I'm up high like
a plane," she said aloud in a soft, high voice. "It's all right."

But she was not in a plane. The wind stirred, blowing wet mist
against her cheek, blowing her hair in her eyes. She looked down again.
As mists merged and parted, she saw glimpses of the earth far below,
squares of ground in different colors, a ragged, patched-up quilt. So
far below that she could never in the world climb down. Never make
a vine ladder long enough. Never hope—this was laughable now, to
think she'd had this hope as she lay on the nest floor—that she could
signal someone below and be rescued.

Summer was alone at the top of the world. The wind was cold, and
stronger now. It battered her face and made her hair sting her cheeks
and eyes. She clung to the edge of the nest as to the prow of a ship in
deep waves. She wanted to go back down, but that would be a surren-
der to thirst and hunger and death. She would only be weaker tomorrow, and the climb would be even harder.

She gripped the edge of the nest and looked up. The tree tapered upward for only another ten or fifteen feet. Very near the top were a few new greeny-gold buds and shoots—branches not quite bare, after all.

But even more surprising, Summer saw what looked like a large fruit, or a cluster of fruits—it was hard to tell. It must have been hidden by the mist before. But from up here she could see it: blackish globs, the size of small tangerines, but rumplier, hanging in a tight cluster.

Summer knew the dangers of eating fruit you did not recognize. On the other hand, without *something*, she would die anyway. She edged her way around the nest till she could grab the thick branch that led toward the fruit. One hand on the branch for balance, she pulled one knee to the edge of the nest, gripped the branch in both hands, and then, with a deep breath, pulled the other knee up as well.

How would you feel if you were balanced on your knees on the edge of a giant nest that was rocking like a cradle, holding a branch tightly in both arms, staring through a cold wind many thousand feet to the earth below? That's how Summer felt, approximately. A sharp gust of wind caught her at just that moment. If it had come a second earlier, when she was only holding on with one hand—but it hadn't.

But now she was afraid to move, not up the branch or back down to the nest. Maybe she would hold onto the branch forever. She could think of worse things.

Then, for some reason, Summer thought of Bird. That charred sleeve. *So it doesn't matter, anyway,* Summer thought, *whatever happens,* and with that thought she swung her whole self onto the branch. She clung there like a baby monkey for a long time, hands slippery, breathing hard. And then, as she had done hundreds of times on trees back home—"It's no big *deal,*" she muttered to herself, "you make everything into such a big *deal* sometimes"—not looking down, she edged her body up the branch, knees and arms working and clinging. Once her right hand slipped, and she almost swung down below the branch. She did not fall, but it felt as if her heart fell, all those thousands and thousands of feet. She pulled and pushed herself on.

After a long time (an hour? five hours?), she came within a long arm's reach of the fruit.

Now that she was close, she could see it was not black at all, but a deep blood red. The fruit was the size of a large watermelon, but like a raspberry it was globular. A blood-colored, watermelon-sized raspberry. Summer wanted to laugh. *I'm sitting on a branch thousands of feet in the sky,* she thought. *The wind is cold and gusts to make me fall. I'm stuck inside a cloud, picking the only fruit from the tallest tree.*

But when she thought *only fruit,* she stopped laughing. Only fruit. Only chance. No mistake.

Carefully, her hand shaking ("Stupid," she breathed), Summer reached for the big red fruit and tested its weight. It looked pluckable on its slim stem, but too heavy for one hand—perhaps even too heavy for two. She locked her legs tight, breathed one breath—and then, saying *brave* and *it doesn't matter* over and over in her head, reached out for the fruit with both hands and pulled. If it pulled free too suddenly, she would lose her balance and fall. Or she could lose the fruit, which might be worse.

The fruit came into her grasp as easily as the hand of a friend. But it was heavy—watermelon-heavy. How could she lift it onto the branch? And even if she did, how could she make it back down the branch, holding it? When she wiggled backward, she twisted and nearly fell, which sent a flash of adrenaline-fear through every muscle. Her legs were aching and losing strength. Still flat on her stomach, gripping the branch with her legs, holding the fruit with both hands below the branch, Summer put her forehead down and cried.

The wind made the tears feel icy. The sound was nothing but alone. Her arms ached, and if another gust came…

A few inches away, someone gave a hoarse cough. Astonished, Summer raised her face. On the branch beside her sat a black bird, its feathers stirring in the wind. It had long black legs and ugly black feet and one blue eye on Summer and the fruit.

For a long time they stayed that way, bird and girl, unmoving, cold high wind ruffling black feathers and pale hair.

Then, without warning, the bird leaped lightly down onto the fruit. "Oh, DON'T!" said Summer, who could hardly hold the weight of the fruit on its own. "PLEASE don't. Get OFF!" she shouted. The bird looked up at her, turned its head, and then pecked at her hand, hard, once. "Oh!" said Summer. Her hand jerked; her hand opened. The fruit fell. Swept by despair, she watched her only chance tumbling away through the mist.

But when a gust pushed the mists aside, she saw that the fruit was dropping directly into the nest, like a raspberry into a big brown bowl.

Summer looked at the raven, the tears still wet on her astonished face. The bird looked back. Then it flapped its wings and was gone.

○⃝

Summer's tree was a special tree, is and always has been a special tree. Partly because it is tall—the tallest thing of green or iron in this green-and-iron world—and partly because its roots run deep, into the center of the planet, where they knot around the world's hot red heart.

As Summer found, the World Tree is a generous tree in some ways, although it doesn't bend to help you, or notice if you fall.

The tree itself will fall one day, because down in the earth's red heart, a long snake, a World Snake, is gnawing at its roots. It has been gnawing for many thousands of years, and will gnaw for thousands more.

The snake doesn't always stay at the roots. Sometimes it slides up the trunk to the very top of the World Tree, to see what it can see.

But Summer hasn't come to the snake yet.

Or it hasn't come to her.

∽

The fruit was interesting to eat. Each globe was thick with sweet, dripping meat, and tasted like a cross between huckleberry and cherry, with a little maple syrup mixed in. The meat surrounded a hidden pocket of juice, the color of grape juice, but better, more quenching, as tangy and fresh as limeade. Summer ate and drank one golfball-sized globule right away, and found that she wasn't hungry or thirsty for the rest of the day. That night, however, and every night she ate the fruit, she had wild dreams, of women and snakes wrestling in the sky; or of a huge pink-and-silver fish that talked like a man and made jokes. The fruit brought her those dreams, which Summer did not like. But the fruit kept her alive, and kept her sore, dark heart beating on.

∽

After she had been in the tree for two days, Summer began to allow her mind to skirt the idea of Bird's journal. It was unbearable to think of reading it at first, but Summer longed to know why Bird had run away. And she was lonely.

Maybe just a little at a time. She could bear it, a little at a time.

So that morning, after her fruit breakfast, she walked to the far side of the nest, picked up the burnt and blackened journal, and opened it to the first page.

The journal was a school-year diary with a page for each day, beginning the previous September. The first pages were in some kind of private code, almost a musical notation. Summer flipped through page after page of these symbols and syllables, finding only one brief passage she understood, in early October:

> *I know Mom could tell me more about this, about why I am like this and who I am. She could teach me, but she won't. I know she thinks I'm too little.*
>
> *I'll find my own teacher. I'll learn it myself.*

The rest of October was the musical code. By early November, some days were left blank. By Thanksgiving they had stopped altogether.

The next entry, on the page for December 21, was written in Bird's scratchy printing.

> *I had a dream last night. But in the dream I knew it wasn't a dream, it was real. And when I woke up I remembered it, I remembered for sure, that that really happened when I was a baby. Only I forgot.*
>
> *I was lying on a yellow blanket in the grass. The grass looked giant, like a grass forest, with giant forest insects crawling along the blades.*

I couldn't see Summer but I could hear her singing a song, like a nursery rhyme.

Then two huge bird feet were in the grass right next to me. It was a big black bird, almost as big as me. It stared at me out of one black eye. When it turned its head, the other eye was blue. I remember that so exactly now.

And then its giant black beak was right over my face. And then the beak came down, so gently, right between my eyes. It kissed me. The bird kissed me. I remember it.

Then the bird flew away. I watched it fly the whole way.

It got smaller in the sky till it was gone.

Summer looked up from the page. One eye blue and one eye black? Could it be that that was a *common* trait in ravens?

But she knew, as much as she knew anything in her life, that it was not.

So that is why I have to talk to birds, and why I know I can. That bird kissed me, and even though I didn't remember it, I sort of did inside.

Before my dream I almost gave up, because no matter how much I kept listening to my bird tape, it didn't work. But now I remember the birds want to talk to me, too.

I will learn to talk to birds. I WILL X 100 X 1,000,000. I will make the birds want to come to me again, the way they come to Mom.

Summer saw in her mind the dusty cassette tape Bird used to play over and over, on an ancient toy tape player shaped like a purse: the tape hand-marked *Brd Sngs of th Grt Lks*. She wanted to *talk* to birds? That was so little-kid, so ridiculous, so Bird, that Summer was swamped again with grief for her little sister. Poor dead Bird. She put the notebook away.

And what was Bird, the very alive little Bird, doing at that moment? At that exact moment, she was making paper birds, and sailing them down the throat of a stone swan, and laughing.

In their first days together, the Puppeteer had told Bird everything she wanted to hear. She had told her that she was meant to be a bird, and not just a bird, but someday perhaps even more. She taught Bird that she was special (which was truer than she knew) and that because she was special, she was better (which was not true at all).

It was everything Bird had wanted to hear from her own mother, but never had. It was as if the Puppeteer could see into her dreams—and perhaps she could. Bird should have noticed that nothing the Puppeteer said was surprising. It was all just exactly what she hoped and planned for. That's the sign of a bad story, and a false one.

But Bird loved to hear the story of herself as bird and perhaps one day something more (*queen*, said her heart: *queen*). She could listen to that story all day.

The one niggling pain, the nighttime anxiety, was for the birds below—the birds who walked on the ground, and spoke English, and seemed so broken and wrong. She pushed those thoughts aside and down, but the Puppeteer saw them. She saw Bird's tender heart reach for the puppet birds, and she decided that her soft heart must be hardened.

And that was why on this day, Bird sat at the Puppeteer's feet, watching her twist bits of paper into lovely little birds, while she told Bird things like "special" and "important" and "better." So Bird followed the Puppeteer, like a puppet herself, as she walked to the edge of the stairway and sent the paper bird sailing, sailing down.

The waddling birds below looked up in astonishment. Up rose a comical squawking chaos, in broken bird-English: Flying was forbidden! What bird was this? It would be made to pay! They flapped and hopped and squawked until the little paper thing finally drifted to the ground.

Then they fell upon it with claws and beaks and ripped it to pieces.

The Puppeteer laughed and laughed at this, so Bird laughed with her. Bird's laughter was a little bit false, because she was a little bit ashamed. She wasn't a cruel Bird. But her heart ached so badly for these sad, broken birds that, just as the Puppeteer had planned, she had begun to hate them. She hated them for making her feel so wretched, when she should be happiest. That happens sometimes.

So when the Puppeteer offered her a piece of tissue paper and said, "You must try it. It passes the time when you're bored," Bird was what she had rarely been: she was obedient. She took the paper, she made the paper bird, and she sailed it down to torment the creatures she loved and hated in her wanting, misled heart.

◌

The climb up the wall of the nest became easier every day. After a week Summer was climbing like a monkey, barely thinking about it at all. Now she took the egg with her and caressed it in her pocket as she straddled the wide rim of the nest and watched the changing sky. Once she saw a glorious half-sunrise, the rays of the sun making gold-and-jewel paths across the ground below, just the way Ben had described.

But Summer's heart did not sing with the sunrise like the chickadee's, because the memory of what she thought she saw in Bird's camp that day still hurt. Still, she kept climbing every day to watch the falling and rising sun. So maybe her heart, like the egg, was not so ruined after all. And maybe that's why one morning, she read more than just a little in Bird's notebook.

March 2:

An owl is trying to talk to me.

Last night before dinner, when it was just getting dark, it came to the edge of the forest and hooted. It sounded almost like a person. I could almost almost almost understand him, but I couldn't. Sarah hissed at him. [Something scratched out here.]

March 7:

Third meeting. I figured out he comes right before dark, on Tuesdays and Thursdays, when Summer stays inside for extra math. So I went a little inside our gate and waited, in the weird color of air before it gets dark. When he came, Sarah lay down flat under a bush, then ran away.

He landed right above me, so I was looking up at him from underneath, his giant claws wrapped around the branch, and it sank down under his weight. A long dark thing like wet, torn paper was dangling from one claw. Then he dropped the dangling thing on me. I freaked out, it was so strange, like a bad dream. But I liked it, too.

It was a snakeskin.

I think it is a secret message.

After a while Sarah wouldn't go outside with her at all, thought Summer. *I remember that.*

March 9:
I figured out the snakeskin. I think it means me—that I am about to do my big change. That I will shed my human skin and find my bird skin.

March 14:
Today he brought a black feather, almost as long as half my arm. I looked at pictures of feathers online and I think it's from a raven. So I looked up ravens.
RAVENS:
Can talk like parrots sometimes
Eat dead things sometimes
Steal shiny stuff
Can do air gymnastics
Live a long time
Then, circled:
The smartest bird
Maybe it means be smart? Do something smart?

March 16:
Stupid stupid STUPID STUPID Summer came out early, so he didn't come. Now I have to wait a week almost. I HATE HER sometimes.

But it proves he's just for me.

March 21:

Today he brought me a bird's egg, a pink one and so tiny. He carried it inside his beak and put it in my hand as gentle as a person. I didn't even know it was an egg at first, I thought it was a pebble or a nut, only so light, like a pink paper nut.

The secret message might be that I am still in an egg, inside a shell. Maybe our house is my shell. Maybe I need to leave this place, to be a bird.

I know he's going to teach me to talk to the birds. But he hasn't started yet. I don't think he has. Or is this part of the lessons?

March 23—and the date made Summer stop. This was the day before that terrible morning, when they woke up and their parents were gone.

I found out what I have to do. It's all I have to do, I think, and then he'll teach me the bird language, or maybe how to be a bird.

He just wants me to open the window in Mom and Dad's bedroom. That's all. He flew to the window, and I ran after, and he stood on the windowsill pressing his head against the windowpane. Then he looked at me. Then he did it again. And I figured it out.

That's just the one thing I have to do, and then I think he'll teach me to talk to the birds. An owl couldn't hurt us; Mom or Dad would just hit it with a baseball bat or something if it tried. Anyway it won't, it's my friend. It's just opening my shell. Open the window, open the egg. A bird comes out.

So I'm going to open their window tonight, while we're having dinner. I'm going to pretend I have to go to the bathroom. And then tomorrow, everything will be different.

Summer flung the notebook aside. Her feelings were a thunderstorm.

And the funny thing was, at just that moment, another egg was almost ready to hatch.

CHAPTER SIXTEEN

SWALLOWED

That night, in the dark, while Summer was asleep, Ben's egg rocked gently, once. It rocked itself upright.

It rested.

Then the egg rocked again, and another time, little rocks, like a grandma in a porch chair. It shook for a moment, and was still.

Then a tap. Then a brighter, harder tap, from the dark inside of the egg, which was held in the dark of the nest, which was held in the dark of the night. A tiny hole appeared between the world and what was in the egg, a tiny crack in the wall between. Something moved against the inside of the shell, stretched and pushed. The egg rocked. A tiny dark beak pushed through the hole, pushed again. The hole grew wider.

The egg rocked again in wider arcs, not a grandmother anymore but a child on a swing: rrrrOCK! ROCK! RRRRRRRRRRRRRRRRROCK! More cracks, and a longer crack: the eggshell came to pieces like a broken heart. Struggling out, still caught in the half-destroyed shell—a bird, of course. A tiny, dripping bird, holding its wings at startled angles, stretching its neck, looking around with moist, blind eyes.

Meanwhile, Summer was dreaming again. She dreamed she was sitting in the nest, the egg beside her, watching a bright, sunless sky. A flock of ravens appeared, carrying a swan on their backs: a black cloud topped by a white one. Summer wondered why the swan didn't fly by itself. And then, in the dream, she was riding the ravens. And then they weren't ravens anymore but one creature, huge and writhing, and in her dream she rode a black dragon across the bright sky.

And then she woke up. She opened her eyes. It was only half-light, the very earliest light. Stretching, thinking of her dream, she turned her head—and saw a terrible sight. Wooden shell in pieces. Naked, bloody creature lying beside it. In one second, the grief of the campfire flooded her again: she had promised, she had promised, and somehow again she had failed.

But then she blinked, and the light grew stronger. The naked, bloody thing was alive, moving. Her stomach turning over with nausea and fear, she forced herself to look more closely.

And she laughed. The little creature wasn't bloody at all. It was a bright red bird, draggled with egg-juice, but straining and turning, and drying fast. Its skin was almost translucent red, with a few stiff bits of deep red down or hair. No feathers. Eyes closed, two dark patches. Its neck twisted. It cocked its head. Its sharp little mouth opened wide. It squeaked.

Summer laughed again. Little peeper. Little bird. Blind bird with tiny limp, bent arms instead of wings. It was hideous.

She loved it.

The peeping red birdlet struggled to its feet, wet and dragging. It raised its head: a pinpoint of emerald in its forehead. Summer put her hand out. The blind wet thing stumbled toward her across the rough floor. It put one tiny claw on her hand, then another. A small thrill of repulsion raced up her arm.

Now the bird was trying to climb her arm, but kept sliding down. Adorable idiot. She lifted her palm up near her face, watched it move uncertainly around her hand, then around two hands. She held the bird up in her two hands like an offering. Its mouth opened cavernously. She reached over to the fruit, pinched a bit onto her pinkie, offered it to the gaping mouth. It worked; the bird ate. She gave it more, till the pocket in its mouth was full and fat.

The bird began to shiver. Summer unzipped the top of her jacket, tucked the bird inside. Made sure its head was near the opening so it could breathe. The bird's tiny heart beat clear against her chest.

Suddenly, Summer was exhausted. And just as suddenly, her heart ached for her wooden egg, gone forever, in shattered pieces.

Then she felt the tiny bird in her pocket rearrange itself against her. *Now I am the egg,* she thought. She lay down, careful of the bird in her jacket, and fell back asleep in the gray dawn.

Ben's red bird lay against Summer's heart, and the pulsing of Summer's blood, like a breathing ocean, rocked it to sleep. All that day and through the night, as they slept, the heart of the tiny red bird beat against her own. That flutter, that dragonfly wing, began to soften her own hurt heart. In her sleep, tears leaked down her face, the first tears since her first day in the nest.

The next morning, the bird peeping from her pocket, Summer found she wanted to read the next entry in Bird's diary.

> *March 24:*
>
> *It's so dark. We're in the forest, deep in, with not enough food and no tent. Summer's asleep.*
>
> *A minute ago I burned the owl feather to make him come. I was so mad at him, and I asked him three questions, and he answered them all the same way.*
>
> *I said, "Where is my mom?" And he digs in the dirt.*
>
> *I said, "Where is our dad?" And he digs again.*
>
> *I said, "Where should we go now, what should we do?" And he digs in the dirt.*
>
> *What does he mean, in the DIRT. Does it mean they're dead? I keep thinking about how much Sarah didn't like that owl. Does it mean he killed them, and now me and Summer are supposed to die, too?*
>
> *It's my fault it's my fault IT'S MY FAULT.*

Bird was feeling all this all alone, and I was asleep, Summer thought. She had no more tears for all the ways she had failed. She turned away from the blackened book and picked up the small red bird. It touched her face with its prickly wing.

The tiny bird needed to eat a great deal, tiny bits at a time, all day. Sometimes Summer took a little juice in her own cheek and carefully squirted it down the bird's tiny throat. More often she just fed it bits of the fruit.

The bird ate and ate and ate, all day. Summer was glad for the boredom and tedium of it. She was glad to serve this tiny bird that had not died, that was alive. She was keeping it alive. "Come here, bird," she said at first. But that made her think of Bird. So she began to call it Ben's bird, or Bensbird. "Come here, Bensbird." After a few days, she sometimes just called it Bens. By that time a few fine hairs had grown into a thicker red down and his prickly red pinfeathers stood straight up. But on one side of the bird's face, the feathers were a dark, charred brown, as if they had been burnt.

Bens thrived on the fruit, as if he and the fruit were made for each other. The day his eyes opened to green slits, Summer opened the diary again. Not many entries left.

> *March 25:*
>
> *The owl didn't mean dead. He meant Down. That's where we are. That's where I am. So Mom and Dad are here, too.*
>
> *As soon as I'm a bird, I'll find them. As soon as I can talk to the birds, they'll tell me where to go. But first I have to go to the one last place the song wants me to go.*
>
> *I'm all alone now. I think it's good.*

At first Summer left the bird on the bottom of the nest, tucked in a smaller nest of fresh leaves and twigs, when she climbed the side of the nest to watch the sky or sun. But left alone, he gave a tiny, piercing wail, like a sad whistle far away. So Summer put him in her jacket pocket, and they climbed together.

Sometimes at night she lay on her back, the bird standing unsteadily on her chest. She told him stories of her life before the nest. The stories never had Bird in them. Sometimes she sang lullabies, including her mother's old favorite. She sang:

> *Two little birdlets*
> *Sleeping in the snow,*
> *One starts a fire*
> *And one turns to go.*

One night, as she lay on her back, trying to see constellations in a traffic jam of stars, she felt a sharp pain in her chest, just over her heart. "Ow, what," she said out loud. The pain grew worse and sharper, like a bite: like a burn. Her chest was burning. She leaped up, pulled off her jacket (but setting it carefully down, to protect the bird inside it), and pulled off her shirt, which bore a small, smoking hole. On the skin above her heart, a hot red rose bloomed, a bad burn. It was a screaming hurt. The air was cold, but not cold enough to stop the pain. She reached out for the fruit, recklessly ready to waste the dwindling juice to ease the pain. She was crying with it; she could not imagine how this had happened.

She did not see the last curl of smoke rising up from her jacket pocket, or the bird squirming out to stand apart, eyes glittering green and red in the moonlight. But she felt the scrabbling claws on her hand, on her wrist, as the bird climbed up. She lifted the bird in her hand. It leaned toward her chest, almost falling off, so she brought it closer, then closer again. "Don't touch, it hurts," she said. But the bird was bending its head gently, touching the blooming red burn with its own soft feathers. Red against red.

And where the bird touched her, the burn stopped hurting, and began to fade.

So the bird burnt the girl, and healed the girl. Then, wrapped together in her jacket, neither of them understanding what had happened, but neither of them afraid, they fell asleep.

And while they slept, something long and thick and dark drew slowly closer to them.

The next morning, Summer picked up Bird's journal again.

> *I am learning from the birds. There was a lot I thought I knew, but I was wrong.*
>
> *The owl brought me a snakeskin. And I made up that that meant, you will change into something new.*
>
> *Then the owl brought me a raven's feather, so I made up that that meant: be tricky, be clever, be sneaky.*
>
> *And when the owl brought me a bird's egg, I made up that that meant, I was still inside a shell, that something special was waiting for me, a world was waiting for me, when I broke out of our house that was my shell.*

"That you needed to destroy our house?" said Summer out loud. She felt suddenly angry. "That you needed to shatter it so it can never be put back together again, like a shell?"

But I didn't understand right exactly. I thought I totally understood. But I only understood a little part. I didn't understand that they all meant more than one thing.

More than one thing. Summer thought of Ben, and flushed. She flipped ahead, but the entry broke off there, and only blank pages followed.

In the morning, Summer woke just as the sky was beginning to gray. The air was calmer than usual, and less cold. Summer pocketed the bird and climbed to the edge of the nest to wait for sunrise. Spring had come, at least here in the clouds. The leaves of the great tree had grown fast since the tiny golden furls of Summer's first day. Now they were long, slim ovals, serrated, many-veined, tapering to a sudden sharp point. Each leaf was paired with a sister leaf—two, four, six up a swingy stalk, with a seventh crowning the top, like a queen. When it was windy, the leaves blew back together like a head of hair, and the air rushing around them made the broad shape of a song.

But now the air was still, and the nest was still, and the leaves hung around her shoulders, green scarves and curtains for a Summer and a bird. The sun was below them now.

Ben's bird felt it before Summer saw it, even buried in Summer's jacket as he was. The sun was just creeping up, red as a ball, casting green-and-gold rays, when Summer felt the bird, shifting, ruffling, unsettled in her pocket. A red head thrust out of the jacket, cocked up at her.

"What, red?" she asked. "What, sunrise?" She liked to give Bens different nicknames. She smiled at his straining, twisting head, trying to see around her. She shifted her weight to make it easier for him to look across the nest. "What, cranberry?" she asked as she swung her legs around. "What, tiny little fireplug? What, mama's lipstick? What, bright red—" And then she stopped talking. Her mouth stayed open.

A sleek, dark knob had appeared along the edge of the nest directly across from them. Like the sun, it was rising. It rose higher. It was a snake. It was a snake, even though at first Summer's mind and eyes could not agree on that, because it was too big, much too big. It could not possibly be what it seemed to be—but it was. It was a snake, thicker than the thickest snake in any zoo, and longer than you could ever guess. The head alone was the size of Summer's torso. This was the World Snake that lies curled in the bowels of the earth, gnawing the roots of the great tree, sleeping and pulsing until it wakes with a purpose in mind. This time, its purpose was in the nest.

The snake turned its head to the left, and Summer saw its pale green eye, its dark green pupil, all of it split down the middle with a vertical line. That's a sight for a sunrise.

The snake swayed a bit, like a cobra in a cartoon. Summer could not move. She was thinking very fast. Summer knew that snakes do not see very well, but their ears and noses are sharp. The snake was weaving its head back and forth to find their scent.

Bens' tiny feet were scrabbling against the inside of her jacket. "Quiet," she breathed, almost no sound at all. She slipped her hand inside her jacket, caught the red birdlet in one hand, pulled him out. She reached out as far as she could, one leg wrapped tight around her branch, stretching her arm to find a branch nearly all the way around the tree. She tucked Ben's bird there, out of the way, out of sight, perhaps out of scenting range as well. "Hold tight, hold tight," she breathed. Ben's bird gripped the branch sturdily, for such a small thing. The air was so still. He would be all right, wouldn't he?

But then she saw that the snake had stopped weaving. Its head was pointing directly at her, as still as a gun.

As the snake melted over the edge of the nest and down, moving across the bottom of the nest toward the two of them, pulsing, relentless, Summer did a strange and surprising thing. It was surprising to her, at least. Maybe she felt reckless and sad; or maybe she felt she had nothing left to lose but Ben's bird. Or maybe she had had enough of lovely things dying. Or maybe she did it in strength and love. In any case, she jumped down into the nest to meet the snake.

She fell as she landed, twisting her ankle. The thump shook the nest. That caught the snake's attention: the hot juices of a terrified mammal. The snake began to move toward Summer. And Summer began to move toward it.

When Summer realized what she was doing, she almost paused; but she didn't pause. She limped toward the snake. It wormed toward her. It opened its mouth wide, and wider, and then wider than was possible.

All snake have teeth, mostly just small ones. Only the poison ones have fangs. This snake's teeth were bigger than most, but they had been worn to softness by gnawing at the roots of the enormous tree. The snake does not eat the tree roots; it just gnaws away at them, year after decade after century. They are at war, the snake and the tree, a silent, many-thousand-year war. Someday the snake will win. That's just the way it is.

Summer looked at the snake's teeth, worn flat by the hard tree roots, but teeth all the same. Her eyes filled with tears. She missed her sister so much. She wished her mother and father were there. It was suddenly as if she were yanked up into space and watching herself in the gray light: a small girl in a high nest, facing a great snake, facing a dragon.

She came back from space, and was in the nest. She walked close to the snake's wide jaws. She was doing it. She was feeding herself to the snake.

She knelt down. She would just fit. At the last moment, almost tender in her fear, she put her hand to the side of the snake's head, sliding her fingers beneath one of its huge, black scales. It came off easily. So no matter what else, she had taken a piece of the dragon in her hand. She had lost an egg, but she had faced a dragon.

She put the scale in her pocket.

The snake's jaws closed around her.

CHAPTER SEVENTEEN

A CAGE
WENT IN SEARCH
OF A BIRD

ird stood near one end of the long veranda that was the eye of the swan castle, a few feet from the stone railing, watching the lake turn slowly far below. At the black edge of the trees, the sky was a warm peach; above that it was pale, peppermint-ice-cream pink; then white-green, like the root of a leek. (Bird was hungry.) At the edge of the green, the sky turned ice-blue, and then, at the spacious center, dark blue, almost ready for stars.

The lake was the opposite: darkest where it met the black ground, but in the center silvery blue, except where a long column of cloud cast a shadow across it.

It was pretty; it was dreamy. Bird felt dreamy, too: hungry and dreamy. She stood near the railing, but not too near. Too close to the edge, and waves of dizziness and fear would swamp her little evening boat. A foot or two back, she was safe, could look out over her lake and feel what it always made her feel: that she had come home.

Her legs ached. She had been learning dances for many weeks now, hours a day, and her legs always ached. Dance was not her natural element, and her short legs and arms struggled to imitate the long angles and curves that sprouted like jets of water from the woman in the mask.

But she didn't mind. She was living in the air with the Puppeteer, as she thought of her, another bird-obsessed soul, learning another bird language. She had her own room, a little round cave with whitewashed walls and a bed with piles of sky-and-lake-blue quilts. Every morning when she woke, soft fresh clothes in robin's colors were laid out on a chair at the end of her bed. She never had to do a chore. After break-fast—which was all she liked of toast and fruit and cheese and other good things, but of course never eggs—she spent the whole morning dancing with the Puppeteer in the long mirror room. In the first weeks, her stubby body in the mirror made a joke of the Puppeteer's elegant movements, some of which were strange and disturbing, some beauti-ful, but all intoxicating, when the Puppeteer did them. But now, after weeks, Bird was finally finding her own way into the dances.

The afternoon was for dancing, too, but at dusk the Puppeteer dis-appeared into her own rooms to talk with the parrot, or sometimes with another bird, a night bird. Bird darkened when that Great Gray Owl, her great betrayer, flew silhouetted against the evening sky and into the Puppeteer's private rooms. Why was he here? Once she dared to ask, but in answer, the impassive mask turned its face and stared at her until Bird excused herself and left the room.

At first, in the evenings, the Puppeteer tried to persuade Bird to teach her the bird language. "I wish to become part of the great song," she said that first night. She stood just outside Bird's bedroom, only half in view. So began the first of the fruitless discussions that Bird and the Puppeteer had over the first few evenings Bird lived there.

"It doesn't work that way," said Bird this first time, and many times after.

"Because you refuse to teach me," said the Puppeteer in a cool and dangerous voice. The long beak of her bird mask turned away.

"I don't refuse," said Bird, many times. "It's just that you can't learn birdsong that way. You can't pay for it or grab it or take lessons. It doesn't work that way. You have to listen."

"I don't have time to listen," said the Puppeteer, half hidden around the corner. "I have waited all this time."

Bird said, "But you have waited inside thick walls. You have waited in a castle in the air, and locked the birds to the ground, and made them speak English. You must wait outside, where the birds live."

"I want to know the language before I wait outside," said the Puppeteer, for the first of many times. "Once I know the language, I will hear the great song. Then I will be part of the Great Conversation." Her voice sounded longing, to Bird, this first day. *Perhaps because I can't see her,* she thought.

"You will be part of the Great Conversation," said Bird, "if you will come out from behind your walls and hear it. Catch bits of it. Sing bits of it back in."

"There must be an easier way," said the Puppeteer. Her mask remained blank and unreadable, but her voice was higher and colder. "Teach me, I command you."

"I can't teach you," said Bird miserably, this time, and every time they had this conversation. "How can I teach what you haven't heard yet? It would sound like stupid squawking and whistles to you. Not like a song, till you hear the song."

"That *is* what it sounds like," admitted the Puppeteer. "That is what it sounds like to me. It makes me angry. I feel angry."

"Then anger's your song today," said Bird. "You can't even hear your own song. Just listen."

But in time the Puppeteer stopped asking Bird for lessons, and her heart turned toward other ways to use her.

After a while, to her relief, Bird was left alone in the evenings: to eat all she liked for dinner, to watch the changing lake and sky, to think. In the old days Bird might have written in her notebook; but she had left that behind. And anyway, she did not quite trust the Puppeteer not to read what she wrote. So she kept her thoughts secret—or so she believed.

It was a good life for a Bird. True, she sometimes felt nagging grief about the strange, sad birds below. But the Puppeteer's paper-bird game was teaching her to chill that sorrow into contempt: they must be stupid birds; they must deserve it.

Still, she never sailed those paper birds unless the Puppeteer was there to urge her. And whenever she looked down on the walking, talking birds below, fury and heartbreak and fear tangled around her heart, and made it hard to breathe. Once, a rhyme their mother used to say came into her mind—"A robin redbreast in a cage/Puts all heaven in a rage"—and her throat felt tight and painful, as if she might cry.

175

So for the most part Bird avoided the puppet birds, and tried not to think of them, which she was good at. And in all these weeks, she had never once gone back down those stairs.

The birds below weren't the birds she loved, anyway. Bird missed Summer more than she would admit, but she missed the company of birds—real birds, wild birds—even more. In this place, she had even begun to sleep past dawn for the first time in her life, because the castle's silent dawn, without the birds' dawn chorus, struck her with new pain every morning. Her recorder lay in a drawer of the small table by her bed, unused.

And what about her parents? Did she miss them as well? She missed them, especially her mother, with a pain so wild she had to tie it up in ropes, and hide it in a box, and put it behind a locked door: Bird's own inside closet.

So why did Bird live at the top of a swan castle, despite the silent sunrise, the dreadful, broken birds, the dark owl, her fear of heights? Why did she stay with a woman in a mask who was not quite human and was certainly not bird, instead of finding her own mother and father?

Bird would have given various reasons, most importantly learning another bird language, the language of dance; and she believed her reasons were true. But the truth was, she stayed because the Puppeteer wanted her to stay. The Puppeteer was a magician and a brilliant dancer, but her greatest genius was to know what you wanted most, and how to use that knowledge to control you. She knew where the tissue-paper bird longed to go, and because of that, with one tweak, she could make it fly wherever she liked. She knew the secret longings of the parrot's heart, and in that way she made it her slave.

The Puppeteer made Bird a puppet as well, not with strings, but with words that caught the strings of her heart. "That tugged my heartstrings": people are right when they say that. Every heart has strings, and it's wise to be careful about allowing a puppeteer to pull them. Bird was a heart girl, easily led by her heart and its hungers. (Summer was a head girl, but that didn't let her off. The head is just as easily tugged around—ask any horse.)

Because the Puppeteer knew one thing—that Bird wanted to be queen of the birds—she could lead Bird around by her small nose. In fact, it was easier with Bird than with the parrot or even the tissue-paper puppets, because of course, to be queen was what the Puppeteer wanted herself. So she understood Bird particularly well. And she knew how to weave knots that were very heard to break. She was weaving one now:

"The queen is a both a bird and a woman, did you know that?" she said to Bird. "It's true. She has a special robe that allows her to become a swan whenever she puts it on, and a human whenever she takes it off. But she chose not to use that robe for over thirteen years, can you imagine? To have such a gift, and never use it?"

(This was true and not true, for it was the Puppeteer herself who had locked that robe away from the swan. But true-and-not-true makes the best strings.)

But to know that such a robe existed stirred Bird's appetites, and stirred her anger at this queen, just as the Puppeteer knew it would. So that was one string attached, with more to come—because the Puppeteer had a secret, which was the true reason she kept Bird in the castle. She planned to use Bird to get the swan robe for herself, so that she could become the true queen of the birds, with language and wings, forever.

That had been her plan for years now. It had taken her a long time to understand there was no way back to the upper world for her; and by the time she understood, she didn't care. By then, she had found the swan's castle, and was planning her campaign to become the queen of the birds and have that swan robe back in her hands, and never let it slip away again.

Back then, when the Puppeteer first saw the castle, it was thick with birds. Birds perched along the stiff stone feathers, nested in the curves of the wings, flitted around the swan's huge head, peering in, or sailed down the castle throat. But none of them ever nested into the queen's apartments at the top. They left those empty, waiting for her return.

The Puppeteer could see it was a queen's home, and she meant to be queen and make it her own. But a bird's idea of a castle is not the same as a human's. The Puppeteer worked a piece of magic, and not an easy piece, to open a door in the swan's side, one she could make appear or vanish at her convenience. Once inside, she found a huge hall studded with birds' nests of all sizes, chaotic with birdcalls and swooping swallows and wrens—no rooms, no tables or chairs, and straw and fluff and bird droppings everywhere. How could any queen have lived here? She needed to know more.

The Puppeteer had moved into a discreet corner where a young sparrow perched in an indentation in the stone. He was preening, his head buried in his wing. Glancing around to make sure she was not observed, she seized the little sparrow, swallowed it whole, and felt the familiar change: the new colors, the sharp smells, the language that burned so bright and clear, a living torch inside her. The torch would sputter and return her to darkness soon, when the bird died. But for now, her second heart, her bird-heart, beat on.

She learned two things. First, the queen's quarters were far above, and the only way to get there was to fly. And—able now to understand the bird chatter and calls around her—she also learned that she had been observed after all. Another young sparrow had seen her in the corner, swallowing his brother alive. He had raised the alarm: Bird-eater! Bird-eater! But there was confusion. She did not look like any predators the birds knew. And this was the queen's castle. He was a young bird—could he be mistaken? Some birds fled, but many stayed, and the conversation sang loud around her.

Quickly, while the language still lived inside her, she called out to the birds, asking them to gather to listen to her. Astonished to hear her speak their language, they came. Here is what she said:

BIRDS. You have lost your queen. I have come as regent, to rule in her place until we can find her and find our way back to the Green Home.

Absolute silence. The Puppeteer was daring; she had no idea what the Green Home was, only that the birds grieved it and longed for it and dreamed it.

In the meantime, I will bring you food and water, she continued. There was plenty of food and water in the forest, in the lake, but a bird is always intrigued to hear of more. *But I bring more than that,* the Puppeteer said. *I also offer the finest of you—the strongest, the bravest, and the most beautiful—a place in my bird army. That loyal army will be dedicated to nothing but finding your swan queen and bringing her home.*

(This was, in fact, what she intended the army to do—but not for reasons the birds understood.)

At first the birds were uncertain. But the Puppeteer's magic was strong in Down, much stronger than it had been above. She used it to clear the wildness from the castle grounds, to establish formal gardens and fill them with everything birds could want: baths and fountains and winter-blooming flowers, and enough different kinds of food to please any kind of bird in the world.

A few birds sensed danger, left the castle, and did not return. But most were drawn by their bellies (as birds can always be drawn) to the food she left, and saw no harm in eating it. And some, the most susceptible to her powers, were inspired to join her army. Above all her other magic, she was a brilliant puppeteer, who knew how to turn longing into puppet-strings.

The most susceptible of all were those who had lived with humans before, or whose parents and grandparents had—parrots and mynahs and the descendants of parrots and mynahs who had escaped their cages (on purpose or accidentally) long ago, who sometimes spoke with regret or affection of the comfortable lives they had led in those cages. And because the Puppeteer laid special emphasis on the promise of power to birds who would speak to her in English—the castle language, as she put it, not the forest language—she also attracted some of the other great mimics to her army, including starlings and even a few ravens.

At first nothing was said about not flying inside the castle. That came later. Not just as a courtesy to the wingless regent—or queen-regent, as she preferred, or (why not?) simply "queen"—but because walking was better. Better because the new queen did it.

She used her magic and her bird army to build stairs up to the queen's quarters—"so that I can keep the rooms ready for her return." One day, she emerged at the top of the stairs wearing the long-beaked mask, black and red with streaks of white. "I am one of you," she announced. The birds were afraid to disagree. After that, she was never seen without the mask.

In the bird army (the birds who had retreated to the forest called it, in disgust, the Puppet Army), the greatest honor was to be chosen to draw the Puppeteer's chariot in the sky. Those birds were at least allowed to fly: allowed to fly in chains, dragging her weight behind them.

Some recruits were failures who could not be made into puppets, who were driven mad by the attempt. She put these birds in cages and hid them away, and told the others that they had become afraid, and deserted.

After a while, most of the birds who had not joined her army abandoned the castle and lake. Some could not bear to see the Puppet Army walking on the ground, talking in English. And although few believed the rumors about the new queen swallowing birds alive, too many birds were vanishing. As the birds outside became fewer, the queen-regent spoke directly to her people less and less. Eventually, she withdrew into the upper apartments and was rarely seen, making announcements only through the generals of her English-speaking army. In time, the grounds of the castle were entirely birdless.

And because of that, one midnight when the swan queen finally did return, there were no forest birds to see her.

On that night, only a week before Bird arrived at the castle, the Puppeteer stood alone in the eye of the swan, watching a full moon ripple across the lake. Most of the bird army was asleep. A shadow passed across the water, the shadow of a huge bird with wings that touched the sides of the lake-moon. The Puppeteer looked up. At first she could see nothing—white bird hidden against white moon. And then the bird broke against the blackness, a huge swan, wings beating hard, throat stretched and tense, aiming directly for the castle.

The Puppeteer was full of dead birds. At the sight of the swan, these began to stir inside her. Each of those swallowed birds had left something behind: a feather, a piece of claw, a bit of beak. Each of those pieces now stirred up at the sight of their true queen.

The Puppeteer fell to her knees. At this most crucial moment, when the prize was almost in her hands, something inside her was rising up, was fighting back. Mutiny. On her knees, the Puppeteer gagged and coughed. Her body twisted. She fell forward, hands on the ground, body heaving, as the thing inside her fought to get out. Finally, she vomited, once.

Out of the Puppeteer's mouth came a tiny bird, all patches of color, made of all the birds she had ever eaten. It was dusty blue and rusty orange and grass-green and raincloud, and its beak was like a sharp bit of sky.

The tiny patchwork bird flew straight toward the swan queen to warn her.

But the patchwork bird was too small, and the swan was too desperate and exhausted, too focused on her goal, seeing nothing but the castle ahead. Never seeing the anxious, fluttering patchwork warning beside her, the swan flew straight into the castle's eye, where the Puppeteer was waiting.

The patchwork bird hovered outside for a few moments, then flew off into the forest. Besides her, only two guard birds had seen the swan arrive. The Puppeteer killed those two later that night.

Many weeks later, Bird stood in the same place in the swan's eye, looking at the same lake. The peach on the horizon was now deep gold, and the deep blue was creeping down lower in the sky. But there was still enough light to see the lake, and Bird was trying to decide whether to wait to watch the whole sunset, or go in and find something to eat.

Then she heard something she hadn't heard in a long time. It had been so long, she almost couldn't believe it. Her whole body whipped around, and she ran to the other end of the stone veranda to see. She had heard—she would swear she had heard—the call of a bird.

But even though she stood as near the stone railing as she dared to look out over the darkening garden and the forest beyond, she saw no birds. Feeders bursting with food, baths full of water, stood undisturbed. A stone of sullen disappointment formed in her heart. She turned around, ready to abandon the sunset.

And then she stopped.

Just where she had been standing earlier, a boy was sitting on the railing. He straddled the narrow stone like a cowboy, one leg dangling in the air. The boy's skin was radiant brown, and his hair was a nest of sloppy dark curls. The corner of his mouth that she could see was turned up, as if he had been laughing, or was just about to.

At her?

Without moving his body, the boy cocked his head and looked at her through one eye. "You're Bird, right?" he said.

Bird stood where she was. "How did you get here?" she asked.

"I flew," said the boy. He swung his legs around so that he was facing her, apparently unconcerned to be balanced on a railing a hundred feet above the ground. "I came to tell you something," he said. He had a dark birthmark like a char across one cheek. "I came to tell you," he said, "that you need to go down."

"I already knew that," said Bird. "The patchwork bird's song said to go down."

"I know," said the boy, with an annoying smile. "She was right. Go down, Bird. It's important."

She hated his big smile. She hated his ease in the air. She hated his terrible advice. But for some reason, she liked him anyway, inside and around the hates.

"It's important to go back down the stairs? To the ground floor, with those pathetic awful birds who don't fly or sing?" She doubted this. Those birds were stupid creatures, and she couldn't bear to look at them again. She couldn't bear it. Her heart beat fast with rising anger and fear. Maybe she would never go back down.

"To the ground floor," said the boy, "but not just to the ground floor. Further than that. If you go down further than that, underneath the place you think you are, you'll find what you secretly want, in your deepest heart."

Bird felt a familiar electricity in her blood. To be queen was her secret desire. Was her crown waiting under the castle? Under the revolting, sad, wrong birds?

"What's your name?" she asked the laughing boy. Sharp as a queen already.

"Oh, my name," said the boy, as if that were a long story he did not have time for. And he fell backward off the railing.

With a high cry she didn't hear herself make, Bird ran to the edge, her stomach already in knots: she knew what she would see on the ground.

But there was nothing at all on the ground, only dry grass and dark flower beds, as usual. In the air, though—in the air, there was something unusual: a small red bird, in this long-birdless place, disappearing into the trees along the lake.

But Bird was feeling dizzy and sick, and had already turned away.

CHAPTER EIGHTEEN

THE GREEN HOME

S ummer was inside the snake.

The light abandons you, when you are swallowed by a snake. Choking darkness takes its place. You're wrapped tighter than a baby in a blanket, wrapped tight in strong wet muscle, when you are swallowed by a snake.

The violence of being swallowed by a snake is like a rough, powerful wave, tumbling you over and over. At the same time your body is gripped and squeezed, and it feels like there is nothing to breathe, and you can't breathe, anyway, you are squeezed so tight. It's the violence of digestion, which tries to turn you from yourself into fragments that once were you, fragments that the digestion can use. It's not a personal violence. The green, vertically slit eye of the snake is friendly and human compared to this relentless machine made of flesh called digestion.

Did Summer's bones crack? They should have, but they did not.

Perhaps once you have been pulled through a keyhole, your bones remember how to soften. But also, Summer was now traveling deep inside the earth, though she did not know it (because the snake was longer than she ever could have thought). Even the rocks there are not like our surface rocks. Inside our world, the rocks are red and pulse like hearts. They know how to soften and bend. So perhaps in this place, Summer's bones also knew how to soften and bend.

With what was left of her mind—the few times she could seize a thought from the crushing, wrenching flesh machine in which she was caught—Summer thought of Ben's bird. Was the bird all right? Would the snake leave the bird alone, now, and go home?

(The snake was going home, back into the center of the earth, though Summer did not know it.)

As her body was battered, beaten, twisted, Summer's thoughts kept coming in fragments. What would it eat? Would it learn to fly?

But mostly she did not think. The sound of being swallowed by a snake is a blank roar that might be your own blood screaming in your ears, or it might be the snake's. It makes it hard to think.

The sight of being swallowed by a snake is patches of red mixed with patches of dark, swelling and shrinking, expanding and reshaping.

The smell of being swallowed by a snake is wet and sick, decaying; sharp and painful, ammonia.

The taste is your own blood in your mouth as you bite your tongue, as you are tumbled and pushed and squeezed.

The feeling is muscle wrapped around you, holding you tight: PUSH, PUSH, release, PUSH, release, PUSH, PUSH, PUSH, release. Peristalsis. The feeling is also the acid that eats at your clothes and eats at your skin, changing you.

Summer was inside the snake for three days and three nights. Sometimes she passed out for a while, although you couldn't call it sleep. But mostly on the long, long journey through the snake, she stayed awake, awake and alive. Lucky Summer. If you call that lucky.

At the end of three days and three nights, she popped out. There was one last PUSH, PUSH, PUSH, PUSH—and she was free. She had gone all the way through the great snake, which meant all the way through the deepest bowels of the earth. And she came out—somewhere else.

∽

When she woke, she was lying on grass.

She was still. There was air. It was quiet.

Her clothes were torn and damp. Her hair was matted. Her feet were bare. Her body ached, every cell.

She moved an arm. The arm was hers again.

The light hurt her eyes, but that was no problem; she kept them closed. She lay on soft grass across a soft pillow of earth. The air was soft, too, warm but not hot, breathing lightly along her length. The air seemed sorry for what she had been through. The soft place was quiet, quiet, quiet.

Eyes closed, she allowed her inner world to reassemble. *I am Summer. There was a snake. There was a bird in a nest. Bird means sister. My sister is dead, because I left her alone. My parents left us alone. My parents are gone.*

These were tugboat thoughts, towing cargo ships of grief. They passed through her. She did not cling to them, or turn away. She watched them pass. Tears leaked from under her eyelids and dried on her cheeks. She was an ocean bearing heavy ships; but she was an enormous ocean.

She opened her eyes, a little. Squinted, a little. Dark green grass and deep blue sky, like a friendly drawing of grass and sky, two long blocks of color, unbroken, except for one dirt path, which began a few feet from where she lay and unrolled to the horizon. One path, dividing one long block of green, meeting one long block of blue.

Summer rose to her feet. She felt sore all over, but she also felt free, felt air on her skin. She put a hand in her pocket and felt the scale of the snake, as big as her whole hand, clean and sharp as a sea-washed shell. She put a hand in her other pocket and found the last match. In her jacket pocket, though the jacket itself was badly torn, she found the crane map, clean and whole: the map that would someday take her home. She was ready.

With pain in each step, but also freedom—with grief in her heart, but also peace in her heart, her wide ocean-heart—she set one bare foot in front of another along the path. The path was soft, cream-colored dirt on soft soil. It was easy to walk.

It was quiet. The field and path were as kind as the air: no insects, no stickers, nothing to hurt or bother. Just green grass unstirring beside her. Just silence. Just one long, unwavering path into the blue. Summer walked.

After a while, Summer thought: *This place holds another feeling besides kindness, besides softness, besides green and blue.* She stopped and closed her eyes. She tried to name the feeling. She thought of the word *bereft*. She thought of a house just emptied of furniture, the moving van gone, the last echo of the car in the driveway fading away.

She thought of the word *lonely*.

Summer walked on, bare feet in soft dirt. The sky never changed; it stayed the same blue. The grass stayed the same green. The world was as steady and blank as a kindergarten drawing.

After some time she saw that in the distance her path crossed another path. In the center of that crossroads stood a tiny black figure. As she got closer still, she saw that the figure was a raven. She had a curious sense of being in two places, and two times, at once: here and now; but also on the path from Ben's camp, which felt so long ago.

When she reached the crossroads, Summer stopped. The raven looked at her with calm, intelligent eyes: one black and one blue.

"Hello, Summer," said the raven.

That was the first surprising thing: that the raven spoke English. The next surprising thing, Summer realized, was that the raven was not actually speaking at all: it was cawing, the way ravens do, in this case a soft, gurgling caw, a friendly caw. The raven was cawing, but Summer understood the caw—it made perfect sense to her. It was almost as if she heard two voices, speaking in one. The impossibility of this hung in Summer's mind, waiting for a resolution.

The third surprise was that when the raven spoke, a violet popped up in the green beside her. It was a surprise, and not a surprise—the violet seemed like just the same thing as the word. It was just a different way of hearing the word.

"It's you," Summer said to the raven. She didn't notice, but behind her a pale blue morning glory sprang up and began to wind across the road toward the violet. "I know you."

"I like your song," replied the raven. Four tall red poppies rose up behind her, swaying. "I like the music of it." Her caw was husky and warm; it pleased Summer's ears. "And yes," she added, "you know me well."

"I met you in the road before," said Summer. "And you helped me in the tree, getting the fruit. And"—she hesitated, because the thought of Bird swamped all other thought—"and my sister, when she was a baby, did you—"

"I have watched you both since you were born," said the raven. An aspen rose out of the ground behind her, hundreds of leaves unfurling from the tips of its fingers as it grew.

"You're my animal friend," said Summer tentatively. "Or my animal teacher, or something like that—is that right?"

"I like the word 'friend,'" said the raven. "Walk with me. I want to show you something. And while we walk, let's talk. Let's make a world."

Summer thought: *Who said that to me before?* But the question dissolved as she and the raven walked side by side, straight along the path. If you could have hovered above them as they walked and talked, you would have seen a world grow up around them: scatterings of flowers, with dipping butterflies; a line of white-barked trees, burning with red and yellow leaves; snowy hills that shadowed one another; a stretch of tumbling creek; a gray boulder; pale, waving grasses. A world.

"Where am I?" asked Summer.

"In the Green Home," said the raven. "It belongs to the birds."

"While the birds fly past/To the Green Green Home, the Green Green Home, the Green Green Home," Summer sang. A ripple of wildflowers ran alongside her. The raven said nothing. Summer laughed.

"Things happen when we talk," she said. "The world changes. What's happening?"

The raven was silent as they walked along the path. Then she said: "Sometimes, in the world—in the outer world, I mean, outside the Green Home—we speak from our hearts. Do you know what I mean?"

"I think so," said Summer. A few strands of her hair became a daisy chain, twining around her head.

"I want to be sure you do," said the raven. "Sometimes there is a seed in your heart. It might feel like a stone, or like a bud ready to blossom. It might feel like a heavy little egg, and you have no idea what's inside. It might feel like a hard, burning ember. No seed is the same. But if you let that seed, that feeling-sound, take root, then it will grow. Sometimes it grows quickly, or sometimes very slowly, especially if you don't tend it. It could take months or even years to grow up through your throat and out your mouth. But when you do finally speak it, the birds call that a heart-song. Do you understand?"

The rough raven voice sounded lovely to Summer. Along the raven's side of the path, a row of young maple trees rose up. Red and yellow autumn leaves drifted down to the path as they walked. The bird herself was glossier, taller.

"Yes," said Summer. A patch of fog appeared and dissolved around her.

"Heart-song is the language of the Green Home," said the raven. "No other language is spoken here. But also, heart-song creates the Green Home, because here your songs take shape in the world. It was first made by a chickadee—"

"I know that chickadee story!"

"Ah," said the raven. "This is the land the chickadee found. When she first came, the chickadee sang a tree to sing in."

A bush sprang up, heavy with peachy-red fruit the size of Ping-Pong balls.

"In some ways it is true to say that heart-song creates the world where you come from, too," said the raven. "But it's easier to see it happening, here."

"I think I see," said Summer. And saying it, she knew that her words had always made flowers and fog and mud and trees, only she had never understood that before. And she knew that flowers and fog and mud and trees had always made her. And to be able to know it, and see it, in this place—that made it the home her heart had always sought and turned toward, as a plant turns to sun. She felt great peace.

They walked in silence for a while, until a question rose up.

"If this place belongs to the birds," Summer asked, "then where are they?"

"They only come here half the year," said the raven. "But they have not been here in a long time—more than thirteen years, which for some birds means whole generations."

A stretch of red desert opened up across the green.

"Every year," the raven said, "as long as we can remember, when the days and nights drew equal at the end of summer, the birds would gather on a huge silver lake beside the queen's castle, and she would lead them on the long and terrible journey."

"To the Green Green Home, the Green Green Home, the Green Green Home," Summer sang softly to herself. There was a brief shower of rain.

"But thirteen years ago, the queen of the birds never came. And she has never come since. For a long time the birds waited at the castle. But she never came back." The wind turned cold, and the sky was dark.

"Where was she?" asked Summer.

The raven told that story with mountains and dragonflies and windstorms and cold. It was the same story Summer told Bird, much later, of how their father, hiding in the brush on a riverbank, saw their mother change from a swan into a woman with one black swan foot.

But of course, the story didn't end there, and so the raven continued:

"As your mother swam, your father gathered up the robe in his arms," she said. "He buried his face in the silky feathers for a moment, because he couldn't stop himself. He ran deeper into the forest, and hid the robe in a hollow log, covering it with leaves. Then he came back to the riverbank, and waited.

"You will think she was angry; you will think she should have been angry. But you need to understand that he possessed the robe now, the robe that contained her swan soul. So he possessed her soul. And so the instant she saw him, she fell in love with him, and wanted to stay with him forever."

"It was cheating to do that," said Summer. "That was a terrible thing to do." A rush of autumn leaves, burnt-red and coffee, whirled around her feet. The cold deepened.

"It was and it wasn't," said the raven. "But your father, actually, agreed with you. He loved her from the moment he saw her. He has never stopped loving her. But in those first weeks, he was wrung with guilt for the way he had won her, and wrung with doubt that he really had her.

"In any case, they married immediately. She almost began to forget her robe and her life as queen. But then one night she woke in terror, crying 'My birds, my birds.' She put her hands to his face and asked, 'Where is my robe?' And he felt ashamed.

"So they drove though and past the dark city streets, back to the country, and the river, where they walked with flashlights and hushed voices to the hollow log.

"But the leaves were scattered, and the robe was gone. And no matter how long they looked over the next days, each torn with a different kind of guilt, the robe was gone. Your mother wouldn't give up, or leave the forest.

"She never did give up. That's why they bought a little house near those woods, and near that river."

"Our house," said Summer.

"Your house," the raven agreed. "When they walked into that little stone house, your mother said 'Oh: my heart is almost whole here.' So they made it their home. She bound her swan foot tightly and kept it hidden from everyone except your father, and began her new life."

"No, I've seen her feet," said Summer. "You're wrong, I've seen her bare feet."

"You have seen one," said the raven. "But have you ever seen them both?" Summer fell silent. Mom with one sock, walking around the house in summer: Oh, I have a little rash, I don't want the rest of you to catch it. Mom's feet in sneakers in the river: I don't like to stub my toes on the rocks.

The raven continued. "Being near the river was useful so that your father could study the river birds, and that's what they told people. But more important to them, your mother could continue to look through the woods for her lost bird-soul."

"She walks in the woods every day," said Summer. Her hair and shoulders were dusted with snow.

"Yes," said the raven. "But what your parents did not know was that someone else was in the woods that sad night, the night they found the robe was gone. Someone else was there, someone who stole the robe and locked it in the same little cottage that later became your home. So your mother slept near her bird-soul every night, without knowing. But even not knowing, it helped her to be happy there."

"But who—" began Summer.

"That comes later," said the raven. "Let me finish my story." The raven was now walking alongside a rocky beach at the edge of a long lake, a mountain reflected in its clear, blank surface.

"So your mother was a kind of Cinderella in reverse," the raven continued: "a queen who gave up her kingdom to scrub floors and cook stews. But as I say, she was happy, except in her dreams. In her dreams, a thousand birds flew into the jaws of a wolf as big as the sky. She ran and ran to stop the birds, but without her wings, she could not fly, and so the jaws slammed down.

"Whenever she had that dream, her next day was haunted and sad, and she spent longer in the woods than usual. Then one night, she dreamed of two young swans with their heads entwined, making an arch. The next day she planted two young willow trees at the edge of the forest, and later she trained the trees together to make a gate."

"That was our gate!" said Summer.

"That's right," said the raven. "And after a year or so, the man and the swan had a daughter, with very human feet."

"Me," said Summer, surprised to find herself entering this long, strange story.

"Yes," said the raven. "And a few years later, they had another."

"Bird," said Summer. A flower patch died at her feet. They were both silent for a long time, and the landscape as they walked remained green and blank.

The raven said, "After you two were born, the nightmares were fewer, and most of the time, your mother was happy. And your father was happy, too, happy and guilty and doubtful, with his own fearful dreams. He dreamed of himself stepping clumsily into a nest full of eggs, breaking them all. Or standing in a marshy field, watching three birds fly away, knowing they took all his happiness with them, but unable to fly himself, so unable to follow."

"Wait," said Summer. Something had been bothering her, and it popped like a bubble on her tongue. "How do you know all this? How do you know what they dreamed? I mean, I don't know what they dreamed. They never talked about it."

The raven stopped walking. A cold rain swept across the lake, stirring the waters, and Summer felt chilled. "I had a friend in your house," she said. A cherry tree bloomed beside her, pink blossoms and sweet scents. "A spy, you might say. My friend knows how to listen to dreams, and told me. Most of what I know about your lives together came from my friend."

"But no one lived at our house except us!" said Summer.

"Who is 'us'?" said the raven, not looking at her.

"My father and mother and me," said Summer, "and Bird." Her heart seized up when she said "Bird," and the ground cracked open beside her. Hot red liquid seeped out, drowning the few small flowers and plants that had emerged beside her.

"No one else?" asked the raven.

"Just the four of us, and Sarah—oh, and Sarah, our cat Sarah!" Summer said. "Is it Sarah? Is Sarah your friend?"

The raven made a pleased bobbing motion with her head. "Sarah is my friend," she said, "and she has lived with you many years, since before you were born. She slept on your parents' pillows, where she could hear their dreams. Sometimes she slept on yours. And I am worried about her," she said. The leaves on the cherry tree withered and spun away in the wind, leaving black branches. "I have not heard from her. Have you seen her?"

"No," said Summer. "I'm sorry. She was gone when my parents were gone."

They walked again in silence, under dark clouds. Then the raven began to speak again.

"Your father watched your mother very carefully. He is an ornithologist, and ornithologists know how to learn from captive birds. So although he loved her, he also studied her. He did both with all his heart. Do you know that ornithologists keep birds in special cages, with ink pads at the center, to track the patterns they make with their feet, pacing, pacing, pacing their cages when migration time comes. Birds have a magnetic soul, and it responds to the song of the earth as it turns. Your father did not use ink, but he watched the swan very carefully. Especially near the equinoxes, when it was time for migration, he watched her very carefully, and watched the direction her feet wished to go. That's how he knew where to follow when she left."

"That is horrible," said Summer. "He was horrible to do that. And he was horrible to steal her robe. And the birds can't come here because of him."

The raven replied, "But he tried to give the robe back—it wasn't he who locked it away. And he didn't know about the Green Home. Your mother knew about it—she was the queen, she was responsible. But she stayed with your family instead."

"Then it is her fault, she was wrong."

"But her robe was gone, what choice did she have? And her one bird foot was bound and broken. Besides, she loved him. And even more than him, she loved her daughters."

There was a long silence. "But if she loved us," Summer asked, "why did she leave us alone?" Her face dissolved into a rainstorm. They were quiet for a long while.

Summer turned to look back on the path they had walked. On the raven's side of the path a whole landscape had begun—the bush, the trees, the patch of desert, the mountain and long mirroring lake; but also a field of peonies, and a wind stirring them, and long grasses, and the beginnings of a yellow hill. On her side was much less: a few lonely morning glories, their long vines longing toward the other side of the road; a patch of snow; a small smoking crater.

The raven gave a laugh like a cough. "Well, I have been doing all the talking," she said. "So tell me something true: speak a heart-word. What is the biggest seed, the hottest egg, living in your heart right now?" She looked up at Summer sideways with her small black eye.

Summer saw that her whole heart was a fat red egg of pain, and that the seed at the center was Bird's blue plaid shirtsleeve in the embers of the fire. "My sister is dead," she said, "because of me." The pain-egg burst, and tears came down her face.

"Oh," said the raven. "Oh, I see. But no, my dear Summer. You are wrong about that."

"You mean it wasn't because of me?" said Summer, through thick tears.

"I mean she isn't dead," said the raven.

Summer could not speak. But her skin, pale from her travels in the snake's belly, turned the colors of a rainbow. Her torso was a bare winter tree, punctured by light.

CHAPTER NINETEEN

THE CHAINED SWAN

Very late that night, after lying in bed a long time thinking, Bird took the advice of the smiling boy and went down. It was no easier going down the hard, shining spiral stairs than it had been coming up—except that it was dark, which was in some ways more dangerous, but also kept her from seeing how far she had to fall. As she walked, she sang, in a shaky half-whisper, a verse of the nursery rhyme song that had popped into her head when the boy said "Down":

> *When the old road ends,*
> *And the sky has teeth,*
> *A cygnet must look*
> *For what lies beneath.*

One shaking step at a time, Bird walked down, her sweating hands pressed out against the air like wings. But she refused to go crawling the way she had come up. She went down on her feet.

Once on the ground, dizzy with solidity and relief, she stopped. When you're on the ground, how do you go further down? Far from the starlight and moonlight of the swan's eye, she was blind. She would have to feel her way in the dark.

The parrots and starlings of the Puppet Army were asleep, she knew, huddled together as near the door as they could. They missed the forest at night. There were guard birds, too, but they were outside, in theory to keep the castle safe from outside threats—but also, she had often suspected, to keep her in. But she wasn't going out. She was going down.

No choice but feeling in the dark (never really any choice but that, even when daylight fools us). No choice but slow and attentive and alive in every sense but sight, above all touch. Feeling along the rough walls, she found crannies, indentations, rough wooden beams with the soft prickle of rotting nests. The silence was a huge animal in the dark beside her.

Throughout that whole night, she felt her way in the dark. A bird with night eyes, watching from above, would have seen a girl, slow and uncertain, hands before her against the wall, head up, listening at an unseeing angle. Sometimes she knelt and crawled along the ground. Always her hands felt along the surface before her.

But she felt no crack or passage. Not even a hint of a way down. It had been so easy to find Down when she knew the patchwork song, but now she had only her own rage and longing to guide her. Hours of blind crawling and fumbling: and then she felt a gleam of gray in the blackness, which meant the dawn was coming—the castle's terrible, silent, birdless dawn. She had lost her chance and would soon be discovered, and would never find her heart's desire underneath the castle. Sitting back on her knees, she pressed her dirty hands against her face. She rubbed one eye with her arm. And then she stretched out on the ground and shook with silent sobs, crying for her heart's desire, no longer even sure what it was.

As she wept, her flung, unsearching hand brushed against what should not be there. A long crack in the floor. A metal latch.

A door in the earth.

Bird knew that the castle spun up into the air, but until now she had not known it spun down deep into the ground as well. The heavy door in the earth opened, with difficulty, onto stone steps that led down into the dark. These steps were not as fearful as the ones going up, since there was nowhere to fall. Walls of damp black earth pressed in around her—she spread her arms and touched both sides as she walked down the edgeless, age-worn steps. Sometimes her hands found things growing in the walls.

After many turns in the spiral stairs, she began to hear noise from below—noise like talking, like an arguing crowd, though she could not quite make out what they were saying. She slipped more than once on the worn, formless steps. As her fear and excitement grew, the clamor from below grew as well. Sometimes it sounded like a crowd, other times like a machine, with metal parts banging, banging, banging.

By the time she reached the ground that sound was so loud she put her hands over her ears. She stood at one end of a long, wide hall, lit by high yellow sconces, a flickering, shadowy light. The hall was full of noise. Bird entered it.

The racket was birds. The hall was lined with caged birds, and all were speaking at once, in a mangled mixture of English and bird, a hideous parody of the dawn chorus.

"I have a question! I have a question!" one large starling shouted again and again. A cardinal, still as a statue, peeped one note over and over: Bird knew it as a call that meant "bird here" or "I am." The cardinal's round eye darted back and forth, but the bird itself never moved, and never stopped peeping.

Although Bird did not know it, she was walking through the Hall of Failed Puppets: birds who had gone mad in the effort to become walkers and talkers, to lose their bird selves. In these birds, the transformation had been incomplete. Now they were neither forest birds nor Puppet Army; they were only broken. They were the Puppeteer's mistakes. She caged them here and kept them alive to eat when she needed a language to know, a secret to learn. She did not want to eat her own army, which was lean enough as it was.

(But in the years of eating mad birds, she had grown a little mad herself.)

The noise was dreadful, and Bird kept her hands over her ears. Frantic birds had tried over and over to spread their wings inside the cramped cages till their wings had become broken and infected. Half-bald birds were pulling out their own feathers one by one. A magpie paced back and forth by a broken piece of mirror, muttering to himself. "That's you," he said, over and over. "That's you. That's you. That's you."

Walking down this row of deranged, desperate birds, fingers covering her ears, Bird felt nausea and grief. It was the worst place she had ever been.

A parrot inches from her face suddenly screamed, "Don't shoot! Don't shoot!" Bird stumbled back against another cage. Her sleeve caught on the rough iron and she fell, dragging the cage down with her. That quieted the hall.

Lying on the ground, shaken, Bird opened her eyes to find herself inches from an ancient, half-bald crow in the overturned cage. He made a soft, murmuring noise she recognized as the crow's "come near to me" call. But he was not calling in bird; he was calling in English, strangely accented English, as if he were trying to fit English words into the half-remembered cadences of a crow's call. She put her hand to the cage, slipped her fingers inside. She saw that one of his wings hung at a wrong, broken angle.

In a strange, bird-inflected English, rocking back and forth in the fallen cage, the old crow began a bird tale. It was familiar, somehow, and Bird almost remembered hearing it before. Were the birds telling it as she fell asleep that last night in the woods, before she came here? Or had she heard it from her mother, in her bed back home?

It was the story of a red bird who had died and come back to life, and died and come back three hundred thousand times since the beginning of the world—or the beginning of birds, anyway. He would die and return three hundred thousand times more, said the story, because he loved the world, and because the world loved him, and could not bear to see him leave forever. Every stone and wind and river of the world loved this red bird, and fire loved him most of all, and was his home. The hall was quiet around them, and the bedlam in Bird's troubled heart calmed, too.

But then a bird at the far end of the hall gave a sudden scream, and instantly the hall was a nightmare of bird-din. "I can't hear you," Bird shouted in English, and scrambled to her feet. She hung the old crow's cage up beside the others and added, impulsively, in bird language, *I will hear the rest another day. I will come back, I will free you, and you can tell me the rest of the story.*

Bird's feet pounded down the long hall, leaving behind the cages and their cacophony. The strange falling boy had said her heart's desire was here, and she would find it.

At the end of the long hall, where Bird's breath gave out, where there were no more cages, she took her fingers from her ears. The hall had seemed to come to a dead end, and there her flying hopes stumbled, almost fell. But actually it opened up on the right, to another hall, long and empty.

As she walked—she could not run anymore—through the dim yellow sconce-light, the cries of the mad birds grew faint, almost like silence. It was a long, lonely walk, much longer than the first hall. Her feet felt the damp earth's cold.

The hall ended, finally, in a sort of dark, rounded alcove, in which a white figure huddled. At first Bird thought it was a human figure, about the size of a grown woman, somehow bent strangely in on itself. Then a draft (from where?) stirred the air, and stirring the air, stirred the white feathers on the white, huddled form. Bird realized with a shock that the figure was not a woman but a swan, its head tucked under its wing.

Bird had seen swans before, floating along her river at home, but never so close, and never so magnificent. Her throat closed up, in fear or awe, and her feet slowed as she neared the white figure. From a few feet away, she watched the great sleeping form. For some reason, for no reason, because her hopes were over, because she was a young, lost girl, because something about the swan made the knot around her heart relent, for the second time that morning she began to cry.

The swan raised its head. Around her throat was an iron collar, attached to a chain that led to an iron post half buried in the dank black earth. Her long beak opened, and Bird, falling back, waited for the husky horn of the trumpeter's warning cry. But all that emerged was a rasp. The iron was too tight around the swan's neck; she had no voice.

The swan drew a ragged breath and dipped her head, caught against the chain, then dipped again. She lifted a wing. She raised her head and looked directly at Bird. Her alien eye shone, familiar as home. And although Bird knew that such a large swan could hurt her, could be mad or diseased, her heart drew her on without hesitation. She knelt down by the swan and slipped against her side. The wing folded over her and pulled her close. Pressed against the warm white silk, Bird cried.

She could not see, but the swan cried also, two long wet tears. Birds do not cry, but this bird had been a woman too long not to cry when she found her lost and youngest child.

As she wept, wrapped in softness, Bird thought of her mother's old nonsense song—some verse that almost—how did it go?

Between sharp breaths and sobs, she said it: "Weeping cygnet/ Pulled from the fire/Under loving wing/With her heart's—"

A hand locked around Bird's wrist and wrenched her out from under the wing, yanked her to her feet. She was back in the cold, dark dungeon, her shoulder throbbing, and the Puppeteer was saying, "You must be more careful—the queen is terribly dangerous. She is only here because I didn't have a cage big enough."

CHAPTER TWENTY

THE ATTAINABLE BORDER OF THE BIRDS

After a while, the rainbow of her face faded, and Summer was herself again, with only a lingering white-gold glow. "Is Bird all right?" was her first question.

"She is physically safe, at least for now," said the raven, "but not safe at all in other ways. She needs our help. And your father needs our help as well. He is in Down. I don't know where your mother is." Slowly, in the sky above her, a massive cloud was forming, mixed sun-gold and gray.

"Can you take me to Bird, or to Dad?" asked Summer, not knowing who she wanted to see more—the one she could help, or the one who could help her.

The cloud moved low across the sky. "I don't know the way out," said the raven.

Summer stopped walking. "But how did you get in?"

"The same way you did," said the raven. "When I saw what you were doing, I fed myself to the snake, just behind you. We took the same terrible road. I woke up before you, that's all—you slept for more than a day after you got here."

"But why"—Summer could hardly form the question, she was so astonished—"but why did you do that?"

The raven gave her one eye, then the other, then shook her head in a near-human way. "Well, I had my reasons," she said finally, "but let's come around to them more slowly. For now, at least, all we need to know is that we can't go back the way we came." She rattled a laugh. A shower of dead leaves whirled around her. "There used to be another way, the way of the birds. But that way has been closed since before you were born."

There was a long stretch of unbroken green silence. Summer's mind ripped like fire along the edges of thoughts. She thought about the crane map, still in her pocket—a map you could use to go wherever you liked, Ben had said, but that you could only use once. She had intended this map, this great gift, to take her home, out of this world of talking birds and World Tree nests and old men who turned to ash. Her fingers ran over the map in her pocket, but she did not mention it to the raven. A rough black stone rose up on the path in front of her, and she stopped, then sat down on it. The raven glanced at her but said nothing.

Summer was seeing something in her mind. "Was it you, before the tree—well, it might have been a dream—" She paused, confused, then began again. "I dreamed, or I remember—but it must have been a dream—a raven, flying ahead of an enormous black bird. I think I was flying, too. The enormous bird was holding me, somehow."

"That was not a dream," said the raven. "I saw you as well. And I saw the egg you held in your pocket."

"How did you know about the egg in my pocket?"

"That egg sang," the raven said. "I heard the small singing rising from your pocket."

A white flower on a tall stalk rose out of the ground. The center of the flower burned reddish gold.

"What did its song say?" asked Summer. She was filled with sadness to think of her egg, and the little red bird who had been her companion in the lonely tree. "And why couldn't I hear the song?"

"You did not know how to listen," said the raven. "It sang about fire. Fire was its word. The egg sang that everything is fire." The flower beside the raven blossomed full, then beyond full; its petals bent backward, the glow died, the stalk bent down.

"I no longer hear the singing," the raven added. "You no longer have the egg. It's a pity. I would have liked to meet that egg."

Summer and the raven sat together on the rock Summer's silence had made. A whirling rainstorm came and went. The sun shone. Summer ran her finger along the rough edge of the snake scale in her pocket. The map in one pocket, the match in another, a piece of the dragon-snake in a third: all she had done, and all she might do.

"My friend," Summer said, "my animal friend, please tell me now why you followed me here, and not just here but all through this place, and even before."

The raven hopped up on the rock beside her, then settled down to sit. "All right," she agreed. "But it is not an uncomplicated story."

In the far distance was a sound of thunder. Summer's body knew that was wrong before her mind caught up. It was a sound in the *distance*—a sound they had not made. She turned, her mouth open to speak.

The raven stopped her. "We are walking toward that sound. You will find out soon enough. Listen to me.

"Many years ago, when we had been without a queen for almost five years, a flock of waxwings came to the ravens with news. The waxwings came to us because ravens have a reputation as clever birds, although perhaps we are merely noisy." The raven coughed a laugh. "In any case, these waxwings believed they had found the queen.

"All birds can move between Down and your world when they choose. They all have doors, though not all choose to use them. Most birds follow a single migration route back and forth all their lives, but waxwings wander wherever they like. Waxwings like surprises. One summer day, from a berry-rich tree, they heard the queen's song. It was a human woman on the ground beneath them, retying two young trees that had grown together to make an arch. She was a human woman, singing in a human voice, but it was the swan queen's song, unmistakably.

"They watched her from their tree. They saw a human man wrap her tight in his arms. They saw her two young: an eager duckling who followed her everywhere and a toothless, frowning baby."

"My mother and father," said Summer. "Me and Bird."

"That's right.

"When we heard this from the waxwings, the ravens made a plan. One of us would go to this human family to watch them and find out what we could, to find out if this was our queen—and if so, why she had left us, and whether she might come back. That first day I arrived, I was intrigued by your sister, and went up close to see what I could see."

"She remembers that!" said Summer. "I read it in her journal."

"I am not surprised that she remembers," the raven replied.

A question rose up in Summer and unfolded like a flower in her mouth. "Why her?" she asked. "Why were you intrigued by Bird?" She did not ask the rest of the question—"Why not me?"—but the raven answered her anyway.

"Because she seemed more bird than you," said the raven, "that little baby, with her wide-set, frowning eyes. Even as a baby she could face a cold wind and feel it very little. And she ate like a bird—still eats like a bird, I've seen it, by which of course I mean, she eats everything she can get.

"And there are other differences you cannot see. Her bones are light, and her blood can live on thinner air than human blood. She has the magnetic soul of a bird. She is made for the sky.

"But when I put my beak to her small forehead, I think that without meaning to, I put a little of this place into her mind. Or perhaps some grains of this land were still in my feathers, and fell on her—it had not been so long then, after all. The Green Home is made of the language of the birds. Do you understand that? This place was created by a song, long, long ago. When the birds are gone, it is made of their silence, and it is made of their song when they are here. Even you can speak and understand the language of the birds here—that was lucky. I do not believe it would be true of all humans.

"So perhaps my bird kiss, or perhaps a fragment of the Green Home—something planted a longing in Bird, a longing for our language. I would call it a gift, but I am not sure that longing has always been a gift to her."

Summer said softly, "Then if Bird was such a bird, and I am not, then why did you—why did you show me my animal soul that day?

212

And help me in the tree? And why did you follow me into the snake, knowing you could not get out?"

The raven replied, "Well, I am in the habit of watching after you now, after all these years. Perhaps it was that. But you should know, I also thought that perhaps we could come back."

"How?"

"Because I thought you might be the next queen. Do you understand? Bird had seemed more likely, but you can never tell, and it was surely one of you. The stories say that the queen can always find the Green Home, and can always find the way out. The queen teaches her daughter the way from childhood. That's what the story says; that's how it's always been. So when you entered the snake, I thought you were going to the Green Home. And you were. And then I thought you could lead me out."

"But I don't know how to get out," said Summer miserably. "And Mom never taught me anything like that." She thought of her mother and Bird, their long walks together alone, her mother's head bowed low near Bird's, whispering. So that's what they'd been doing.

A weeping willow tree grew up behind her, and the wind breathed through its leaves. A silence.

"So how did the birds used to come, before I was born?" Summer asked suddenly. "The snake couldn't swallow all of them."

"They came the only other way I know to come here, by crossing the attainable border of the birds. But that way is not passable now."

"I have heard of the attainable border," said Summer, "but I don't understand exactly what it is."

The raven almost sighed, or something like a sigh. "The attainable border is the place where earth and sky meet," she said. "Before the queen disappeared, she led the birds there every year, and earth and sky opened gladly to receive them. But since the birds stopped coming, the attainable border has changed. That's what I wanted to show you. Let's keep walking."

They walked an hour or two, or three, and they talked much less. At one point Summer asked about her father, and the raven said, "Everything that happened to your father is a long story, and a story for another day. I will tell you this. He has never stopped looking for her since the day she left. Never stopped once, even now, when he can only seek her with his restless mind and heart." Then they were silent again.

The thunder grew louder as they walked. It was like thunder but not like thunder: how thunder would sound if you were inside the storm cloud, a violent inrushing of air, and a violent emptying. But Summer thought it was too regular for thunder, as regular as a machine. An outrushing of air, and then a crash that might be metal or water crashing. Then the great inrush of breath again.

The hammering thunder, louder with every step, distressed Summer. But worse was her growing, bewildered sense that the horizon was beginning to foreshorten. The parallel child's-drawing lines of the green earth and clouded blue sky seemed to pull toward each other; the sky and earth curved together. It was as if she were walking inside a snow globe and were about to reach the glass.

The raven raised her voice. "We're coming to the end of the horizon, the place where earth and sky are closest. We're almost there."

After that, the crashing was too loud for conversation, and they were silent. As the sound grew louder, its threads grew more distinct. After the inrush of air was a terrible pause; then, alongside the outrush, came a long whistle or keening, the sound of something falling. Summer thought of bombs dropping in old movies. The huge swallowing inbreath; the pause; the long keening wail. Then the crash, which rattled the ground under her feet.

In the distance, Summer could see the horizon stopped short, like two tight, closed lips. She stumbled, the sight was so disorienting. Then it sighed open, with that great inrush of air, which brought a cold gale from the winter of the world outside the Green Home. Summer's hair was blown back, and she looked down with anxiety at the raven beside her. But the raven stood on sturdy legs, head up to meet the wind.

Now the keening sky was heaving itself down toward earth. Summer tasted metal in her mouth, a bright, electric taste, as air from the highest stratosphere swept downward. Then a warm outbreath of wind swept from behind her, making her stagger. Earth, though bent and straining toward sky, remained fixed. But sky moved, opened wide with that inrushing breath—then fell toward the earth, a screaming, sky-sized bomb. Earth and sky had become jaws, opening and slamming shut, breathing in and out.

All around the spot where earth and sky crashed together, the earth was broken and cracked by the blows. As the jaws swept open again, Summer could see on the battered ground the bodies of birds who had been caught between. She smelled their rank, decaying smell. Every one of Summer's senses was overwhelmed, and she felt a deep, physical panic. She wanted to scream, or run, or both. She turned her back to the ferocious horizon, put her hands over her ears, and screamed.

The earth cracked beside her, a miniature of the cracked, bloody earth where the sky had pounded it. Earth and sky were screaming, too.

The raven had retreated a few dozen yards. She stood still, her beak lifted. Although Summer could not hear her, she had the posture of a bird who is singing. A low, rocky mound of earth grew up beside her. In the mound, a dark hole opened against the earth. The raven had sung open a cave. Glancing back at Summer, she moved into the low, dark entrance she had made.

Summer, her body sound-racked, followed, first stumbling and crouching, then on hands and knees, and then crawling on her stomach along the low, rocky passage. The light went from twilight-dim to midnight-black in minutes. As the ceiling grew lower, the passage narrowed. Worming her way along, hoping the raven was still ahead, Summer thought of her journey through the snake and felt a wave of nausea. She might have gone back, even into that awful noise and smell. But there was no way to turn around.

Without warning, the passage opened into a larger space. Unsteadily, Summer got to her feet. It was too dark to see. The racketing horror of the jaws was now a distant, regular crash, but the darkness made the sound seem louder. Summer's feeling of nausea returned.

Then she heard the raven singing. It was not the harsh croaks of a raven's song as she heard it in the world. It was a true song, low and musical, passionate and clear. It was a song she had never heard before, but that felt familiar all the same. Listening, she thought of Ben, and her dream of the red bird who held her safe inside a soft red wing.

The darkness broke apart, and the raven stood in the new glow, beak open, singing. A flame floated in the space between them, fed by the song as it came to an end, filling the cave with warm, dim light.

The raven said in a conversational voice, "If we had come at night, you could have touched the stars. You would have been killed doing it, of course, but it would almost be worth it."

Summer did not answer. The metallic air still tasted wrong in her mouth. Her ears still rang from the sound. But the crashing sky seemed much farther away now, in the glow of the fire. Finally she asked, "Why does it happen? Is it, is it—" She paused, confused by what she wanted to say. "Is it *hungry*?" she asked. "It seems hungry."

The raven looked up at her. "That is a very good question," she said. "That is a useful way to see it. Streams of birds, millions of them, used to fly through the border's open mouth every year. But without the queen to lead the birds here—without your mother to lead them here... Well, the attainable border was always narrow, earth and sky closer together than at any other place. And now: Yes, it is hungry; that's a good way to put it. It is ravenous. These days, even birds who have found their way here, through accident or desperate luck, are sucked into the great jaws when the wind rushes in, and crushed when the sky slams down." A little stream flowing through the cave alongside the raven turned muddy red. The fire that hovered between them dimmed a little.

Summer made herself form words. "So we can't go out that way." Stupid thing to say.

"No, we can't," said the raven.

Summer fingered the crane map in her pocket. Her only way home. She thought of this beautiful place, the Green Home, which also felt like home, never visited by birds again. She thought of the horror of earth and sky, which should never meet, crashing together, over and over, forever. She thought of the dead birds lying on the bloody ground between the jaws.

She said out loud, "My mother did this." She paused, and tried it another way. "Because she loved us, my mother let this happen."

The raven was silent, watching.

"I think I know how to get out," Summer said.

CHAPTER TWENTY-ONE

THE SILENCE
INSIDE THEM

As they sat in the dimly lit cave, Summer told the raven about the crane map, and how she had found it. When she described Ben and what he had told her about it, the raven made a small sound, like someone holding a puzzle piece who cannot quite see where it goes.

Summer sat down beside the raven and spread out the map so that they could look at it together. The song-flame sank down to illuminate it. As she carefully smoothed out the creases, Summer recalled her fear that she had got some of it wrong. But no use worrying about that now. She felt a sudden, wrenching sorrow for the hopes she had put in this map, the trust that it would take her home. She was about to set fire to that hope.

The raven's black eye gleamed at the map with something Summer could not read. Her long beak opened fierce for a moment, then closed. Finally, she said, "I am glad to have seen a crane map before I died. I am not a young bird. But the cranes are the oldest of all. They see time from a great distance, the way a flying bird sees the world from a great height. Do you know how to use it?"

Summer recalled the day she had told Ben about the map. In her mind she could see, in her hand she could feel, the words she had written in her notebook: *Where you are, and where you're going. And remember to choose your north.*

"You start with where you are," Summer said. "I am in the Green Home, at the attainable border of the birds. I know that."

"From what I have heard," said the raven, "you must understand it in your bones. You must be in it, and still, and not resist it, and not confuse it with where you want to be. It is your map to use, not mine," added the raven shyly, "but I believe that means you will have to go back outside."

Summer rested her head on her knees. "And you have to know where you want to go," she said. "I want to go—" She stopped, and lifted her head, uncertain.

"That one is trickier, isn't it?" said the raven with her rasping laugh, raspier in the echoing darkness of the cave.

"I will think about it," said Summer. "I will decide."

"Deciding is one thing," said the raven, "but you must also want to go there, and you must want only to go to that one place."

"The last thing," said Summer, more doubtful every minute, "is you have to choose your north. I don't think I even know what that means. What is my north?" she asked. Her voice echoed in the darkness. There was a moment of quiet, except for the trickling of the stream, and the whisper of the shrinking flame as it consumed the last of the raven's song. The bird flickered in the low, unsteady light.

"I am only a raven," said her friend. "But as I understand it, north is the direction you look when you are lost. I would choose carefully. I wish you luck, Summer." In the near-darkness, her voice seemed to come from all over the cave. Then the flame went out.

In the darkness, Summer's searching hands found the rocky wall and felt along it, low, until they found the opening. She wormed, then crawled, then crouched, then walked toward the cave's entrance. The closer she came, the louder the crashing and metronomic thunder. Her stomach shrank back, but Summer pushed on.

Once outside in the noise-shattered air, she pulled out the map and sat on the ground. *I can only be in this place,* she thought, *if I let the sound in. Or if I stop trying to keep it out.* She breathed out, and with the next breath in, she allowed the grinding crash, the screaming wind, the shuddering earth inside her. She made the rhythms her own, and breathed with the sighing and keening of earth and sky.

Now, she said to herself. *Now the place where I am is no longer spoiled by the place I want to be. I am the crash, the scream, the shudder. Or I am the silence inside them.* She looked at the map in her hands, and her eyes fell on a chaotic nest of lines, straining against one another. Shaking as the earth shook from the sky's furious blows, she laid her finger on that place on the map. In a voice made of the thunder around her she said, "I am here."

And then the silence at the center of the chaos said: "Where do I want to go?" Then it answered itself: "To Bird."

But then the silence wavered, and was almost sucked into the chaos. Because in the deepest part of her heart, Summer wanted to go to her mother. That was where she truly wanted to go.

But to Bird was where she *must* want to go.

"Bird," she said aloud into the wailing inbreath that passed for silence here. "Bird, Bird." She focused her mind on her sister, alive, needing her. She remembered her arms around her as they lay by the red-bird fire that first night, finally warm except for the cold against her back. She remembered Bird's blue charred sleeve in the ashes of the later fire—the sleeve that through some grateful magic was not what it had seemed to be. And that thought—*It was not what it seemed, I was wrong, I was wrong, so happily wrong*—overwhelmed her longing for her mother, just for a moment. At least, Summer thought it did. She looked down at the map and saw lines like her sister's face in profile, the stubborn mouth and soft jaw, the bird-flip of nose. The profile so much like their mother's. She put her finger against that face and felt an emptiness, a hunger. There. That was where she was going.

Now Summer knew where she was and where she was going. But she did not have her orientation; she did not have her north. She did not know how to hold this map against the sun and stars, how to lay it against the world.

The world shuddered from another crash. Ben had said, "*Choose your north.*" So it must be hers to choose. But the raven had said, "Choose carefully." What would a wrong choice mean? Anxiety rose up her spine, and as the anxiety rose, her bones fell out of sync with the rhythm of the crashing world, and it became unbearable. She let her breath fall back in time with the sighing, bellowing horizon.

North is where you turn when you're lost.

I know how to find north in the world, she thought, remembering her father's lessons about stars and sun and shadow.

But, said the keening air, do you know how to find north on the map?

222

For a moment she felt despair. But then she remembered Ben's kind, rough voice.

A map is a song, she thought.

She stood up, because she knew you should stand to sing. She felt a pause. The bellowing horizon seemed to hold its breath.

Summer sang north. She sang cold and white. She sang slowness of blood, and thickening down. She sang a ringing silence made of wind in ice caverns and the cries of alien birds. The wind in her song made a song of its own, and Summer's song harmonized with it. She sang north.

She looked at her map. She saw her song. She said to the raven, watching from the entrance to the cave: "Let's go."

Sure of her direction, Summer turned and began to walk.

The watching raven saw what Summer never saw—that when Summer sang, the Green Home had responded. Near the thundering earth-sky jaws, a wide, flat river came up from the ground and flowed, clear and strong. It was the largest and most beautiful thing Summer's voice had made in the Green Home. But she did not see it arise, and would not recognize it as her own.

Summer and the raven walked a long time, following the map. They ate and drank what their conversation made. When it was dark, they slept on soft ground. Summer's heart broke to leave the Green Home, to leave the certain knowledge that she and the world were one, the world making her as she made the world. But no matter how far from the terrible horizon she walked, that joy would always have been spoiled by the knowledge of what her mother's absence had made here.

They walked many days, following the crane map. Sometimes the raven flew ahead for a while to see where they were, but she always returned with the same news: still the Green Home. But after a time, the landscape became less green, and less malleable. In time, it was very difficult for Summer to conjure up so much as a sigh of wind, unless her feelings overwhelmed her—and she was too exhausted now to be overwhelmed by feeling. For a while, the raven could still produce food and water. But the land was changing, the green transforming to dry, rocky brown.

One morning, in a place where the landscape was red dirt with stone outcroppings, the raven lost the power of speech. Or so it seemed to Summer. Over the course of an hour or two, her speech became first studded, then riddled with rough, coughing cackles. Then it was only that.

The truth was not that the raven had lost the power of speech, but that Summer had lost the ability to understand the bird language. Without drama, without even realizing it, they had emerged from the Green Home.

They continued to follow the map in silence. Summer felt lonely, walking beside this small, newly alien creature. In the Green Home, she had felt many things, but never lonely. This rocky landscape was stubbornly what it was, unmade and untouched by them.

Now they ate and drank what they found, which was little— berries, and an occasional sweet succulent plant.

One hot evening, Summer lay by a stream and drank for a long time, then slept. She dreamed she was floating on a lake that was covered with tiny white feathers, the glassy water furred with white. In the dream she saw a swan, its head buried in its own breast, plucking, plucking, plucking.

When she woke, the raven was gone. Summer waited all morning, but the raven did not return. She was abandoned again. She put a hand in her pocket, felt the sharp edges of the snake scale, so much less comforting than the warm egg had been. She thought of Bensbird, and wondered if he had lived, or if he was still in the World Tree. Thinking of Bens made her think of Bird, and so she stood up and walked on, following her map. The ground was steep here. She picked her way through reddish rocks as the sun beat down. She clutched at outcroppings to keep from falling, half pulling herself up the rough slope; her nails tore and bled. She scanned the sky for the raven. But she slept alone that night, cradled by two boulders.

In the morning, hungry and thirsty and sore, she came to the end of the land. At the top of the slope, where she had expected a rocky decline to the other side, she found herself at the edge of a long, high cliff that stretched as far as she could see in either direction. The map said to go forward, in an almost-straight line from here. But forward was a sharp drop, thousands of feet. It seemed that the only way to go was back.

So she had read the map wrong. She had chosen the wrong north. This is what it meant to choose the wrong north: to be a small girl who had come to the edge of the land, to a high cliff that stretched as far as she could see in either direction.

Summer sat down on the edge, one leg tucked beneath her. The day was still and bright. A bird wheeling above her would have seen a tiny figure swinging her leg against the side of an enormous canyon. But no bird came, and Summer didn't care, and didn't fear. She looked without longing at the unreachable land ahead, a long dark horizon with a series of mountain slopes, like cutouts, one behind the other. She sat like that a long time, as the sun moved across the sky. There was nowhere to go, so she didn't move. She set the crane map down beside her, and she watched without feeling as the wind swept it into the sky and away.

In the late afternoon, a cloud moved between Summer and the sun. Its edges glowed, but the face turned toward her was dark. It drifted slowly toward her.

"Cloud," said Summer in a rough voice. She had not spoken since she emerged from the Green Home.

The cloud came closer. It moved so purposefully that Summer began to imagine it was coming for her. She held still. The cloud floated close, growing blacker as it came, trailing charcoal mist, close enough almost to touch. It blotted out the sky. Its dark face roiled.

"Who is it?" asked Summer softly.

Then she heard the singing. She heard raven voices from inside the cloud, singing together. And maybe because the air of the Green Home still clung about her, or maybe because the ravens' harsh song rang out over and over, faint and then stronger, all those wings and hearts beating out the song at once, she almost began to understand the song. It sounded like a nursery rhyme, or a marching song:

Four sought it.
Three found it.
Two watched it.
One told it.
A thousand bear the prize away.

The cloud was not a cloud at all. It was a thousand ravens, moving toward her. Soon they surrounded her in a clamor of soft black wings. They lifted her up and bore her away.

The sun shone on the empty cliffside.

CHAPTER TWENTY-TWO

THE TRIAL
OF THE SWAN

U p the dark stone stairway from the dungeon, and then up the long shining stairway, the Puppeteer dragged Bird, clutching her arm the whole way, "to help you up, to keep you safe." Bird feared the Puppeteer now, but she feared the plunge through the golden steps far more, and did not protest.

As they climbed, the Puppeteer spun out a new puppet-string, like the spider she was. She had already planted one string in Bird—the knowledge of the swan robe. That story was true. This second mixed truth with lie, which makes the best stories, and the strongest strings, and the tightest knots.

"Those poor birds," the Puppeteer began, tightening her long fingers around Bird's shaking arm. "Those poor birds. The cages are to keep them safe, of course. Otherwise they would kill one another, or themselves. This is what the swan queen has done to them."

"The swan did that?" asked breathless Bird. She recalled the swan's eye, alien and intimate, and her homey, tender wing. "She *hurt* them?" Bird asked in disbelief.

The Puppeteer loosened her grip for a moment, so that Bird wavered on the stair and had a terrible moment of clutching at air. "She abandoned them," said the Puppeteer. (This was true, of course.) Bird grabbed for a stair, but the Puppeteer took her arm again and pulled it hard. "She left them alone," the Puppeteer said. "Without any warning or explanation, the queen who kept them safe, the queen they loved, who directed their lives, was gone. Can you imagine what that felt like?"

Bird could.

"She left them alone and terrified. It broke the birds' hearts. And for some of them, it broke their minds as well."

The Puppeteer knew Summer and Bird's story, or parts of it. The lie she made was calling out to the lost and angry Bird of that first terrible morning (that lost and angry Bird, that guilty Bird), who still lived inside this braver, strutting version of herself.

"She just left them," the Puppeteer said. "Just flew away one morning, as if they were nothing."

As if we were nothing, thought Bird. And the fear in her heart turned to dark rage. "You don't just abandon people who love you," she said, thinking out loud. Bird did not know that the swan was her mother, but she felt her mother's abandonment, and the queen's abandonment of her birds, in the same place in her heart.

"I agree," said the Puppeteer.

"It's wrong to do that," said Bird. "It makes people broken. It breaks things." And then: "I hate her, for doing that."

So Bird picked up the second string and tied it on herself.

The next morning, the Puppeteer spun out the third and final string that would make Bird do just what she wanted her to do. She rarely joined Bird at breakfast, in part because she rarely ate. But this morning she sat across from Bird, a tall narrow glass of clear red juice in front of her, and said, "Bird, I need your help."

Bird looked up from the orange she was breaking into segments.

"Bird, I think it may be time to take the queen's robe," the Puppeteer said. "After all she has done—I believe she no longer deserves the robe."

The fruit did not feel right in Bird's stomach. She stopped eating.

"Bird," said the Puppeteer (saying the puppet's name over and over helped fasten the strings, she had found), "Bird, it is a very serious thing to do. Only the one who possesses the swan robe can be queen. Normally, the robe belongs to the queen until she dies, and then passes on to her daughter.

"But Bird," the Puppeteer continued, "there is one exception: if someone challenges the queen in bird court, and a jury of birds takes it away. If a bird court decides that the queen no longer deserves to wear the robe, then the challenger may claim it. And then she—the one who deserves the robe, who will use it the way it was intended—becomes the new queen, and becomes bird or human, whenever she likes."

All of this was true. But the Puppeteer had left out one important detail. Not just anyone could challenge the queen in a bird court. Only the queen's own daughter, the one due to inherit the robe at her death, could win the robe in a challenge. That was why the Puppeteer had waited so long in this castle for Bird. That was why, with the help of the owl, she had reached her claws all the way to the stone house by the river, and set a story in motion to bring Bird here.

And that was why she had driven too-human Summer away. The Puppeteer had learned from her swallowed victims about the queen's half-bird daughter, hollow-boned, hardy against cold, the one who had already learned the bird language. That was the one she wanted. She had laid her traps not just for the swan queen, but also for Bird, because only Bird could win the robe at trial. And once she had won it—well. It is easy to take things from a child, especially one who trusts you.

Bird knew none of this. She did not know she was the queen's daughter; she did not know she could have a claim on the robe. So when the Puppeteer said, "I have thought of challenging the queen myself," Bird believed her.

"I feel so strongly the terrible thing she has done to the birds," the Puppeteer continued. "I have devoted my life to trying to care for the birds she abandoned as best I can. And I can't deny that the idea of becoming a bird whenever I liked—to fly, to sail down a river, to speak the bird language, to lead my people through the skies to the Green Home…"

Bird was still as a cat.

"But the queen should be young," the Puppeteer concluded regretfully. "And I am much older than I look." (True; although she was also likely to live many years more.) "They have suffered so much—it would be unfair to give them a queen they would lose to death in a few short years."

The Puppeteer stretched her neck, then lifted the narrow glass of juice and downed it in one swallow. She did not look near death.

"Bird," said the Puppeteer, laying out her last string, "can I ask—would you consider challenging the queen in bird court? It is a great responsibility if you were to win—not just to be a bird, but also to be queen. Do you feel ready for that?"

Greedy Bird: her appetite opened wide as a hatchling's beak. Ready to be queen of the birds? Yes.

And yet: Bird did not say yes right away. Something in her drew back from the thought of harming that swan, with her strange splendor and somehow-familiar warmth, the swan who had sheltered her under her wing. Bird was greedy; but Bird was also warmhearted, and kind, and stubborn.

The Puppeteer was patient. For three days she stirred Bird's fears, desires, and righteousness like a pot of evil soup. Then, one evening, as they stretched out on the floor after a long, fierce dance, Bird looked up at the stone ceiling above her and said: "All right. I will do it."

The Puppeteer smiled. "Good," she said.

A bird court is never held indoors. This court—as everyone involved knew, except Bird—was something like a puppet-theater version of a court. But when the Puppeteer designed a performance, she was particular about the details, and it looked as much like a real bird court as she could make it. So the queen's trial was held outdoors, at dawn, in the clearing between the lake and the high breast of the swan castle. Twelve birds chosen from the Puppet Army stood in a circle around a wooden stake plunged deep in the frosty ground.

The Puppeteer herself led the queen out on a leather leash knotted and double-knotted tight around her long throat. The swan limped badly. Her swan foot, the one part of her that had never changed in her long years in the stone house by the field, had been cramped too long in human shoes. In her wild run that first night, away from the house and everything she loved there—when she had to run, because she didn't want to go—the foot had been damaged more seriously. Now it looked badly swollen, perhaps broken. So the real queen stumbled after the Puppeteer, graceless and low to the ground, while the masked queen glided over the frosted earth, tall as a spear.

The Puppeteer tied the swan's leather lead to the stake in the center. In a real bird court, all the birds come freely, even the accused. So within the puppet jury's breasts, their hearts felt hot and strange to see their queen—the queen for whom they had searched the skies so long, who had broken their hearts—to see that queen shamefully tied and silenced before them. They looked at the ground.

The Puppeteer kept the swan chained and leashed for two reasons—to keep her from speaking, and to keep her from flying away. But a swan who cannot run, who cannot get up the speed to take off from earth or water, cannot fly. Leashed or not, the swan queen could not leave.

A light, cold breeze off the lake stirred the fir-tops.

"My people," said the Puppeteer. She had caught the scent of unease and sorrow in the hearts around her, and bent her mask toward them. The long stripes along the eyes gleamed in the sun.

"Today you face a terrible responsibility," the Puppeteer continued. "Do not fear it. Do not shrink away. The queen, once so beloved by all birds, has returned to you for the ancient judgment. The decision is yours alone, freely. I will leave you to it." She left the circle and walked back toward the castle.

The birds continued to look down. They knew this trial was theater, was a puppet show. But they also knew that the Puppeteer would be watching, as would another set of eyes: a gray, long-taloned owl who sat on a branch above them in plain sight.

From the same great door where the Puppeteer had disappeared into the castle, a small Bird now emerged. The birds watched her uncertainly. They had heard rumors of the queen's human daughters, but none of the birds in this circle had ever seen them. How would they know whether this girl had the right to challenge the swan? And could even a mock trial, even a puppet show, come to any conclusion if she did not?

Bird walked toward the circle slowly, chin high, watching the dark of the sky dissolve into gray. She thought: *Ever since I first came here, it has been winter, almost ready to turn into spring. But why hasn't spring ever come?*

Crisp brown grass broke and bent beneath her feet.

As she approached the circle, the queen lifted her head, and her adoring, anguished eye told the birds without question that Bird was her daughter. They stepped aside for Bird to enter the circle and bowed their heads.

Ignorant Bird stood facing her mother, not seeing what was plain to every bird around her. The court stood silent.

The Puppeteer appeared in the eye of the stone swan above, watching. The owl shifted his feet on the branch. The bird court began, overseen by two predators in the sky.

Bird spoke.

"I charge you with three crimes," she said. She had been up nearly all the night, planning what to say; she was ready. She spoke in English, because these birds spoke English, and the Puppeteer had ordered it. Still, in case it came to speaking bird language, she wished she had her flute.

"First, you abandoned us," she said, then stopped. She had not meant to say it like that.

"You abandoned your people," she corrected herself. "You abandoned those who depended on you. You were supposed to take care of them. They trusted you, and waited for you, and you never came back. And now they can't find their way back to their home, to the Green Home. They are stuck here in these woods where it has been winter since you left, dreaming of home. But they don't know how to get back there. Because of you."

The swan watched without moving. Her black eye burned, but with what Bird could not tell. She took a deep breath. The bird court stood still in the still, cold air. The predators watched from above.

"My second charge," said Bird, "is that you abandoned your gift. You could become a bird whenever you liked. You could *fly*, you could sail down a river at dawn. You could join the Great Conversation. You could fly. But you let that gift lie useless for years. You didn't even miss it. You didn't even care. You might have let your beautiful gift go to waste forever."

The swan's eye glowed with unreadable fire.

"So you abandoned your people, and you abandoned your gift," Bird continued. "And my third charge is that you abandoned the Green Home. I don't know very much about that place. But I heard that it's dying without you, and without the birds. And so everything you should have cared for is ruined or lost, or almost ruined. And so you deserve to lose your robe and your crown." Bird turned her back on the swan's burning eye and faced the silent court. The sun was higher now and bright in her face. She frowned.

"Someone who would use that gift should have it. Someone who would respect that crown, and respect the birds, should have it. I would respect them. I would use the gift. I would never just let them— I would *treasure* them, the robe and the crown and the birds. With all my heart. For my whole life."

There was silence. The birds shifted uncomfortably from foot to foot. Then one bird, the smallest bird—a sparrow with a black mask, streaky brown feathers, and a slender frame, for a sparrow—spoke up.

This isn't fair, said the sparrow, in the language of the birds. *She should be allowed to speak.*

The owl's head turned slowly and stopped dead at the sparrow. The Puppeteer leaned in closer, trying to hear, unable to understand.

"She can't," said Bird shortly. Her voice changed: "I mean I don't think she can, anyway, because of the knot. And I can't untie"—she glanced up at the Puppeteer, who though she could not hear well from her height, leaned over the railing like an arrow aiming—"I can't untie the knot," Bird continued, "or she might escape." She felt lost. She had said everything she planned to. She had not expected this.

The sparrow was relatively new to the Puppet Army. He had joined believing he would defend the castle until the queen came home. But life in the army so far had not been what he had expected. He spoke up again. *Then I will speak for the queen. Otherwise it isn't fair. The bird on trial must have a defense.*

The owl's wings flapped, and his shadow passed across the little group. The birds of the court looked up and saw that the great gray bird was now perched on the railing next to the Puppeteer. On the horizon, a low, dark cloud was drifting toward them. But the sparrow went on.

Here is what I say, said the sparrow.

First, it is true she abandoned us. But it is also true that she returned. We don't know where she was, or what she was doing. We don't know what kept her from us so long. We only know that she left, and now she is here. No birds died because she left us. It is true, we could not find our Green Home, and that was— That was hard.

The bird court nodded and shook their heads, looking at the swan from one eye; and now, finally, the swan bowed her head.

But some of us tried to find it, and found new worlds, looking. At least the ones who came back.

The swan's head sank lower.

*And some of us kept her castle safe—*the sparrow glanced up at the Puppeteer's hungry, seeking mask, and then back down—*or at least we tried. We were braver than we thought we could be, and learned things we never knew we could learn. I am glad for that.*

The bird court shook and nodded their heads again.

And if she abandoned her gift, said the sparrow—*well, it is her gift. That's what I say. It is her gift to use or not. Some of us might be jealous of it* (no one looked at Bird), *but that does not mean she owes it to us to do what we would do in her place.*

The sparrow paused for a moment, then stepped back to join the circle of the court. Bird held her ground. She was thinking hard. She felt she was losing; she felt her dream was slipping away; and she did not like the feeling. She said, in English, "What about the mad birds?"

The bird court glanced at one another—they did not know about the mad birds. Seeing that they did not know, Bird felt triumph rise inside her. From the castle's eye, seeing Bird's posture change and straighten and her confidence return, the Puppeteer felt triumph rise within her as well. Soon the robe would be hers—would be Bird's, but that was the same as hers, since she could take it from the child the first moment she let it out of her sight. Almost, almost.

The dark cloud floated nearer.

"She did this," said Bird, walking slowly around the circle, pointing at the swan, "she drove birds mad. The basement of the castle is full of them—mad birds, talking English and bird mixed together. Pulling out their own feathers, screaming over and over. She did that to them. Maybe some of you became soldiers, or went looking for the Green Home, and maybe some of you even came back. But some of you were driven insane—by her, by being abandoned. And she should pay for that."

Bird paused at this point and turned to the swan, stubby finger pointing. The storm cloud now loomed almost directly above them. The swan lifted her head, and lifted her wings, just for a moment, as if to protest what Bird was saying. As she lifted her wings, the scent of that soft, warm silk breathed through the cold air and wrapped itself around Bird. She felt herself back in that tender place where she had hidden her face and cried, melting in the familiar/unfamiliar warmth. Tears rose in her throat, and she furiously fought them. Unthinking, raging, she dropped into a mixture of English and what bird language she could sing without her flute.

You did that, she said in bird language. *You LEFT them.*

"You're not ALLOWED to leave, you're not ALLOWED to," she continued in English, looking straight into the swan's alien, loving, terrible eye.

You saw what it did to them. You see—I mean you saw: you did that. You did that!

Then in English: "And I hate you! I hate you, I hate you, I hate you." Bird was flailing now toward at the swan, striking her on the chest and throat; but she was too close to strike hard. "I hate you!" she cried into the warm, familiar scent. "I hate you, I hate you!"

From this point, Bird never quite remembered, or perhaps never quite wanted to remember, everything that happened.

She remembered the sparrow flying at her face, wings beating and feet clawing at her hair, protecting the tethered swan. She remembered the Puppeteer screaming from far away. And she remembered the terrible, true swoop of the owl, who scooped the sparrow in its talons and flew away toward the forest.

But then, somehow—did that dark cloud descend from the sky, in a wild confusion of black wings? She was sure it was Summer's voice she heard, calling from somewhere, "Bird, stop, don't—Bird, she's our *mother*!" And then time held, suspended, and all she saw were Summer's long clever fingers at the leather knot—Summer was good with knots—through the beating of a thousand black wings around her.

Time started again with a loosened knot, with the swan's long, muted-trumpet call of pain. It was Bird's own name, cried out, that call of pain, and now she knew it was her mother, she knew, and in the cacophony of raven wings she was cut through with shame. "She can't fly!" Summer was shouting, but to whom? "She can't fly, her foot is hurt."

Bird shouted to the swan through the raven-storm, pushed on by the blacker storm inside her. Still speaking in English, she cried, "You shouldn't have left!" Her voice was raw. "You shouldn't have left! You don't deserve that robe. I should have the robe now, I should!"

The swan tried to move toward Bird, but the raven cloud surrounded her. And then, *No, Bird,* said the swan, through wing beats flickering like black flame. *No, Bird, my darling girl, you don't understand—you are not the one. You will never have the robe, I am so sorry, my darling girl, but you are not the one.* And the ravens bore her and Summer into the sky. A phalanx broke off to come for Bird as well, but she beat them off with her arms, staggering with grief and shock.

"Bird, COME!" screamed Summer. "Please come!" The swan gave wail after terrible wail of anguish. But Bird swung furiously at the ravens who tried to rescue her and ran back into the swan castle, the words echoing in her ears. Not the one. Not the one.

As Bird entered the castle, the swan's call changed, became deeper, more urgent. Bird, crumpled at the base of the golden stairway, did not hear; nor did the furious Puppeteer, striding down the steps to meet her.

But the birds of the court, and the birds of the Puppet Army, and even some forest birds half a mile away—they all heard the swan's cry, pleading and commanding, the cry of a desperate queen, as it echoed over the trees. *Protect my daughter from that usurper,* said the cry. *My people, I beg and command you: protect her, protect her, protect her.*

Deep into the forest, the owl finally landed, seizing a high branch with one long claw. The other claw still held the sparrow, who shook within the owl's talons from cold and fear. The owl lifted the sparrow to his face and looked at him for a long moment. Then, with care, he set the trembling bird on the branch, and flew away.

CHAPTER TWENTY-THREE

HARROWING

Bird flew. She flew away, from her sister's human voice, and from her mother's swan voice, that trumpet of agony as the raven cloud lifted her away. *Bird, Bird,* they called. But Bird ran from her own name, ashamed of herself and her deeds and her hopes, which she now saw would never come true.

Not that Bird was thinking: *I betrayed my mother* or *I will never be a bird, or be queen.* She hardly thought at all. She only felt terrible pain, and ran from it, to the place she had tried to think of as home.

But this was not her home, and the Puppeteer was a false and dangerous mother. Bird was sobbing at the bottom of the golden stairs when sharp talons seized her shoulder. "Come with me," said the Puppeteer, and her hideously strong hands dragged Bird up the winding ribbon of steps. Unable to catch her footing, Bird stumbled, then screamed as the Puppeteer's nails drew blood from her arm.

But the Puppeteer, raging, never heard the scream. She did not know bird language, but she was a master of hearts, and she had recognized the look on Bird's face when the swan told her who she was, or who she was not. She had chosen the wrong daughter; all her work had been for nothing.

As they climbed, to indulge her own pain and rage, the Puppeteer tormented Bird. She told Bird the story of her parents—the story of the swan maiden and the student who saw her swimming in the river. She told it in the most hateful and hideous way possible. In the Puppeteer's mouth, the story turned ugly. Your father a kidnapper, an enslaver. Your mother a lazy, selfish coward. She smeared soot and excrement across Bird's green and lovely memories. Now she saw a home built upon a field of dead birds. By the time they reached the top of the stairs, Bird's sobs were no longer from the piercing talons, but from grief and confusion.

But the Puppeteer was not finished. Master of hearts, malicious tyrant, she knew which strings to tug. "She left you," said the Puppeteer, dragging Bird along. Her voice was low and even, but it pierced through Bird like a sword through a hand. "She left you, just like she left the birds. She abandoned you. Her own child. Remember that morning you woke up in the cold alone?"

(Bird remembered. And she remembered something worse: the evening before, when she had opened her parents' window to welcome in the owl, to start this story, because she thought he had promised to teach her to be a bird if she would. That meant it was all her fault— or so she thought, as children always think, though everything began long before they were born.)

So in this way, dragging Bird up the stairs, the Puppeteer poisoned her heart, for no reason except that she had poison handy, and it pleased her to. It wasn't part of a plan; she had no particular reason.

After all, once they reached the top, she was going to throw Bird over the stone railing, and watch her fall a hundred feet to the hard ground.

On the lower floor of the swan castle, the remaining bird court had rejoined the Puppet Army. The birds paced restlessly around the floor of the swan, but in silence, without conversation. In every bird-heart, the words of their queen echoed: *Protect her, protect my daughter.* They felt stirred and confused, torn between two queens. Here and there wings fluttered along the floor, struggling against the forbidden impulse to fly. These birds had served the Puppeteer for years; but the voice of their true queen spoke to their true natures, so long repressed. The impulse to flight and birdsong burned inside each one.

When, from the golden stair, Bird screamed in pain, the birds on the floor fluttered as if in pain themselves. A spotted starling leaped into the air, beating awkwardly with long-unused wings. At first other birds squawked in protest at the forbidden act. But then, in pairs and trios, more followed the starling into the air. Soon the whole Puppet Army was in restless flight, circling inside the castle's belly, faster and faster, a gathering inner storm.

From above them, high on the winding stair, Bird no longer screamed but wept, only wept, as the Puppeteer filled her breaking heart with poison. At each echoing sob, the birds swirled faster. It was not the kind of poison a bird understands, but heart-sobs are the language of the Green Home itself.

When they reached the top of the stairs, the Puppeteer dragged the sobbing girl to the stone railing. And now, seeing at last what the Puppeteer intended, seeing the worst of her oldest nightmares shambling toward her, Bird began to wail, a deep and primitive wail of fear. Ancient terror, the most ancient of all, seized her body and wailed through her throat.

In the swan's belly, the birds swirled faster. Their wings began to beat in unison, a true army now.

At the balustrade where the smiling boy had perched, the Puppeteer jerked Bird up by one wrist, trying to twist her up to the top of the railing. Bird screamed wildly now, fierce with terror, clinging to the railing with her other hand.

Faster and faster, the swirling birds beneath.

"Can you fly?" whispered the Puppeteer from behind her mask, jerking Bird's arm almost out of its socket. "You can speak like a bird, but can you *fly*?" A hard pull. "Can you *fly*?" Another jerk. "Can you *fly*, little Bird? Well, let's find out."

Bird lost her grip on the railing. She clawed for the Puppeteer's dress with her free hand, desperate for something to hold, kicking wildly at the stone ledge, trying to push it away from her.

"Let go of me," said the Puppeteer, and wrenched the small brown hand free of her dress.

Half blind with fright, writhing and flailing at the stone, Bird, from the depths of her terror, spoke her deepest word, her last resort, her heart's root.

"Mama!" she screamed. "Mama, help!"

And the castle's belly exploded. Up the throat of the swan castle surged a mass of birds, like one arrow shot from one bow. In less than a second, each beak open in a single furious call, the birds were on the veranda.

The Puppeteer, still holding Bird, whipped around to face them. "You—" she began.

It was all she got out. In an instant, she was herself a feathered mass, covered with all colors of beating wings, no inch of her showing. She raised bird-crusted arms to beat them off, releasing Bird, who crawled into a corner and hid her face.

It was good she hid her face; but even with covered eyes, Bird could still hear. She heard a single rising scream from a thousand tiny throats, thousands of wings battering the air in unison. She heard the Puppeteer's furious screams turn to high, wild panic, and then her final, harrowing scream of terror, fading as it fell through the air.

Bird never forgot that scream, or the sickening, thudding crunch that followed. Those two sounds haunted her worst dreams for the rest of life.

She kept her eyes shut, face buried, in the corner where she crouched. She heard the birds, the object of their rage gone but the rage still pulsing inside them, continue to spin around the air in a tight circle. Then she heard the circle dissolve, heard wings fall out of step. She heard single birds cut through the air and away.

She heard the circle grow smaller and fewer.

She heard the last few chirping, exhausted birds fade into the forest. She was alone.

Much later, when the swan heard what had happened, she wept— partly from relief, and partly from sorrow and guilt. She knew that she had made herself a kind of Puppeteer, and made her birds a killing army, as they never would have become on their own. It broke her heart, to have done such a thing. But to save her daughter, she would have done it again, and again, and again.

$$\sim$$

For almost an hour Bird sat curled against the stone wall of the swan's eye, shaking. But at last she wiped her face, stood up, and walked on unsteady legs to the railing, to see if the Puppeteer was really dead. Looking was a mistake. The Puppeteer was certainly dead, an awkward and hideous shape staining the dead grass below. It was the only ugly shape Bird had ever seen her make, and it was more food for future nightmares.

Bird turned away and stumbled for the stairs, ready now to make her way outside, back to the forest and her beloved birds. She watched her feet settle uncertainly on each golden step, humming the old rhyme to herself to keep the falling-fear away.

Halfway down, feeling more secure, for the first time she glanced up. What she saw stopped her cold, made her sink down to a gleaming stair and sit there in shock.

The castle door was closed. Not even closed; there was no door at all. The door in the side of the swan castle had been conjured by the Puppeteer, and when she died, it had vanished with her. It was a bird castle again, with its only door high in the air.

So there was no way out, and Bird was as caged as she had ever been. The castle was hers alone, and she was its lonely queen, after all this time.

Just what you always wanted, Bird?

You might think Bird sat on that golden stair and sobbed then; or ran back up to the stone railing to scream to the empty forest for help; or in some other way cried out against this terrible thing that had happened to her.

But Bird was a surprising girl. Ben, who liked surprising people, would have liked Bird a great deal. Maybe she wasn't the true queen, and maybe she was poisoned with anger and fear. But Bird had something like a queen within her. Or maybe it was something like "hero." Maybe a hero is what Bird was born to be.

Because yes, she understood, she felt it like rapidly hardening ice in her chest, that she was locked in a stone castle, with no way out except a door in the air, which is no way at all for a flightless Bird. But at this most terrible moment, her first thought was not despair for herself.

Her first thought was to remember the birds trapped in the dungeon below.

And that was the thought of a hero.

They are in cages, just like I am, she thought, with the icy clarity of pain. *And if the door had been open, I might have forgotten and run out, and left them there to die. At least I can free them now.*

And that is what she did. She strode through the Puppeteer's dungeon and harrowed it like a champion. She found the keys, and she opened every cage. And once a cage was open and the bird inside was free, she smashed the rusting iron under her small, furious boot.

Some of the birds flew straight out of the dungeon and through the swan's throat to freedom. But others could not understand that they were free. These Bird led out gently, coaxing them with bits of food from her own tiny store. Some had forgotten how to fly at first, and these she carried in her hands to the swan's great room so that they could practice, skidding and tumbling across the air, mumbling to themselves in broken English.

$$\backsim$$

When she had followed the last tattered bird up the golden stair and seen its safe flight to the forest, dipping and weaving, but flying and alive, Bird was once again alone. And alone in her bedroom, with no more birds to see to, no more purpose to carry her on as the dark swept slow across the sky, the bars of her cage rose up around her again. The Puppeteer's last evil act had been to poison Bird's heart, to make a cage of evil words and leave her trapped inside it.

And so Bird was angry.

With the Puppeteer?

No. Angry with her father, for stealing and caging her mother—or so she thought, so the poison made her believe.

And angry with her mother, for being the queen of the birds. With her mother for owning the robe, and with it everything Bird had ever wanted, and now would never have. Above all, with her mother for letting herself be enslaved, letting the robe lie locked in that closet, while the birds to whom she owed protection wandered the world, lost without her, trying to find the Green Home.

At least, that is why she believed she was angry. But locked in the inside closet of her heart, she was angry with her mother not for letting herself be caged, but for leaving that cage, and leaving her Bird behind. That's how hearts work sometimes. Summer might have pointed out how funny it was, but Summer was not there.

As her room grew dark, Bird began to cry. It was a dry, coughing kind of crying like the wheezing of a small animal. She was trapped and might die in this place, but she could not even long for the family who loved her, because the Puppeteer's words, and the knowledge that Summer would have what she most wanted, had left her so full of bitterness and hurt.

She lay on her bed and closed her eyes, letting the noises come out of her, detached. Eventually she felt herself dissolve into sleep, still crying the small dry sobs.

In her half-sleep she heard a creaking voice, like an old gate. "Hush now hush now hush," creaked the voice. "I tell you a story now, hush." She felt something soft brush against her eyelid. She jerked awake.

At first she could see nothing. Then, up on one elbow, blinking, as her eyes adjusted, she caught a gleam at the end of her bed. A dark shape formed around and below the gleam. A black bird—a crow, she thought—was standing next to her. His rough outline against the dim light suggested unpreened feathers, maybe some pulled out. He shook his head and shifted from foot to foot, compulsively. She leaned closer. The bird was muttering in something like English.

It was the mad crow, she realized: the one she had met the night she found the swan, the one who had told the story of the red bird who died and came back to life.

In the language of birds, Bird asked the crow why he was still here. The old crow shook his head and held up his misshapen wing. "Oh, your wing is still broken," she said in English. He bobbed his head and stepped from side to side.

"I tell you a story now," said the crow. "I tell you the phoenix. I saw this, I saw with my eye."

"What is a phoenix?" asked Bird.

"Only one phoenix," the crow persisted. "Red bird, jewels. When he a bird. Five hundred years, then he burns. And then he born. Burns, then born, then burns again. Then born again. Phoenix old as world. World love him. Stone and water and wind love him. And fire his home. Where he touch the world, the world heal."

"I remember this story," said Bird. "But what—"

"Listen," said the crow. "Five hundred year comes. He go to egg-wood tree, to make he egg. But she saw. And she came."

"Who came?" asked Bird. The crow shook his head, back and forth, back and forth, and did not answer.

"Across the moon she came. Two hundred puppet birds pull her chair. Puppet birds." The crow spit. "She mean to kill he phoenix. But phoenix cannot die."

"Why did the Puppeteer want to kill him?"

"He other map to Green Home. He and swan queen, only maps. Puppeteer, she would be swan queen. And she would be only map." The crow paused, and scratched at the quilt. "Also. The birds they love he phoenix. And if you love, you no puppet. Never." The crow shifted from side to side. Unexpectedly, Bird felt like crying again.

"She came. Phoenix stand alone in moony night. He call out to puppet birds, 'Brothers, sisters.' Puppeteer, she scream, she throw she magic knife. But no knife kill a phoenix, even magic knife. Knife love phoenix, too.

"But knife strike egg-tree, split him open.

"'Put him in tree!' she scream. And two hundred puppet birds attack." The crow spit again. "The phoenix will not harm a bird. But he touch some to his heart. And those who touch his heart are free. They turn, they fight for him. They fight for him!" the crow croaked.

He stopped, then added, "I was one of puppet birds. I he heal. I turn to fight. I turned. I fought.

"But puppets too many. They hang phoenix in eggwood tree, upside down. She magic-close the tree, and there he stay. There he stay, long legs bent in long bent branches. Long arms twist in twisted branches. Old head pressing hard gray wood. There he stay."

"But how long?" asked Bird, heartbroken, not sure why.

"Thirteen years," said the crow, shaking, shaking his head. "If he still in there."

But he was not.

CHAPTER TWENTY-FOUR

A DOOR
IN THE AIR

After that, the old crow and Bird spent their days together. His soft, rough voice made a rope she clung to. It kept her from drowning in her own mind's black and echoing well.

The Puppeteer had kept little food in the castle, and Bird soon finished what was there, and nearly finished the water. Although birds from the forest, alerted by those Bird had freed, brought them berries or nuts to eat, or little acorn-cups of water, she was wasting to bones. How much food or water a bird can carry, even a good-sized jay, is not enough to keep a girl alive, even one with hollow bones. But some of these envoys were kind, and made extra trips to bring a little more, and this kept Bird at the edge of life.

Still, she grew so thin that even under the covers, even birdlike Bird, impervious to temperature, never felt warm, not once. She lay curled in her bed with her mind echoing black, and did not dream of her past, which was smashed to fragments by her mother's betrayal (of the birds, not of me, not of me), and those fragments smeared with her father's kidnap and the blood of dead birds. Pain like that, you can't even get your hands around. It's not even pain, just a thing smashed on the floor, ruined.

And she did not dream of her future, smashed in just the same way, in almost the same moment. That fast, that easily: just a sentence or two—"She's our mother," "Not the one"—and past and future were finished.

So although the Puppeteer was gone, her story was not over: she had trapped Bird in more ways than one. Day and night she lay in her small round room, her robin-colored clothes growing filthy and dull. She was empty as a pot tipped over, and she dreamed of nothing. Empty stomach, empty eyes, empty heart.

Through it all, the crow sat beside her. Some days he told his phoenix story again, or said strange old bird poems or tales. Nights, too, he sat near her, sometimes sleeping, sometimes nodding or shaking his head in the dark. His presence comforted her, and was her only comfort.

One night, when Bird had lain buried under blankets for more than ten days, the crow finally ventured a little bird language. She could see it was hard for him. He sang her a fragment of a song, just one verse in his quavering, creaking voice: *A young swan, hidden in a burrow-nest, like a seed before it opens and grows.* "Like you, this song," he added in English.

The song rattled and turned in Bird's empty mind.

"Like you," said the crow again.

A young swan, hidden in a burrow-nest, like a seed before it opens and grows. And suddenly there was an answering rattle inside Bird's empty heart. "One little cygnet," she said in English. She sat up. "One little cygnet/Buried in the earth/Dark as a seed before its birth." Then she turned to the crow and said, in the bird's language, *How do you know that song?*

After a long pause, he spoke in bird again. *It's an old song,* said the crow. *Old, old, old.*

"I know that song," said Bird in English. "My mother sang that song. It's been in my head the whole time I've been in this place. Do you know the rest? Like 'When she hears the song/That a true map sings,'" she began.

And then she stopped. The song that a map sings. The song her mother sang. *He and swan queen, only maps.* How did that song end?

"On a mountain crossroads," Bird rasped through dry lips, "The little house stood,/Two little cygnets say,/ 'Something smells good.'" She turned to the crow. "Have you been to the Green Home?" she asked urgently.

"I have, I have," he said, nodding.

"Does that sound right? Is there—'on a mountain crossroads, a little house stood,' and something cooking in the house? Does that happen on the way?" she asked.

The crow nodded vigorously. Bird did not see it, but he was too full of emotion to speak.

"The song is a map," Bird breathed. "It's a map to the Green Home. Oh, I wish I knew the whole song, but I know some, and I can remember more. How much do you know?" she asked the crow.

I only know small pieces, he said, as if mention of the Green Home had brought bird language more easily to his throat. *Though I know*

254

more than most. I don't know who knows all. Maybe the queen. Maybe the phoenix.

Sing it, please, said Bird in bird language. Her empty heart stood under a waterfall, filling up again.

Over the next few nights, Bird pieced together as much as she could of the song, partly through her own memories and partly with the help of the crow. She asked the berry-bearing forest birds if they recalled other parts of the song, but only one did, a gray parrot who could sing one verse in broken English. A few others had heard of it, but had never heard it themselves.

All day, sitting alone in her messy nest of a bed, Bird would rock back and forth as she sang the bits of the songs she remembered or had learned from the crow. She remembered her mother singing as she stirred cookie batter; singing over a knee Bird had scraped in a bicycle fall; singing to herself as she and Summer dawdled behind on her long walks along the river. She picked up pieces of her exploded past, cleaned them off, set them right. She saw her mother's smile, heard her voice, as she called the song, half-heard background of her childhood, into the foreground of her mind. She felt out the right order for the fragments she had; she put it deep in her body, just like the patchwork bird song. She pulled out her long-unused recorder, and played it.

But if the Bird who two weeks ago had flown a mocking paper bird down to the miserable puppets below—if that proud Bird had seen herself now, thin and filthy, with wild hair, rocking back and forth singing a nursery rhyme over and over—she would have said: "This is a mad girl, and they are right to lock her up alone."

One night, after she had fallen asleep with her mother's rhyme on her lips, a breath of air swept across her face, as if from wide wings. Her eyes opened.

At the end of her bed, the owl's ghostly gray face wavered before her in the dark. The crow was nowhere to be seen.

Hello, Bird, the owl said.

Bird was flooded with fear, and then with shame, and then with anger. The owl had done all this.

"You lied to me," she said.

I did not, said the owl. *You chose to understand me in a way that pleased you.*

"You knew that I would do that."

Yes, I did.

Why have you done this to me and my family? she asked in bird language.

I? Why have I done this?

Bird reddened, and asked in English, "Why did you make me do this?"

The owl was silent. Bird blushed again. Then he said, *There are truths beneath the truths you see. I am here to free you, but you must grow stronger first. Here.*

Opening one claw, he dropped on the blanket a nest of small, salmon-colored eggs. At first Bird did not understand; but when she saw that she was supposed to eat them, she hid her face in the hot pillow, crying uncontrollably. The lovingly tended eggs of some bird, perhaps a bird she knew—who might be even now flying frantically around a tree, *My nest, my eggs, oh help me, where are they?*—even to see them here made her sick.

The owl watched her for a moment, then flew off. When he returned, carrying a freshly killed fish, the tears were still wet on her face. At first she resisted eating a raw fish. The owl was her enemy, had ruined her life. Was this a trap? She felt paralyzed. But hunger overcame her, and it was not so bad after all, mild tasting, only so wet and slimy that it was hard getting it down. While she ate, the owl vanished again, then returned with a small pail, one that the Puppeteer had used to gather berries. It was full of cold water, which she drank gratefully.

But you hate me, was all Bird could think of to say when she had finished.

You are wrong, said the owl.

∽

When she woke, the sun was in the west. She had slept most of the day, and the owl was gone, though he had left another full pail of water. The crow was by her side again. "Where did you go?" Bird asked.

The crow shook his ragged head. *I was near,* he said. *I watched, in case you needed help. But the owl is not my friend. The owl is no bird's friend.*

They spent the rest of the afternoon working on the cygnet song, until Bird fell back asleep. She woke that evening to find the crow gone, and the owl on her bed again, a silhouette against the dying blue of the sky through the door of her room. *The crow says you are no bird's friend,* Bird said.

So the birds believe, said the owl. *Eat this.*

This was an uneasy answer. Although she ate, Bird lay awake that night letting anxiety hunt across her mind. *The owl says he will help me leave this place when I am stronger,* she thought. *But how? Where is the door I can use?*

It went on this way for two weeks, with Bird sleeping much of the day and spending the rest with the crow, sharing the food and water the owl brought her every night and singing and piecing the song together. After the first few days of regular meals Bird felt much stronger. Sometimes she walked around the castle, searching for that hidden door the owl must know about, the door or crack or something—there must be a way out, some way that was not a door in the air.

One very early morning, after bringing Bird her meal and several pails of water, the owl said, *Tonight, we leave this place.* Then he disappeared into the graying dawn.

Bird had a moment of terror, then a moment of relief. *No, I can't leave,* said Bird into the dim air. She had remembered: the crow. She knew he was nearby, listening. *I can't go,* she said, *if it would mean leaving you, my friend.* She would stay out of friendship; but she was relieved to her core.

Girl, said the familiar, creaky voice. *You must go.*

I can't leave you until you can fly, she replied, certain. She searched the still-dark space for the old black bird.

Wings flapped on a high corner perch. Ragged black against the iron-colored air, the old crow flew, flew perfectly, through the door and to the stone railing outside. Bird followed just in time to see him

258

leap off, coasting and flapping in a lazy circle out and back again.

Bird was astonished. *You can fly? You could fly all this time? But why did you stay with me?*

The crow replied in English, "To honor phoenix, who free me."

But you stayed in a cage, when you could have been free, said Bird.

"Heart free," said the crow. "Better freedom. But now we both will fly." Then, switching back to bird language he said, *I know you are afraid, Bird. But I have watched the owl all this time. I do not know why he has come to help you, but I trust him, this time. Fly, Bird,* he said. *And now I will help you leave.*

Then he flapped off into the forest, and Bird never saw him again.

That night, Bird couldn't sleep. For all her anxious hopes of a hidden passageway, she knew there was no other way. This castle's only door was in the air. The only way out was down.

Down, how? On a rope? Twisted sheets?

Dangling so far above the ground.

Think of something else. The boy with the crooked half-smile, and the burnt slash across one cheek: how he fell, and lived, or at least did not die. *If he could fall and live, maybe I can do it, too,* she thought.

(But the Puppeteer fell and died, Bird—what about that? Remember? She did remember that. She did.)

The night was deathly quiet and moonless black. When she heard the low *wooo-oof* outside, Bird stood with difficulty, ripples of adrenaline running up and down from chest to feet, trembling her hands. She could see the owl at the far end of the veranda, standing on the rail. Like a small gray ghost, he turned his gray mask full around to stare at her. *Follow me now,* he said, *and I will show you the way out.*

Bird took a step toward him—then, impulsively, ran back to her room. She found her recorder and stuck it in her pocket, in its old place. *All right,* she thought. *That means I will live.*

It was brighter at the veranda railing, at the swan's eye, this edge between the castle and the world. This was the door. She could see the stars. A light night breeze caught her sweat-damp hair and made her shiver. Fear made her senses too sharp: the green of dark and distant trees too vivid; the rustle of feathers, shattering.

The owl disappeared around the corner. Like a person in a nightmare, against her own will, Bird leaned over the abyss to see where the owl had gone.

He was walking slowly down the back of the swan's long stone neck.

But he can fly, was Bird's first thought. *That doesn't make sense.*

Then she saw what the owl meant her to see: that the swan's neck, a smooth pearl-gray when seen from the ground, was actually pitted with small holes, some as big as half a peach.

Big enough for a small foot, small sweaty hands.

He meant for her to climb down. He was showing her the way.

She could not go. It would kill her. The idea was hilarious and mad. She stood, small and trembling, at the edge of the long drop.

And then she thought: I'll show them.

My sister will be queen, and be a swan, and fly. But I can do this. Only I can do this.

My mother left me before I learned how to be a bird, and never taught me what I most wanted to know. But I can do this; she will never do this.

I'll show her, I'll show Summer, I'll show my father: I'll show them, I'll show them. They'll see.

A bird circling above the castle that night (and was that a black wing and a blue eye flashing against the stars?) would have seen a small brown form, a sparrow-colored creature, clinging and climbing down the graceful neck of an enormous swan. Once or twice a foot slipped, or a hand, and then the creature stopped and clung. Sometimes its shoulders shook and heaved. But it never let go.

One endless hour later, the longest hour of her life, Bird lowered herself to the swan's broad back, dizzy with relief. She sat for a few minutes, safe, catching her breath, hugging her sore, torn fingers under her arms.

Then she rose and stumbled to the swan's side, to peek over the carved stone feathers and see how much farther there was to go. The top of the feathers came just above her knees. It was far, very far, farther than jumping off a roof. She turned, her back to the edge, to look for the owl for what to do next.

The owl was flying straight toward her. In that split second she saw a furious gray angel, legs extended, talons unfurled. She threw up her hands, but it was too late.

That black-eyed, blue-eyed raven, still circling above, saw an owl and a girl, falling through the air together. The owl's talons clutched the girl's shirt, and its wings beat hard and harder as it pulled fierce against the strength of gravity.

She had to fall, the owl knew that. The owl had known that all along. But he did his best to break her fall.

They could not go far into the woods—not as far as the owl wanted to go—because Bird was too weak, and she had twisted her ankle in the fall. Twice she stopped walking, fell to the ground, and lay there, just as she had lain in her bed so long. But the owl fluttered down, pulling at her hair and clothes and whispering, *Not far, not far, almost.*

At the bank of a stream, where the light of the million stars filtered through tall trees, they paused. Bird drank as much as her shrunken belly would hold. When she finished, she looked up and past the owl. "And the old woman watches on the mountain alone," she recited. "While the birds fly past to the Green Green Home, the Green Green Home, the Green Green Home."

The owl did not reply. Bird was looking over his head at the wheeling stars, her eyes bright and hot. She had climbed down the long swan neck. She had fallen from the swan's side, and lived. There was nothing, nothing, that she could not do.

The song is a map, she said. *It's a map to the Green Home.*

Do not do this thing, said the owl.

I feel better now, she said, as if he had not spoken. *And I know what I am supposed to do. My mother cannot fly. So I will lead the birds to the Green Home. I can save them, because I know the song, and because I know the way. I am not the queen, but I can still save them.*

Wait, the owl said. *We will talk in the morning.*

All right, said Bird. She curled up on the ground where she was and fell instantly asleep.

But when the owl came back with Bird's breakfast the next morning, she was already gone.

CHAPTER TWENTY-FIVE

FOUND

Ravens scattered in a storm of black wings and were gone, their cries echoing in the bright, dry air. Summer and the swan stood alone on a rocky dirt path, in a clearing made of many greens, deep inside a forest. Summer studied the trees for her raven, but she was gone. They were alone.

The swan began to limp along the curving path, then paused to look at Summer. *So I guess she knows the way,* Summer thought, and followed. It was hard to think of this bird as her mother, and Summer walked beside the swan self-conscious and shy. Swans are for water and air, not land, even when their feet are whole and well, so the daughter and bird-mother moved very slowly, much more slowly than Summer would have gone on her own.

Summer's bare feet were gray with the grime and dust of the road out of the Green Home. The Green Home, where you could be only yourself. Here she had to worry and plan: *Where are we going? How can we get back to Bird? Is she all right? Is the swan? Is my father all right, and where is he, where is he?* The thoughts made her step heavy.

They walked on. Once in a while the swan would open a wing toward Summer for a moment—just a brush of wing against Summer's arm or hair. Then Summer felt a physical, electric thrill along the skin, and she wished the swan would never stop. But the swan, uncertain, always stopped.

As they walked together, barefoot girl and dirty, limping swan, Summer remembered how, in the chaos of the swan rescue, the swan had sung a plaintive trumpet call to Bird; how Bird's face had twisted into fury and tears; how she had run away, beating back the rescuing ravens who fluttered around her. What could the swan have said to make her run like that? Would she ever know? Bird had understood the swan, and here, so far from the Green Home, Summer never would.

Experimentally, she said aloud, "I'm sorry about your hurt foot." The swan dipped her head in acknowledgment.

So the swan understood her, at least, if not the other way around.

But Summer could think of nothing else to say.

They walked for an hour or two. The sun was past its crest, and Summer wondered how cold it would be, and where they would sleep when it was dark. But she was growing too tired to think. Reflexively, she checked her pocket for the last match. At least they had that. She ran one finger along the edge of the snake's scale in her other pocket.

Although the swan was slow, she stopped only once, to approach Summer and tug gently at the shirt beneath her jacket, then tap at her numb, blue feet. Oh, Summer saw: she means I could tear my shirt to wrap my feet.

Her feet secured, her jacket pulled close, they walked on in silence.

Summer kept telling herself: *my mother.* But when she looked at her face she saw the long black bill like hard rubber, reaching up to an arrow point at the beady black eye; she saw the head feathers stained dirty brown but smooth as a baby's combed hair. She could not see through to her mother.

After they had walked what felt like most of a day, their path crossed another, narrower path. This second path led off to water on the right—a pond or small lake, it seemed to be, from the glints of pale blue between the thinning trees. The other two paths led farther into the forest. Summer tried to see down the two dark paths to know which one was right, but before she could choose, the swan gestured toward the left. She herself limped off toward the right. Summer hesitated, but the swan stopped to watch her turn. "But are you coming this way later?" Summer asked. The swan nodded, and gestured again. Then she limped toward the water.

Summer walked on alone. *It should be getting dark,* she thought, but the light seemed to hang in the air here, lingering among the trees. Why is there always farther to go? She was on a path, but she had no idea where the path was going: a different kind of lost. Inside the strips of shirt her feet were sore with the cold, and in every clearing, the wind caught her. Stepping around patches of snow, she walked toward a snowmelt creek that roared over rocks a few yards away. The water tasted good, though it numbed her hands and face. She crouched by the running water, drinking, then raised her face.

Just on the other side of the creek stood a small, alert animal. Although Summer recognized the animal, for a moment she did not know why. It was in the wrong context, this animal, with its silky black back and white front, its green-and-golden eyes. It was not supposed to be here. It should be a fox, or a squirrel, or an otter, standing at this forest creek.

But it was a cat. A little black-and-white tuxedo cat.

"Sarah," said Summer. As if she had been waiting for the call, Sarah crossed the water in one leap and pressed her head hard against Summer's leg. "Sarah, Sarah," said Summer. Her hands were full of black fur. "You are such a good jumper, you always are. You are such a strong girl," she said—this, and more of the kinds of things we say to cats, to keep our minds busy so that our bodies may lovingly meet.

Summer lay on her back now, with Sarah on her stomach, in their favorite old way. "I don't know how you got here, but—" The cat's head pushed with urgent love under Summer's chin, and she laughed. Her mother would be so glad to see Sarah, her little cat that was no hazy gray, but black and white in decisive patches. Sarah, who would let a bird sit on her shoulder and be safe; who would fold herself into a small, polite package, taking up less space than she had a right to. She was a cat like a bird—no wonder their mother had loved her so much.

"Sarah," said Summer, and rolled on her side, still holding her cat. And then she remembered what she had learned in the Green Home. "You know the raven!" she said, sitting up. "You listen to dreams!" Sarah's eyes gleamed up at her, green and gold.

Then her cat ears pricked high, and she turned to face the creek.

A cat's ears are sharper than a girl's, so at first Summer heard nothing—but then: long, swinging steps through the woods from across the creek. Not a cat's steps, or a wounded swan's, or a boy's. A man's steps. Summer jumped to her feet, ready to run. But Sarah, though erect and alert, was not running, so Summer waited.

As the man cleared the trees, swinging a stick, a hawk flew overhead and caught his attention, so Summer had a moment to see him without being seen. *That man looks like Bird* was her first thought. She had never seen before just how much he looked like Bird—brown all over, though now with white mixed into his hair and his new beard. He was like Bird, and he was too thin, and he somehow had a beard now, and he was her father.

Now it was Summer's turn to cross the creek in one leap. His embrace was too bony, and his beard scratched, and his voice was exactly right, and so was the scent of his shirt, and when he said her name over and over she said nothing, but only cried.

Impossible to have found Sarah, more impossible, more wonderful, to have found her father. But almost as impossible as finding her father was the house he now led her to: a small red house on an autumnal carpet of red leaves, one thread of smoke curling from its black chimney. It was that house, the house of dreams that were somehow real, the house that had pulled her through a keyhole and into the top of a tree. Only this time, the battered black door was wide open to reveal a warm fire and delicious smells inside.

But that day, Summer had little time to think about the house. That evening was talking and laughing and crying and tumbled stories, first as she and her father ate at the small wooden table, just the right size for two people, and later by the fire, where Summer warmed her red, battered, bare feet.

First Summer told her story, or the outlines of it. She did not tell the private parts, like the egg, or the parts that still made no sense to her. She told him that she had stopped at this little house, but not what had happened there.

So, as it happened, she left quite a bit out; but that didn't matter, she thought.

When she told him about Bird—choosing her words carefully, not saying how long they had been apart, leaving out the terrible time when she thought Bird was dead—he stood up and paced the room, and at the end he demanded to know where the swan castle was, so that he could go get Bird. But Summer had arrived on a raven cloud, and had no idea how to get back. "Maybe the swan will know," Summer said, and her father looked up. "So she's here?" he said, his face all sadness and hope. Summer said she was near, and would be here soon, she thought. They both looked down, uncomfortable.

After a while, looking at the fire and not at her, he told Summer his own story, beginning with the story of when he first found their mother, by the river, stepping from her robe. Summer had already heard this story from the raven, although this was among the growing list of things she did not tell him. (The room was beginning to fill up with these unsaid things, feel a little stuffy with them.) In any case, with a mixture of shame and pride and loss, her father told her many details she had not known before.

He also told the story of that night, the night of the open window, the night her mother left them. "I don't understand how the closet was opened, but it was." Summer opened her mouth, then closed it again, and thickened the air with her silence. He had always felt guilty about losing her robe, he said. He had hidden it in the first place only because he didn't want her to go. Sometimes he had dreamed he was buried the way he had buried the robe, he said, under leaves in a hollow tree, folded, choking on the dry, dirty air.

And when their mother found the robe that night, he said, it was like another dream, something he had lived in his mind over and over happening before his eyes, because he knew someday she would find that robe, and that on that day, she would leave. He had been planning for this day since the first day he found her, studying her all those years. Every spring and fall, when the birds move on, he saw which way her feet turned, her body longed, as her voice grew distracted and her hands fluttered like useless wings. At those times of year, her whole body turned toward another home. And twice a year, on one of their canoe trips, her yearning oars drew their boat off balance, toward a little inlet on the north side of the river, almost masked with overhanging vines and brush. He would feel her yearning and fear it, and pull strong on the other side. For a while, they would paddle this way, in silence, each pulling at their oars as hard as they could, in opposite directions. But their father always won. He kept the canoe sailing straight. And their mother relented and seemed to forget, though she was quiet and sad for days after.

That night, the night she found her robe and ran, he was far too late and far too slow, no matter his strength at the oars. You can't catch a bird in a boat.

He followed her as long as he could see her, which he knew would not be long. But he remembered the spot where her oars would pull, and he watched for it, skimming along the north side of the river in the moony darkness. He turned his boat into the almost-not-there space, so swaddled in nettles and branches and vines that no one would ever see it, who had not been there before in a boat with a homesick swan.

Did he think of the two girls then, as he pushed his way behind the veil of willow branches and vines? He did not. But as he told Summer—and now he did look up at her, with pained eyes—he was only planning to see where it led, to investigate, to be scientific for now, and come back later. He didn't realize that as soon as he pushed in far enough, space would shape itself around him and—"Well, you know how it works," said her father, "since you are here."

It had fit her, and it fit him. He was swept Down. ("That's funny," a smiling boy told Summer much later. "I only know one other way here that fits two people, and that's the way you and your sister came. All the other ways are for one person alone. Or all the ways I know, at least.")

When he arrived, of course, she was long gone. The air was quiet, but the river was loud underneath him. He thought of his daughters, sleeping alone in a dark house, and his heart was sick.

But there was no way back. Behind him was not where he had come from. And so he paddled on.

He saw his wife everywhere at first. He saw curving white throats that were snow-dashed branches. He saw white wing beats that were flashes of sun through the trees. He listened for the sweet, muted trumpet calls and clucks of the swan: *hwaaah, wah-haw, hwah, hwah.* But he heard nothing but crows and sparrows, robins and jays, or occasionally the low, dark hoot of an owl.

His canoe traveled too rapidly down the river, which was different here, rocky black water jangled by slush and ice. He forgot that when you are lost, you shouldn't push hard ahead. You shouldn't move as fast as you can, when you're lost. At night, he would stop to pile dead leaves by the bank and sleep beneath them.

He had left barefoot, in his pajamas, with no food or supplies. He was terribly cold and hungry. Once he tried to kill a fox for meat, but it laughed at him, slipping away and stopping, slipping away. He was an excellent nester, but looking for his bird-wife, frantic for his abandoned half-bird children, he could not bring himself to try to kill a bird, or even eat an egg. He pulled berries from the trees and bushes.

He had a plan for finding the swan: follow the river hoping to find a lake, hoping it would be the lake where the swans congregated before migration. He knew swans well, and he was not far wrong about the lake. But the forest eats all plans. The river became narrower and shallower and finally dove underground, where it would run for many miles before it reached the lake. So now he had to walk over cold ground, over snow in some places, with nothing but hope that the river still ran below him. He dragged his canoe behind him. His mind was hot and wrong from starvation. Animals no longer feared him; they came close to watch his scarred, battered bare feet stumble through dirt and brush, the scratched and tarnished canoe flattening the ground behind him. They watched the feet stumble, and stop. They watched his legs sway, and collapse.

He lay in his grounded canoe unconscious for a day, maybe two days. When he finally swam up from the blackness, it was because something hard and sharp was striking his forehead between the eyes, over and over.

He opened his eyes and looked into the face of a raven with one blue eye, holding a map in its mouth.

$\sim\!\!\circ$

Later that night, when the swan arrived, the house changed. Nothing worked. Nothing was beautiful. Her father reached out to touch the swan and then pulled back. He made a joke that wasn't funny. They kept bumping into each other. The swan looked wrong inside a house, and she seemed to feel that, bending her head away, avoiding their eyes.

So Summer left her sad, tense parents to explore the red house. It was the same plank floor and the same blue, peeling, star-shot walls that she remembered; the same fireplace, inlaid with the same plumed bird's head. But there were doors and halls and even stairways she had not seen in her first visit. How could she not have noticed? (And how could the house look so small outside, and contain so much space within?) Summer wasn't sure if she was sorry or relieved to find that the flowers and vines painted around the shelves no longer looped and crawled downward to show her a secret latch and a secret door. They were just flowers painted on a wall, and the wall below them was smooth and whole.

Upstairs, Summer had a long, hot bath, with three changes of water, her first bath in weeks, her first bath since home. She came downstairs flushed and damp in a long, clean gray shirt she had found, which hung past her knees, and fresh socks. "The swan—" her father said, then stopped. "Your mother, I mean. She went upstairs."

At the table, the two of them ate bread and beet stew and a warm, salty cheese. "Did you make this?" she asked. "No, it just…the food just comes," he said, awkwardly. Then they were silent, thinking about the bird upstairs.

Finally, without warning, exhaustion ran through Summer like a wind, and her father half guided, half carried her upstairs to a small attic bedroom with a sloping roof, a square window, and a small fireplace. In the light of the moon and the fire, the walls looked warm and yellow-red. He kissed the top of Summer's head, and left.

Summer lay in bed, her first bed since home, close to sleep; but something in her mind kept dragging back the corner of that heavy curtain. Oh! She jumped up, ran to her dirty clothes crumpled in the corner of the room. She found the snake scale, the last match, and Bird's journal: all her only treasures. She tucked them under her pillow.

As she fell asleep, she thought with pain of her raven friend, whom she had seen in the cloud of ravens that brought her here, but not since. "My friend, my animal friend, where are you?" she whispered into her pillow.

The next morning, Summer found her clothes on a chair, washed and folded, with a new blue shirt and soft blue boots beside them. ("Did you wash my clothes?" she asked her father later. "This house," he said, gesturing around, and then his hands dropped. "I don't understand how it works. But no, I did not wash them.") Sitting on the small table beside the chair were the backpack and tomato-red sweater she had left here on her first visit. The house had kept them for her.

But when she ran downstairs with a light heart, the tension in the house had thickened. Her father was restlessly wild to go to Bird, and Summer sensed a similar restlessness in the swan, who stood outside staring hungrily above the tree line. But both of them were ill and weak, and the swan's damaged foot would not allow her to fly.

Summer was worried about Bird as well; but something inside her also felt hard against her. "She chained the swan up," she said to her father, feeling disloyal, but saying it anyway. "She wanted to steal her crown. And when we came to save her, she ran away."

"Bird is very young," said her father.

Not that young, Summer thought.

Part of Summer was still the small head in the window, watching her mother and sister walking, whispering. That envy made it hard for her to understand Bird. All she could see was her mother's favorite.

If she had wanted to know, she might have learned from her father that each time their mother was pregnant, she had nightmares of half-bird children, of beaks set in human faces, raw pink bird legs and claws sticking out from under pleated school skirts. When each girl was born, she wept with relief to see them fat and red and human.

What her father did not know was that as the years went on, their mother learned that she had been wrong about Bird, a girl who looked fully human, but had a bird's magnetic soul. Twice a year, child though she was, she felt a call, an overwhelming call to move, no matter how difficult the journey, to find the place she ought to be. She was born on the first day of autumn: the earth itself was pulling her, and calling her on, even on that first day. But she had no flock to show her how to answer the earth's wild call. She was a little girl, spun in circles like a wild compass. She only knew with absolute certainty that there was something she must do and be. She was young. "Queen" was the best she could make of it.

But Summer knew none of this, and she might not have softened if she had. Her heart didn't want to soften. She had had a lifetime of strange, special Bird, called by the turning, burning earth, specially taught (and specially loved?) by their mother, while she herself was only pale and practical, with an unmagnetic, unhearing soul.

Besides, Bird's willful, stubborn absence had devastated her parents. When her parents looked at Summer, she saw their eyes looking past her, for Bird.

It's because Bird's not here that everything is wrong, Summer thought. *If Bird were here, it would all be better. We would be a family again.*

So she thought, so she thought, and the more she thought it, the more angry she felt, and the more alone.

The Puppeteer, this family's great enemy, is dead now. But the wrong she did them continues to simmer and boil among them, and they have added their own wrongs to the pot:

A kind and clever man—whose human love and single mistake set this story in motion—lies awake at night, unable to restore his shattered family, unable to protect the daughters he loves.

A crippled swan queen limps away from a house not made for a creature like her, head bowed, wondering how to restore her ruined kingdom without further harming her own beloved children.

Summer, still seeking the bird inside her, blames Bird for tearing her family apart.

And far away from these three, a Bird who will never be queen rages at her sister, her mother, her father, rages at all the world except her own beloved birds.

The Puppeteer may be gone, but her strings are still tied tight, and the puppets yank and grieve one another's hearts.

CHAPTER TWENTY-SIX

I WILL NOT LET THEE GO EXCEPT THOU BLESS ME

Later that day, her father told Summer the rest of his story in those first days in Down: how he had read and reread the raven-sent map and tried to understand its pattern. It was a tangle of lines, almost impossible to follow, but he knew that the X and the O must be himself, and the sun and the bird his children, and that drove him on. He even pulled out the map to show her, and explained how he had deduced that this line meant to turn from the underground river, and this meant to turn left, not right, into a clearing of autumn leaves, to a small red house. (He would never know how close to this house he had been the day he got the map—how the map led him far away before it led him back.)

But when he arrived at this house, with the smoke curling lazily up from the chimney, it was empty. Empty, but ready for him, with a fire and food. "I knew it wasn't right to come in, but I was so sick and so hungry," he said, "and I thought I could smell food." Summer remembered herself kneeling at the black door, her hungry eye at the keyhole.

"I stayed here by myself for weeks," he continued. "At least, I think I was by myself. I never saw anyone, or heard anyone. But the fire was always stoked, and there was always fresh food on the stove when I woke up."

A thought came to Summer: *This is a house like a heart.* (Heart, flute, claw.) *It's always the right size, and it never runs out of what it has to give.* She was not even quite sure what this meant, but she thought it was true.

Once his story was told, her father retreated, and mostly slept—healing, too, like the swan, though he did not know it. And in the rare times they met, her parents continued to treat each other with painful politeness. After that first night, the swan mostly avoided the house; Summer sometimes watched her from the woods as she floated, delicate as a reflected cloud, alone on the pale blue lake. She took her meals at the lake, too, after that first night, and slept near a sheltered bank. But she seemed to avoid the company of birds, almost hiding from them, almost as if she was ashamed.

The days ran on like water. Summer often walked in the woods alone, and whenever she saw a flash of black wings, she would stop, searching, hoping for a raven with one blue eye. But the blue-eyed raven never came. Summer remembered from Bird's journal that she had burned one of the owl's feathers to make him come. She wished she had one of the raven's feathers, but she only had a match, and nothing to burn.

Every night in the great tree, what she now knew must have been the World Tree, she had longed to be with her parents. And now she was, but she was as lonely as ever. When her father was awake, he was mostly silent. Her mother in swan form seemed to daze him. His eyes were red and dry, as if they had seen something that hurt, and his hand on Summer's head was light and forgetful.

At least her father was himself. The swan was not her mother, would not be. Summer was a good girl and she felt an obligation to love this bird like a daughter, but it seemed like a joke. "Why can't she take off her robe and be my mother? Just for a minute?" she asked her father once.

He said, sadly, "I think she is afraid. That robe was lost for so long—I think she is afraid that if she takes it off even for a minute, it will be stolen forever. And from what you say, she has a powerful enemy." (They had not yet heard of the death of the Puppeteer, so she often hovered in their thoughts.) "So maybe she's right," he concluded.

Summer looked off at the bird-busy trees and saw no raven, still, still, still. "I miss my mother," she said. "It wouldn't be so terrible for her to be my mother again, just for a few minutes. She should want that. She should want to be my mother."

Her father followed her eyes to the firs swaying against bright blue. "She is your mother now," he said. "You just don't see it."

One evening, Summer left her spy-place in the woods and stood on the lake's rocky shore, between the now-indigo water and a stand of dark green. She had been staying in the red house for weeks. It was a sort of home now, but Birdless, and ravenless, and with only half a father and almost no mother at all.

And so although her parents were here, this place was not home, after all.

I am hungry, Summer's heart said to the lake. *I am hungry. Food never lasts. Food is for every day, not once in a while. I need an everyday food. I need an everyday love. The worst thought is that nothing can, nothing can feed me, it's me and my hunger alone together forever. I want my mother.*

A flutter, a turmoil of water nearby, and she looked across a spur of earth into a small cove. The sound brought Summer's mind to the day she saw the cranes dance, first in the water, and then against the sky. It felt like that day. Only this time, instead of cranes, she saw a magnificent, lonely swan.

But Summer had had enough of magical birds. She had had enough of loneliness.

The swan was floating on the shallow water, leaning its long neck to drink. "Feed me," she said softly to the white bird, who was too far away to hear. "I am not my sister, I can't live on air and song. Feed me, heart and stomach, feed me, I am starving. My mother left me. My father left me. One friend died, and the other has left me here alone. I thought I killed my sister, and now she is a stranger. My father sleeps and shakes his head. No one is left who can see my real face. This is my real face," Summer said to the water. "This is my face," she said to the great white bird.

Then, with no thought, she ran. Summer ran across the rocky earth and into the water, splashing across to the swan, who raised her head but did not move. She splashed deeper, past her knees, dragging her legs through the lake, until she was on the swan and holding her long throat in her hands, not to choke her, but because it was the only part she could hold. "I hate you," said Summer, "I hate you, I love you. I don't know you, I can't see you at all."

The throat swelled and twisted in Summer's hands, bigger and bigger, but she did not let go. The swan's body shrank from her, twisted, changed, curved, but Summer hung on. The throat grew thick as a young tree. Hair spilled from the swan's head, black hair with white chalk-streaks, a curtain over Summer's hands. She let go. The swan, no longer a swan, turned toward her.

"Mom," said Summer, and burst into tears. "My girl," said her mother. She pulled Summer to the shore and held her as she cried, pushing her hair away from her face.

When the tears had stopped, when they had held each other in silence for long minutes, Summer's mother began to whisper to her. She whispered about the robe, and what would happen to it when she died.

She whispered "bird." She whispered "fly."

She whispered "queen."

Summer's mind and body both stood still, with shock and with hope. "But why me?" she asked.

"It goes to the queen's daughter," her mother said.

"Then Bird should have it," said Summer quickly. It was not a decision; it seemed more like a fact. "You should let her. She's the one—she's the bird one. She's the one who wants to be a bird more than anything."

Pulling her closer, her mother whispered into Summer's hair, "But don't you want to be a bird?"

Summer felt a trembling in her heart, as if a gentle arrow quivered there. "Yes," Summer said, after a moment. "I do want that." She straightened a little in her mother's embrace, and said goodbye to a beautiful friend she had only just realized was her dearest love. "But Bird wants it more. It should be hers." She felt calm, and certain, and utterly bereft.

But her mother said softly, "My love, it isn't a matter of *should be,* or *let*, or *wants*. It's a matter of how it is. And the robe will be yours: the robe and all that goes with it."

Summer thought of Bird, and her heart went hot, and she thought: *It will kill her. I will have killed her again.* (And strangely, that only made her angrier at Bird. *Bird, why are you always being killed by me, please stop being mine to kill.*)

"She already knows," said her swan-mother. "I told her that day you came to free us, the day of the trial. I think that's why she ran back into the castle. Because she couldn't bear it."

In the bird queen's arms, in her mother's arms, Summer felt that Green Home feeling, that she could say what was true in her heart, that it was the easiest thing in the world. She said, "I don't know how to be a bird. I don't know how to be their queen. I will let everyone down."

"You will have bird teachers," her mother said. "You have already had bird teachers, I think."

Why didn't she say, "I will teach you"? Summer didn't think to ask. She was remembering the cranes at the lake, writing her map on the sky. She was remembering Bensbird, and the blue- and black-eyed raven who had taught her her own animal soul, for whom she scanned the trees every day.

"Yes," Summer said, "I have had bird teachers." And she began to cry again, for happiness and grief at the newness of her life, which lay before her now like an egg broken open, with light pouring out.

Smoothing and kissing her forehead, whispering love in her ear, Summer's mother held her for a long, long time, until she fell asleep, and then held her all night while she slept.

In the morning, the swan was gone. But Summer found a small white breast-feather in her hand. She kept it the rest of her life.

That night, Summer crept out of the little red house to walk in the dark woods, because she couldn't sleep. She had lifted an apple from the table on her way out, but now she slipped it into her pocket. She wasn't hungry.

After that radiant night in her mother's arms, after the news that she would be bird, and queen, she had walked straight into a wretched day: her father agitated and angry, wild to find Bird, wild to see his wife, not a swan. Summer heard him at the pond at dusk, shouting and pleading, then maybe crying, too. She wasn't sure; she shut the door, so as not to hear.

The moon's belly swelled half full, but treetops splintered her little light. So Summer walked a path she'd walked before, but with one hand along the trees to guide her. Turmoil, good and bad, kept her awake: bird, queen, family.

"Family" hurt to think about. And "queen" was a high, fearful tower, a tall stone castle, with no way in that Summer could see.

But what will it be, to be bird?

What she knew: To be a bird meant to speak the heart-conversation of the Green Home, so that your heart makes and is made by the world around you.

What else she knew: To be a bird is to be present and alive in the world, with an animal mind untormented by future and past. That's what the raven had taught her at the crossroads; that's how she found the egg in the ruins of Bird's fire.

The egg. To be a bird also meant to hatch from your egg, and to leave the nest.

Summer walked through the night forest, her boots crunching dead leaves, her hand stretched against rough bark. *If I could find my raven,* she thought, *then I could find Bird. I could bring her back, and we would be a family again.* What had been faint and bird in her blood had begun to stir and listen. Her blood told her to find her raven, her own bird, and get her help in finding Bird.

Summer had the impulse to flight, although as yet she had no wings.

All their lives, Bird had been the difficult one, the unmanageable child, and Summer the good girl who could always be relied on. But Summer could see that Bird had always found her own story and chosen to follow it, and Summer envied that. Most of all, she envied the magnetic bird-soul that had told Bird what to do.

So she would see what it was like to be Bird, to just try it on for a night.

She only meant to leave the nest this one night, to find her raven. She only meant to learn more about what it meant to be a bird.

But in the back of her mind, under it all, ran *queen queen queen.*

An hour later, deep in the forest, Summer stood in a thick tangle of brush. She had walked off the path, as the old Summer never would; she was following, or trying to follow, for the first time, the faint call of her own bones. Now there seemed to be no way forward or back.

But Summer looked around her with her animal soul's open and scavenging eyes. She spotted a space between two trees, an opening in the hopeless brush: a small clearing. She fought her way into that empty space.

Across the clearing stood a silver maple, a spreading skeleton against the blue-black, cloudy-starry sky. Three Summers could not have held hands around that tree. It waited for her. The bark was rough and thick; she ran her hand along it, found fingerholds, ridges deep enough for small boots. She looked up, up. The tree was enormously tall. Thin clouds sailed behind the branches. The moon was broken in half.

Her face turned upward to the shivering stars, her eyes closed, Summer listened to the faint, pulsing call inside her. Half whispering, she sang: "One little birdlet/Sitting in a tree." Her strained and beating heart was louder than her voice. "Fear in her pocket," she sang softly, "but—something something free."

Her mind was stripped like flesh from bone. Nothing was all that was left in Summer's skeleton mind. But her bones said: higher. Said: raven. So she dug her fingers into rough bark as high as she could reach, scrabbled for bootholds, found them.

She had climbed the World Tree; she could climb this one.

A scratched and breathless half-hour later, panting Summer, legs dangling, sat astride a fat branch, wrapped in cold. She floated above all the trees around her. A white plain—Ben's plain?—hovered in the distance like a ghost. As if she knew what she would find, Summer put a hand on the trunk behind her. Her fingers followed the channels of the rough bark, careful, seeing. Tree, tree, tree: ah—nothing, where tree should be. Careful, with seeing fingers, arm twisted behind her back, Summer traced the outline of the nothing. Big. As big as her shoulders. Which was big enough.

Summer swung her feet back to the branch. On her belly, she wormed her way feet first into the opening. How deep does it go? What's in there already? Her skeleton-mind didn't ask; her animal hands and feet moved.

What did her boots find in the hole? First: air. Then: softness. A pallet of feathers and grass. Bits of bone and fur. She wriggled and slid her way in. It was not comfortable. She was hunched like a baby in a womb. She didn't care.

Up in her tree, Summer waited for sleep, inner eyelids closed, outer open, like a bird of prey. Summer was an owl that night, tucked in an owl's nest.

Just as sleep came, she recalled her dream of the red bird, how she had peered through the warm curtain of silky feathers and seen the world stained with red: red-stained fire; red-stained stars; the place where a sleeping, red-stained Bird should be, but wasn't. In her black nest, Summer fell asleep dreaming of red.

A weak yellow light lined the horizon. The same chilly breeze that blew damp hair from Summer's face made dead pine needles stir and swirl far below.

But Summer noticed none of this. With only head and shoulders out of her nest, she held still as a new flower. A raven with one blue eye sat inches from her face. "Raven," she breathed, soft, soft, so the raven would not fly away. "Oh, raven. I missed you. I looked for you everywhere. I came here for you."

Raven's head dipped once, twice. Then, like that time on Ben's plain so long ago (not so long ago, but it felt like years), her eye gleamed at Summer. The last time it was the black eye that had gleamed. This time it was the blue. But once again the air swam and shimmered between them, and their eyes burned together.

And then, again, the world leaped into sharper focus, with new colors. With new sharp and open eyes, Summer took in the dirty, yellow-haired girl across from her, still half inside an owl's nest: the girl she also was.

Where have you been? Summer raven-croaked.

"Waiting for you to find me," whispered the yellow-haired girl hoarsely. "Listen: this time look deeper."

So the girl inside the raven's mind looked within, and saw Bird, tiny, climbing down the neck of an enormous stone swan. Bird, stumbling back, pushed off a ledge by an owl. Bird limping, running into the woods.

The raven saw this, thought the girl inside the raven's mind. *This is a memory. The owl tried to kill her.* (Summer misunderstood that part; but owls are easy to misunderstand.) *The owl tried to kill her, but Bird escaped.*

She saw Bird, no longer limping, walking through the woods, a Pied Piper of the birds, singing and playing the old rhyme, gathering the birds to lead them to the Green Home.

Oh, thought a corner of the girl inside the raven's mind: *the song is not just a nursery rhyme; it's also a map. Not just one thing, but also another. Like me right now: I am a raven and also myself. Like me, like me, like me.*

"She is taking the birds to the attainable border," said the hoarse raven-in-girl. "If she succeeds, millions of birds will die."

But when they see what has happened to the border, they'll stop, croaked Summer-in-raven.

The girl across from her shook tangled yellow hair. "No," she said. "By the time they are close enough to see, instinct and longing will carry them on against their wills."

What can we do? asked the girl in the raven.

The raven-in-girl spoke slowly. "I believe the queen could restore the border. But she is not yet ready to fly."

When will her foot heal? croaked girl-in-bird.

"I don't know when, or if it ever will," said bird-in-girl.

They were silent for a while, the two creatures on a high branch who were both raven and both girl. Finally, girl-in-raven said, *I think it's up to us then. Let's find my sister.*

CHAPTER TWENTY-SEVEN

I AM BIRDS

The day the owl returned with food to find Bird gone, he flitted through the woods, seeking her. She was not hard to find; she was enormous, easy prey for an owl, who could hear a mouse breathing under the earth. Not hard to find a girl snoring under a pile of leaves.

She walked to find the birds. It took days. She knew the owl must be tracking her. Sometimes she played him a song, then laughed her small hoarse laugh. It took days of walking, following a creek she remembered from her bird-beset walk in. She looked for berries, recalling her father's rule never to touch a white or yellow berry, and to avoid the red ones, but to look for black or blue ones instead—clustering berries like blackberries being safest and best. The season still hung static between winter and spring, but this part of the forest had been abandoned by birds for so long that Bird was able to find a few. She sat by the creek in the golden dusk, watching for fish. She caught a few minnows in her hand and ate them.

She walked for over a day before she met a bird. The first ones had never heard the rumors of the half-bird girl, so she astonished them. She lay under a tree and sang and played to them, in her half-human birdsong, the song she had learned from her mother all her life. She told them that she was a bird-princess and the birds' hero, who knew the way to the Green Home. Word whipped around the forest, and more birds came.

But soon the birds came who had tried to stop her from going to the Puppeteer, or who had heard that tale. These did not trust her. They sat in distant trees, watching her for signs of puppetry. To them, she had to tell the truth. The truth is the last resort of the strategist, and it's a good one. She told them the truth about her dance-language lessons with the Puppeteer. She told them how she had wanted to be queen. Then she told them of the trial of the swan, and the queen's wounded foot, and the raven rescue, and how she learned the swan was her mother. She told them about the killing of the Puppeteer, of how she was trapped there, and what she learned from the old crow. She told them everything.

(Or she thought she did. She did not tell them about the flying boy, but that was because she forgot. She could not quite keep that boy in her mind, because he did not fit with the story she was making. That's the trouble with making stories—what doesn't fit tends to drop away, no matter how important.)

Truth has a wild beauty and power, and this new story—this true story—pulled in many more birds. At first dozens came to hear her; then hundreds; then many, many more. Bird collected followers; she collected a host. She told them all: *I know the way to the Green*

Home. I am the queen's daughter, and she gave me the map. Follow me.

Some birds argued that they should wait for the queen to heal, but Bird said: *No one knows how long that may take, or where she is, or if she will ever heal. I am here now. I have the map.*

Bird walked on, singing her human nursery rhyme, then singing and playing the song in bird, translating it verse by verse. The smaller birds, who live only a year or two at most, had never been to the Green Home, though they had heard the stories told by other birds, as well as the deeper, aching stories told by their own magnetic bones.

But with so many birds following the princess now, from so many places, there were always one or two who recognized the landmarks in a verse. Some birds who were older, or who had known older birds—raptors, or seabirds, or one who had once spoken to an ancient albatross—had their own fragments of knowledge about the way to the Green Home. So as Bird played and sang, the birds chattered and sang: *That verse must mean this mountain, that lake, that desert. I know that place. I know.*

So Bird walked, and the trees around her filled with chattering birds. And as the mass of birds around her increased, so did its gravity, so did its pull. And more and more birds joined Bird's host.

The owl watched. Owls know how to hide and watch. When there were almost a million birds, he flew off to inform a friend.

As the owl flew, for the second time in her life, Summer also flew: on a cloud of ravens, in a rain of beating wings and harsh cries, small muscled bodies struggling beneath her, the ripple of beating wings under and around her, little claws digging into her clothes.

In her first ride on the raven cloud, she had lost her balance, turned and tumbled across a throbbing blanket of birds, always about to fall, but never falling. This time she rode the ravens like a boat on a black, stormy sea.

Once, when they had flown for hours, Summer saw her own raven beating the air beside her, looking at her through one blue eye.

Summer looked back through one of her own.

Through one eye each, their minds met on the thread of sight, and Summer felt the comfort of the raven mind within and around her.

"I'm still inside myself," she said, over the wind, but in her own voice, from her own mouth. "But I am inside you, too."

And I am still inside myself, and inside you, too, said the raven, in raven caws—and Summer understood her, just as she had in the Green Home.

"Is it because we're flying to the Green Home that I can understand you?" Summer asked, then added, "But I can't understand the other birds. Only you."

The Green Home so near, that may help, said the raven. *But also, maybe we have just visited within each other enough that now we are at home in each other's hearts. I don't know. I have never had a human friend like you.*

Summer smiled. "Me either," she said.

Soon the ravens approached a low mountain—soft grass at the bottom, dark trees in the middle, and snow at the very top. As the ravens sank to the ground, Summer heard, from the other side of the mountain, a faint, rhythmic crash, like enormous jaws crashing slowly together, over and over. They were that close to the attainable border. She felt cold.

The ravens placed Summer gently at the edge of a white plain, as white as her own plain, that first plain, Ben's plain. But this one was far larger, stretching farther than she could see. In the mass of black feathers, Summer sought out her own raven friend, blue- and black-eyed, and with deep relief, found her nearby. Her attention, like that of all the ravens, was fixed to the sky. Summer could see nothing there, but she was a girl standing among the ravens, so she gazed up as well, and waited.

The sky changed. A line of greenish-black clouds came up on the horizon. *Tornado weather,* Summer thought. The line of clouds stretched as far as she could see, twisting and roiling, as if they were alive. As the clouds covered more of the sky, it grew dark as evening, the whole sky obscured by a cloud like an enormous sea creature, muddy gray-green-black, moving and twisting restlessly.

Out of the turbulent sky came a single sharp sound. A bird. And something in that cry changed what Summer saw: not a twisting mass of clouds stretching across the sky, but birds, millions of them, un-countable millions of birds.

A second cry, and a smaller mass of birds detached from the large one, sailed toward them. And there she was, a small, dirty girl, hair streaming behind her, riding this cloud of birds. Bird's head was flung back in triumph or ecstasy, and she was gazing at the sky. *What is she looking for?* Summer wondered, following Bird's gaze. Then she saw that Bird was not looking for something in the sky. She was looking away from the ground. She was afraid. "Oh, Bird," said Summer to herself. Her sister, who had always been so terrified of heights, riding a flock of birds across the sky.

The flock that bore Bird settled on the clay a hundred yards away from Summer. Then, after a long, eerie silence made of wings on wind, the whole black sky descended. Now millions of birds ranged the plane behind Bird, as far as Summer could see. Hundreds, even thousands, still darted in the now-blue sky above.

The birds held their silence. The wind caught Bird's sky-tangled hair and pulled it up behind her, then let it go again. She looked fevered and strange. Even from this distance, her eyes were electric.

Magnetic soul, thought Summer. She felt triumphant to have found Bird so quickly, but she also felt afraid.

Stepping toward Bird, Summer felt all that stood thick and hard between them. And she felt reluctant to tell this strange girl, ozone still swirling in her hair, that she had come to fetch her home. She spoke as if she had seen her the day before, and her fear made her smile a false smile.

"Hey, Bird," she said. "Wow, you've got a lot of birds with you," she added, in a pretend voice.

Bird watched.

"Bird, I was worried for you. Bird, I brought—I have food with me if you want some."

Bird watched.

Summer rained inside. Abandoning the pretend voice, she called, "Bird, I'm scared. You're scaring me. Please talk to me. Please."

Bird watched. A crow hovering above her coughed out a crow-call. Bird looked up. (Thinking what? What? Summer used to be able to tell.)

Summer pulled the apple from her pocket and walked toward her sister. She is only a small Bird, she said to herself, hiding her fear. Foolish to fear her own little Bird.

But this was not her own Bird.

Pale beneath the brown. Thin, dirty, tired. "Can you hear me, Bird? Why don't you say something?"

For a moment, Bird looked lost. She lifted her recorder to her mouth and looked at Summer. Then Summer saw: she had forgotten how to talk. It might have been funny—forgotten how to *talk*?—except that it was not funny to Bird, lost between two worlds, nor to frightened, uncertain Summer.

Bird put the recorder down. "Ah," she said.

"That's right," said Summer.

"Ach-gg," said Bird.

"Keep trying, please," said Summer.

"Bah," said Bird.

"Yes!" said Summer. "That is almost you!"

"Bah. Bahd."

"Bird, Bird."

"Brr. Brrrrd." Her tongue fumbled. She looked at the apple in Summer's hand.

"Yes, apple!" said Summer. "Here, please." Bird's eyes were burning, her whole body was like a thin brown flame, but her hand did not lift to take it. So Summer broke the apple into fragments and slipped them into Bird's mouth with her own fingers.

Oh Bird, look at me and say "Summer," thought Summer. Bird said nothing, only ate the apple and looked at Summer with too-bright eyes. But in a little while, she began to look better, more present in her own skin, less pale.

"Bird, why are you here?" asked Summer aloud. After a silence, she said, "Bird, why did you leave me that night?"

"B. B. Bird," said Bird, carefully.

"You are Bird," said Summer.

"I am birds," Bird agreed. Her voice was raspy and strange.

Standing before the million-bird host, the two girls touched each other: face, shoulders, chest, arms, hands. In silence, Summer pulled leaves and sticks from Bird's hair. In silence, Bird ran her hand up and down Summer's sleeve. After a while, they sat on the ground. Summer wrapped her arms around her sister, who was shivering as she never did, and continued to pull bits of forest from Bird's hair.

Then Bird pulled away from Summer and stood, hand out into the air for balance, like a wing, her face turned toward the great mass of birds. Her eyes darkened; her throat must have darkened, too; and she began to sing. Something like singing—a sound that followed a pattern, at least. But it was no song Summer could sing along with her, nor even understand. It was singing like sticks breaking, like chips of ice flying from under a chisel, like little whistles, like coughs and sighs.

But it did make a song, even Summer could tell that. It made a birdsong.

"Bird," said Summer. "I don't understand."

Bird was silent, and her birds were silent, too—until one song answered her, and then another. And then the songs wove together in a little symphony of song.

Summer looked at Bird, who was crying. "It's my heart," said Bird.

(*Heart*, thought Summer. *Heart and flute and bird claw. Her song is all three.*)

"Bird?" she asked. She saw that Bird was worn and tired, caught between her world and the birds. She saw that Bird was just a little girl. But resentment had stepped to the front of Summer's heart, so she pushed on. "What are the birds saying now? What did you say to them?"

"I said you are my sister and my—" Bird paused in confusion. "I said you are my sister, and my nest."

For a moment Summer's heart half broke, half cracked, opening to let her sister in. But Summer's own envy and fear pushed her cracking heart closed. Stiffly, she plowed on, describing the ruin of the attainable border, the danger for the birds. Bird backed away from Summer as she spoke, as if to set herself apart from this news.

"But Mom and Dad are safe," Summer finished, "and they'll be so glad to see you, they've been crazy-worried. They've been fighting, I think. And you'll be so glad to see them."

"Mom I'll be glad to see," muttered Bird, and Summer felt a stab of misgiving—it would not be all right, her family, not all right ever again. Again, her heart tried to crack open, and again she pushed it shut, talking right over Bird.

"But so the point is, it's all right now," said Summer brightly. "We got here in time. You just have to stop them now. You just have to tell the birds it's not time yet, that they should turn back, and then I'll bring you back and everything will be—"

"Summer," Bird interrupted her in her clear, husky voice. "Stop talking a minute so I can tell you. It might be too late. I thought I was bringing the birds here, and I think at first I was. At first I really was. But it's been different for the past couple of days. It seemed like I wasn't bringing them anymore. It seemed like they were bringing me." She looked uncertainly across the plain, at the waiting birds. "I don't know if I can make them do what I say anymore. It's different now. But I will try."

Bird turned to face the bird-covered earth, and an answering quiver rippled across her host. She pulled her recorder from her pocket. Summer understood none of it, of course, but this is what Bird said, in her girl's bird-voice, singing and playing on the small flute:

We have to wait. Wait. The Green Home is not ready for us yet.

As her message was passed backward, there was a stirring and a rising chatter, mile after rapid mile. The crest of noise moved like the patter of a storm, gathering sound as it ran.

Bird sang more loudly: *We have to—because the border isn't open. It's dangerous, right now.* Her voice felt small. She did not feel like the princess who had flown on the backs of her people through storm and night sky. She felt like a girl who was near crying because seeing her sister reminded her of home.

But Bird was enough of a princess to feel the uneasy throb in her host, their bird-bodies longing to lift from the ground and fly over this mountain to home. She felt it herself. Almost there, how could they wait? More and more birds were now joining the birds in the air, darting and circling above the host, swinging in wide arcs together, every arc closer to the mountain. The million birds on the ground felt like a single bird trembling on the verge of flight.

Flight to death and destruction.

Bird felt panic. To be so close, to have brought the birds so far, and into such danger. For a moment, in her mind, the bird-thick ground ran with blood. She turned back to Summer.

"I can't keep them," she cried over the rising, roaring protest of the birds. "We're too close. Even I feel it, I feel this pull to just go, just be there, no matter what. It's hard." Bird turned back to the trembling host. "I don't think they can wait, or at least I'm not strong enough to make them," she continued, almost to herself. "They're fighting their own bodies as hard as they can. But they can't fight that hard for very long. I brought them here, and now they're all going to die." Her face was pale and set and wild.

Summer was at a loss. Even she felt the faintest ache as her blood pulled beyond the mountain. Her own raven stood on a rock a few yards away, but the other ravens had already joined Bird's millions. The mass of birds on the plain felt furiously powerful, a single engine ready to explode. How long could they wait?

CHAPTER TWENTY-EIGHT

QUEEN ENDGAME

The two sisters faced each other on the plain.

"Bird, come on," said Summer. The wind tossed her hair across her face and back again, and fear made her chest tight and her voice too loud. "Stop freaking out. You must know some way. Think of something to say to stop them."

Bird was staring straight ahead, just past Summer, as if Summer weren't there. Her face was blank. "I'm not freaking out," she said.

"Look, don't worry then," said Summer, thinking hard. "I'll deal with it. If you can't stop them—maybe I can ask the ravens."

"Ravens won't help," said Bird, almost too softly to hear.

"Well, we have to try something," said Summer. "It'll be fine, I'll fix it, I'll figure something out." She spoke lightly to hide her rising panic.

"Don't want you to fix it," said Bird, still soft, not fooled.

"Well, we don't really have any choice, do we?" said Summer, more sharply than she meant.

"Maybe I can do it," said Bird, "if you just—"

"Don't worry about it," said Summer.

"I can—"

"I'll deal with it," said Summer.

"DON'T INTERRUPT ME," Bird shouted, and behind her, a million birds started up into the air with a sound like roaring water. "STOP INTERRUPTING ME, SUMMER. NEVER INTERRUPT ME AGAIN."

The blue-eyed raven flew to Summer's shoulder. There was absolute silence. Summer's heart thudded as if she'd been slapped. She felt afraid of her little sister, and saw that her plan to lead her home by the hand had been wrong and small.

The bird host hovering above them pulsed like a single heart.

"I—" said Summer.

"STOP TALKING," said Bird. Her face was red and wet but her voice was hard. "It's my turn to talk."

Summer felt anger rising up like a wave, but she held her tongue.

"You think you're queen," continued Bird. "But you're not the queen of me, and you never will be. You NEVER will be. You're not my queen and you're NOT MY MOTHER."

Now Summer's face was red, but she said nothing.

"You don't just get to BE a queen," said Bird. "You have to earn it. I learned the bird language. I learned the map. I led these million birds here. What have you done?"

Summer's mouth was flat and her eyes were bright.

"WHAT HAVE YOU DONE?" shouted Bird. The pulsing birds surged out, withdrew, surged further.

"I found a bird to be my friend," said Summer, her voice quiet and shaking. She heard how small it sounded next to what Bird had done. "And I can talk to this bird, my friend, at least," she added. "And I—I helped an egg to hatch, and I—"

"How is that QUEEN?" shouted Bird. "SO WHAT, an *egg*. I'll show you what a queen should be."

"But Mom said I'm the queen. I'm sorry, Bird, but she told me I'm the queen—"

"But how can that be right? It's not fair! I should be queen!"

Summer's anger boiled over. "I have been to the Green Home, and you haven't!" she shouted. "I have been to the border, Bird. I gave up my map that would have got us home to find you, TO FIND YOU. I have *been a bird*. I have been a bird, have you done that?"

"All right all right shut up!" screamed Bird. She looked ready to fight or collapse. "But then who am I?" She fell down to one knee, put her hand on the ground to balance, through tears of fury and grief. "Then Summer, who am I, who am I, if you are queen?"

From the sky above them came an echoing, terrible trumpet call. Both girls looked up, blinking against the bright sky. Both saw a motley flock of forest birds bearing a swan as still and proud as the prow of a ship.

But only Bird understood the swan's call: *She is not queen,* said the swan's trumpet. *Neither of you is queen. I AM THE QUEEN.*

An energy ran through the pulsing bird host, like fire along a fuse. *It is the queen,* said the energy.

The swan's flock turned again, closer to the host, like a dog chivvying a mass of sheep. The swan lifted her throat and called, a long trumpeting cry, so loud it echoed against the mountain behind her and sprang back into the air, doubled in sound.

Even those birds who had been born long after she disappeared heard her voice in their blood and responded. *It is the queen.* Bird's eyes filled with tears as she listened.

Wait, called the swan. *I ask you to wait. Allow me to protect you and your children, as I have failed to do for so many years. Wait, just a little while, and I will open the border for you, and we will meet in the Green Home. I know it is difficult, but you must wait.*

The throbbing bird-heart slowed. Its pulse became ragged, uneven.

The swan-bearing birds—crow and cardinal, sparrow and wren, blackbird and robin—descended to the open space between the bird-mass and the mountain. Summer saw that behind the swan, sprawled unsteadily on his stomach, was their father, holding a small black-and-white cat in one arm. Sarah leaped lightly to the ground, while their father scrambled and rolled off. Finally, the swan dismounted, wincing as she landed, and her bearers flew off to join the greater mass.

The swan limped toward the bird host and stood, a few yards away from Bird, her head high, breast pressed against the wind as if it alone could hold back the host. Birds swirled above her head, a whirlwind of wings.

What do you say, my people? she asked. *Will you wait?*

One by one, and then in twos and threes, the birds swirling in the air returned to the ground. Their fiery silence was like a single animal poised to spring: *We will wait, queen, because you ask. But we cannot wait for long.*

Summer turned to her father, who was standing next to her. "How did you—" she said, just as he said, "It's crazy how we—" But then they both stopped talking. Bird was approaching the swan, and the swan was limping forward to meet her.

For a moment the two stood facing each other. Summer's father, misunderstanding the silence between them, called out, "Bird! She's your mother!" The swan, startled, turned toward him.

And with two fast strides across the white ground, Bird threw herself on the swan's back, hands around her throat. The swan's throat twisted in her hands, just as it had in Summer's hands, but, like Summer, Bird did not let go.

The swan's throat was one long muscle, and as the swan twisted her neck Bird was flung from side to side. But she wrapped her legs tight around the bird's fat stomach, silk against her ankles and arms, and held on. Summer had the curious sensation that she was watching an old home movie. Is that me or is it Bird, this time? Her father, distressed, walked a few yards from the wrestling bird and girl, but no closer.

Silk against Bird's skin, silk over powerful muscle. Her mouth was pressed against the swan's side, and she spoke in broken, urgent bird language. *It should be mine,* Bird said into the silk and the power. She was sobbing, but she was not letting go. *I brought them here. I brought them to show you. I proved it, I proved I am the leader of birds. I am a bird, I am almost a bird, I am!* She wrapped her legs tighter. *I tried so hard!* she cried. *I am so close. I am not letting go, I am not letting go, until you give me the robe, or make me a bird. Just make me a bird! Mama,* she sobbed, and her hands loosened, and now it was only her arms around the swan's neck, and the swan twisting to pull one protective wing over the weeping girl. *Mama,* she wept, *why won't you, why won't you make me a bird like you.*

"What is she saying?" said Summer to herself, or to her raven, still perched on her shoulder.

But no one could hear them now. In the curtain of white silk, two heads, one slender, white, feathered; one brown, tangle-haired, wet with tears.

Listen, said the swan, in their private space apart from the millions-host, apart from the hovering father and the sister, puzzled, hanging back. *Listen,* said the swan, *listen sweet, listen birdlet, best girl. I named you Bird the day you were born. I felt the air in your bones, I saw your open hungry mouth. Your blood called to me in the old way, the way your father and your sister do not know. Summer will learn it someday, I hope. But you have always known—you have been my Bird from the day you were born. You were my only connection to my true life, to my people, to my home. You shared my bird soul. Yes, you are your father's girl, too, but you are also mine. You are half and half, with a foot in two worlds, in Up and Down, in air and earth. There is no one else like you, in any world. My love, my bird-girl, you are the only one. Don't you see how special you are?*

Two humans, a cat, and a sea of birds silently watched the swan with the girl hidden inside her wing. The wait felt long. Jealousy slid like a snake through Summer's heart, and she saw it slip across her father's face as well. The two birds together, their two magnetic souls. The two dull humans, left aside. Summer turned her face toward the raven on her shoulder, to feel the brush of black feathers again, the warm life against her face. She had this, at least, her animal friend.

Silence, except the breeze ruffling a million feathers, a million tiny feet shifting on dirt.

At last, the swan opened her wings and lifted her head, and Bird rose up, squinting and pushing an arm across her face, wiping snot and tears.

Then, giving her father a birdlike, sideways look, Bird took a hesitant step toward him. He intercepted her in three steps, caught her up in his arms, and held her there, though she was too big to be carried now. At first she struggled to get down, but he whispered in her ear until she cried and held him closer, and kept whispering until she laughed.

Still, when he set her down, she frowned, and walked a little apart from him. As she did so, a small, triangular shadow passed across her body. Summer looked up, afraid the birds were beginning to fly again. But it was just a single bird.

A raptor.

An owl.

"Owl," said Summer, not sure who to warn first. Then the ground disappeared beneath her feet and the air disappeared from inside her, as the owl landed at her mother's side, and the swan bent her head to listen.

Summer could not move. It was an owl who had betrayed Bird, had caused all this—all *this*—in the first place. Destroyed her home. Driven her parents apart, maybe forever. "That owl—" she began to her father.

"That's how we came here," her father was saying. "That owl. He came to visit the sw—your mother, and they talked a long time. Afterward—you know how she'd been avoiding the birds? But afterward she went into the forest and called and called. It was the call a swan uses to gather her young. I assumed she was calling you. You shouldn't have left."

"But she wasn't calling me."

"No. She was calling those birds, all the birds that could hear her, and more, hundreds of birds came, maybe a thousand. And they brought us here. And I have no idea what's happening."

You brought them here, the owl was saying to Bird. *I did not think you could.*

Bird said bitterly, "I thought I did. I thought I controlled them. But that was stupid. Their whole bodies wanted to come. I just had the song, I knew the way. It was barely a touch, and they came. Now I don't know how to stop them."

It was not your strength then, said the owl. *And it is not your weakness now. You might as well stop water from running downhill. Even the queen's word will only hold them a few hours, at best.*

"Why is that owl *screaming*?" asked Summer. "It's ugly." Her voice was black and angry. She hated being deaf to birds. She walked away.

As Summer stalked down the white clay, the raven brushed her wing against her, tiny bird-bones under soft feathers skimming the down on her face. Summer's sore heart felt a surge of gratitude.

She sat down in the shade of a mountain pine, far from her family. She looked at the dirt, and the raven looked at the sky. The silence comforted her, and gave her room to say her heart. "Everyone is a bird but me," she said. "Everyone but me and my father. We're the clueless ones. We're like foreigners here. I don't understand what's happening. And I will never be queen."

The raven said nothing.

Summer said, "Can I ask you something about the owl?"

Of course.

"I know he's the one who—" This was hard. "He's the one who, he found Bird and told her—and because of him, my family—" She stopped.

The raven rocked back and forth on her tough little claws. She looked out over the rippling, sighing sea of birds. Light filtered through wind-shifting branches and played over her face, light and dark.

The owl does not fit inside the birds' story, said the raven, at last. *That makes him hard for us to understand. Maybe impossible. Even when he helps us, his help looks like hindrance or hurt.* She paused, began again. *Sometimes his story…intersects with the birds' story, as it did with your family's story. When that happens, he is sometimes a villain, for the birds. Or for you. But it's just the intersection, do you see?* Summer was not sure she did see, but she tried. *And sometimes he is something much different from a villain,* the raven continued. *But then, too, it's just the intersection. At least, this is what I believe.*

They were silent as Summer turned this over in her mind. Then the raven continued, *The queen knows him, and seems to trust him. And we may need his help. Your mother is not yet healed, but we have no choice. The birds are so close that the pull of the Green Home is almost irresistible. Your mother did what Bird could not in holding them a few hours. But if she does not open the border soon, they will pour into its jaws and be killed.*

"How can we even get there that quickly?" asked Summer. "It would take us more than a day, maybe two days, to get to the top of that mountain. Let alone down the other side." She remembered her trip here on the back of the raven cloud. So: "If we have to? If there's no choice, can't you make the ravens—"

The ravens are not my puppets, or yours, said the raven. Her caws stayed calm and level, but Summer felt ashamed. *Not anyone's. But you're right: we'll have to ask them for help, one last time.*

"Why are you so sad?" asked Summer.

It will be dangerous for them to fly so close to the attainable border, replied the raven. *They may not be able to stop themselves from flying through. But of all the birds, the ravens have the best chance of returning safely. Even then, we will have to walk the last mile or two ourselves, though it will be very hard on your mother's foot.* She was silent for a moment. *I will ask,* she said finally, and leaped into the air.

As Summer watched from a distance, the raven soared above the million birds and the little group of man, Bird, cat, swan, owl. She cawed and cawed her message to the ravens: *It is dangerous. We may die. Will you join me?*

The shifting among the birds became a tremor, then a rolling movement across the whole host. Then, as far as you could see, here and there across the host, black birds began to lift into the air. Black flecks dotted the sky like pepper in soup, then coalesced into a swelling black cloud.

We need all of us, the raven cawed, *every one.*

Stand together, she cried to the swan and her party. *We will come for you.*

The ravens left them near the foot of the mountain, on the far side. They circled for a few moments, whipped on toward the border by bones and blood. Summer's raven called, *No! Go back!* The owl flew among them, diving and snapping, pushing them back. The swan gave a long, commanding call. Finally the ravens turned and flew back toward safety, to join the mass of birds on the other side of the mountain—all but one, who swept back low through the air, to land on Summer's shoulder.

"No, it's too dangerous," said Summer.

But you might need me, said the raven. *And I think it will be all right, if you hold me close to you.* So Summer carefully tucked the bird inside her jacket, allowing only her head to emerge. She was warm and throbbing there, a second heart. *That was the bravest and hardest thing the ravens have ever done,* she said. *To come so close to the border and go back. I am so proud of my people today.*

They walked for an hour or two, mostly in silence, toward the border. They were seven: in the lead, a swan whose limp, which at the little red house had nearly healed, was now returning, and a young girl, recorder in hand, walking beside her. Back behind, following the others who seemed to know the way so surely, were a taller, paler girl, her hand to the blue- and-black-eyed raven peering from her jacket; and a tired, bearded man. The sixth, an owl, darted from branch to branch above them. And Sarah the cat kept her own way, moving from tree to brush near the others, but never beside them.

They rarely spoke, but the woods were not silent. The distant, regular thunder was getting louder.

Bird, staying close to her mother's white silk, was bird enough to feel drawn certainly along the way. *We're leading the others,* she thought. She felt a wild excitement. She felt that a gift was coming. She felt the birthday feeling: soon, soon, and almost there, to the perfect day, the new life. Even the smell of the air filled her with intense joy and longing. Almost there, almost there. This was her bird-bones sensing the Green Home.

The path forked. "Should we—" said their father. "It's this way," Bird interrupted, and the swan nodded.

Drawn by joy, focused on what might be around the next corner, Bird was deaf to the rising, crashing noise ahead. But Summer felt sick;

she had to push herself to go on. She knew what they were approaching, the unbearable crashing of heaven and earth. Bearable now; soon not.

They broke through the firs, and the land flattened out before their feet. Only one stand of trees, just a little ways away, kept them from seeing the horizon that lay ahead.

"And now that the Puppeteer is dead," Bird was saying as they walked, "you know what this means, Mom? It means you can have your castle back. You can go back to live there, as soon as you open the border."

The swan stopped walking. She pushed her face against Bird's side, but said nothing; her bird face was hidden in the folds of Bird's shirt.

Then she lifted her head and said, *That's right. We hope I can. But first I must do something difficult and dangerous. More dangerous than I have told you. I'm sorry.*

Bird translated, and Summer began to speak, but her father interrupted her.

"Tell us now," he said.

CHAPTER TWENTY-NINE

THE LAST
MATCH

When the swan explained, and Bird, with increasing distress, translated, there was chaos. Their father shouted. Bird buried her face in the swan's side, sobbing into the white. The swan herself remained still, tucked neatly into herself, her head down, whispering to Bird.

Summer said fiercely to the raven, "My mother says she needs to fly into those jaws. But that will kill her. She will be killed. I don't understand why. Tell me why."

Think of what you said yourself in the Green Home, Summer, said the raven. *You asked if the attainable border was hungry.*

"But what does that mean?" said Summer. "What does it have it do with—" she asked.

The border is hungry. The Green Home is hungry. It needs a sacrifice.

"What about all the birds who have been killed there already—why aren't they enough sacrifice? Why does it need more?"

Because when those other birds died, it was only tragic. It was only a terrible, sad accident. It was not done with intention. It was not done intending to create something sacred. That's what a sacrifice is.

"It was my mistake, not hers," said the father. His voice was harsh with not crying. "It should be me."

The raven said, *It only wants the one who leads the birds to the attainable border.* She glanced again at the owl here, uneasily, then resumed. *That is the only sacrifice the border will accept. So we have to hope that her foot has healed enough to allow her to run, so that she can fly through. Otherwise—not just those million birds on the other side of the mountain will die. If the Green Home remains closed forever, all the birds will die without it. They are near to dying now.*

Summer asked, "Are we the mistake?" Her voice felt small in her throat. "Me and Bird, is that the mistake that closed the border?"

The swan lifted her head and called, a long, sad clarinet line of melody.

"She says," said Bird hoarsely, turning her face but keeping it pressed to the swan's side, "that we are a beautiful mistake. A precious mistake. A mistake she would make ten thousand times over." At this the swan shook her head, furiously.

"Then, no, wait," Bird said, straightening a little. "Not 'mistake.' She isn't saying 'mistake,' exactly. I think it's more like—" The swan called again, one poignant measure. "It's something more like 'out of balance,' what she's saying. Like she made the world go out of balance. Like she leaned over too far into human, into us"—she glanced at her father—"into all three of us. And she forgot birds. She forgot she was a bird. And she's the queen, so what she does, or doesn't do, or forgets, that affects things, in the world, in her world. In this world."

She paused while the swan crooned another forlorn and tender phrase. "She says she loved to lean toward us," said Bird, her voice breaking again. "She says she would do it a thousand times again."

Their father reached out to touch the swan; pulled back.

But that made this place a wasteland, said the swan, a clarinet playing a slow sad song in a dark room. *And the birds are dying without their true Green Home. I must correct the imbalance. I must lean too far in the other direction. I must offer myself to the Green Home. And trust it to take me back, or to destroy me, as it sees fit.*

The raven softly translated for Summer while Bird wept, louder now. Summer said, "But, no" in a shaking voice.

I think I might live, sang the swan, as the raven softly repeated the words beneath her. *I might, somehow. I am the largest bird, and the strongest. My ancestors were goddesses, were choosers of the slain. And I am the queen. Only I wish my foot had healed completely. I should not have bound it up for so many years.*

Her daughters wept and clung to her. Their father turned away. "Why can't it be me," he said to the dark trees. "It's my fault. It should be my sacrifice."

This time Summer interpreted for him, following the raven's low, rough translation. *No,* said the swan. *I forgot my soul was hidden. I let myself forget. That's the only part I regret, the forgetting. You should make a sacrifice like that with eyes open and clear. Just as I am doing now.*

∽

In the rising noise of crashing sky and earth, but in a silence of their own, they walked through the darkest wood Summer had ever known. Even her raven, as the noise grew unbearably louder, had hidden herself deep within Summer's jacket. She was alone. Her mind, her clever, searching, solving mind had turned its back on her, closed up, left her alone. Her body knew her mother was about to die, and that was all she was made of now. And she could not even be with her, because this large, limping white bird, ungraceful and foolish on land, stood between them.

Instead, Summer walked behind, with her father, who did understand, who still thought of ways to fix it, to make it right, thinking hard to keep his heart from breaking open and spilling a thousand seeds of grief that would grow into vines that would strangle him.

They broke through the last of the tall trees into open, rocky ground. The horizon was still far away, much farther than when Summer first saw it in the Green Home. But the distorted, curving landscape, the sealed mouth of the horizon, the slow, widening jaw were all the same. Bird's fingers dug into the swan's feathers. The swan herself had turned her head away. All the terror of her time at the border rising up, Summer turned to her father for comfort. He was on his knees, vomiting. Beyond him, in the trees, Summer saw a flash of black and white—Sarah taking cover back in the woods.

The swan turned to give her family one last, loving look. Then she began to limp down the rocky hill toward the border. She picked up speed, but awkwardly, thudding heavily on her injured foot. Finally, she raised her wings—but she did not lift into the air. She had not been fast enough.

She trudged back a few yards, limping more painfully, to try again.

"She can't do it," breathed Bird.

"Thank God," said their father.

"She will this time," said Bird, defensive.

But once again, the swan pelted awkwardly down the hill; again, her lifted wings took her no higher than the lifted arms of a child running down a field.

"She should give up," said Summer.

"Then a million birds will die," said Bird. "She will never give up,"

"Then she will die," said Summer. Her own heart was a forest fire, but her living second heart, her raven heart, still beat against her chest.

"Bird," she said softly.

"What," said Bird, not looking, wiping her nose.

"We can't let her die," said Summer.

Bird laughed a sharp, hiccuping laugh like a sob. "Yeah, what are you going to do?" she said. "Do you have a magic feather in your pocket you can burn, to call some super-bird to save her?"

"No, I don't," said Summer, "but there must be some way. Because it can't be right that Mom has to die, that we did all this so that Mom could die. That can't be right. There must be some way to—to make it safe to go through, to find a way to, to, like, prop up the sky." As she said it, she heard how stupid it sounded, and she was opening her mouth to take it back.

But Bird—because however angry she was, Bird still had a younger sister's belief in her older sister—had turned to face her. "You mean like with a tree?" She frowned. She watched the swan limping back up the hill.

"I guess but—it would have to be such a tall tree and such a strong one, and there aren't any trees like that here, so—"

"Well, there aren't any trees like that anywhere," said Bird.

"No, there's one," said Summer, defensive. "I saw it, I lived in that tree, a thousand feet high, for a long time before we—" even now it was hard to say. "Before we found you, that first time at the castle," she concluded awkwardly.

Bird looked doubtful. "So how did you get down, then, from such a tall tree? Did the birds come get you there?"

"No," said Summer, distracted "No, look, it's complicated, but no, something came up to—"

She stopped. Something hovered at the edges of her burning-forest heart, some idea, some way out. Anger and terror still washed over her, waves and waves of hot rain, but suddenly, for a moment, she was not the rain, only herself. She was listening to her heart, to both her hearts, animal and human.

When the sky has teeth, said her heart.

A line from the old song. She looked up at the horrific jaws the sky had become. The sky had teeth now, that was certain. So what did the song say? "When the sky has teeth,/And the road is closed…" Was that right?

"Bird," said Summer, as if she were half asleep. "How does it go, that one part of the song, about when the sky has teeth. Tell me. It might help."

"Oh," said Bird, too dumbstruck to argue. "Oh, yeah, I know that part, but—but Summer, I already know what it means, it's this thing that happened in the castle."

Summer heard Ben's voice under her own as she said, "Bird. Nothing important means only one thing."

"But…okay. Okay! So it goes 'When the sky has teeth'—wait, that's not right."

"Bird, hurry, hurry, please."

"'When the'…oh, I know! 'When the old road ends,/And the sky has teeth,/A cygnet must look/For what lies beneath.'" She paused. "But how can that, I don't see how that can—" And she broke off. A noise, over the mountain. A noise getting louder, a hurricane wind, a thousand squeaking gates: the biggest flock of birds you ever heard.

The birds were coming.

The owl was already in the air, scouting, swinging back. He landed on the grass between the swan and her family.

They will be here in two minutes, said the owl. *Perhaps three. They could wait no longer.*

Then if I can't fly across, I must run, said the swan.

Running may not work, said the owl. *And even if it did, you will not make it in time.*

I have to try, she said, and once again began her limping, loping run down the hill. But a swan does not run fast at the best of times, and a swan with an injured foot is slow, slow.

She will never make the border before the birds arrive, said the owl. *All those birds will die.*

"No!" said fierce Bird. "I brought them here. I can't let them die. There must be something we can do!"

The owl turned his head to face her. His eyes burned gold at her. *Only the one who leads the birds here can make the sacrifice,* he said. *Normally, that means the queen. No one but the queen has ever led the birds to the border. Before today.*

He watched. Bird stood stock-still for a moment. Then, without a goodbye, without a speech, without a word, she turned and ran directly toward the border's clashing jaws.

From the swan came a cry of pure terror as her youngest daughter ran past her.

From their father, a scream of rage as the owl came at him hard, wings spread and talons outstretched to stop him from running after Bird.

The owl's help always looks like hindrance or hurt.

And Summer stood still. She watched Bird run, and the swan run after her, and her heart said, *No*.

No, my sister won't die. My mother won't die. A million birds will not die. No one will die.

I say, No.

She felt the snake scale in her pocket. *Do you have a magic feather in your pocket?*

Snakes are old birds.

Without another thought, Summer ran, ran straight toward the roaring border with the snake scale in her hand. And as she ran, she reached into her other pocket and pulled out the last match.

Behind her, her father's shouts, her mother's bird-screams.

Ahead of her, the bravest girl she knew, short legs pumping wildly down the slope. She remembered the day Bird had found the way Down and led her there; she was leading the way again. Summer caught up, grabbed her by the arm, swung her roughly to the ground, shouting, "Wait, Bird, WAIT, please, just one second. WAIT!"

Summer stopped as close to the border as she dared, lit the match, and held it to the scale. It exploded in a shower of sparks, and Summer remembered the moment she threw the burning match onto Ben's tree. She dropped the scale to the ground, watched it move and sizzle like a living thing until it lay melted, black, and still.

Nothing happened. The jaws of the sky were sighing open, up, up, up, and in the windy silence Summer heard her father's shouts and the swan's trumpet behind her, coming closer.

She heard the noise of a million birds cresting a mountain.

She saw Bird standing, holding her arm, preparing to run again.

"Please, please, please," she said to nothing.

The soft ground beneath the burnt scale began to move. A ridge of crumbling black earth rose up, as high as Summer's knee, then higher. The shouts and calls behind her died away. Summer waited, trembling. Only she knew what was coming. The raven at her heart trembled too, unless it was only the wind.

The earth swelled and stirred, as if the dirt were a blanket over some sleeper, and the sleeper was waking up.

Then the ground erupted, scattering dirt for yards around. Summer's teeth began to chatter; she was overwhelmed for a moment by the memory of the snake's jaws closing around her.

Out of the ground, shaking off dirt, rose an enormous snake. Its eyes glowed yellow and green in the swirling air. Its huge head swept through the air, weaving, seeking. Smelling.

"Rise up!" said Summer. But as the sky-jaws neared the top of their arc, the snake's head rose no higher. The great head rocked and wove, searching for what it smelled and what had brought it here. "No! Rise up! Go higher!" she shouted.

And then somehow she was running straight at the snake, somehow she was grabbing the snake's cold, scaly side. With one pull of her hands and push of a foot, Summer leaped on the snake's back and began to climb. She climbed it like a tree, as if every tree she had ever climbed—every oak and ash at the edge of her forest at home, the owl nest's silver maple, the World Tree itself—as if all those trees were practice for climbing this writhing, twisting, scaly trunk. She dug feet and hands into scales like bark, she clung with legs made strong by wandering, she pushed up and up until she was at the snake's head.

"Get up!" she screamed, as the snake tossed its head and snapped around toward her. The snake was every tree she had ever climbed, but this tree was alive and squirming. Digging her heels beneath the scales, she glanced down to see the swan limping toward the twisting horizon and the crayon-green expanse of the Green Home behind it.

Now. The sky was descending. Summer thrust her hands into the sides of the snake's long flat mouth and pulled with all her strength.

With a deafening hiss—a furious steam engine, a dragon beneath her—the snake rose up, up, thirty feet, forty feet, more. The great black trunk twisted and rolled, but she kept her grip, knees and hands, holding all the darkness and destructive power of the world beneath her own small body. The sky descended, and the blast of air became a gale, but she clung on and on.

And then without warning: stillness. The snake was still. The sky was still. The wind receded.

The World Snake, drawn out of the world's burning heart and bridled by a two-hearted girl, girl heart, bird heart, had caught the sky on the end of its snout. Time hung frozen. Summer held her breath and looked down.

The swan was running. Fierce with terror for her children, the swan had found a new, more desperate speed. Watching from high above, Summer saw, for just a moment, instead of a limping, straining swan, her own tall, black-haired mother, in their own green field, taking down laundry ahead of a storm, when a sudden wind whipped a white sheet around and around her.

Watching, Bird remembered her mother running down that field between their house and the river, chasing a black-and-white cat who was always just ahead of her, pausing, then running again, her mother's black hair tumbling out of its ponytail and over her face as she laughed and ran.

We lose our mothers, and look for them everywhere.

(They did not know, but their father, released by the owl now, saw her running ahead of him that night it had all gone wrong, the robe in her hands, one arm inside it, two, and her lifting into the air: gone.)

The swan's unsteady run grew faster.

"Please," said Bird on the ground.

"Now, now," said Summer in the air.

The limp was gone. The swan lifted into the air. "Oh," said Summer in anguish and pride.

The swan rode the still and silent air between jaws of earth and sky. Summer's heart broke with the rightness of it: a beautiful white bird crossing the border into the Green Home, leading the way for her people.

And then the snake wrenched itself free of the sky, and flung Summer off his back. Her body sailed through the attainable border, just as the swan had.

But Summer was no flier. The raven, her second heart, exploded into the air just a fraction of a second before Summer's body hit the ground.

CHAPTER THIRTY

AND SOMETIMES
AN OLD MAN

A dreadful pause. The snake swayed low and dangerous against the ground, but did not cross the border where Summer lay, where the raven fluttered in circles just above her. The swan was already with her, her small head running over Summer's limp body, her wings arched high with grief.

Bird and her father began to run toward her, until the owl fluttered in front of them, wailing his high, ghostly cry. "Stop!" said Bird. "Wait, stop a second, let me listen." She listened, replied in a brief, soft call, then said, "He says it might not be safe. He says wait." They waited. But the jaws sighed open, open, open—and then held. The crashing and screaming that had seemed like part of the landscape was silent.

And then the sky darkened with birds. The million birds who had waited so long poured across the border with screams of joy, one long, multicolored creature, undulating through the air and into the Green Home.

Who had opened the border? The wounded swan who sailed through? Summer, who held the sky open to save her? Or Bird, whose bright, mad courage inspired her mother and sister to do more than they thought they could?

All three?

✺

"Stay here," said Bird's father grimly. "Stay away from that snake." But the snake was already slithering backward, subsiding into the ground it had erupted from, and Bird, disobedient and afraid, ran behind her father like a small shadow. She slowed down as she approached her family. Around Summer and her parents, both bent low over their daughter, a winter landscape was arising. Frozen brooks. Low, leafless trees hung with ice. The green grass was withdrawing, blackening, lying flat across the land around them. The raven wove anxious circles overhead.

"She's not dead," said her father. But Summer was badly hurt, so badly hurt that it was hard for Bird to look at her. There was blood, and an arm bent backward at a wrong angle, with bone coming through. She lay on the soft grass of the Green Home, perfectly still, breathing fast and shallow. Like the patchwork bird, Bird thought, just before it died; and her heart was swamped with grief.

Their father had torn his shirt to strips, sent Bird to find sticks for splints—"What the hell kind of place is this, no trees, nothing—no, wait, Bird, there's one behind you, don't know how I missed that, bring me sticks." He looked pale and thin and furiously concentrated in the cold air. Summer cried out, though her eyes remained closed.

"You're hurting her," said Bird in tears.

"I'm trying to save her!" he snapped, but he looked near tears himself. His hands and arms were soaked with blood.

The Green Home trembled around the four of them, the swan, Bird, her father, Summer on the ground, as if it did not know what to become or be.

Bird turned her face away; it was unbearable. But as she did, from the corner of her eye, she caught a flash of red in the sky. It was a bird, a small red bird, boring through the air like a flaming arrow, directly toward Summer.

Summer lay on her back, floating on a dark river. Her mouth and eyes were filled with black water, and the river bore her away.

Away from? Away from family, away from self, away from life. To a new and lonely country.

Summer wanted to cry out, to say that she was lost; that she was afraid; that the river was pulling her away. But her voice drowned in the black water, and she was only alone.

And then: someone was floating beside her, a warm, dry hand on her own. A boy's voice soft in her ear: *Hello, forget-me-not eyes. Hello, sunshine hair.*

Who? she said, in bubbles of black water. *Who are you?*

Cranberry birdlet, murmured the voice. *Little fireplug. Mama's lipstick.* He laughed, and his laugh was a shower of light through her wracked body.

The black water beneath her began to drain away.

Bens, said Summer, still water-blind, as she sank toward the riverbed.

My name is Ash now, said the voice.

How did you find me? she asked.

Someone called my father out of the earth, said Ash. *I heard him rumble and hiss. I came to see why.*

They lay together on the warm, dry riverbed, companionable and still. *I would live here forever,* thought Summer.

Now close your eyes, my mother, said Ash. *And be well, be well, be well.*

✺

The others saw a boy who sang softly as he kneeled beside Summer, stroking her, feeling along the lines of her bones. His song made a pool of clear green water, which grew and deepened and became a lake. In the center of the clear green lake was an enormous white water-flower, lower petals spread flat against the surface. Summer lay on the flower, half hidden in the flower's upper petals, and the boy kneeled beside her, touching her wounds and singing.

The swan circled the flower, swimming, sometimes making low sounds of grief.

On the shore, Bird's father reached out a hand to her. But Bird turned away from him and walked to the other side of the lake, where she sat on the blank grass of the Green Home, watching him from across the water. Her heart was a swollen flood held back by a cracking door. The Green Home called her to pour out her heart, but she could not trust human words, so she took her recorder and played a bird-song, a song of sorrow and anger and loneliness.

Behind her arose a cypress tree, long-veined, bending over the lake. It sheltered her as she played, and she let herself lean back against it. When she finished her song, she put down the flute and buried her face in the tree's great roots. She felt a small weight, four delicate paws, on her back, and Sarah slipped down beside her, curled in her arms.

Her mother circled the lake-flower, over and over.

Her father sat across the broad green lake, alone.

So, far from one another, Bird and her parents waited through a long, deep night. The Green Home around the family stopped growing as they fell, first silent, and then into troubled, anxious sleep. The swan slept with her head tucked under a wing, floating a few inches from Summer's flower. Their father stayed awake the longest, but as the air began to turn gray just before dawn, even he fell asleep, face down, fists clenched near his head.

Bird woke up around the same time, but she did not move. Curled in her tree-root nest, cat in her arms, she watched her father's prostrate form with fury in her heart. *All of this is your fault,* she thought, the Puppeteer's poison still flowing in her veins.

So in that cloudy gray light, only Bird was watching when the phoenix-boy stood up in the center of the flower, where Summer lay hidden, and walked across the water. At least, that was how it looked; but then Bird saw a streak of stones that scattered before him across the lake, each stone appearing just before his foot reached it. He walked along it as trustingly as if it were a sidewalk, never even glancing down.

She saw the boy speak to her father, saw her father drop his head down to cry. A rank, icy river ran through her. She pulled Sarah closer: no, no, no, no. The boy walked around the lake toward her, and with each step her body cracked a little open, tiny piercings of air and fear.

The boy stopped a few feet away. Standing above her, he was outlined against the pale morning sky.

"She will sleep for a long time now," he said. "But she will be all right."

He reached out and touched Bird's hair, lightly, lightly. Something red and sore inside her dissolved. She cried, and as if through a rain-drenched windowpane, she saw her father across the lake crying, too. They cried together.

Summer slept for three days and three nights. The others slept a good deal, too. It had been a long journey.

When Summer finally woke, she felt light and unsteady, as if something heavy she had carried for many miles had vanished. A boy was smiling at her, his wide-set eyes creasing down in a way that made her think of Ben. Over his shoulder, her raven perched on the edge of the lotus flower, watching.

Listen, said the raven. Lying on her back, still not fully in this world, Summer listened. She heard something in the distance: a high, excited sound.

"Look," said the smiling boy. "Word must have spread. The sky is full of birds."

Led by the cranes from one direction, by the owl from another, all the birds of the world were coming back to the Green Home.

A little while later, Summer lay on her lotus flower with her head against the swan's breast. A rather damp Bird (she had swum from the shore) sat close by, stroking the swan's neck absently.

"But Bird, how could he be a phoenix?" Summer was saying. "A phoenix is a pretend bird. It isn't real, it's a myth."

"It is a real kind of bird," said Bird. "I heard it was. I heard from a bird he saved. I heard he burns up and then he is born again. And I heard he can heal you, your body or anything, no matter how bad. But ALSO I heard," she added hastily, before Summer could interrupt, "the phoenix I heard about is maybe locked in a tree. She put him there, the Puppeteer did. But I guess there was another."

Summer looked doubtful. "Ash can heal, I know," she said. "But I don't know if I believe in phoenixes."

There is only one phoenix, said the swan. *And he is real, Summer. I met him once before, long ago.* She paused for a long moment. *The stories say he is a red bird with a jeweled crest. But sometimes he takes human form as well, as I do. When the phoenix is near death, he makes an egg to live in until he's ready to be reborn, an egg carved from the wood of trees that are only found in certain places. One of those places is a small white plain that lies near my castle. I wonder if the Puppeteer found him there, and—*

"Wait," said Summer. She had been standing very still. "A red bird, with a jeweled crest?" she asked.

Yes, said swan.

"And sometimes a man? An old man?" she asked.

Sometimes old. In my time, old, yes.

"I think—I might know him. I might have known him. But he— the old man—died. But he gave me an egg, and it hatched a bird, a little red bird—but that was far away, at the top of this—and it was just a baby bird—"

"SUMMER," said Bird. "That was him."

That night, the swan had a long private talk with Ash. The others watched a garden of white flowers grow up around them as the sun set. Afterward, he came to Summer, took her hand, and placed a long red feather inside her palm. "Call me when you need me," he said. "And I will come. I will come even when you do not call."

"I know you, Ash," said Summer. "You are my Bens."

"I am," said Ash. "I am Bens, but I am also more than that. I gave you my red sweater. And you stayed in my house."

"I didn't know that was your house," said Summer, but as she spoke she realized, yes, of course: the pot of food, of course she knew that pot. And the stone like a bird's head with mosaic plumes above the fireplace. And the kindness of the house was Ben's kindness, was Ben's heart: of course it was, of course.

"And you found the door to the sky," Ash said. "And the thunderbird took us to my tree, which has my fruit, so I could be born again, and eat, and live." He moved to her, took her hand, and held it to his forehead.

"Are you the phoenix?" Summer asked.

"I am," he said. "And I love everything on this changing, burning earth, but I am most grateful to you." Then he smiled his wrinkle-eyed smile, so like Ben's that Summer's heart swelled and moved.

Ash visited Bird that night, as well, on the tree limb where she slept. He gave her a feather, too. It was dark, and their hands touched in the dark as she reached for the feather. "I like you, brightness-Bird," said his silhouette against the indigo sky.

"I like you too, Ash," she said, because she knew he couldn't see her.

By dawn, he was gone. That morning, Summer asked the raven, "Is he Ben?"

No, said the raven, *at least as I understand it. He is never Ben again. He is Ash, this time.*

"But is Ben still part of him? He remembered the sweater he gave me. He knew what happened when he was in the egg."

He is a bird. His memories are in his bones, even when his mind is new. Like the memory of a bird who knows it must leave when the sun begins to slant a certain way, and does not ask why.

Behind them, a group of red rocks appeared.

"He thinks I am his mother."

You cared for the egg. You brought it to the thunderbird, you brought it to the World Tree.

"It's so stupid, I thought that big bird saved me. But it wasn't saving me. It was saving the egg."

Or both of you.

Summer was quiet. The rocks had grown into red boulders behind them, like a group that had gathered to listen. Then she said, "But the red bird, Bensbird—he only hatched a little while ago."

The raven coughed her raspy laugh. *Birds grow out of their babyhood much faster than humans do.*

"Ben looked like a human, though."

The raven looked out at the growing landscape. *I saw him once as a bird. An enormous red bird, taller than a man, with jeweled crest.*

Summer remembered her dream on the plain, the red bird who was her mother that night. She remembered the red house that had mothered her through her worst time, when she thought Bird was dead; that had provided a haven for her broken family.

We lose our mothers and look for them everywhere.

CHAPTER THIRTY-ONE

AFTER
THE END

The next morning, the rising sun made the sky pale gold. Summer let the wind run across her face. Scents of pine and smoke and snow came with it, touching her face, rushing past: news from elsewhere, across the border, brought by the beating of a million wings. Summer stood in the sun and let everything fall away—her wishes for what her parents would be; her fear for Bird and her anger at Bird; her love for them all; her love for this place and her fear of it; her exhaustion. With everything fallen away, she was empty. Summer stood, empty in the sun, letting all the smells of the woods and water fly past her and disappear.

In her emptiness she heard, just faintly, a few birds—finches, she thought. They were far off, perhaps by the lake the boy had made, in Bird's cypress tree. She thought she heard a cardinal, too, and sparrows. She understood them, understood the meaning of their calls and song, the feeling and the intention.

"The Green Home," she said gratefully.

A jay rattled past.

Summer listened again. The sound of the wind mixed in with the faint bird sounds, and Summer could not always tell them apart. The whistle and clack and chuckle floated along the air and mixed with the rushing, the whisper, the swish.

Then Summer saw that they spoke to each other. The birds and the wind spoke to each other, and their sounds knitted together to make some new thing.

Summer listened. Heard among the birdcalls something like a chime, but what bird sounds like a chime? The sound died away. Summer let the question go, and let the names go, and listened for that chime again.

After a moment the chime-sound came, then tripled. Then a *click-click-click* sound. Then silence. Then the wind rose a little, stirring the leaves of the cypress. A trilling birdcall followed the wind. Another, making a different, shorter run of notes, followed that. Then three excited chucks: *chuck-chuck-chuck*. The wind waited, then rose again suddenly and shook the leaves. A long, questioning whistle. *Click-click-click.*

And suddenly Summer heard. Heard not just the single calls, but heard the conversation, the way it worked, heard the larger song inside, the wind and the birds and the leaves speaking to one another, asking questions, answering one another, no question unanswered.

"No question unanswered," said Summer aloud. The words she

spoke lifted and twined and knitted among the wind and bird and leaf sounds, and became part of them. A field of sound and meaning loomed together, her own thread caught into the warp and weft of the Great Conversation and woven tightly into the whole.

And Summer knew it would be the same with whatever she said, whatever sound she made, this green field would pick it up and weave it in. And she knew that she was a bird, too, and always had been.

To know that, to know that.

"Heart, flute, claw," she said. And she thought: *Heart is love, and the Puppeteer eating the hearts of the birds, and Bird's half-destroyed heart when she lost her dream. And heart is my second heart, my raven heart, my friend who taught me my animal soul.*

Flute is the conversation that carries the heart, and stories and songs and maps, and that old nursery rhyme. And flute is Bird's flute, and bird-songs.

Claw is our mother's broken foot, and the phoenix's protection, and the raven on my shoulder, and Bird, all birds. And me.

She looked at the tree beside her. *And heart is the heart of the wood,* she thought, *and flute is the branch, and claw is the roots that grasp a handful of earth.*

Her father said, "What a racket, huh?" He was walking up, smiling at her. Summer's heart broke for him, that even in the Green Home, he could not join the conversation.

◌

When she was fully healed, Summer found herself spending more and more time alone. Her father's deafness to the world they lived in made her too sad to be with him for long. Once he came across the owl and tried to strike him. The owl flew up to a branch, just out of reach.

"He's angry because of what you did at the border, when you stopped him from saving Bird," said Summer.

I knew the queen had to run faster, said the owl. *I thought that to save her daughter, she would find the strength. I was right.*

Summer translated this for her father. "That doesn't make it all right," he said angrily, and walked away. She saw less of her father after that. And Bird stayed with the swan or with the other birds, and did not seem to care about Summer's human world.

Or perhaps Bird was angry about the robe.

So Summer spent much of her time alone by the river she had made that day with the raven, the day she had sung her north. Although she did not know it was her river, she knew she loved it and was comforted there.

She sat on its banks, thinking about the robe. She knew she should be delighted, to know it would someday be hers. And already she felt the beginnings of "bird" inside her, already hints of what was electric, magnetic, aloft.

But she felt nothing at all—the idea was horribly hilarious—like any kind of queen, let alone a queen of the birds.

As she turned over these thoughts, her swan-mother, still as a carving, rode her own river reflection toward Summer. Feeling the old heart-seed impulse of the Green Home, Summer spoke.

"I know a little about birds now," she said to the swan, "although I have so much more to learn. But queen—I don't see how I will ever be that. I am made of mistakes. I couldn't even take care of one little sister.

She could have died because of me, more than once. How will I ever take care of a world of birds? I will fail, and ruin everything."

As she spoke, the green of the river clarified, the river bottom deepened.

The two swan-pictures stirred and trembled and opened their mouths, and Summer heard the bird's doubled voice: the swan's low call—a wavering trumpet, a low coo, a throaty clarinet measure—and her mother's rich voice, at the same time.

Oh, Summer, said the doubled swan, in her one-but-two voice. *You are too young. That's why the crown feels so heavy now, because you are still so small. But at the border, you showed the queen that you will be. You used my gifts, and your father's gifts, and every gift the world has given you to make the world you wanted, to fight a world gone wrong. You have many years before you will grow into your crown, but Summer: what a queen you will be. Look in your dreams; they will help you know. They always have.*

That night, for the first time, Summer visited her dreams wide awake and trusting.

"Mom says she has to stay," said Summer miserably to their father. He was angry. The two girls and their father were standing near the edge of the lake, days later, as the sun sank into evening. Summer's raven sat on a branch nearby.

The swan floated nearby, near them, but not of them. The swan had been avoiding their father. She would swim up to her daughters, or even the little black-and-white cat, but she turned her back on him.

"She says she has to stay in Down, to serve the birds, and to make it up to them. Dad, I'm so sorry."

"But I can't stay," said their father.

"You could," said Summer, with hesitation. "But—"

"But I don't belong here," said their father flatly. "I don't hear the conversation you and Bird keep talking about. My words don't make things, or they hardly ever make things. Everyone sees it, even I see it. This place doesn't work for me. It's for the birds." He smiled a wry, tight smile at his joke. "I have to go back," he concluded. "I don't fit here." He added: "I will take the girls, of course. Girls?"

Summer turned her head away. Over the lake, toward the west, a single bare tree stood in black silhouette against the golden-peach sky. Three cranes stood around the tree like black shadow puppets, lifting their heads to the sky, lifting their wings.

Bird was already answering their father, her voice sour. "I won't go back there," she said, as flat as her father. "You belong there. But I belong here."

You will stay with me then, called the swan, *because you are my little girl, and I will care for you.*

Bird turned half away. "But I need to learn to be a bird," she said. "If I won't get the robe, I have to learn another way. I don't want to be only your little girl. I have to go back in the forest."

The swan said, *No, not out in the forest alone, no.* Her call was almost an alarm call.

"What is she saying?" asked the father impatiently.

"Why can't you try to listen?" said Bird.

From above them came a high, soft, guttural cry. *Like a bird purr-*

ing, Summer thought: *cranes.* It was the three cranes, making a wide circle above the water, long legs trailing behind them, crying their long, strange cries. Summer could not understand what they were saying and turned to the raven, her mouth open to ask.

They are old, said the raven. *They speak an old language, one that I do not know.*

The cranes landed to the left of the small group, in the shallows of the lake. They were tall and elegant and alien. They lifted their wings and stepped long, high steps into the air. They nodded and dipped toward one another, and then toward the group.

Bird walked toward them.

"Be careful, Bird," her father called.

Bird ignored him. She heaved out a high, guttural cry and began to dance. It was a dance of angles, lifted arms like wings, the dance she had learned from the Puppeteer. And though Bird was no crane, only a stubby little girl, her dance was exquisite and strange, because she danced not just with her body and not even just with her heart, but with her wounded, hopeful soul. Summer held her breath. Even her father was silent, watching.

When the dance was finished, the three cranes approached her. Now they spoke in the language common to all birds, albeit with a foreign, unaccustomed inflection. *We can teach you,* said the first crane to Bird. *We can teach you more language, and more of the dance. But we can teach you more than that. We can teach your bones to hollow. We can teach your back to sprout wings. We can teach you to fly.*

What you did not inherit, we can teach you, the crane said. *You will never be a common bird, but you can be a true Bird. We will teach you to grow wings.*

Bird decided to go. Her father's anger, the swan's trembling trumpet cry, nothing could dissuade her.

Half with me, the swan begged. The cranes agreed: *You are half one thing and half another,* they said. *It will be better for you that way.* Even Bird looked relieved at that. She would spend half the year in school with the cranes, and half with the swan.

"When will you see Dad?" Summer asked. But Bird had not yet forgiven their father for capturing their mother, for hiding the robe. She had heard the story the wrong way the first time, from the Puppeteer's twisted mouth, and that is hard to forget. The way a story is told has power.

"If he hadn't done it, we wouldn't be here," Summer argued. "Mom says she isn't sorry. And it was the Puppeteer who stole the robe. Dad tried to give it back."

But Bird was stubborn: to capture a bird, to put it in a cage, which was how she saw what their father had done that first day at the river, was the worst thing to her.

"When I am a bird I will lead the other birds to rescue any bird that is in a cage," she said. "Or else I will go alone."

Her father argued furiously, and then reasonably, and then in tears. In the end he had no choice. Summer tried to comfort him. "She's only little," she said. "She's just mad. She'll change her mind. She'll miss you." But he shook his head and turned his face away so that she could not see it.

The raven said: *Bird. Your mother loved your father. He did trick her at first, but the first time she asked for her robe, her soul, he tried to give it back to her. It wasn't his fault that he could not. And she loved him anyway. Love is complicated, more complicated than anyone understands.*

But one day she had to free herself. It doesn't mean she didn't love him, or didn't love you. But when you find your soul, you have to take it. When you remember who you are, you have no choice.

Bird looked at her stubborn, sad father, who had not heard any of this, and although she said nothing, her heart in that moment softened and began a slow turn back to him.

Then Summer spoke. "I am half, too," she said. She turned to face her parents. "I am half mind and half heart, half gladness and half fear. And I am half bird and half human. So I will live half and half, too. Half my life here in the Green Home, with my mother and sister, learning the bird world. And half human, with my father, up above. Can I do that, please?"

The Green Home around her chattered with birds, their conversation its landscape. "I think…" said her father hesitantly, but Summer was thinking of the two rivers she loved, the one by the stone cottage and the one in the Green Home, and her heart was torn in two. He saw it on her face.

"Yes," he agreed. And the swan echoed him from the river with a sad song of assent.

Then Summer had another thought. "Is it possible?" she asked. "I mean: can I leave, and come back? How can I come back?" She turned to her raven, her second heart. "Can I?"

High thin clouds crossed the sun, so that the grass was light and dark, light and dark beneath them.

And then the raven said, *I have an idea. I think you and Bird must* build a bridge—a bridge between the two worlds. A bridge to the world of humans from the world of the birds.

"How?" asked Summer.

I don't know, said the raven. *It has never been done before. You two must decide how. It's your bridge.*

Summer and Bird walked off alone to talk it over.

"A bridge needs to be deep in both worlds, or it won't be safe," said Summer. "It needs to be dug in on each end."

"I will dig the bird side," said Bird.

"And I will dig the human side," Summer said. And they were quiet again, thinking.

"But how will we dig?" asked Bird. "How will we build it?"

"I guess we will have to talk," said Summer. She looked at Bird shyly. Bird was looking straight ahead. They had not really talked for a long time. Maybe they had never talked the way they were about to talk, at least not since they were very, very small.

"I'll start," said Summer. And she began to tell Bird the story of what had happened to her while they were apart. When she got to the part where she found the burned campsite, with Bird's clothes in the fire, Bird put a hand over her mouth.

"You thought I was dead," she said, and her eyes turned red and wet. A wound in Summer's heart began to heal.

Bird told why she left the campsite that day, how she wanted so badly to prove that she could be bird and queen. She told how what she wanted most led her into the Puppeteer's trap, and how she put their mother on trial, and how she chose to go back into what she knew was a cage, because she was too ashamed to go back with Summer and the swan, knowing her dreams had been a stupid, pretend lie.

"But they weren't a lie," said Summer fiercely. "You can still be a bird. You're more than half a bird already, and you did that with no help at all. You were always the special one. With the cranes to teach you, you can be anything, I know." And a wound in Bird's heart began to heal.

Finally, they talked about the robe, which would be Summer's one day, though it was Bird who wanted it more than anything. And that wound did not heal, and could not be healed; but it was shared and sad between them. And when their hearts relented and opened up, to each other and to this wound, a bridge arched in the air between them like a rainbow, strong and light and threaded with color.

"We are the bridge," said Summer. And Bird laughed. She said, "I asked Mom yesterday what that picture letter meant, what she really meant it to say. She said it meant 'My heart is broken. You are swans. Support each other now.' So I guess we are."

They took the bridge and set Bird's end in the ground. "But how will we set my end on the other side?" Summer wondered.

"Birds," said Bird. And she sang out a long, loud call, full of joy and strength. Flocks of birds made their way to the clearing, and when Bird explained what she wanted them to do, a thousand tiny claws delicately seized Summer's end of the bridge and pulled it across the sky and out of sight. "They will take it straight home," said Bird, then blushed because she had called it home. "To the river by our old house," she said.

When they told the raven, she said, *Don't forget that a bridge must be maintained.* So they made plans to make their six months with the swan at the same time every year, when Summer visited the Green Home and Bird came back from the cranes. Their half-years together would keep the bridge alive.

"You and me, we will be like a flock," said Bird. "To be a flock, there are three rules. First, you have to stay a little bit apart. But the second rule is: never too far apart. And third, you all have to be going in the same direction. When you follow those rules, you're a flock."

"Apart, but not too far apart," repeated Summer. "And going in the same direction."

$$\sim\!\!\!\!\sim$$

And now all four of them stood on the arching bridge. Bird stood alone at the end, while the swan limped up to the top of the arch with Summer and her father. Summer embraced the swan and whispered to her, then walked quickly on. But her father and the swan each stayed in the middle of the bridge, a step or two apart. They bent toward each other, in the middle of that bridge, the swan stretching her graceful neck forward, the man leaning in. And in the middle of the bridge, the man kissed the bird, and kiss and bridge made a double arc against the sky.

The kiss ended, and the swan pulled away, and turned back. Their father waited a little longer, watching her go. To Bird, watching, he looked for a moment like an eagle, hunched and folded in.

Then he and Summer turned away to follow the bridge toward home.

$$\sim\!\!\!\!\sim$$

Back in Up, neighbors and teachers heard a sad, familiar story: divorce, split custody. "See what it's done to him," they said of the older, thinner, sadder man Summer's father had become. It was an unusual arrangement, the neighbors and teachers learned: Summer would spend half the year with her father, attending school just like before, and the other half with her mother and sister "in the country somewhere, being home-schooled." Bird lived half the year at a boarding school, they heard—bad feelings with her father, they guessed, from the divorce—and half with her mother and Summer, in the country.

"Sad," said the neighbors and teachers. And it was sad, and not sad, both. It was their life now.

In the months she lived with her father, Summer spent long hours in the forest, to be nearer the birds, and to watch them. Sometimes her father came with her. In those many hours, he taught her everything he knew about birds, which was quite a lot.

And sometimes on a Saturday afternoon, her father would see her from a distance, sitting by the river, leaning against a large white shape that must be a swan. He didn't go near them; he left them alone. But it made him glad to see it, glad and sad.

Although he didn't notice it, the cat was usually there, too.

ACKNOWLEDGMENTS

Summer and Bird began as a vague idea for a story to tell two little girls I was babysitting. They had already picked out bedtime stories to hear that night, so they never heard mine, but I wrote down those first few pages anyway. The story has changed a great deal since then, but I still see those girls in the faces of Summer and Bird.

I borrowed a few of my chapter titles from better writers:

- "A Cage Went in Search of a Bird" is a line from the writer Franz Kafka. Someday you might check out his great story about a man turning into a cockroach.
- "I Will Not Let Thee Go Except Thou Bless Me" is a line from a strange and lovely story in the King James version of Genesis, in which a man named Jacob wrestles with an angel.
- "And No Birds Sing" is from an eerie poem by John Keats called "La Belle Dame sans Merci." That's French for "the beautiful woman without mercy," which, now that I think of it, might fit the Puppeteer—although of course, we never see her face, so who's to say.

Bird is wrong, by the way: "A robin redbreast in a cage/Puts all heaven in a rage" is not a nursery rhyme, but a line from William Blake's "Auguries of Innocence."

"The attainable border of the birds" is a real story the Chukchi people of Siberia tell, though I have changed it quite a bit for my purposes. I first read about the story in *The Language of the Birds*, by David M. Guss. Other books that taught me facts and folklore about birds include *The Folklore of Birds*, by Edward A. Armstrong; *Birdsong*, by Don Stap; and *The Folklore of Birds*, by Laura C. Martin.

"Brd Sngs of th Grt Lks" (only spelled out properly: *Bird Songs of the Great Lakes*) is a real CD by John Neville; I listened to it a lot while I was writing.

By the way, I am sorry to say that ravens might not have such a good sense of smell as I gave them, as it turns out. But it's not settled yet, so we can hope.

I feel tremendous gratitude toward my first readers: Jonelle Patrick, a writer herself, whose thoughtful comments on my first chapter helped me understand what I was trying to do; Jeanne Frontain, who read the first chunk and delighted me by demanding more; and Meg Worley, the first to read the whole book, whose astute comments and generosity helped more than I can say. Thanks also to my other early readers, Janet Catmull, Diane Morrison, and Tim Hanson—and especially to my first young readers, Ari Polgar, Hannah Dunton, and Rosalind Faires. Their feedback helped me make this book.

I am also grateful to my smart, patient, funny agent, David Dunton, whose enthusiasm for this book, combined with first-rate agenting skills, upended and transformed my life in ways I didn't think possible. Thank you, Edward, for introducing us.

I also want to thank my terrifyingly superb editor Julie Strauss-Gabel, whose comments had me sitting on the floor with the whole book in pieces around me, like a car I was rebuilding. Sometimes I was in pieces on the floor, too. But with Julie's intelligent and unflagging assistance, I got it all put back together and running better than it did before.

Finally, and most of all, to my husband, Ken Webster, my best love and gratitude. His kindness and love have held me up like a raft in the scary, uncertain, thrilling sea of making this book.

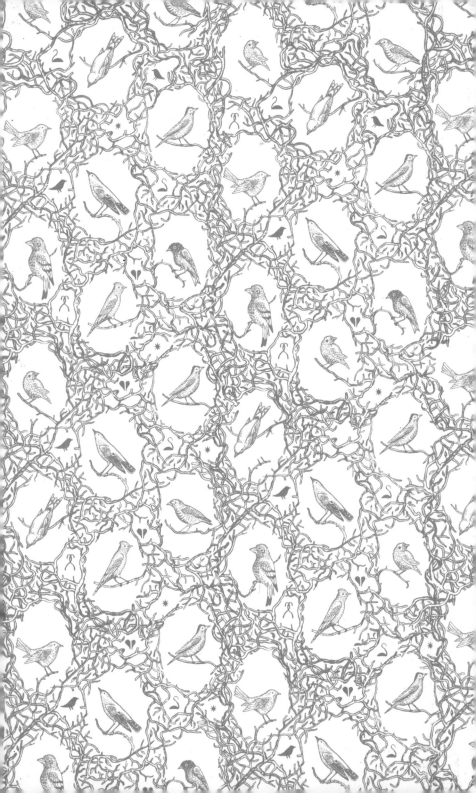